And still there are demons to conquer. There has been justice – of a sort. Indigo's recklessness released the seven evils: she alone must track and slay them . . .

Now Indigo has come to Simhara, the Jewel of the East; city of the world's greatest merchants, artists, inventors, and birthplace of her own mother. But evil is alive in the city, and the omens are ambiguous.

What is the destiny of the innocent child whose fate seems so entangled with Indigo's? What is the nature of the malignant darkness that threatens Indigo's sanity and, perhaps, her very existence? And what do the opium-inspired words of the ancient fortune-teller signify?

BEWARE THE SERPENT-EATER . . .

And, most important of all, where and *what*, is the demon? Indigo must find and destroy it. The price of failure is unthinkable . . .

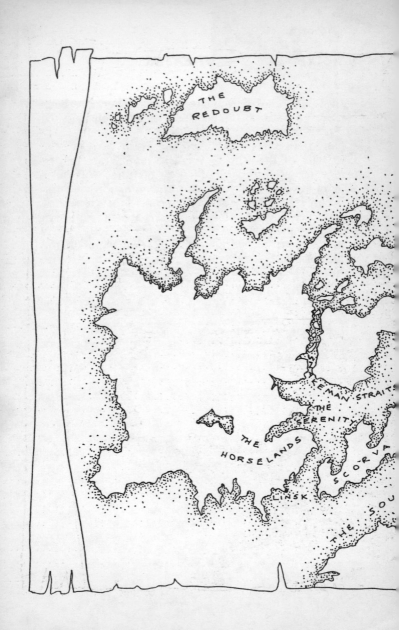

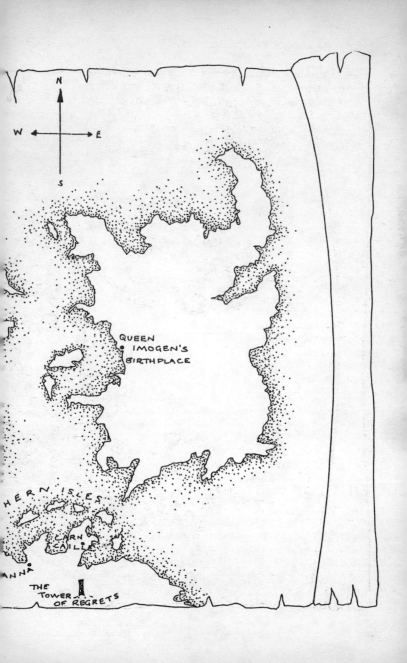

N

W ← → E

S

QUEEN
IMOGEN'S
BIRTHPLACE

HERN ISLES

CARN
CAILLE

ANNA

THE
TOWER
OF REGRETS

INFANTA

Book 3 of

INDIGO

LOUISE COOPER

UNWIN
PAPERBACKS

LONDON SYDNEY WELLINGTON

First published in Great Britain by Unwin® Paperbacks, an imprint
of Unwin Hyman Limited, in 1989

UNWIN HYMAN LIMITED
15–17 Broadwick Street, London W1V 1FP

Allen & Unwin Australia Pty Ltd
8 Napier Street, North Sydney, NSW 2060, Australia

Allen & Unwin New Zealand Pty Ltd with the Port Nicholson Press
Compusales Building, 75 Ghunzee Street, Wellington, New Zealand

---

British Library Cataloguing in Publication Data

Cooper, Louise, *1952–*
    Infanta.
    I. Title II. Series
    823′.914[F]

ISBN 0-04-440303-8

Set in 10 on 10½ point Times by Computape (Pickering) Ltd,
North Yorkshire
Printed and bound in Great Britain by
Cox & Wyman Ltd, Reading

The stars move still, time runs, the clock will strike
Marlowe: *Doctor Faustus*

For Tanith Lee
in knowledge of true friendship

Prologue

On a lonely and barren stretch of tundra, where the borders of a small kingdom meet the vast ice-ramparts of the southern glaciers, the ruins of a solitary tower cast their unnatural shadow across the plain. The Tower of Regrets – it has no other title – was the handiwork of a man whose name is now long forgotten; for, as the old bardic story goes, his was a time and a time, before we who live now under the sun and the sky came to count time.

In those ancient days, mankind's foolishness and greed brought his world to the brink of ruin. At last Nature herself rose up against him, and the Earth Mother wrought Her vengeance upon the children who had betrayed Her trust. But through the dark night of Her retribution, the tower remained unsullied. And when it was done, and a wiser mankind raised his head from the wreckage of his own folly to begin life afresh in a cleansed and untainted world, the tower became a symbol of hope, for within its walls the evils which man had made were at last confined.

For centuries the Tower of Regrets stood alone upon the plain, and no man or woman dared turn their face towards it, for fear of the ancient curse that lay within. And so it might have remained – but for the recklessness of a king's foolish daughter.

Her title then was the Princess Anghara Kaligs-daughter; but now she has forfeited the right to name and heritage. For she broke the one law that had endured since her people's history began, when she breached the sanctity of that eon-old tower in a bid to learn its secret.

Oh yes; the princess had her wish, and the secret was revealed to her. But as its chains were released, the Tower

1

of Regrets sheared in two; and mankind's ancient curse came shrieking from darkness to fasten again upon the world – and upon Anghara's soul.

In the black night of the curse's reawakening, Anghara lost all she had ever held dear to that deadly power. Her father, Kalig; her mother, Imogen; her brother, Kirra. Good friends, kind companions. And, hardest of all, her beloved Fenran, son of Earl Bray of the Redoubt, who would have been her husband. And in the wake of the destruction, she took upon her young shoulders a burden that now haunts her day and night, waking and sleeping. For the Earth Mother has decreed that she must make reparation for her crime, by seeking out and slaying the seven demons which came laughing into the world when the Tower of Regrets fell.

Anghara is Anghara no longer. Her name now is Indigo – the colour of mourning – and her home is the world itself, for until her task is completed she cannot return to the hearth at which she was born. Nor can she age, nor can she die, until the quest is done. And when each night she cries out in her unhappy dreams, How long? Great Mother, how long?, she hears again the reply of the bright emissary, avatar of the Earth Goddess Herself, unyielding, implacable, yet redolent with pity.

Five years. Ten. A hundred. A thousand. Until it is done, Indigo. Until it is done.

One demon is dead now. Fire was her weapon, and the ghosts of many innocent souls walk in her wake. She sang their elegy, and then she turned her face to the rising sun, following the sure guidance of the lodestone which was the Earth Mother's gift to her. Half a world and seven more years have brought her to the shores of a new country, and it is time for her second quest to begin: a responsibility which she cannot and dare not shirk.

But she is not entirely alone. With her travels a loyal friend who, although not human, has chosen to share her curse and her obligation; for the friend, too, knows what it is to be an outcast among her own kind. And with her goes an undying spark of hope that one day, in an unimaginably distant future, she might free the man she *loves from the torments of the life-within-death to which her crime has condemned him.*

But while her task remains unfulfilled, Indigo also has one eternal enemy. This enemy will dog her footsteps wherever she goes, for it is a part of herself, created from the blackest depths of her own soul and grown to independent life: Nemesis, who lurks in every shadow and whose mark is the colour silver. And Nemesis is a deadly adversary indeed.

For thirteen years now a new dynasty has ruled in Carn Caille, stronghold of the kings of the Southern Isles and Indigo's one-time home. The legend of the Tower of Regrets no longer exists; for the Earth Mother decreed that all memory of the tower's purpose, and of its fall, should be erased from the mind of man. So Kalig and his family live on only in sad ballads of the fever that, it is believed, took their lives. And King Ryen grows older in peace and dignity, never dreaming that Kalig's daughter still lives . . . and that upon her shoulders rests the ultimate fate of his world . . .

Chapter I

The quaymasters had established a strict order of precedence for the docking and unloading of ships that put in to harbour at Huon Parita. Wharfside facilities were limited, honest labour hard to come by, and the crowds of hawkers, tricksters, fortune-tellers, itinerant opportunists and outright beggars thronging the quays were a constant hazard to cargoes and passengers alike. Under normal circumstances, the three trader vessels from the west would have had to ride at anchor in the bay for two days or more before being allocated berths. But when word reached the shore that the traders came from the Jewel Islands, hasty rearrangements were made, and within an hour of the ships' arrival the wooden semaphore arms atop the masters' tower clacked out the signal to bring them and their cargo of gems in to harbour.

As the big traders docked, a smaller, sleeker vessel, with a ballista mounted on her foredeck and the ferocious head of a battering-ram gleaming just below the waterline at her prow, skimmed in under their shadow to tie up in the shallows of an adjacent quay. A crowd was already gathering about the traders, but the *Kara Karai – Little Sea Mother* in the language of her home country – was largely ignored. Anyone who knew anything of the merchant fleets recognised the distinctive yellow and black hull of a Davakotian hunter-escort, and knew the fearsome reputation of such ships and their crews. Only a single official, a young man whose splendid scarlet sash and cap seemed to do little to boost his confidence, stationed himself at the foot of the emerging gangplank; beyond the necessary formalities, the *Kara Karai* would be left well alone.

5

The Davakotian captain was the first to disembark. Thirty years old at most, the top of her head came level with the official's shoulder, and he wasn't a tall man; but her diminutive frame was solid with well-developed muscle. Her amber-skinned face looked as hard as seasoned wood, and in both cheeks, just below the eye, a small diamond had been implanted into the flesh, surrounded by a pucker of scar tissue. In the brisk breeze her cropped black hair stood out like a bizarre, stiff halo. Her appearance – not to mention the fact that she was a woman, and here in the east a woman's place was not at the helm of a ship – upset the young man's sense of propriety; as he stammered out a request for her documents he saw the *Kara Karai*'s crew, again mostly female, hanging over the ship's rail and leering at his discomfort while they waited for business to be completed. Most were heavily armed. Sweating, the official hastily sealed the embarkation papers, and barely waited until the captain had put her thumbprint to the berth allocation docket before giving an abrupt salute and hastening away with a burst of raucous laughter from the hunter's deck ringing in his ears.

Within minutes, the crew had dispersed. Escorting the gem-traders was always a profitable commission, and this had been a trouble-free voyage; they had coin to spend and seven days to indulge their pleasures before putting to sea again. Most vanished quickly into the frenetic mêlée of colour and noise and human activity that waited like a tide beyond the docks, until the only crew members remaining on the hard were the captain, and a tall young woman who had been among the last to disembark.

The newcomer was no Davakotian. Like most of her peers, the captain wasn't overly interested in her crew's origins; *Kara Karai* boasted recruits from a dozen different parts of the world. But this woman, with her blue-violet eyes and long, copper-coloured hair that was prematurely greyed, was more of a contradiction than most. Her skin was burned brown by the sun and her hands were work-roughened, yet her features had the unmistakable stamp of aristocracy. And though her face

6

and figure were youthful, there was something in her look that made strangers turn quickly away from too close a scrutiny; a shadow of experiences best left unprobed, a hint of something old and desolate behind the young mask.

For a few moments the two stood together at the foot of the gangplank; then the captain said:

'You're sure you won't change your mind and stay with us, Indigo?'

The girl shook her head, smiling. 'You and *Kara Karai* have been good to me, Macce. But no: I must go on to Simhara.'

'Ah, well.' Macce hunched her shoulders. 'Then say a prayer for all of us at the Shrine of Mariners, won't you? Keep our good luck running.' She looked down, then grinned. 'I'll wager Grimya will be glad to see the last of the ocean for a while, at least. Won't you, Grimya?' And, bending, she rubbed the head of the big, brindle-furred creature who sat at Indigo's feet.

Grimya's tongue lolled between her jaws and she made a pleased sound at the back of her throat. Those who knew no better – Macce included – took her for a large, shaggy-coated and unusually intelligent dog; an impression which Grimya and Indigo had taken pains to maintain. But anyone bred in the cold lands of the distant south, in Scorva or the Horselands or the Southern Isles, would have recognised the grey pelt and distinctive form of a forest wolf.

'If you take my advice, you'll join one of the southbound caravans,' Macce continued. 'They're slow, but a good deal safer than travelling alone.' She nodded towards the milling throng. 'Especially for a woman. The eastern countries don't share our Davakotian attitudes; the moment you walk into that crowd, you'll be looked on as fair game.'

Indigo smiled thinly. 'I can take care of myself.'

'Oh, I know that. And Grimya will soon enlighten anyone who gets the wrong idea. But all the same, be careful. If you fall prey to some thief or slave-trader, it'll reflect badly on my training!' She grinned. 'Besides, I'm planning to be in Simhara myself at some time, and if you're still there I'll want you back on my crew.'

'I'll remember that. Thank you.'

'Well, then. Best be on your way, eh?' Macce reached out and pinched Indigo's upper arm; a gesture of farewell. 'The best of fortune, Indigo. May the Sea Mother's tides flow well for you.'

'And for you, Macce.' Indigo laid her hands on the little Davakotian's shoulders and kissed both her cheeks, feeling the rough facets of the diamonds scratch her skin. 'Good hunting!'

She settled her two packs more firmly on her back and, with Grimya at her heels, started to walk away. Macce watched her for a few moments, then yelled after her in a voice that carried shrilly over the general hubbub. 'Don't pay more than five zozas for a riding-animal! And don't let anyone sell you a halfbreed – make sure you get a full-blooded chimelo!'

Indigo looked back, smiled and waved an acknowledgement. Then the crowd mingled like a tide around her and she was gone.

Huon Parita was something of a paradox. For centuries the deep, natural harbour on the northern shores of the Agantine Gulf had been uninhabited, for though the waters were a near perfect shipping haven, the surrounding terrain was too hilly and uneven for a port of any real size to be built. But the Gulf kingdoms, ideally placed to trade north, west and south alike, were fast becoming the mercantile centre of the world, and as their prosperity and influence grew, so too did the need to accommodate more and more of the great merchant fleets. Thus suitability had finally given way to necessity, and Huon Parita was born.

The great coastal cities to the south were renowned throughout the world for their beauty, civilisation and sophistication; but Huon Parita boasted no such qualities. Even after two hundred years it was still little better than a ramshackle sprawl of a place, consisting of a jumble of harbourside wharfs, a covered market flanked by a pleasant but poorly maintained merchant quarter, and, radiating from this centre of activity, a conglomeration of huts, shanties and even tents that were home to the port's vast itinerant population. Pickings were thin in the cities for the human parasites who traded on the weakness or gullibility of others; but here the militia were so few and so inefficient that they could ply their crafts without interference. And so, as Indigo moved into the throng, she found herself in the midst of a sea of noise and colour and excited activity. Hands thrust fruit or trinkets or lucky charms at her, while voices exhorted her to buy, eat, drink, learn her destiny, even to sell her hair. Alerted by a surreptitious tug at the strap of her pack she turned swiftly and angrily; but the would-be thief was already scuttling away into the crowd. A gaggle of young women, scantily clad and glittering with ropes of mirror-beads, shouldered past her with an air of brash confidence, and the pale-eyed, heavy-jowled man in rich robes who walked behind them paused to eye Indigo speculatively; but before he could speak, Grimya growled and, seeing the wolf for the first time, the whoremaster made an oily gesture of apology and hurried on. A short way off, a fight was breaking out between two sailors and a wizened little fortune-teller: Indigo smiled faintly as she recognised Macce's brawny and short-tempered second mate at the heart of the mêlée.

The press of humanity at last began to ease as the dockside gave way to the less frenetic merchant quarter. Here, some semblance of order had been established; the licensed market traders took pains to keep competition from charlatans and tricksters at bay, and it was possible to walk in relative ease. Indigo was thankful to be clear of the chaos. For the past two years, since taking service with Macce, she had known little beyond the closed and comradely world of the *Kara Karai*, with the sea her only horizon, and to find herself amid such a press and bustle of humanity after a long absence from the shore was unnerving.

She wished she hadn't had to leave the ship. During those long voyages she had come close to finding surcease from the black shadow that lay upon her life; but always she had known that the interlude couldn't last. In her dreams, and in unguarded waking moments, she had felt the goad of an obligation that she could neither deny nor fight, and with the ship's arrival in the east she had been forced to face her destiny, sever the ties and move on.

Unconsciously, Indigo raised one hand to her breast and fingered the small leather pouch that hung on a thong about her neck, carefully concealed beneath her shirt. Her fingers tightened on the hard, uneven contours of a small stone, and she felt a familiar mixture of thankfulness and loathing flood into her mind. The stone, and the tiny pinpoint of light that moved constantly within it, had been her guide now for nearly twelve years: where it led, she had no choice but to follow. And in the chaos of Huon Parita, she felt her fate closing in on her, as the town closed in, like a breathless and claustrophobic assault upon her mind.

Her uneasy thoughts were broken by a voice that spoke silently in her head.

Indigo? I am hungry. And I do not think that this is a good place for us to stay any longer than need be.

Indigo looked down, and saw that Grimya was watching her hopefully. Born a mutant, the she-wolf had an extraordinary – perhaps unique – ability to communicate with human minds and speak in human tongues. She and Indigo had shared a telepathic link since their first, chance meeting, now almost thirteen years ago; it was a closely guarded secret, and the foundation of the great bond between them.

The girl smiled, glad to be able to shake off her darkening mood and think of more mundane matters.

Remember Macce's warning, Grimya, she projected back. *It isn't advisable for us to travel alone; and it may take some while to find a southbound caravan.*

I know, and Macce's advice is sound. Even I could not protect you from an arrow or crossbow bolt. But I would still prefer to make haste, if we can. Grimya hesitated, then added a little diffidently, *If you are . . . reluctant to set out, I understand.*

10

No, I'm not reluctant. But despite her reassuring tone, Indigo felt a sharp stab of inner pain. In truth she would have preferred almost any other destination in the world to the one that lay ahead of her; for though she had never before set foot on its shores, the eastern continent – and in particular the wealthy land of Khimiz – held associations that tore at her soul. Her own mother, Imogen, had been Khimizi by birth: Imogen, wife of King Kalig of the Southern Isles, who with her husband and son Kirra and so many others had died hideously at Carn Caille, when the Tower of Regrets fell. Her daughter, the Princess Anghara, should have perished with her family in that same carnage thirteen years ago. But Anghara had survived, to take the new and bitter name of Indigo – the colour of mourning – and to carry the curse that had made her immortal, unageing, unchanging, until she had undone the horrors she had wrought.

Imogen, whom Indigo had indirectly murdered. The borders of her mother's homeland lay perhaps twelve days' journey south of Huon Parita. And Indigo knew with a sure and terrible instinct that the lodestone she bore was guiding her inexorably towards Simhara, Khimiz's first and greatest city.

Grimya, aware of the nature of her thoughts, was watching her anxiously, and Indigo took a deep breath, tasting the mingled hints of dust and brine and spices on the air, and dragged her thoughts, with a great effort, back to the present moment. She forced a smile, and deliberately skirted the subject, returning to Grimya's earlier plaint. *I'm hungry, too. Let's buy something to eat before we decide what else is to be done.*

At the far edge of the market, Huon Parita's food-sellers were shouting their wares. Most stalls were busy; people haggled for candied fruits, squares of sugar-cake, slabs of some dark, sticky confection that smelled sickly-sweet. At an open firepit several traders were cooking and selling spiced meats wrapped in thin, crisply-baked circles of dough. Grimya sniffed appreciatively, and Indigo – who had learned enough of the local tongue from Macce to know how to bargain – bought

11

four of the meat parcels, which the stallholder wrapped carefully in a fine, white paper the like of which she had never seen before.

Leaving the stall, they were looking about for some relatively quiet spot where they could eat undisturbed, when a voice shrilled closed by.

'Learn your fortune, copper-haired lady? Learn what lies in store for you in Huon Parita?'

Startled, Indigo turned, and saw an old woman squatting on a multicoloured mat and surrounded by good luck charms. With one hand the crone held out the stem of an incense pipe, while the other beckoned jerkily in time with the nodding of her head. 'Just one puff of my fine potion, lady, and all your dreams will be revealed!'

Indigo shook her head. 'No. No, thank you.'

But the fortune-teller wasn't easily deterred. 'Cards, then, handsome lady?' she persisted. 'Red cards, yellow cards, blue cards like your own blue eyes.' She grinned, showing shrivelled brown gums. 'Or silver? Silver cards for my lady and her fine grey dog?'

The blood drained from Indigo's face, and she felt sweat break out on her body. 'What did you say?' she whispered.

'Silver cards, lady. My very best. They never lie.'

It was a hideous coincidence, Indigo told herself; nothing more. It could surely be nothing more . . .

'No.' She heard her own voice, sharp with an involuntary stab of fear. 'I said, *no*!'

The gnarled hand made a complex, placatory gesture in the air. 'What my lady wants, my lady does. But have a care, foreign lady. Be wary of where you bestow your smile as you travel south. And watch for the serpent-eater!'

Grimya's hackles rose and she showed her teeth. *Indigo!* her mental voice was urgent. *I do not like this! She knows where we are going – and she spoke of silver!*

'Hush,' Indigo said aloud, touching a warning hand to the she-wolf's head. For a long moment she continued to stare at the nodding crone, seeking some hint of familiarity in the wizened features, a clue by which she might identify something less human lurking behind the

12

mask. But there was nothing. Save for the fact that on her thumb, the old fortune-teller wore a silver ring . . .

Indigo swung round. She had to force herself not to run from the creature on the mat, and Grimya had difficulty keeping up with her in the crowd. But at last the press of people eased, and Indigo halted. Turning, she stared back into the heart of the market, but the old woman was no longer visible.

'Damn her!' Indigo hissed. '*Damn* her!'

Grimya looked anxiously up at her friend's taut face. *It could have been co . . . co-in . . .*

'Coincidence. Yes; it could have been. Or it could have been Nemesis.'

The she-wolf lowered her head, blinking. It was a long time since they had encountered the demonic being that was, in a sense, Indigo's own alter-ego, but they had both known that in its own time and its own way Nemesis would return to plague them again. The demon was capable of adopting any form it chose – though in her nightmares Indigo always saw its first manifestation, a vicious-faced, sharp-toothed child – but the one constant that it could never disguise, and which was a warning of its machinations, was silver. Silver eyes, silver hair, a silver or even silver-coloured brooch . . . Indigo shook that particular memory off quickly, before it could gain a hold. Now, silver cards and a silver ring. And a warning which had seemed to carry more than a hint of irony. It could, as Grimya said, have been coincidence. Or it could have been a sign that the second of the seven demons that had cursed her life was perilously close at hand.

She turned away from the market's bustle and walked with Grimya to the shadows of a trellis-roofed arcade where a drinking fountain played sluggishly into a small tiled pool. The she-wolf slaked her thirst and then, a little apologetically but with great relish, devoured two of the meat parcels. Sitting on the pool's raised rim, Indigo nibbled at the edges of the third, but the encounter with the fortune-teller had killed her appetite: after a few minutes she abandoned it and took out the leather bag that contained the lodestone. It could tell her nothing that she didn't already know; but, for the fifteenth time since the eastern shore had loomed on *Kara Karai*'s horizon, she wanted to look again, to be sure.

South. The tiny pinpoint of golden light shimmered at the stone's edge in a clear and unmistakable signal. South, on the great trade road to Simhara.

And Nemesis walked in her footsteps.

Grimya looked up. Her jowls were greasy with meat juices, and the parcels were almost gone. She licked her chops, then said aloud:

'Is it j-*ust* as before?'

Her speech was guttural and halting; her larynx and throat weren't designed to cope with the intricacies of human language, but she took a stubborn pride in speaking aloud to Indigo when there was no one to overhear them. Indigo nodded.

'Just as before.' She slipped the lodestone back into its pouch. 'Southward. And I have a terrible feeling, Grimya, that Nemesis knows of our destination.'

'That may not be trr-*ue*. The old w-woman was a – seer.'

'I know. But my intuition tells me she was something else, too. Or the agent of something else . . . '

Grimya whined softly. 'If she . . . was, we ca-*annot* change matters. And we knew, I think, that such a th-ing as this must happen. The demon will not be con-tent to leave us alone.'

She was right. Logically, they could have expected no less, and to delay the inevitable seemed a futile exercise. Best to get their business under way; she had no true wish to linger in Huon Parita.

Indigo sighed, and looked at the barely-touched food in her lap.

'You sh-ould eat,' Grimya said. 'The meat is vv-*ery* good, though it makes me thhirsty.'

She could force herself to eat the third parcel, and would be the better for it, Indigo knew. She picked it up, and held the fourth out to Grimya.

'Here, love. I'm not very hungry. We'll finish these between us, then be on our way.'

14

'You are . . . sure?'

Not knowing whether the she-wolf referred to the food or the journey ahead of them, Indigo smiled. 'Yes, I'm sure.'

'And the . . . demon?'

She looked over her shoulder, back into the hubbub of the market, and her eyes narrowed. 'We'll wait and see. At this stage, we can do no more.'

Chapter II

A rustling in the tall palms that fringed the beach was the first herald of the breeze, and a welcome signal for the evening's activities to begin. The caravan – some twenty wagons, seventy pack and riding animals and the motley assortment of humans whose business was in one way or another connected with the train – had halted an hour earlier, but no one had thus far done much more than sit in whatever shade they could find, slake their thirst and allow muscles aching from the day's exertions to relax. With the coming of the breeze, though, the makeshift camp began to stir. Lanterns were lit, anticipating the darkness that was already encroaching from inland, and as the sun started to slip below the horizon and the sea's vast expanse turned to molten silver, the small, fierce flickers of camp-fires glowed in the gathering dusk. Cooking pots clattered with comfortable familiarity, animals stamped and snorted, talk and an occasional burst of laughter intruded on the quiet.

As she walked with Grimya up the gentle slope that led from the shore to the road, Indigo thanked her luck – and not for the first time – that Vasi Elder's caravan had been delayed in Huon Parita for a day beyond its planned schedule, and that she had therefore been in time to join it. She had taken an instant liking to the flamboyant Vasi, who, despite his villainous looks and extravagant style, had a strict code of honour and efficiency that was rare among his peers. Grimya's unerring instinct had backed her judgement, and so for the past nine days they had travelled southward with the caravan along the broad coast road that would bring them eventually to Simhara. It was a slow journey but a safe one; the road was good, the weather kindly, and

16

there had been no sign of the shrivelling hot winds that often raged out of the great Falor desert, some twelve miles to the east.

These evening walks along the shore had become a pleasant habit. With the rising of the sea breeze that always cooled the day at sunset it was good to stretch her muscles and stride out along the beach, and to watch Grimya running with all the speed and graceful energy of her kind on the hard-packed sand at the tideline. The entire vastness of the Agantine Gulf was laid spectacularly before them, fringed by a bay that curved north and south as far as the eye could see. Here, Earth's greatest continent met Earth's greatest ocean; and the serenity and awesome beauty of the scene had a cleansing power that made Indigo feel, if only for a short while, at peace.

There was another kind of peace, too, in the friendly evening gatherings around the camp-fires. It hadn't taken Vasi long to discover that Indigo not only spoke his own tongue but was also fluent in the elegant language of Khimiz, as spoken in the great southern cities. With several Khimizi merchants travelling in the convoy, her skills as an interpreter were much in demand – and when Vasi also realised that one of the bundles she carried contained nothing less than a lap-harp, he had wasted no time in persuading her, each night when the eating and drinking were done and the fires stamped out, to sing and play the company to sound, untroubled sleep.

The comfortable crackle of the fires and clatter of cooking utensils greeted them as they reached the camp. In the last few minutes the sun had sunk to a fierce, orange-red sliver on the unbroken line of the sea, and dusk was sweeping in from the east to turn the sky overhead to dim violet. Beyond the reach of the flamelight people were little more than silhouettes; someone called a greeting to Indigo and she acknowledged with a smile and a wave before finding herself a place near one of the larger communal fires. A little way off, the tall cone of Vasi's silk tent showed sharp against the skyline; a smaller fire burned nearby and she heard the caravan owner's distinctive laugh among the small group gathered round it.

The evening meal was served, and for a while the camp fell silent as everyone satisfied their hunger. Indigo was eating the last of a dish of sugared dates, with Grimya sated and almost asleep beside her, when new sounds at the edge of the camp drew her attention. The thump of animals' feet, the jingle of harness; looking up, she saw that a group of riders on chimelos had emerged from the dark and were dismounting near the tall silk tent. Grimya tensed, sniffing the air; but then Vasi's voice carried across the short distance, and they both relaxed as they heard the bland and faintly ingratiating welcome in his tone. The she-wolf settled back to somnolence, but for a few minutes Indigo continued to watch as the silhouetted newcomers gathered around Vasi's fire and squatted down, seemingly deep in conversation. They were, she surmised, probably of the Falorim, the proud, self-sufficient and self-possessed nomads who somehow struck a living from the hostile inland desert after which they had named themselves. They considered the coast-dwellers weak and degenerate, but were not above conducting business with anyone if there were some advantage to be gained from it, and though they shared no common tongue with Vasi, the sign-language of barter was universal. Doubtless they would be haggling and drinking far into the night, and Indigo yawned, losing interest. Their dealings were of no concern to her, and tomorrow they would have an early start; best to follow Grimya's example and get some sleep.

She finished her food, rinsed plate and knife in one of the water-pails set by for the purpose, and turned towards the small tent she shared with the wolf. But before she could open the flap and crawl inside, she was alerted by a voice calling her name, and looked up to see someone, unrecognisable in the dark, hurrying in her direction. She sighed, and rose to her feet to meet him as he approached.

'Indigo.' It was Vasi himself, and he seemed agitated. He kissed her hand in the eastern manner, but it was a

18

courtesy only, with none of his customary exaggerated flamboyance. 'I apologise for intruding on you, but I am in great need of your services.' He glanced back over his shoulder, uneasy. 'We have visitors – a band of Falorim – and they seem to have urgent news; but I can't understand what they are trying to say. Can you help me?'

'Yes, of course.' For no reason that she could discern, something moved deep in her mind; a quick, barbed frisson of uncertainty: and she felt the swift, telepathic flicker of Grimya's curiosity. 'I'll come at once.'

Vasi hurried beside her as she strode towards his tent with Grimya padding a pace behind. As they neared the figures gathered round the fire Vasi laid a hand on her arm, slowing her.

'You'll forgive me, I hope, for mentioning the matter, but . . . the Falorim are not what one might call enlightened men. They have peculiar attitudes to those they consider foreigners, and a strict and formal code of behaviour. They also tend to look upon women in much the same way that they look upon their chimelos.' He shrugged an apology, and Indigo smiled slyly.

'Unlike the men of Huon Parita, eh, Vasi?'

Vasi bridled. 'I can't speak for the portside scum, but in higher circles, I assure you, there is no comparison!'

Amused, she let it pass and only said, 'I understand. And I shall take good care not to offend your guests.'

'Thank you, Indigo. Under the circumstances I feel it would be prudent not to arouse their ire.'

The Falorim didn't rise to greet them as they approached. There were five of them in total, all big men but without an ounce of spare flesh, and the similarities between them suggested that they might be brothers, or at least closely related. All had sun-bleached hair and harsh, bony faces, mahogany-brown from exposure to desert winds, and their eyes were startlingly dark, almost black. One, who appeared to be their spokesman, cast back the loose hood he wore and fixed Indigo with a cold, hostile stare before addressing Vasi.

'Who is this?' He spoke in the tongue of Huon Parita, crudely accented.

Vasi bowed. 'Desert lord, may I present to you my trusted friend Indigo, who alone among us speaks both your language and mine with fluency.'

The Falor clearly didn't fully understand the reply, but he nodded, then the gimlet stare focused on Indigo again.

'To which of the men here do you belong?' he demanded in Khimizi.

Indigo flushed angrily. Vasi saw her look; frantically he made a surreptitious, negative gesture, and Indigo bit back her retort. She forced her face muscles to relax, and smiled coolly.

'Among my people, who revere their traditions as you revere yours, sir, there is no such distinction,' she replied. 'I belong to no man, but am simply a servant of the Earth Mother.'

Vasi looked nervously from one stern face to another, unable to follow the conversation. Then abruptly the Falor tribesman nodded.

'So be it. We may pity a foreigner's ignorance, but pity is not enmity.' He pointed to the ground. 'Sit.'

Indigo took a place facing him on the opposite side of the fire, and as soon as she was seated the Falor said, 'Tell the little man that he would be well advised to go no further on his journey.'

Indigo translated, and saw Vasi's face tense. 'Why?' he asked. And, in a whisper for Indigo's ears alone, 'Is something amiss, or is this some attempt to threaten us? Ask him, quickly!'

Indigo looked at the Falor, choosing her words carefully. 'Vasi Elder thanks you for your advice, sir, and begs to know the reason for it, so that he may put it to the wisest use.'

The tribesman gave Vasi a withering look. 'It is not a question of wisdom, but of fact. This caravan is travelling to Simhara, yes?'

'Yes.'

'He may not find the welcome he anticipates. Khimiz has been invaded, and for three days past the city of

Simhara has been under siege. We believe that it may by now have fallen.'

Vasi grabbed Indigo's arm. 'What does he say? Tell me!'

She told him. Vasi stared at her for a long moment, then snatched at a little amulet he wore about his neck. 'Mother of All Life! Simhara under *siege*? It's impossible!'

'Wait.' Indigo gestured him to silence and turned again to the Falor. 'Vasi Elder is greatly distressed by this news. He asks who is responsible for such an invasion.'

The tribesman shrugged eloquently. 'The details of the matter are of no concern to us. We believe the invader to be a warlord from far to the east, but we have no further information.'

'And you have sent no help to the Khimizi? Not even scouts or spies?' Indigo ignored Vasi's urgent mutterings; the Falorim's careless attitude was rekindling her anger.

The spokesman smiled superciliously. 'We have no interest in the squabbles of the city states, and no cause to quarrel with the invader unless he should offend us. However, we also have no quarrel with those who use the caravan roads, and so we have seen fit to impart this news.'

Indigo understood. The Falorim were well aware of the value of the cargoes that traversed these roads, and what their loss would mean to the traders. This information would be worth a substantial reward.

Disgusted, she turned at last to the agitated Vasi, and recounted what the nomad had told her. When she was done, Vasi stroked his chin.

'This is an unhappy state of affairs,' he said softly. 'I'd be inclined to discount it as wild rumour, but the Falorim aren't liars, whatever else they may be.' He sighed. 'They expect to be well repaid for their trouble, I presume?'

'That was the implication.'

'Ah, well.' Vasi didn't like parting with money. 'I suppose I must look upon it as a worthwhile investment.

21

I'm indebted to you, Indigo; though I might wish the news had been happier, I'm thankful to have it.'

'What will you do?' she asked.

'I must consult the merchants who travel with us. It's their gold that's at risk, after all.' Another, heavier sigh. 'I'll satisfy the requirements of our friends here and see them on their way, then I'd best break the bad news. Thank you for your assistance, Indigo.'

She nodded. 'I'm only sorry the circumstances weren't happier. I'd best return to my tent and leave you to barter. Goodnight, Vasi.'

'It is not a good night. But I acknowledge the sentiment.'

As they walked away from Vasi's tent, Grimya looked up at Indigo with troubled eyes. *This is not good news,* she communicated. *This city* – she had not yet mastered the name Simhara – *is the place where we believe we must go. Yet if we cannot now reach it* . . . She licked her muzzle. *What does the stone say?*

There seemed little point in consulting the lodestone yet again, but none the less Indigo drew it from its pouch. The tiny golden eye winked back at her, and she shook her head.

It hasn't changed. Aware that others were in earshot, she too spoke telepathically. *It still leads us southward.*

Then what are we to do?

I'm not sure yet. But she was dissembling, and knew it. Whatever Vasi and his merchants decided, her own road was clear. Siege or no, invasion or no, she must reach Simhara, even if it meant leaving the caravan and travelling on alone.

And perhaps, she thought, the demon she was seeking might find its purpose well suited by the ambitions of an invader . . .

Within an hour the camp was in uproar. At the centre of the chaos was Vasi, who had broken the news to his companions and was now trying to bring the babble of

22

questions and arguments under some semblance of control. Indigo was drawn into the mêlée to interpret for the Khimizi merchants, and gradually, as the details of the Falorim's news became clear to everyone, a consensus of opinion emerged. The Khimizi, whilst protesting their concern for their homeland and loyalty to its ruler, the Takhan, were pragmatists above all else and, like the northern traders, were unwilling to risk themselves or their cargoes. Vasi, listening for dissenting voices and privately relieved to hear none, finally called the babble to order, raising his arms and flapping his hands for silence. Quiet fell, and everyone looked at the caravan-master's grim face.

'My friends,' Vasi shouted. 'We have no reason to doubt the word of the Falorim – we must assume that Khimiz has been invaded, and the city of Simhara has fallen. In my view we have no choice, and I believe that everyone here agrees with me. We must turn back, and return to Huon Parita!'

Voices were raised in eager assent, and Indigo and Grimya exchanged a look. Grimya said silently:

And our path . . .?

She didn't expect an answer. She had already seen it in Indigo's eyes.

He reasoned with her, he argued with her, he even threatened her; but Indigo was resolute. The caravan was almost ready to move, and Vasi couldn't believe that she and Grimya would not be returning with them. She was, he told her, committing suicide.

'Woman, you're out of your mind! This country is at war. *War.* D'you understand what that means? Your dog won't be able to protect you from an invading army – you'll fall prey to some drunken band of soldiers, or be captured as a spy, or find yourself in the middle of a battle – you will *die*, do you understand me?'

But his entreaties fell on deaf ears, and at last Vasi admitted defeat. With a gruff stolidity that was quite out of character and which Indigo found touching, he bestowed on her one of his best chimelos, and ample food and water for several days. He refused to accept a single zoza from her in exchange, grumbling that to take money from the dead was bad luck and that he might as well consider Indigo dead as of now. When this gloomy prediction made no impression, Vasi finally gave up. He kissed her, full on the mouth and with considerable relish, then wiped his eyes, announced that she was a fool of a woman who should have stayed at home to bear children, and stamped away, yelling at his overseers to move out.

From the side of the road, Indigo and Grimya watched the caravan lurch slowly away. A few people looked back at her; she waved, and they turned quickly aside, shaking their heads. At last the final wagon was past, and she reined the reluctant chimelo's head towards the south.

Grimya looked at the road stretching away into the distance, following the vast sweep of the bay. The scene was utterly undisturbed; the sea glittered under brilliant sunlight, the palms rustled gently; there was nothing to show that this peace might be an illusion.

'It is . . . hhhard to believe that the no-mads told the truth,' the she-wolf said.

'Yes.' Indigo checked her mount, which didn't like being separated from the caravan and was trying to back round and follow the departing wagons. 'But as Vasi said, we've no reason to doubt them. As we go south it probably won't be long before we see the first signs for ourselves.'

'You are – *sure* that our choice is w-wise?'

Indigo continued to look at the quiet road. Then she smiled with more than a hint of irony.

'No, Grimya. I don't think it's wise at all.'

She touched her heels to the chimelo's flanks, and the animal moved off.

They came upon the first refugees before noon; a grim, silent column trudging stoically northward with the few meagre belongings they had been able to carry with them as they fled. Indigo wanted to speak to them and

24

ask for news, but it seemed that the sight of even a single rider was enough to terrify them, so instead she guided the chimelo well clear of the road to show that she presented no threat. From a distance she watched the pathetic procession straggle by, and her pity deepened as she realised that there were no men of fighting age among them. Just women, children and old folk . . . any man who could wield a weapon, she surmised, had gone to the aid of his country.

The pattern was repeated three more times that day, and as dusk fell Indigo and Grimya reached the village – or one of the villages – that the fleeing folk had abandoned. There were many such small settlements on the gulf shores, peopled by fishermen and smallholders who grew crops in narrow strips of fields along the fertile coastline. But there were no signs of habitation here now. The houses all appeared to be undamaged, crops stood untouched in the fields, and several fishing-boats lay among the dunes. A small herd of goats milled by the gate of their fenced compound, bleating hungrily for attention, and a few chickens scratched in the dust; a scrawny puppy scampered away to hide at their approach, but there was not a human soul to be found.

For a long time Indigo stared at the empty village. It seemed that the invaders had not reached this area; yet if the villagers had been moved to abandon their homes, the enemy army could not be far away. She didn't relish the idea of travelling further with the daylight failing, and so suggested to Grimya that they should strike a makeshift camp among the dunes, where they would be well hidden from anyone who might come by. They dared not light a fire, and so spent a frugal night eating only uncooked food and taking turns to sleep while the other kept watch. During her first watch, Grimya reported, yet another band of refugees had tramped past, though she could not tell how many; but otherwise the night was uneventful, and with the coming of dawn they took to the road again.

The second abandoned settlement came in sight at mid-morning. Like the first, the buildings were unscathed; but the air of desolation here was given an ugly tinge by the stench of food left behind by the fleeing villagers and now decaying in the heat. Buzzing clouds of flies were everywhere, and Indigo and Grimya veered out on to the beach to give the village a wide berth.

'This is just the beginning,' Grimya said sombrely as she eyed the empty, silent houses. 'It will be w . . . *worse* as we continue on the rrr-oad.'

Indigo wasn't looking at the village but at the landscape that lay ahead of them. In the distance, a greasy pall of smoke stained the sky; its source was hidden beyond low hills, but she had more than an inkling of what it might be, and pointed it out to the wolf.

'If Simhara has fallen, we'll encounter more than deserted homes before long,' she said. 'Even if there are no soldiers in the district, there'll be bandits looking for what pickings they can get. Vasi was right; the road isn't safe.'

Grimya caught the train of her thoughts. 'The desert?' she said uncertainly.

Indigo glanced speculatively to the east. From this distance it wasn't possible to see where fertile land gave way to the Falor desert; but she could feel its presence beyond the horizon, a sense of hostility, barrenness, emptiness.

Yet for all that, the desert might hold fewer dangers than the road now. She had maps she had bought in Huon Parita: doubtless they weren't wholly accurate, but they would do well enough. And the lodestone wouldn't fail her. Better, she thought, to face the perils of the Falor than to risk continuing on their present route.

She said: 'We have enough food for several days. And there are oases in the desert. If we travel inland for a day or two and then turn, we should be able to reach Simhara from the northeast. No invader would trouble to set guards in the desert.'

'We may not be able to ap . . . p*roach* the city,' Grimya pointed out.

'I know. But I have to try. I *have* to. You understand, Grimya, don't you?'

'Of course I do. And where you go, I sh . . . all follow.'

26

Not for the first time, Indigo felt shamed. Yet again she was leading the she-wolf into deprivation and danger, but never once did Grimya's loyalty to her waver. She had no right to expect such devotion, for she had done nothing to earn it, and softly she said, 'Grimya . . . this is my battle, not yours. There's no reason why you should risk your life to stay with me. And if you –'

The she-wolf interrupted her. 'No, In-digo. You have said such things b . . . before. I did not heed them then, and I will not heed them now. I am your fr-*iend*. That is all that matters.'

'I don't deserve such friendship.'

'That is for me to decide.'

Indigo knew – as she always knew – that Grimya wouldn't be swayed. And though the knowledge did nothing to ease her conscience, it warmed her heart.

'Grimya, I think you must be very foolish.' She blinked, then laughed self-consciously to cover the surge of emotion she felt. 'Listen to me: I'm beginning to sound like Vasi! But it's true.' She smiled down at the wolf. 'And I'm more grateful for it than I can say.'

A hot breeze blew suddenly from inland, stirring her hair and bringing a dry, sharp scent that banished some of the stink from the village. A breath from the desert, like an invitation . . . Indigo liked to think that it was a good omen.

She swung the chimelo's head around, saw its ears prick forward as it, too, scented the desert. Then she touched her heels to its flanks, and, with Grimya pacing beside her, turned her back on the road and set off eastward.

Chapter III

The sun was beginning to wester behind them, though there was as yet no breeze to relieve the terrible heat, when Grimya first glimpsed a speck of green in the distance that broke the sand's unending monotony.

They had been travelling through the desert for a day and a half, and as the journey progressed Indigo had begun to understand the meaning of the phrase 'sand-madness', which she had heard from the lips of some of the Huon Parita merchants. For as far as she could see in any direction, there was nothing but the relentless emptiness of Falor, buff sand meeting buff sky in smooth and seamless unity. The sun reflected from the arid land in huge, fearsome waves that blurred the scene under a rippling heat-haze, and only with the coming of night did the undulating shapes of dunes and crescents, sculpted by the wind, emerge from the blinding glare and restore Indigo's sense of perspective. In the Southern Isles, her own homeland, she had heard tales of people caught on the open tundra during the great winter blizzards, who had lost their direction, their orientation and finally their sanity as land and sky and snow all merged into one and their minds snapped under an onslaught of total whiteness. The desert had close parallels with that deadly illusion, and she was thankful that she wasn't alone.

Thus far, the journey had been uneventful. They travelled during the cooler hours of morning and evening, and by starlight through much of the night, resting – though shade was almost impossible to find – during the worst of the noonday heat. The chimelo seemed tireless; the creatures were desert bred, and although superficially they resembled unusually long-legged and long-necked horses, their splayed, open-padded feet, pale, loose-haired coats and ability to run for hours – even days – without drinking made them perfectly adapted to the harsh life of the sands. Indigo was accustomed now to the almost hypnotic quality of the chimelo's peculiar, loping gait, and calculated that at their present rate of progress they could turn south-westward tomorrow morning and be in sight of Simhara's walls within another day.

They had just climbed the slope of a broad dune, the chimelo's feet making easy work of the soft, drifted sand, when Grimya yipped an alert. The she-wolf was poised on the dune's crest, her shadow starkly elongated before her, and her voice carried sharply.

'Some-thing ahead! Green!'

Indigo strained her eyes, but the endless sand shimmered back at her and she could see nothing. Cursing, she rubbed her eyes, shaded them with one hand and tried again. And this time she thought she glimpsed a dark smudge on the horizon, a splash of colour breaking the desert's monotony.

The chimelo pulled against the bridle, wanting to go on, but she held it back. When she looked again, the smudge was still there. It could be a mirage. Or it could be a group of Falorim. Or an encampment of soldiers...

The wind rose suddenly, flinging particles of sand that stung like wasps against her unshielded face. Grimya raised her head and tasted the stirring air: then she cried out, her voice excited and barely decipherable.

'Wa-ter! I smell wa-ter!'

An oasis. Indigo laughed with delight, remembering her last consultation of the map she carried. She had seen the green mark depicting a waterhole, but had reluctantly decided that to visit it would take them too far out of their way, and had regretted the decision as their supplies grew more brackish and unpalatable with every hour. Now though, it seemed that her calculations had been wrong, and they had come upon the oasis after all.

Sobering, she urged the chimelo level with Grimya, who was waiting for her, tail wagging eagerly.

'We'd best go carefully, love,' she warned. 'If anyone else is there, they may not take kindly to us.'

Grimya's tongue lolled. 'There is – no one,' she said. 'I can see. And I . . . want to drr . . . ink!'

The thought of fresh cold water, of being able to wash the sand from her hair and clothes, was wonderful. Grimya's eyesight could be trusted: there was no need to hesitate, and Indigo spurred the chimelo on down the slope of the dune.

The featureless blur ahead of them changed rapidly, resolving into a cluster of spindly trees and shrubs through which the glitter of water was clearly visible. The oasis was a large one, set in a natural hollow where grass grew thinly, and as they neared it even Indigo, with her inferior human senses, could scent the change in the air as the wind carried hints of moisture towards them. The sun was a wild orange flare at their backs now, the sky ahead changing through gold and green to soft purple, with a few faint stars shimmering on the horizon. They were only a few hundred yards from the trees when Grimya suddenly halted.

'What is it?' Indigo had to fight the chimelo to slow it; it, too, had smelled the water and was eager to reach it.

The she-wolf's ears were flattened; she showed her teeth in an uncertain snarl. 'I – do not know. I th-*ought* there was no one here, but . . . I was . . . wrong.'

Indigo's pulse quickened and she peered ahead, frowning. 'I see nothing.'

'You w-would not, not yet. But there is . . . an animal . . . ' Grimya sniffed the wind. 'Wait here. I will see.'

'Grimya!' But her protest went unheeded; the she-wolf was already streaking away across the sand. Indigo watched her approach the oasis and drop to a crouch, slinking forward on her belly as the ground began to slope down towards the trees. Ten paces, twelve – then she froze. Slowly her head came up, her ears flicked forward . . . and she sprang to her feet, and her telepathic voice called in the girl's mind.

Indigo! Come, quickly!

There was urgency in Grimya's call but no fear; rather a note of surprise. Indigo gave the chimelo its head and it broke into a rapid canter. They reached the top of the hollow, and as she saw what Grimya had seen Indigo pulled hard on the reins, slewing her mount to a halt in a churning wave of sand.

'Great Goddess!'

The still mirror of the oasis with its fringe of vegetation was clear now in every detail. On the southern side, some twenty yards from the water, a chimelo lay motionless. And beneath it, pinned by its body, was what looked from this distance like a bundle of brightly-coloured fabric.

Hastily, Indigo urged her mount down the slope and across the grass to where the fallen beast lay. She slithered from the saddle and, with Grimya behind her, ran to its side. Reaching it, she looked down – then swore softly as her fears were confirmed.

The chimelo was dead, its saddle panniers scattered about it. The accident must have happened very recently, for its corpse was still warm and rigor mortis had not yet set in. It had clearly stumbled and, by some freak of ill luck, fallen in such a way that its neck was broken near the poll. And, as Indigo had suspected, the bundle of rags trapped beneath it was the body of its rider. He was swathed in the folds of some flimsy fabric, and lay face down so that she could see no detail but for a stray lock of fair hair. Then she saw the outflung arm that protruded from the fabric's folds, and realised that the rider wasn't a man at all.

Swiftly she dropped to a crouch and took hold of the woman's slender wrist, feeling carefully. There was a pulse, erratic but quite strong . . .

'She's alive.' Relief coloured her voice.

Grimya peered at the prone figure. 'Is she . . . b-badly hurt?'

'I don't know. We'll have to try to move the chimelo's body and pull her free.'

'That will not be easy. It may make her hurts w . . . worse.'

'I know. But we have to take the risk; we can't leave her as she is.' Indigo eyed the chimelo speculatively. She was strong enough to lift it a few inches perhaps, and

31

only for a few seconds; but with Grimya's help it might be enough.

'Take a hold of the rider's clothing, near to the shoulder,' she said. 'And as soon as I lift, pull as hard as you can.'

Grimya looked dubious, but went to obey. As soon as she had gripped the prone figure's garments firmly between her teeth, Indigo put her shoulder under the chimelo's dead weight and, using all the leverage she could muster, heaved. At first she thought she couldn't do it; but then the animal's body shifted, rose a fraction – and with a ferocious tug Grimya pulled the woman free.

'Earth Mother!' With considerable relief Indigo let the corpse drop, and went on her hands and knees to where Grimya was already sniffing tentatively at the unconscious rider. As gently as she could she turned the woman over, and lifted aside the veil that obscured her face. She was young – certainly no older than her middle twenties – and a true Khimizi. Dark gold hair, curling about her cheeks and brow; skin the colour of honey, a full-lipped and faintly petulant mouth. An aristocrat, Indigo guessed, and her clothing confirmed it. Swathes of jewel-coloured silk, elaborately embroidered with sea-pearls; rings on each finger, gold ornaments at her brow and on her wrists that clinked delicately in the rising night wind . . . no one in their right mind would wear such finery in the desert, and she couldn't believe that the woman was any ordinary traveller. If, as she suspected, the woman had come from Simhara, then she must be a fugitive.

She turned to Grimya and was about to voice her thoughts when, from somewhere on the far side of the dead chimelo, a high, thin wail rose on the air.

Grimya yelped in alarm, and shock made Indigo jerk round. She sought the source of the wail, then Grimya cried: 'The basket! I saw some-thing move!'

Indigo scrabbled wildly to her feet, goaded by an irrational suspicion that she found hard to credit. She ran round to the far side of the chimelo, and when Grimya caught up with her she was staring down incredulously at a baby which lay, kicking feebly and waving its tiny fists, in one of the panniers among the scattered debris.

The infant opened its mouth and cried again, shutting its eyes tightly and beating at the air. By a miracle, the basket must have been thrown clear when the chimelo fell, and the baby had sustained no injury; in fact it seemed to have been sound asleep and had only just awoken. Indigo gathered up the basket and immediately the child became silent, opening its eyes once more and regarding her with solemn interest.

Grimya said: 'A w-oman and her young one, alone in the desert? It makes no ss . . . sense.'

'No. Unless they were with a refugee party, and somehow became separated?' But the theory wasn't convincing. Carefully, Indigo carried the infant back to where the woman lay; and as she set the basket down, the woman stirred. She tried to raise her head and her hands clawed in the dry grass, seeking purchase, but she was dazed and had no co-ordination. Suddenly she started to retch, and as Indigo went to help her she vomited helplessly on to the ground.

'J . . . Jess . . . *ohh*!' The woman sagged forward as Indigo held her shoulders. One hand clamped feebly on the girl's wrist and the contact seemed to startle the woman out of her daze, for suddenly her whole body stiffened. She pulled her hand away as though it had been stung, and her head snapped round, eyes brilliant with terror.

'*Who are you?*' she said in Khimizi.

'It's all right – I'm a friend,' Indigo told her soothingly, 'I'm not going to harm you; you're safe now.'

'You're . . . from Simhara?'

'No. I've come from Huon Parita; I was on my way to the city when I heard of the trouble in Khimiz. My name is –' but she got no further before the woman burst into a violent storm of tears.

'No, no, *no-o-o*!' Her voice rose in a shrill lamentation punctuated by racking sobs, and she rocked back and forth, trying to tear at her own hair. 'Great Sea Mother, please, let it be a dream, let it be a nightmare,

33

oh, *please*!' She retched again and started to choke; Indigo signalled frantically to Grimya and the she-wolf ran to where the chimelo stood grazing, reared up and snatched at the thong securing one of Indigo's water flasks. She returned with the flask gripped in her teeth, and Indigo held it to the woman's lips. In her distress she could hardly swallow and a good deal of water was wasted, but at last enough went down her throat to check the spasm.

'Th . . . Thank you . . . ' She coughed, and struggled into a more upright position. She didn't seem to be seriously hurt, Indigo saw with relief; there might be concussion, but nothing worse.

She squatted down and took the woman's hands in hers. 'What happened to you? Can you tell me?'

'I . . . ' she frowned: then suddenly the wild look returned to her eyes. 'Je . . . Jessamin! My child – where is she?'

Indigo glanced at the basket. The baby hadn't uttered a sound during her mother's outburst and, as before, she seemed to be gazing at the proceedings with infant fascination.

'The child is here, and uninjured,' Indigo said gently.

'Give her to me!' The woman's body jerked spastic-ally as she tried to reach for the basket, but she only succeeded in rolling over on the grass. Indigo helped her to sit up, and, when she tried again to rise, pressed gentle but firm hands to her shoulders.

'Hush,' she said. 'Don't distress yourself. Your child is *safe*, I promise. Now, can you tell me what has happened in Simhara?'

The woman drew a harsh, gasping breath. 'Gone,' she said. 'It has *gone*!'

'Gone?' Indigo was appalled.

'F-fallen. They – they besieged us, and we . . . had no defence. Our army was scattered throughout Khimiz, trying to fight them off, and . . . and . . . ' She snatched her hands from Indigo's grip and covered her face. 'They broke down the walls and they poured in like a floodtide, and we . . . oh Goddess, we . . . '

She sucked in a gasping breath. 'I had to get my

34

daughter away. I *had* to, don't you see? My uncle; he – got us out in the minutes before we were overrun – he sent me into the desert, and I . . . don't know what happened after that!'

'Who are they?' Indigo hated herself for such cruel persistence in the face of the woman's distress, but she had to know: something she didn't comprehend was goading her and she couldn't control it. 'The invaders – who are they?'

'I don't know! Curse you, I don't *know*! Isn't it enough that they *destroyed*, and they *killed* and – and – oh, Great Mother, I feel *sick*!' She tried to lurch to her feet, one hand clutching at her abdomen. For a moment she swayed, doubled over – then she slumped to the ground in a dead faint.

Indigo stared down at her, shocked by what she had heard. She had only the barest picture of what this woman had been through, but her mind was conjuring dreadful parallels as she remembered Carn Caille, her own home, and the monstrous horde that had shattered her world. The ugly reverie broke only when Grimya, anxiously investigating, pressed her muzzle against Indigo's hand and startled her back to reality.

She has fainted? the she-wolf communicated silently.

'Yes . . . ' Forcing the memory into the dark recess to which she had learned to banish it, Indigo leaned over the woman, lifting her tangled hair back from her face. She was completely unconscious, and her skin felt unhealthily cold. The girl glanced at the sky. The sun had almost vanished now; shadows were merging into heavy gloom and darkness was falling rapidly. The woman needed shelter and warmth urgently, if she was to survive the bitter desert night.

She turned back to Grimya. 'I must make a fire. Keep watch on her, and tell me if she wakes.'

There was plenty of dry brushwood among the trees and shrubs surrounding the oasis, and by the time the unconscious woman began to stir, Indigo had a good blaze going. She was unsaddling the chimelo when Grimya's silent warning alerted her, and she hastened back into the circle of firelight in time to help the woman as, dizzily, she opened her eyes and tried to sit up.

'What . . . ' One hand reached out, but without co-ordination, and she blinked uncertainly at the flames. 'What are you – '

'You fainted,' Indigo told her. 'It's all right; all's well. Look.' She indicated the basket and the infant, which with extraordinary placidity had fallen asleep again. 'Your child sleeps soundly, and we have a fire to warm us. There's food in my saddlebag; we can rest here safely for the night.'

'No!' The woman's eyes widened as comprehension dawned. 'We can't stay here! *They* will be searching for us – we must flee!'

'Searching for you?' Indigo was nonplussed.

'Yes! Oh, don't you understand? Don't you know who I am?' And, when Indigo's expression remained blank: 'I am Agnethe. I am the Takhina!'

Indigo stared at her, stunned. The Takhina – wife to the ruling Takhan of Khimiz, around whose court the entire city of Simhara revolved. With the city fallen she had assumed that the ruling family must be dead or taken captive.

More tears began to fall on Agnethe's clasped hands. 'Now do you see?' she said desperately. 'There's no time for fires, or for resting! I dare not stay here – I must go north, before they find me! And they will be searching.' Her face twisted into a look of bitter hatred. 'Sea Mother, they will be *searching*!'

Indigo dropped to a crouch before her. 'What of the Takhan?' she asked urgently. 'Does he live?'

'I don't *know*.' Agnethe shook her head violently. 'But if he is dead . . . Oh Goddess, if he is dead, then Jessamin – my baby – she is our only child!'

Indigo understood. If the Takhan had been killed, then the infant who now lay sleeping in the basket a few paces away was the rightful ruler of Khimiz. And if the invaders should find her before Agnethe could get her to safety, it was unlikely that either of them would see another dawn.

'Please!' Agnethe begged. 'You must take her away

from here, far away from Khimiz! *Please* – I will give you anything I have, anything I own; but Jessamin must be got away *now!*'

Indigo knew that she had to help them if she could. Her own mission was in ashes: to approach Simhara now would be utter folly, and she had nothing to lose by turning back. Once the Takhina and her child had been taken to sanctuary, she and Grimya would need to make new plans, but for now she had to think of the immediate future.

'Takhina, I don't want your money or your jewels,' she said. 'But we *can't* leave here before morning. You're in no fit state to travel – '

Agnethe interrupted her. 'No, *no!* You must leave me, and take the child! Find the Falorim, tell them – '

'I can't abandon you!' Indigo was shocked. 'If the searchers come – '

'I don't *care!* All that matters is to keep Jessamin from them at any cost! Take your chimelo now, and *ride!*' Agnethe's voice rose hysterically. 'You must! You *must!*'

'*No*, Takhina. I won't leave you to die!'

Agnethe clenched her fists and pressed them to her temples. 'Oh, why won't you *understand*?' She grabbed Indigo's hands. 'They will kill her, don't you realise that? They will kill my child! She was born before dawn of the fourteenth day under the constellation of the Serpent – *do you know what that means?*'

Indigo started to say, 'Takhina, I don't – ' but before she got any further, Grimya sprang to her feet with a snarl. The she-wolf had been sitting at the far side of the fire, not wanting to alarm Agnethe who, it seemed, was as yet unaware of her presence: now she was up and staring into the darkness beyond the oasis's smooth mirror, her hackles raised.

'Grimya?' Unease coloured Indigo's voice.

Grimya's lips drew back to expose her teeth. 'Ssss . . . *scent!*' The word came out as a warning growl, barely recognisable.

'What?' Agnethe shrilled. 'What is it?' And at the same moment Grimya cried aloud: '*A-larm! A-larm!*'

Indigo sprang up, instinctively reaching to her belt where the wicked-bladed knife that had been a parting gift from Macce hung in its sheath. She glimpsed a blur of movement in the treacherous darkness among the trees, but her pupils were contracted from staring into the fire's glare, and patches of brilliance danced on her vision, confusing her.

'Grimya, *no!*' She saw the she-wolf make to spring forward and ran towards her, grabbing the scruff of her neck and pulling her back. Then Agnethe screamed – and from the black tangle of vegetation came a dozen or more men on chimelos.

'*Jessamin!*' The Takhina shrieked like a madwoman and flung herself towards the basket. Scrabbling on hands and knees, she gathered it into her arms and scrambled to her feet. Male voices shouted in an alien language as Agnethe began to run crazily towards the oasis, and something whistled through the air with a vicious, singing whine that was horribly familiar to Indigo's ears. The archer's aim missed and there was more shouting; Indigo saw a figure struck from his mount's back by one of his fellows, then another man had jumped down from his saddle and was running after Agnethe. She heard the Takhina's cry as he overtook her and threw her to the ground, and the baby's thin howl of protest as the basket spilled.

Indigo snatched out her knife as anger and fear burst in confused turmoil into her mind. She started forward, not stopping to think but driven to help Agnethe, and from the darkness three more men appeared, blocking the way. Indigo skidded to a halt. Panting, she raised the knife, brandishing it – then Grimya whirled, snarling, and she realised that more warriors had moved in behind her, trapping her.

Very slowly, Indigo turned. The light from the fire fell on her assailants, touching them with an eerily hot glow and illuminating the weapons that pointed at her stomach. With a sick sensation Indigo recognised the sleek, metallic shapes, strings drawn and heavy bolts poised. Crossbows. She knew their deadly accuracy and efficiency only too well, for the crossbow had always

38

been her own favoured weapon. And these were huge, brutish, lethal. She couldn't hope to prevail against them.

One of the warriors smiled, and, still hefting his bow one-handed, made a beckoning gesture. Grimya growled, but he ignored her and beckoned again, more imperiously. Indigo didn't move. She could hear Agnethe sobbing, but the sound seemed to come from another world and she couldn't relate to it. She watched the bow, then very slowly, aware that one mis-interpreted move could earn a bolt through her ribcage, started to lower the knife. She was, it seemed, too slow for the warrior's liking, for suddenly he lunged towards her as though to snatch the knife from her hand – and, unable to control her instincts, Grimya uttered a furious, challenging snarl, and sprang for his throat.

'Grimya, *no!*' Indigo shrieked, horrified, but she was too late. Grimya's solid weight bowled the man off his feet and he fell, flailing, with the enraged wolf on top of him. His companions rushed to help him and Indigo, too, flung herself into the fray, frantically trying to reach Grimya and drag her clear before they could harm her. Something – an elbow, a shoulder, she didn't know – rammed into her, knocking her off balance, and she sprawled among a confusion of trampling feet. Before she could attempt to get up, a boot caught her on the temple, stunning her; through a fog of nausea her brain registered the sounds of a thump and an animal yelp, then powerful hands hauled her out of the mêlée and she was dropped unceremoniously on the hard ground.

She must have passed out for a few minutes, for when she regained her senses the fracas was over. As the world swam into focus, Indigo heard the low murmur of voices a short way off, punctuated by the sound of a woman sobbing. Agnethe . . . but what had become of the baby? And Grimya –

Suddenly she remembered the yelp she had heard, and panic gripped her. *Grimya!* she called silently, struggling to overcome the giddy inertia in her head. *Grimya, where are you?*

I am . . . here. They hit me . . . The she-wolf's

answering message was weak, but to her intense relief Indigo heard the underlying indignation that told her Grimya was uninjured.

They have bound my legs, Grimya said. *I cannot come to you. Indigo, are you all right?*

Yes. The warriors could easily have killed them both, she realised: the fact that they were relatively unharmed was surely a hopeful sign. *Don't resist unless they try to hurt you,* she added. *I think we'd be wiser to wait and see what they want with us.*

Before Grimya could answer, a shadow cast by the firelight fell across Indigo, and she saw that two of the men had seen her stirring and were now standing over her. One of them spoke to her, but though she caught the interrogative in his voice she was unfamiliar with the language, and shook her head to show that she didn't understand. The man grunted impatiently, and hands reached down to haul her to her feet. Still giddy, and nauseous, she tried to fight back sickness as she was led towards the chimelos that were mustered under the trees.

The attack, it seemed, had been as efficient as it was swift, and the warriors were ready to move out. Agnethe, silent now, sat before one of the soldiers on his mount's saddle: Indigo thought she was bound, but couldn't be sure. A second mounted man carried the baby's basket carefully in his arms – but Indigo could see no sign of Grimya.

She turned on her captors, forgetting in her anger and fear that they wouldn't understand her. 'Where is Grimya?' she demanded in her own tongue. 'What have you done with her?'

The men looked at each other and shrugged, and Indigo swore under her breath. 'Animal,' she said, switching to Khimizi in the hope that they might comprehend. 'Dog! *My* dog.' And she tried to wrench her arms free, to pantomime a creature on all fours.

One of the warriors shook her to stop her struggles, but the second grinned, comprehending. He pointed to another chimelo, and Indigo saw a grey shape draped over the animal's saddle. Grimya had been trussed like a hunter's prize, all dignity lost, and Indigo's anger resurged. But before she could vent her fury on her captors, Grimya's mental voice spoke in her mind.

No, Indigo. Remember what you told me, and do nothing yet.

With an effort Indigo bit back her outburst and forced her muscles to relax. Dignity aside, she and Grimya were under no immediate threat, and so she submitted wordlessly as the two warriors led her to her own chimelo and, when she was mounted, tied her hands to the saddle pommel. The animals were mustered into line, and she caught Agnethe's eye briefly before they were separated. The Takhina's face was a tight, miserable mask and she made no attempt to speak: but as they began to move out there was a small disturbance at the head of the group. A chimelo sidestepped out of line, as though something had frightened it, and Indigo heard Agnethe cry out one damning word.

'Traitor!'

She had only a momentary glimpse of the errant chimelo's rider, but it was enough. A young man, his face disfigured by a sword-cut that had only just begun to heal, his posture hunched and defensive. And his hair and skin the unmistakable honey-gold of a Khimizi aristocrat.

Chapter IV

The walls of Simhara came in sight during late afternoon of the following day. Under other circumstances Indigo would have been entranced by her first glimpse of the city's great towers rising against the brilliant sky: Simhara had been dubbed 'The Jewel of the East', and the epithet was well-chosen, for its myriad stained-glass windows glittered with shades of ruby, topaz, sapphire, emerald in their settings of pastel stone, and the brazen sheen of the semi-precious metals that adorned the roofs of the spires and minarets reflected the waning sun like a hundred dazzling heliographs. Although her mother had been born in Simhara her family had lived in one of Khimiz's lesser cities further to the south. Imogen had often visited the city of her birth, and as a child at her mother's knee Indigo had been enthralled by the tales she had heard of its magnificence. But now she felt too weary and disheartened to do anything other than stare dully at the shining walls and the shimmering spires and the vivid gemstone brilliance of the sea that formed Simhara's backdrop, and her only emotion was one of intense relief that the journey was ending at last.

The warriors had set a punishing pace across the desert, stopping only three times, and then briefly, to refresh themselves. Indigo and Grimya had been given water but no food; their captors' care for their well-being, it seemed, extended only as far as ensuring that they stayed alive. But still the men showed them no overt hostility; several times the warrior who led Indigo's mount had turned his head and smiled encouragingly at her, though she stonily ignored him, and ignored, too, the intermittent sounds of Agnethe's sobbing and occasional infant tantrums from Jessamin.

She had communicated, though desultorily, with Grimya, but as the day wore on and the heat intensified, even that effort had become too great, and a numbing and dreamlike exhaustion had set in, eclipsing all other feelings.

As they drew closer to Simhara, however, her mind was dragged forcibly from its torpor as the havoc that the invaders' siege had wreaked upon the city became clear. For a mile outside the walls the desert sand was churned into chaos, and the signs of a recent encampment – remains of fires, abandoned cooking-pots, animal dung, even a few tents – littered the ground. And a large section of the walls' northern face, where the city's vast and gracious main gates had stood, was reduced to a tumbled mass of rubble. Great stones had crashed down in fire-blackened ruins, and the gates themselves, shattered and twisted almost beyond recognition, lay amid the wreckage like the broken wings of some fabled bronze bird.

There were guards at the wrecked gateway, and the riders' leader halted briefly to speak to them. The sun was a hot furnace, and Indigo shifted on her sweat-slick saddle and clasped the pommel more tightly, hoping she had the strength left to stay on the chimelo's back until they reached their final destination, and wishing that she didn't feel so sick.

After a few moments they moved on again; and as they entered the city, Indigo realised that the chaos she had already seen told only a small part of the story. Simhara had been ravaged. Though the high towers and minarets visible from beyond the walls were undamaged, little else had escaped the siege and the ensuing battle unscathed. The broad avenues were choked with debris, and the trees that had once lined them now lay torn and broken in the gutters. Elegant houses had become shells overnight, their balustrades smashed, their facades caved in, their interiors gutted by blazing missiles from the invaders' ballistas. And of Simhara's fifty bazaars, with their mosaic murals and silk awnings and vine-covered pergolas, nothing was left but an ugly waste of charred, bare stone adorned

43

with tattered remnants of fabric like the mournful banners of a ghost army.

And the signs of death were everywhere.

The worst of the carnage had been cleared, but there was still more than enough evidence of the toll the battle had taken. They passed two of the slave gangs who laboured, under the stern, silent command of invader guards, to gather up the corpses of both sides from the streets and load them on to burial carts. The gangs paused in their gruesome work to let the riders go by, and the resentful eyes of Khimizi nobles and peasants alike stared up at them. Some covered their faces or made religious signs as they recognised their Takhina: one man tried to break free and run towards her, but was struck back into line by two club-wielding soldiers. Agnethe hung her head and began to cry again, softly, hopelessly: as the party rode on, Indigo tried not to look down at the dark runnels of dried blood that lurked in the gutters, tried not to heed the acrid, greasy smoke that rose from the far ends of the avenues along which the ox-carts lumbered. Sick now in spirit as well as in body, she kept her gaze tightly focused on the swaying neck of her chimelo, and tried to control the sweating, shivering spasms that threatened to overtake her with every breath she drew.

It soon became clear that the worst of the destruction had been confined to Simhara's outer limits, for as the returning party neared the city centre, a peculiar quiet settled over the scene. It was more in the nature of a hiatus than a true sense of peace; but even so the devastation seemed less, the reality of war and battle more remote. And when at last they reached the palace of the Takhan, at Simhara's very heart, it seemed that the ancient building stood aloof from and untouched by the smallest sign of trouble.

As she gazed at the high, trellised marble walls with their green cloak of rambling foliage that surrounded the palace, then watched the bronze gates opening and glimpsed the gardens and quietly playing fountains beyond, Indigo's memories of her mother's tales resurged like an old but cherished dream. The guards at the gates – not Khimizi guards but alien men, out of place here – had exchanged no more than a few brief words with the riders' leader: news of their arrival had travelled before them, and they were expected.

And welcomed. For the guards bowed to Agnethe as she passed, and bowed again to the baby Jessamin in her basket. Indigo didn't understand: it was as though time and circumstances had slipped out of true and she was witnessing nothing more than the return of Khimiz's Takhina from some minor social event, rather than the delivery of a fugitive into the hands of her enemies.

But she had no time to think on the implications of what she had witnessed, for the chimelos, scenting water, were hastening eagerly through the gate – and as it shut behind them, muting the sounds of the city and the sea to a dim murmur, it was as though Indigo had left reality behind and entered a closed world of dreams.

Siege and battle hadn't touched the palace of Simhara. They stood in a courtyard filled with flowers and cooled by the glittering play of a dozen fountains and waterfalls that fed an artificial pool surrounded by trailing plants. Indigo glimpsed the gold-silver flicker of fish in the pool, untroubled and tranquil; raising her gaze, she saw a shaded walk of pillars flanking the palace's wall, and muted movement reflecting in multi-coloured glass as servants hurried silently about their business. It was as though the invasion and the siege and the battle had never taken place; as though this regal household continued in its routine, unsullied by any disruption.

The warrior who had led her mount turned his head, startled by the inarticulate gasp that broke from his charge's lips. He was in time to see Indigo sway uncontrollably in her saddle as exhaustion, confusion and numbness finally overcame her self-control, but not in time to catch her as she slipped from the chimelo's back and fell in a dead faint to the elegant marble flagstones.

She woke to a sensation of cooler air on her face and the sound of a faint, rhythmic creaking. For a moment she thought she was still in the desert, and opened her eyes expecting to see the gleam of yet more endless acres of sand under the remote moon. But there was no sand, no vast and empty landscape. Instead she was lying on a low couch, her head and feet pillowed by silk cushions, and the light that met her gaze came not from the moon, but from an ornate lamp with an amber glass chimney that shone softly at the far side of a spacious and high-ceilinged room.

Disconcerted, Indigo sat up and looked about her. Though full dark had fallen and the lamp's glow provided the only illumination, she could see that the chamber was furnished with spare but impeccably rich taste. A painted frieze ran along the top of the otherwise bare white walls, woven rugs covered the floor, and among the soft shadows she made out the silhouette of another couch, and a round table whose copper surface gleamed dimly like a huge, polished coin. And on the floor a few feet away, amid another pile of cushions, Grimya lay fast asleep.

Indigo got slowly to her feet. She had been too exhausted by the time they reached the city to even begin to speculate on what manner of treatment she might receive at the invaders' hands; but certainly she could have anticipated nothing like this. It was as though she were an honoured guest rather than a prisoner.

Movement glimpsed on the edge of vision made her start, and she turned again, to see that behind her were tall double windows stretching from floor to ceiling. They stood part open, and the flimsy draperies that hung across them were blowing in the light breeze from outside. Treading carefully so as not to disturb Grimya, Indigo moved round the couch – her legs felt weak, but that would pass soon enough – and stepped out on to a balustraded balcony that, she found, overlooked one of the palace's many inner courtyards. Moonlight showered down on pale flagstones, and cast complex shadows among the shrubs and vines that wreathed the court;

tiny artificial lights among the foliage augmented the moon like glow-worms, picking out a cluster of honey-suckle here, the velvet petals of oleander or hibiscus there; and though its source was invisible Indigo heard the faint tinkling of water over pebbles somewhere close by.

She breathed in, tasting the spicy-sweetness of the flower scents mingling with the faint tang of the sea. The night was warm but not stifling, and the palace seemed bathed in peace. All around the courtyard she glimpsed other balconied windows, most unlit now but one or two betraying a faint glow of lamplight beyond drawn curtains. The atmosphere was so tranquil that she wondered for a moment if she might still be asleep, and dreaming; and if she would wake suddenly to find herself in some dank cell with this magical scene nothing more than a fleeting memory. But then she felt a familiar stirring in her mind, and a familiar voice impinged gently, silently on her consciousness.

Indigo? Are you there?

Grimya had woken, and now came padding to the window to greet her. Indigo crouched down and hugged the she-wolf, thankful to see that she had suffered no ill-effect from her ordeal.

'Grimya.' She buried her face in her friend's fur, rubbing at her ruff in the way Grimya liked best. 'Are you all right, love?'

'I am . . . very well,' Grimya said aloud. 'And rr . . . ested.' She ventured on to the balcony and sniffed the air delicately. 'This is a *strrrange* place. But I th . . . ink I like it.'

'A strange place, and a strange way to treat captives. I don't understand it.' Indigo straightened. 'When you consider that we were caught abetting the Takhina, it makes no sense.'

'I . . . know. After you f-fainted, the men were very sol . . . sol . . . ' Grimya shook her head in frustration. 'I cannot remember the word!'

'Solicitous?'

'Yes. That word. They called for ser-vants, and they brr-ought us both here and saw that you were com-

47

fortable. They gave me w . . . ater, and some meat to eat. And there is a strrr*ange* device in the room, that keeps us cool. I do not know how it works, but it creaks the whole time, like an old tree about to f . . . fall.'

A fan? Indigo had heard of such things from her mother; wings of silk or feather affixed to the ceilings of wealthy homes and worked by a complex system of pulleys connected to a waterwheel or turned by servants. As a child she had begged to have one, but there was no need of such things at Carn Caille; better, her father had said gloomily, if the artisans of Khimiz could have invented something to still the air, not stir it to greater activity.

The unwonted scrap of memory brought a quick stab of pain and she turned away from the courtyard. As she returned to the couch, she heard the sound of a key turning in a lock, and looked up in time to see three women come in. From their dress she knew at once that they were servants; two went barefoot with gauzy veils over their faces, while the third – considerably older – wore kidskin sandals and no veil, and was clad in soft, loose trousers rather than the pleated linen skirts of the others. She was clearly in charge of the two girls, and as she took in the dark hair and swarthy skin Indigo realised that the woman was no Khimizi but bore a strong racial resemblance to the invading soldiers.

The girls made graceful obeisances, while the older woman stared at Indigo with a mixture of suspicion and uncertainty. Indigo looked back at her, eyes narrowing with instinctive dislike, and said in Khimizi,

'What do you want?'

The woman's brows knitted but otherwise her expression didn't change, and one of the girls – a slight, doe-eyed creature with cheeks pockmarked by old child-blight scars – spoke up deferentially.

'I beg your pardon, madam, but she speaks no Khimizi.' The woman's suspicious stare turned on her; the girl hesitated, waiting for permission to continue and received a curt but uncertain nod. 'We were told to see if you were awake, and to bring you refreshment and new clothing.'

Indigo glanced at the older woman, who was watching the exchange carefully. 'You served the Takhan's household?' she said to the girl.

Another hesitation. Then, cautiously: 'Yes, madam.'

'Then tell me what's happened here. Where are the Takhina and her child? And the Takhan – ' She saw the girl's eyes widen with fear, and added more vehemently, 'For the Great Goddess's sake, girl, I'm not about to betray you! My own mother was from Simhara; I'm no traitor!'

The girl shook her head nervously. 'I can't tell you anything, madam,' she said in a low voice. 'I *dare* not!' She gestured, her former grace and co-ordination gone. '*Please* – eat, drink – '

Indigo sighed. There was no point in pressing her; she was too afraid to speak freely. Turning away she sank down on the couch again and, with obvious relief, the girl signed to her companion. Ice clinked against glass as the other girl came forward carrying a brass tray, which she set on the low table.

'We have brought iced lime-juice and honey, madam, and seed cake, and olives, and dates.' The second girl cast a quick, furtive look in the direction of their guardian, then added softly, 'The Takhan is dead, madam, and Au– ' she checked herself hastily, aware that she had been about to speak a name that the older woman would have recognised. 'Another rules here now. I can tell you nothing more. I am sorry.'

It was little enough, but it confirmed Indigo's worst fears. She cast her eyes down. 'I understand. Thank you.'

They fed her and bathed her, and left her as comfortable as any noblewoman could expect to be made in a house where her name was honoured. Only one thing betrayed her true position: the quiet but emphatic click of the key turning in the lock again as her ministrants finally left.

Indigo sat back on the couch and sipped at her third glass of iced and sweetened fruit juice. She felt truly clean for the first time since leaving Macce and her crew;

her hunger was satisfied, her new clothes were soft and comfortable, and the atmosphere in the room soporific; all contributing to lull her towards sleep. And until she could learn more of her jailers and their intentions towards her – which, she reasoned, she couldn't hope to do until such time as they chose to reveal the truth – there seemed little point in staying wakeful only to torment herself with unanswerable questions.

Grimya's view was unequivocal and pragmatic. To wait, the she-wolf said, was their only option. And the waiting would pass more quickly if they slept as much as they could. Indigo couldn't have argued with her logic even if her own instincts hadn't been urging her to the same conclusion, and so when the soft pad of the servants' feet had diminished into silence beyond the door she set her glass down and lay back, closing her eyes and letting the night's quiet wash over her.

She fell asleep in seconds, and dreamed disjointed dreams of ships and deserts and withered fortune-tellers. The nightmares and the heat made her restless; several times she woke and lay for a while in the close, dark room, listening to the steady creak and rustle of the fan until she slipped into sleep again. But each time the dreams came back, and finally culminated in a hideous, fragmented image of unhuman silver eyes staring at her out of smothering darkness, and a sense that some great and unshakeable weight was pressing down on her body, stifling her, choking the breath from her lungs –

She woke with a violent start, biting back her cry for help before it could take physical form, and found morning sunlight streaming into the room. She sat up, pressing the palms of her hands to heavy eyes, then as her vision cleared saw Grimya also awake, and yawning.

'I am hh . . . *ungry*,' Grimya said aloud.

The prosaic complaint released Indigo's tension in a rush of relief that banished the nightmares into frac-tured memory. She smiled. 'Perhaps we should call for the servants. If last night was any indication, it seems they haven't yet decided whether we are prisoners or guests, so we should make the most of their indecision while we can.'

Grimya stared at her. 'I do not thh-ink it is a joking matter. At the water place, there was little doubt of our p . . . position.' She got to her feet, shook herself. 'Yes; we have been trrr . . . eated well enough since we arrived in the city. But I do not tr-*ust* it. And then there is the l . . . lodestone . . . '

Indigo's mood sobered abruptly as she realised what Grimya implied. It had been easy, with food and drink in her belly, and clean clothes on her back, and a comfortable couch to lie on, to forget the circumstances that had brought them here. And easy to forget the plight of the Takhina Agnethe and baby Jessamin, who had slipped from her thoughts as easily as she might have cast off an old shoe. But the she-wolf had reminded her sharply that this seductive hiatus was just that: a hiatus.

She touched the thong at her neck, feeling the weight of the lodestone in its pouch. An intuition that she didn't welcome told her what the stone would indicate, without the need to look at it. The golden pinpoint of light would be at rest, centred at the stone's heart; telling her that the demon she sought was here in the city, and that she must not, *dared* not, allow herself a moment's complacency.

Then, as though some capricious power had read her mind and chosen with a sour sense of irony to emphasise her conclusion, someone rapped sharply on the locked door.

Indigo started as though she'd been physically struck. She expected the key to grate, the door to open; but instead there was silence in the wake of the knocking. Grimya's hackles were up, her posture aggressive and defensive together; then after perhaps half a minute the unseen knuckles rapped again.

'Wh– ' Indigo's voice caught; she cleared her throat and took a grip on herself. 'What is it?'

'Madam.' A male voice; a native Khimizi speaker by the sound of it. 'May we have your leave to enter?'

Yet again the careful courtesy, as though she were an honoured visitor . . . Indigo glanced at Grimya, her eyes conveying a warning, and called, 'Yes. Enter.'

51

The door opened. Two men stood on the threshold, and as she looked at the first of them Indigo recognised him instantly. A young man with honey-gold hair, hunted eyes, and a newly healing scar on his face as though he'd taken a sword-cut. She had seen that face once before, in the desert moonlight, turning guiltily away as Agnethe screamed '*Traitor!*'

She swallowed her surprise, masking it by reaching down to lay a hand on Grimya's shoulder as though to restrain her. 'Yes?' she said again. 'What do you want with me?'

He was less deferential than the women had been. But his eyes were still hunted, the fear in them painfully real. 'We are instructed by the Takhan to bring you – '

Indigo interrupted him. 'The Takhan?'

His face coloured. 'The Takhan Augon Hunnamek, madam, new Overlord of Khimiz and protector of our beloved city.'

She stared at him as the import of his words sank in. The *new* Takhan. The warlord. The invader. The usurper.

Her visitor's companion, who had dark hair and swarthy skin and carried a short sword in his belt, reached out and touched the young man's shoulder.

'Do not waste time.' The words were accented but recognisable Khimizi, the clipped tone of a foreigner who was learning fast. Indigo began to understand.

'If you will accompany us, madam.' A swift, sidelong movement of the young man's eyes, not intended for his companion to see. 'The Takhan has much to attend to, and would prefer not to be kept waiting.'

Indigo's pulse began to quicken with nervous excitement. 'Very well,' she said, and rose. Grimya, too, started forward, but the swarthy man said 'No. Animal must stay here.' He moved to intercept her, and Grimya showed her teeth, growling.

Quickly, Indigo caught hold of Grimya's ruff before she could do anything foolish, and said silently, urgently, *It's all right, love. No harm will come to me.*

I do not trust them! Grimya argued.

We have no choice, for the present. Wait here, please.

52

Reluctantly the she-wolf relented, and Indigo followed the two men from the room. They locked the door again, and a faint whine issued from the far side before subsiding into silence.

They led her through light, airy corridors whose outside walls were mosaics of multicoloured glass, down a flight of broad, pale marble stairs decorated with urns of trailing plants, along yet more corridors where painted glass mobiles hung before the windows and chimed softly as the hot air moved them. Outside, Indigo saw flower-filled courtyards, and beyond them the graceful, intricate lines of walls and towers and minarets against the hard, dazzling blue of the sky: and despite the heat she shivered. This was the Simhara her mother had so lovingly described to her long ago, and though she'd never set foot in the city before, its familiarity was unnerving. She felt that a part of her had come home, and the feeling awoke memories that were safer buried and shunned.

When her escort turned abruptly towards another flight of stairs, leading upward this time, she realised that they must be approaching their destination; for at the top of the flight the way was barred by double bronze doors overlaid with gold filigree and guarded by two invader soldiers. And on the doors' surfaces Indigo recognised the shapes of a stylised net, trident and anchor; the threefold emblem of Simhara.

They were expected. The guards stepped aside, one reaching to open the doors. They swung wide, and Indigo found herself on the threshold of a surprisingly small but opulent room. Fringed and brocaded tapestries hung on the stuccoed walls, heavy velvet curtains covered the windows, shutting out daylight; a haze of aromatic incense-smoke hung stilly on the air, diffusing the soft yellow glow of oil-lamps and giving the scene an unreal, almost dreamlike air.

There were two people in the room. One sat cross-legged on a cushion at the feet of a carved chair; as she looked up, Indigo had an impression of a bony, ageing

53

face, steady and intelligent eyes, greying hair coiled into a complex plait at the nape of her neck. But her scrutiny lasted only a moment before the room's other occupant rose from the chair and riveted her attention.

He was a giant of a man, almost seven feet tall and massively built, with dark, gleaming skin and hair that by startling contrast was almost pure white. Pale, heavy-lidded eyes gazed coolly down at Indigo, and the full, sensuous mouth widened in a faint smile. A powerful hand, the arm decorated with several heavy, jewelled bracelets, stretched out in a courteous gesture.

'Welcome.' He spoke in Khimizi, though with an accent that no native would have recognised. 'I am Augon Hunnamek.'

Indigo stared at him – and from nowhere, a thick, stifling and utterly irrational sense of revulsion rose to grip her. She opened her mouth, but words wouldn't come: the shock of her violent reaction, without rhyme or reason to it, had taken her completely unawares.

And a voice in her mind said: *demon!*

Chapter V

He was a shrewd and intelligent man: she couldn't help but acknowledge that, whatever else her instincts might be telling her. And from the first moment he addressed her, Indigo also knew that Augon Hunnamek was no petty tyrant. Ruthless – yes; she could see it clearly in his pale eyes, and he made no effort to hide it. Ambitious – yes also; but unlike many ambitious men he had the strength and skill to make his ambitions bear fruit. And charismatic. That charisma was an almost physical aura, and she knew instantly that it was the source from which Augon Hunnamek drew his power. Power to lead, power to command and inspire . . . enough power to have crushed Khimiz in the space of a few days, and set himself upon the world's richest throne.

But beneath that glittering surface lay something else, strong enough to have triggered an intuition that made Indigo want to turn and run. Grossness? Lust? It was both and yet neither; she couldn't accurately pinpoint it, but it lurked behind the cool scrutiny, was implicit in each small movement of his limbs or torso. And when he smiled at her, dispassionately yet with an underlying implication that she couldn't name, cold claws raked her spine.

The ornate doors closed at her back as her escort went quietly out.

'Please, sit.' Augon Hunnamek pointed to a cushion on the floor near her feet. 'I have questions, and you will oblige me by answering them truthfully.' He turned the pointing hand palm upwards to make a gracious gesture in which Indigo thought she detected a hint of threat.

She inclined her head, and sat down. She was nervous and her hands were beginning to sweat; surreptitiously she rubbed them on her skirt, not wanting to betray her unease and therefore increase her disadvantage.

The warlord lowered his bulk back on to the chair, and tapped the arm with a ringed hand. The older woman watched Indigo with detached interest, but said nothing.

'We will conclude the formalities to begin with,' Augon said. 'I understand that you are a foreigner. Is this correct?'

Indigo nodded. 'Yes.'

'Your name? And your home?' He was gazing at her, chin resting on a curled fist, and as Indigo caught his eye momentarily she recognised something less than platonic in his look. He was assessing her as he might have assessed a harlot in a whorehouse, or a slave in a market, and anger rose in her. With it came a reckless urge to spring to her feet and damn this upstart, tell him that she was no peasant plaything for his amusement, but royal, of a rank that he could never worm his way to achieving, a king's daughter, a queen in her own right –

And an outcast who could never claim her throne.

It hit her like cold water in the face, and the fury evaporated in an instant, leaving chill and miserable dismay as Indigo realised that she had almost lost control and broken the taboo that bound her. Anghara Kaligsdaughter, princess of the Southern Isles, was long dead. Indigo had forfeited name, identity and rank, and the throne that by blood-right should have been hers belonged now to a stranger. And that was the way it must always be . . .

Bleakly, her self-control restored, she said, 'My name is Indigo. I am a Southern Islander.'

He raised inquiring eyebrows. 'Indigo? It is not a name I have heard before.'

'It is the only name I have.'

A faint shrug. 'As you please. And your business in Simhara?'

Despite the sobering effect of her near-blunder, a spark of Indigo's anger still remained, and she replied a little sharply, 'Without intending discourtesy, sir, I think that my business is my own.'

56

The woman glanced at Augon, and the warlord smiled gently.

'Indigo.' This time he pronounced her name with punctilious politeness, yet a sensual note coloured his voice, as though he were stroking each syllable. 'You will, I am sure, comprehend my position. You are a foreigner, and yet you were discovered in the desert, in the company of the Dowager Takhina. You have, therefore, some involvement in the unfortunate episode of her attempt to flee the city. I merely wish to establish the nature of that involvement.'

The woman was watching her even more keenly, and Indigo didn't think it would be wise to lie. It was possible – not certain, but possible – that this companion or adviser or whatever she was had some seer's skill; she'd sensed a hint of it in the woman's first glance. And Augon Hunnamek wouldn't be easily duped. No; she'd best tell them the truth. Or at least as much of the truth as she dared reveal.

And so, forcing herself to meet the pale, frank scrutiny, she explained that her encounter with Agnethe had been sheer happenstance; that, heading for Simhara but hearing of the troubles, she had ridden across the desert to assess the situation with her own eyes, and had come upon the Takhina at the oasis, pinned beneath her dead chimelo.

'I see.' The warlord nodded, and his smile broadened a little. 'And if my men had not intercepted you, Indigo. What would you have done then?'

Indigo could feel the woman's gaze like ice, like fire. She said:

'I would have done what any civilised man or woman would have done in the same circumstances, sir – seen to it that the Takhina came to no further harm.'

Augon chuckled, a rich sound that emanated from stomach and lungs rather than simply from his throat.

'A diplomatic answer, I think.' The woman smiled too, but more reservedly. 'Very well: we shall say no more of the episode, Indigo, as I believe that you have performed a service for me in your concern for the welfare of the Dowager Takhina. I have one question

57

further. What was your purpose in wishing to visit Simhara? Do you have acquaintances in the city?'

'No, sir.' Indigo looked at him, unflinching.

'Then what do you want here?'

She knew what she would say, and believed that the answer would satisfy him. And if her surmise about the woman was right, she too would accept it willingly enough.

'Sir, I am a mariner,' she said. 'I was a crew member on the *Kara Karai*, which put in at Huon Parita a few days ago and – '

'From where?' the woman demanded, interrupting.

'*Kara Karai* is a Davakotian hunter-escort.' Memory of Macce's hard little face flashed briefly, nostalgically, through Indigo's mind. 'Our last commission was to the Jewel Islands, and I disembarked with a year's earnings to my credit.'

The woman looked up at Augon, and spoke for the first time. 'Her belongings have been examined,' she said in Khimizi. Her voice was husky but less heavily accented than the overlord's. 'What she says is true.'

Again the little flicker of anger: Indigo quelled it. 'Then if you understand the ways of seafarers, you may know that the Temple of Mariners in Simhara is a place of pilgrimage for us.' She watched the woman's eyes carefully, and saw what she had hoped for; a momentary softening, a tiny light of fellow-feeling. She lowered her gaze. 'Those of us who sail the seas do so only with the indulgence of the Great Mother. Her greatest shrine is in Simhara, and I wanted to make an offering at the shrine, give thanks for safe voyages and ask Her blessing for the future.' She looked up again, candidly. 'That is my only reason for coming to the city.'

The two exchanged another glance. The woman spoke again.

'And when you have made your offering,' she said, and her tone had changed, softened. 'What then?'

Indigo lifted her shoulders as though to convey the inevitability of her place in the world. 'I will find another ship.'

Silence descended on the room for a few moments.

58

Then the woman turned to Augon, who leaned towards her, and spoke quickly, quietly in his ear. He nodded, the smile still playing about his full lips, while Indigo watched them both and tried fruitlessly to guess the nature of their exchange. At last Augon looked at her again.

'Very well, Indigo. The story you have told to us seems satisfactory. However, as I am sure you will understand, I am in a position where I must for the time being take the greatest care, and so certain facts will need to be verified before I can sanction your release.' He made a gesture intended to convey his own helplessness. 'I must therefore insist that you remain in the palace a while longer; but I assure you that you will be treated as a respected guest. I hope, for the moment, that you will be content with that?'

So precise, so punctilious: and yet Indigo knew that he was offering her no alternative. But it was a good deal more than she might have expected, and – for the moment – she was prepared to accept it.

She nodded. 'Of course.' Her eyes met those of the grey-haired woman, and saw a new interest that she didn't know how to interpret.

'Then I will bid you a good morning.' Augon Hunnamek rose, and tugged at a gold-threaded rope that hung beside his chair. A bell jangled harshly somewhere in the distance, and the double doors opened. 'You shall be escorted back to your chamber. And – ' he smiled, and the hint of lasciviousness underlying the smile made Indigo's blood run cold – 'I am indebted to you for your co-operation.'

Indigo got to her feet. That half-hidden look was like a breath of hot wind on the last embers of her anger, making her want to rise to the challenge in his eyes. She smiled, with her mouth only, and said: 'One question for you, sir.'

He inclined his head. 'Ask.'

'The Takhina Agnethe, and her daughter.' She wouldn't use the term *dowager*, and a finely-honed edge had crept into her voice. 'Where are they? What has become of them?'

Augon smiled a broad smile. 'Indigo, your concern does you only credit. They are well, and they are safe, and they receive all the honour that is due to them. You may depend upon that, as you may depend upon the fact that it would not be in my interests to harm them in any fashion.' The smile faded to a moue of amusement, and he tilted his head quizzically. 'Will that content you, lady?'

Indigo's face whitened, but for two spots of high colour on her cheeks. She could stare down most men, but under Augon's steady gaze she was the first to give way.

'Thank you for the assurance,' she said distantly, and turned on her heel. She thought, as the bronze doors closed behind her, that she heard the sound of muted laughter before it was masked by the heavier footfalls of the men who escorted her from the room.

Augon Hunnamek watched the doors come together and lock once more, then sat back in the carved chair, wiping a hand across his mouth and detachedly enjoying the taste of his own saliva. The incense that had been kept burning in this room for the past twenty-four hours was starting to lose its efficacy, and he had rejected suggestions that the brass bowls should be refilled. The sweet, heady smoke had done its work, aiding him to stay awake in spite of his body's demands for sleep; but now the main task was achieved: he had the vital prize, and in a few more minutes he could rest.

The prospect of sleep roused a pleasant, sensuous feeling of anticipation, and he stretched his muscular arms like a huge and self-indulgent cat. He had ordered the old Takhan's bed taken out to the city perimeters and burned; superstitiously, he was unwilling to sleep in a dead man's sheets. But the Takhan's private chamber was another matter. A pity, Augon thought, that he was too weary to take full advantage of such stimuli at present. Tomorrow, or the day after, it would be different . . .

He became aware of a vortex of silence at his left

hand, and looked down at the woman who still sat cross-legged at his feet. A sigh welled in his ribcage, and he quelled it, rising and moving to hack aside one of the heavy curtains. Sunlight streamed into the room, contrasting sharply with the artificial glow of the lamps, and Augon opened the glazed door that led on to a balcony more ornate than most in the palace. He stood for a few moments looking down on the courtyard below – the Takhan's private sanctuary, tended by servants who might anticipate the loss of a finger, or even a whole hand, if a single flower was permitted to wither before its time – and breathed in the hot but fresher air, before speaking at last.

'Well?' He used his native tongue, taking oblique pride in the knowledge that no one born in Simhara could understand it. 'What do you think?'

The woman rose a little stiffly and came to join him at the window. 'She spoke the truth, at least in part. She had no hand in Agnethe's escape, and I don't think she has any idea of the child's significance. But there's something else . . .'

'What?' And, when the woman didn't answer, he put a finger under her chin and turned her head, obliging her to look at him. 'Phereniq. Tell me. Or I shall be angry with you.'

A flicker of emotion that seemed to combine resentment and resignation showed momentarily in Phereniq's eyes before her shoulders relaxed. 'I don't know; not yet. But there's something about her that troubles me; something she's keeping from us.' She shivered, staring at the sky but not seeing it. 'I must consult my auguries.'

'As only you can.' He kept his finger on her jaw and drew her towards him, kissing her mouth lightly, in a brotherly way that might, under other circumstances, have promised something more. 'You are my ears and my eyes, Phereniq. You're my good luck. You know it, don't you?'

'Yes.' She raised her head to be free of him, and turned away.

Augon laughed, very softly. 'You've nothing to fear

61

from her. She's a simple seafarer; that much we can believe, though it seems a shameful waste that such a face and body should be confined to the deck of a ship.' He saw Phereniq stiffen, and his smile became vulpine. 'It might be expedient to do as you suggest and investigate her a little more closely.'

'Expedient?' Phereniq sounded faintly bitter.

'Yes.' Augon's fingers traced the line of the corded muscles that stood out at the nape of her neck. 'Don't forget the value of expedience, dear seer. I'd advise you, *always*, to remember it. And I will be most interested to hear the results of your divinations.'

Phereniq's head drooped and she shut her eyes. Only when his hand at last released her did she allow herself to breathe again. She heard his footfalls as he crossed the carpeted floor – though he moved softly, her hearing was very acute – and when she judged that he had gone, she risked looking over her shoulder.

The room was empty, the bronze doors swinging gently to on their hinges. Phereniq reached to a reticule that hung at her waist, and brought out a small cut-glass phial with a stopper carved from a single amethyst. It was one of the many gifts that Augon had given to her, and he knew the use to which she had put it in recent years.

She unstoppered the phial and put it to her lips. Not too much; not too little. Just enough to ease the overstrung tension within her.

The cordial – her own euphemism – was cloyingly sweet. She allowed a pool of it to form on her tongue, then swallowed and put the phial away, aware of a warm sensation already beginning to tickle the back of her throat. One last glance towards the sunlit courtyard . . . then Phereniq moved, with shoulders hunched as though from some slight pain, to the door, and quietly left the room.

Chapter VI

For the next two days, Indigo and Grimya lived in a strange limbo between imprisonment and honour in Simhara's royal palace.

They wanted for nothing. Indigo had only to pull on the tasselled bell rope in her room, and servants would bring her food, wine, fresh clothes, warm water and perfumed oils to refresh her. It was, on the surface, an idyll: but Indigo was constantly haunted by the reaction that Augon Hunnamek had provoked in her. She had tried to explain it to Grimya, but the words still eluded her, and her efforts to define the peculiar subtleties of what she had felt were lost on the she-wolf. Evil, however, was a concept Grimya understood well enough: and when Indigo described the instantaneous alarm that had sounded in her mind when she looked into Augon's eyes for the first time, the wolf's eyes darkened with disquiet.

'If, then, the demon is here, as we be-lieve,' she said sombrely, 'perhaps we have already f . . . *ound* it.'

Indigo shut her eyes, remembering the warlord's face, his smile, the pale, peculiarly intense stare, the sheer charisma he radiated. She didn't want it to be true, for she could see no way in which she could ever hope to destroy him. Elevated as he was now to the most powerful throne in the world, it would take an army greater than the one with which he had usurped rulership of Khimiz to topple him.

But if that smoothly civilised mask did indeed conceal the horror she had come to seek, then she would have no choice but to face it. And the price of failure was unthinkable.

She tried not to brood on her fears, but they were

insidious, catching her out in unguarded moments, stalking her dreams, lurking in shadows. She was also uncomfortably reminded that her own future was very far from assured. She thought that Augon had believed her story – or, if he doubted it, didn't consider her enough of a threat to be worth eradicating – but she was well aware that to rely on such an assumption was dangerous. Until she was granted her freedom, her fate lay entirely in the warlord's hands; and the knowledge wasn't reassuring.

In her efforts to distract herself, Indigo spent most of her waking hours either playing her harp, which had been returned to her with the rest of her belongings, or looking through the dozen or so books that she found in the room. The books were fascinating in themselves; the text on each heavy parchment page had been inked by carved wood-blocks, an ingenious process invented in Simhara but still rare outside Khimiz, then the finished sheets bound with a bone spine and covered with fine, dyed leather. Most were texts on religion or astrology, with one history of Khimiz which seemed to do little more than list and extol the virtues of successive Takhans. But despite the fact that the subject matter held little to interest Indigo, the books helped to keep less pleasant thoughts at bay.

Then, just before sunset on the second day, a message came from Augon Hunnamek, and with it a curious invitation. The Takhan proffered his compliments, and his regrets that she had been inconvenienced for so long. As of this moment, Indigo was to consider herself freed of all constraint and obligation.

No caveats; no conditions. Indigo was taken aback; despite her efforts to reassure herself, she hadn't expected to be dismissed so lightly. And her release posed a new problem in itself; for once she left the royal palace, she would have no further contact with the warlord.

The message-bringer – a young Khimizi accompanied by the inevitable surly invader guard – spoke again. 'The Takhan trusts, of course, that you will do him the honour of accepting his hospitality at least for one more night. And I have another message, from the lady Phereniq Kala.'

The name meant nothing. 'The lady . . . ?'

'Phereniq Kala. Astrologer and adviser to the Takhan.'

Of course: the woman who had sat at Augon's feet during their interview. Indigo frowned. 'What does she want of me?'

'I understand, madam, that you spoke of your intention to visit the Temple of Mariners. The lady Phereniq also intends to visit the temple tomorrow morning, and asks if you will accompany her.'

There was some ulterior motive in the invitation; Indigo sensed it instantly, and suspected Augon Hunnamek's hand behind it. She couldn't guess what the motive might be, but doubted if it posed any threat. She might learn a good deal from Phereniq Kala; and any information, however insignificant, could be valuable.

She looked at the messenger, who gazed back stoically. 'Please thank the Takhan for his kindness,' she said. 'And you may tell the lady Phereniq that I will be glad to accept her invitation.'

They met the next morning by one of the palace's lesser gates. The sun was climbing in a dazzling, cloudless sky, and the dry summer heat was already intense. Grimya padded at Indigo's side; though the weather wasn't to her liking she had refused to consider any suggestion that she stay behind.

Phereniq was waiting in the shade of a fig tree by the wall. She was dressed in a loose silk robe of Khimizi design, and carried a mahogany walking cane inlaid with silver. Their greeting was courteous but a little stiff; Indigo, still suspecting some hidden purpose in the invitation, wasn't prepared to offer open friendship until she knew where the land lay, and the older woman reacted to her reserve with wary formality.

'The Takhan suggested that we might take a litter to the temple,' she said, 'but I said that on such a fine day I would prefer to walk. I hope you don't mind?'

'Not at all.' So the warlord *did* know of this meeting . . .

They stepped through the gate, and emerged into a broad avenue whose close-planted trees provided welcome shade from the sun. Two cats bounded away on silent paws at sight of Grimya, but otherwise the avenue was quiet, and, like the palace itself, strangely unscathed by the horrors of recent days. Indigo recalled her first, ugly sight of the city in the aftermath of battle, and glanced at Phereniq.

'You're not afraid to go out unescorted?'

'Afraid?' Phereniq's eyes – which were, she noticed, a warm brown – focused on her face in mild amusement. 'No, I'm not afraid.' She gestured with her stick, pointing behind them, and Indigo looked over her shoulder.

Two dark-skinned men were following them, keeping a discreet distance. They were armed with knives and crossbows, and although their manner was casual enough, their purpose was obvious.

'I have my faithful watchdogs, as you have yours,' Phereniq said. 'Don't worry; they won't intrude on us, and they won't draw attention to us. They are simply a precaution.'

'A wise one.'

'Perhaps.' Again, that odd little smile. 'Although I think you may find the city less menacing than you imagine.'

They walked on. Gradually, the quiet began to give way to activity and an increasing hum of sound as they reached the end of the avenue and moved into Simhara's more populated streets. There were more people about than Indigo had anticipated, and, though Khimizi and invaders alike mingled on the thoroughfares, little sign of tension or hostility. With curious fascination, she realised that life in Simhara was already beginning to return to normal. And in the wake of his swift, thorough and brutally efficient conquest, it seemed that Augon Hunnamek was making every effort to repair the damage his army had wrought. The corpses of both sides were long gone; all but a few last traces of debris had been cleared from the paved roads; and mingling with the more mundane sounds of the city came the hammering and sawing and shouting of men set to rebuild shattered houses and broken facades. But there were no slave-gangs now, no sullen drudgery; in fact most of the toiling figures that Indigo saw were of the invader rather than Khimizi race. And in the first of Simhara's many squares, the silk awnings of the bazaar were back in place, and – though their numbers were small as yet – a few traders sat on their embroidered rugs and called their wares to those who passed by.

Indigo heard a soft chuckle at her shoulder, and turned to see Phereniq watching her.

'You are surprised?' the astrologer said.

Indigo shook her head, not in denial but in confusion. 'I hadn't expected such . . . order.'

'Nor the peaceful resumption of everyday life, eh?' The astrologer cast her gaze over the square with, Indigo thought, a satisfied and faintly proprietorial air. 'You're not alone in your misapprehensions, Indigo. The people of Khimiz have a great deal to learn about their new Takhan.'

Her voice was warm and a little fierce when she spoke of Augon, and Indigo caught the hint of something more than respect in her tone. Aware that it was the first of the clues she sought, she was about to prompt her companion to continue, but Phereniq needed no urging.

'The people expect their new overlord to be a barbarian,' she went on, with more than a trace of acerbity. 'But they will soon discover that they are wrong. Warrior Augon may be – but he is *not* barbaric.'

That defensive pride again. Indigo said nothing.

'Look about you.' Phereniq indicated the scene with a sweep of her stick. 'Our army and Simhara's citizens, side by side. Do you see strife? Do you see hostility? Do you see hatred? No; you do not. What you see is men working for a common cause: to restore Simhara's beauty. And that is exactly what Augon wants, because his desires and the desires of all Khimizi are one and the same.'

It was quite an impassioned speech, and Indigo didn't

know how to reply without risking seeming either sceptical or patronising. She decided that tactful honesty might serve her best, and so said, 'I appreciate your point, Phereniq. But do you think that all Khimizi will see it that way? You can't deny that Augon is, after all, a usurper.'

'Yes, he is.' Phereniq glanced obliquely at her, and smiled. 'Don't be afraid that you'll offend me by frankness, Indigo. I have as firm a grasp of reality as you: but I also have the advantage of knowing what the future holds.'

'As a seer?'

'That, yes; although my seeing comes from the science of the stars rather than from true clairvoyance. But I was speaking in a more mundane sense.' The smile took on a tinge of superiority. 'As Augon's astrologer and adviser, I understand his intentions perhaps better than anyone. You see, Augon prizes the finer qualities of life above all else. Art, music, beauty, erudition, invention – all the things that are the epitome of Khimizi culture. To him, Khimiz is not merely a conquest; and to the Khimizi he will not be merely a conqueror, but a ruler whose love of all that Khimiz stands for is equal to their own.' Her eyes took on a peculiar, faraway look. 'Augon Hunnamek will rule with justice and wisdom, and under his guiding hand Khimiz will achieve a peak of prosperity and glory that will make it the envy of the world.'

Indigo stared at her, taken aback by the angry edge in her voice. Then before she could think of any suitable reply, Grimya's mental voice intruded gently on her mind.

She loves the usurper, as female loves male, although he is not her mate. I see it in her mind. And it causes her great distress. That, I think, is what makes her rise so quickly to his defence.

A simple observation, yet, as so often happened, Grimya had touched the heart of the matter with unerring instinct. Indigo looked at Phereniq again, and wondered how she could have been such a fool as to miss the all too obvious signs. Defensiveness, as the she-wolf said. Pride in Augon Hunnamek, yet with a hint of bitterness lurking behind it, as though in a corner of her mind that she refused to acknowledge, Phereniq resented the emotions that had a hold on her.

And, remembering the hot speculation in the war-lord's eyes as she had met his gaze for the first time, she began to understand Phereniq a little better.

They walked on in silence for a while, and Indigo found herself seeing her companion with a new perspective. She was, she realised, older than she had appeared in the softly-lit room at the palace; the hard sunlight revealed the truth more cruelly, emphasising the greying of her hair and the lines on her face. And the walking-cane wasn't an affectation; though she seemed fit enough, Phereniq's gait was slightly stiff and the stick gave her a modicum of support. But there was a kindly set to her mouth and the composure of wisdom in her features. She must have been very handsome in her youth, and it was hard to imagine that she could truly be in love with such a man as Augon Hunnamek, who seemed to be her antithesis in almost every way.

They were nearing the great harbour of Simhara by this time, and the sharp tang of the sea mingled with the city smells. Though they couldn't yet glimpse the water, the sunlight was taking on a diamond-hard, coastal brilliance that for a moment made Indigo feel as though she were back on board the *Kara Karai* under a huge, clear sky. She smiled wistfully without realising it, and Phereniq said, 'Something saddens you?'

'What? Oh – no. Just a reminiscence.'

'I'm glad. This isn't a day for sadness.'

Indigo couldn't help but agree with her. This part of Simhara, furthest from the desert, had been all but untouched by the siege and battle, so that there was little sign of the damage wrought elsewhere. Despite its mercantile power, Khimiz had no military seagoing force to speak of; smaller nations like Davakos or even the Southern Isles could always provide warboats to protect the trading fleets, and the prudent merchants of Simhara agreed that even the most generous fees for such services were cheaper than the cost of maintaining an entire navy. So it was that on almost any day of the year Simhara's vast natural harbour was filled with ships of every kind from all parts of the world, from the huge cargo-carrying square-riggers, triremes and galleons to the escort warboats of a dozen different nations. But as the street began to widen and the glitter of the sea came into view ahead, one great difference between this and a normal day became clear; for the harbour was all but empty.

Indigo and Phereniq reached the end of the street, and stopped as the entire vista of the great harbour spread out before them. It was an impressive sight: a huge and broad paved crescent stretched away to either side, flanked by stately, porticoed buildings, while to seaward a network of wide steps and ramps led down to the quayside. The harbour itself was gigantic, sectioned by stone piers that jutted proudly out into the sea; but the smooth blue-green water was broken only by the hulls of a mere half-dozen small coastal vessels riding at anchor. The barques, the triremes, the galleons, the warboats, were gone.

'The merchant fleets and their escorts put pragmatism before loyalty, I understand, and left when the siege began,' Phereniq said drily. 'News is already abroad that they have nothing to fear. They will return soon enough.' She turned, looking right and left and seeming to drink in the atmosphere as though it were some well-aged wine. Despite the lack of shipping, the paved crescent was crowded, the sun beating down on a vivid panorama of moving forms, mingling colours, a hum of activity. 'There is so much to see. I could stand here all day, simply watching the bustle.' She linked her free arm with Indigo's in a companionable manner. 'However, we must resist the temptation and make our way to the temple. I understand it is no more than a short walk.'

Indigo allowed herself to be led into the crowd, Grimya padding alongside her. Within a few minutes they reached a place where the buildings lining the crescent gave way to a sweeping flight of steps that led up to a great, semicircular plaza – and before them was the Temple of Mariners.

Indigo could only stare in awe. The steps, which were cut from marble the colour of sea-spume, drew the eye up to the vast double doors that stood eternally open. The temple itself curved skywards in soaring triumph, and every inch of its outer walls was carved with images of the ocean; curling waves with latticed edges of foam, schools of glittering quartz fish, dolphins leaping exuberantly. Real water, too, fell among the carvings in sparkling cascades, creating a stunning illusion of life. And crowning the roof, a massive dome of shimmering glass shone like a single, huge diamond.

Phereniq's fingers tightened convulsively on Indigo's arm, and when Indigo turned her head – though it was almost impossible to tear her gaze away from the temple – she saw that the astrologer's face was rapt, her eyes shining.

'I had not realised.' Phereniq's voice was a whisper; then with great effort she dragged herself out of her near-trance and forced herself to focus on the pavement beneath her feet. 'I have heard of its beauty, but . . .' She shook her head, incapable of expressing what she felt.

Beauty? Indigo thought. Yes, the stories she had heard were true; it must be the most beautiful artefact ever created by human hand. But the temple was speaking to her in another way, a deeper way. And it said: *Peace*.

In her mind she saw again milky golden eyes, hair the brown of warm forest earth, a cloak of new green leaves. The face of the Earth Mother's emissary swam before her inner vision, and she felt the bittersweet, giddying sensation of the great Goddess's sorrow and anger and pity that had haunted her dreams for so long. She was swamped by a desire to run, up the steps and through the ever-open doors, to throw herself facedown upon the temple floor and cry for the peace that she knew lay within, hurl herself upon the mercy of the Great Mother and plead for forgiveness.

Forgiveness. Her mind lurched abruptly back to earth

71

as the word lodged in her brain. It wasn't forgiveness that she sought: the Great Mother had granted her that long ago, though in Her own, ironic way, when the emissary had taken her hand and led her from the carnage of Carn Caille. She craved *release*. Release from wandering, from searching, from striving. Release from the curse that she had brought on herself and on the world.

And the temple's spell shattered as something deep within Indigo's consciousness reminded her, as it had done so many times before, that the key to release lay in her hands alone, and that was the way it could only be.

Until it is done, Indigo. Until it is done.

The vivid scene around her swam back into focus, and she felt the hard paving under her feet, the faint pressure of Phereniq's arm against hers, the touch of Grimya's fur.

' – if you do not mind waiting for me?'

Phereniq's words hadn't fully registered, and Indigo turned, blinking with confusion as reality impinged. 'I'm sorry . . . what did you say?'

Phereniq regarded her with detached curiosity. 'The sellers of offerings. I have brought my own, but I would like to see what they display.'

The last of Indigo's miasma dissolved, and she realised that among the crowds on the temple steps were a number of pedlars selling small gifts for visitors to offer at the Sea Mother's shrine. Phereniq was already making her way towards them, and, a little shakily, Indigo followed. Half way up the steps Phereniq crouched down to speak to a blind man sitting on a woven mat. As Indigo caught up with her she raised her head, her eyes alight.

'Look at these! Such clever craftsmanship – have you ever seen the like of it?'

The blind man had carved some tiny ships which ran on wheels and were pulled along by coloured ribbons. The models were biremes, and as they moved, the twin banks of miniature oars rocked up and down.

'I must buy one,' Phereniq declared. 'For the little Infanta.'

'Infanta?' Indigo was nonplussed.

'The Takhina-Infanta. For Jessamin.' And suddenly she frowned. 'Ah, but of course. You don't yet know, do you?'

'Know what?'

Phereniq hesitated, then abruptly her expression changed again and she forced a smile. 'All in good time,' she said. 'There's much to explain to you, but this is not the place for it.' She drew a purse from under her robe, fumbled with it and handed the blind pedlar a whole zoza; four times the worth of the little carved toy. 'There, craftsman. And now my friend and I must be on our way.' And she hurried on up the steps.

Indigo made to start after her, but suddenly the blind man spoke.

'A gift for you, mistress.' His voice was frail, though he wasn't old; and his words were a statement, not a question. Indigo turned, and saw him holding out what looked like a delicately fashioned spider's-web in which tiny bronze shapes glinted.

'I scent the sea in your hair, mistress, and what better gift could a mariner give to the Sea Mother than a net to adorn Her ship?'

The web was made from fine metal thread, and the tiny bronze forms were fish, each scale painstakingly crafted, zircon chips shining in their eyes. Indigo gazed down at it in admiration, and the blind man smiled.

'A net to harvest the bounty of the sea, lady. One of the Three Gifts enshrined in legend. And who but the Mother knows what else it might catch, when the time is right?'

Something clutched at Indigo, like a chilly, unhuman hand clenching on her spine from within. A hint, no more. But . . .

Buy it. Grimya looked up at her, and the she-wolf's message was emphatic and urgent. *I don't know why. But you must.*

She groped for her coin-pouch, feeling suddenly that she rather than the pedlar was the blind one. 'How much?' Her voice was unsteady.

'What you will, mistress. What the Mother wills through you.'

Her fingers clasped a single coin; she didn't know its value and didn't care. It changed hands, and she felt the metallic-silky touch of the net as the pedlar draped it over her arm.

'The Mother bless us all,' he said. 'Or we are lost.'

Under the dazzling heat of the sun Indigo's skin turned cold, and she spun on her heel and ran in Phereniq's wake.

Chapter VII

'I have heard that at night, when the moon rises, the dome reflects her light as a beacon to call home ships at sea.' Phereniq spoke with soft reverence, her voice echoing in a muted cascade of whispers through the temple's soaring vault.

Indigo didn't answer. She stood on the marble floor, gazing up at the shrine, and words were beyond her. She had found Phereniq waiting for her by the temple doors, and together they had slipped off their shoes and walked through the shallow, flower-strewn pool that stretched across the entrance, to emerge into the cool, green-lit interior and stand at last before this incredible symbol of the Sea Mother's bounty.

The shrine took the form of a giant ship. It stood on marble pylons, and its hull had been made from nine different rare woods, which now, hundreds of years on, were all but invisible under a crust of gems and precious metals. Three masts towered into the temple's dome, adorned with a network of rigging, and white silk sails shone with eerie beauty in the gloom. At the ship's side a massive anchor, carved from wood and polished to a burnished glow, rested against the floor, secured to the hull by a heavy and exquisitely wrought chain. And at the prow was a figurehead in the form of a wild-eyed woman, arms outflung, carved hair streaming, mouth open as though she sang a never-ending song to the gales; worshippers had garlanded her with flowers, hung bracelets from her outstretched hands, crowned her and draped her with silk ribbons. And at sight of that serene figure flying before the ship, Indigo had forgotten the blind pedlar's strange allusion, and forgotten Phereniq's cryptic words and her own doubts and fears, and felt something akin to the peace she had craved flood through her. It couldn't last – she knew it couldn't – but while the spell was on her, she wanted only to immerse herself in it.

The temple was thronged with people; a far bigger crowd, Indigo surmised, than was usual, and a sure sign that a good deal of fear and uncertainty still lurked beneath Simhara's calm surface despite the restoration of order. Among the multitude the temple attendants – mostly, so she had heard, retired mariners – moved quietly in their sea-green robes, passing here and there to smile and answer a question or guide some frail individual towards the shrine. Indigo and Phereniq were carried with the throng, until they reached the flight of steps that would lead them up to the ship's deck.

The means of making offerings at the Temple of Mariners was beautiful in its simplicity. Since the temple's inception, all gifts to the Sea Mother had been given in the form of some adornment, great or small, to enhance the shrine; so that every part of the ship was laden with tributes, from the rich gems encrusting the hull, to lanterns and ropes and pennants, and even wooden nails and pins crudely but lovingly carved by the poorest sailors. Standing on the deck with the temple crowds a moving, muted sea in the dim light below her, Indigo gazed up at the towering sails and felt a strange, exhilarating blend of awe and familiarity course through her. At her side, Grimya too looked upwards, and the she-wolf spoke softly in her mind.

It makes me think of being on the ocean again. But there is something different here. Strength. Power. I cannot find the right word . . . but it is a good feeling, like it was when we sailed with Macce but more so.

Indigo had been thinking of Macce, and remembered her promise to say a prayer for the little Davakotian and her crew. She smiled down at Grimya, and walked slowly across the deck to the ship's starboard rail, where an earlier pilgrim had draped a heavy fishing-net hung with green glass floats over the side. Phereniq, she saw, was standing by the foremast, head bowed over something clasped in her cupped hands and her lips moving

76

noiselessly; Indigo watched her for a moment, then dropped to a crouch. For a moment she recalled the blind pedlar's face, and again heard his words. *A net to harvest the bounty of the sea. And who but the Mother knows what else it might catch, when the time is right?*

A chill breath seemed to pass across her, as though something unseen had cast a brief shadow. A net to harvest the bounty of the sea . . . and the blind man had referred, obliquely, to a legend of which Indigo had learned in childhood: the Three Gifts of Khimiz. Of all Khimiz's many treasures, the greatest and most precious were three golden artefacts – a net, a trident and an anchor. It was said that the Sea Mother Herself had given these gifts to Khimiz as symbols of Her blessing on the land; the net for fecundity, the trident for strength, and the anchor for stability: they were the foundations upon which the land's peace and prosperity would forever rest. For centuries past the Three Gifts had been kept and carefully guarded in an inner sanctum of the Temple of Mariners, brought out and displayed only on the most solemn ceremonial occasions. What, Indigo wondered with an inward shiver, would become of those blessings now that Khimiz had fallen to a usurper? And had the pedlar's strange words been, in some subtle way, connected with her own quest?

Indigo? Grimya said gently in her mind. *What is wrong?*

She shook her head. *I don't know. Perhaps nothing – it was a stray thought; a feeling . . .* But she couldn't articulate it.

Make the offering, the she-wolf said. *It is the right thing to do*.

Yes. She smoothed her fingers for a final time over the net with its shimmering bronze fish, then carefully spread her gift across the carved bulwark, trying as she did so to push away and forget her unease. She closed her eyes, felt Grimya's thoughts blending with hers, and together they stayed still for some minutes in silent dedication. Gradually, calm came to Indigo, the doubts giving way to a kaleidoscope of other emotions: love, sadness, fear, hope . . . and finally a quiet strengthening of the sense of peace she had experienced on first entering the temple. When at last she opened her eyes again she felt for a moment that she was held somewhere between the Earth and another, less tangible but ineffably beautiful world; the sensation shivered away in an instant, but its after-image tinged her vision as, very slowly, she rose to her feet and turned around.

Phereniq had also completed her devotions, and stood waiting for her. The astrologer's face was rapt, as though she too had been touched to the core by what she had experienced. Only when Indigo stepped into her field of vision did she blink rapidly, as though coming out of a trance. Her face broke into a smile that was both childlike and sad, and suddenly Indigo pitied her. But she said nothing, only took her hand as they began the descent to the temple floor.

Neither spoke as they left the temple. They emerged into daylight that dazzled them, and paused for a few minutes at the top of the steps to allow their eyes to adjust to the brilliance. At last, Phereniq broke the silence.

'Well, Indigo,' she said quietly. 'What will you do now?'

Indigo flexed her bare toes on the hot paving, and stared towards the harbour and the sea beyond. 'What I've always intended to do. Find another ship.'

There was a long pause. Then: 'So quickly?'

Was she probing? Or was this a first hint of the ulterior motive Indigo suspected behind the morning's excursion? Appearing careless, Indigo shrugged. 'I have no reason to stay in Simhara. Beautiful though it is, Grimya and I must eat.'

'Yet you sound regretful.'

She smiled slightly. 'Who would not be?'

They began to walk down the steps. Unobtrusively Indigo looked for the blind pedlar; but it seemed that he had either left the plaza or moved to another pitch. Then, as they neared the foot of the flight, Phereniq said suddenly: 'Indigo – this evening there is to be a small feast in the White Courtyard at the palace. No great occasion; merely a small celebration and thanksgiving

78

for the Takhan and his closest advisers. Will you attend, as my guest?'

It might have been imagination, but Indigo thought she felt the lodestone pulse suddenly beneath her bodice. She looked at Phereniq, her calm expression belying the quickening of her heart.

'I'd be honoured. But . . . ' She hesitated, then decided she had nothing to lose by being blunt. 'Why should you wish to invite an outsider to such a celebration?'

Phereniq smiled, though her eyes seemed to carry an echo of something less clear-cut. 'Look on it as a small recompense for the inconvenience you have suffered during the last few days.'

Indigo's instincts told her that there was more behind this apparently casual invitation than was as yet apparent, and again she sensed Augon Hunnamek's hand stirring the cauldron. It could lead her, she knew, into murky and dangerous waters – but if her suspicions were right, she had no choice but to swim wherever the tide chose to take her.

'Thank you, Phereniq,' she said. 'It will be a great pleasure.'

'Indigo.' Augon Hunnamek held out one hand in a gracious gesture, and smiled the smile of a predator. 'Your beauty would grace the table of the highest king tonight. Please, do me the honour of sitting here by me.'

From her place a few feet away Phereniq looked up, and under her fringed cap of gold mesh her eyes were cool with interest. Indigo inclined her head, not trusting herself to reply to the glib compliment, and allowed the warlord to take her hand and lead her to the central group of couches.

The feast had been set out in the traditional Khimizi manner, without obvious formality yet to a strictly observed order. Low tables set at intervals around the White Courtyard's central pool were laden with delicacies, while couches and cushions had been brought out for the guests' comfort; couches for the higher orders, cushions for those less favoured. Lamps glowed at the pool's edge and among the shrubbery, and the mingled scents of honeysuckle and jasmine hung heavy on the still air. At the far side of the courtyard, separated from the guests by a screen of trellis, three musicians provided a melodic but unobtrusive background.

There were some twenty people present, and Indigo was surprised to see no less than four Khimizi among them, one of whom was the young man with the facial scar. Agnethe's traitor, it seemed, had progressed rapidly in his new master's service; from messenger to courtier in the space of a mere three days. He caught her eye briefly; his look mingled speculation with a hunted sense that she interpreted as guilt, and, coolly and deliberately, Indigo turned away.

She sat down, feeling unnatural and restricted in the formal court gown that Phereniq had insisted on lending her for the occasion. Augon released her fingers with a final squeeze, then turned and spread his hands out. All eyes focused on him.

'Now that my friends are all gathered,' he said in Khimizi, 'we may begin our entertainment. Eat your fill, drink your fill, take pleasure in splendid surroundings and intimate company. And let us thank the Mother of us all for the blessings She has bestowed.' He smiled at the assembly with, Indigo thought – though the lamplight was deceptive – a touch of private and supercilious amusement, then repeated the speech in what she presumed was his native tongue. The guests, Khimizi and invader alike, acknowledged the language precedence with inclinations of their heads, and as Augon seated himself the hidden musicians changed to a livelier tune and the feasting began.

For the next hour wine was drunk and food eaten, the first course followed by dishes of fruit and sweet biscuits brought by soft-footed servants. To Indigo's relief, Augon made no attempt to monopolise her; he simply exchanged a few inconsequential pleasantries before turning to the wider company, and as no one else claimed her attention she was able to concentrate on her private impressions of the occasion.

80

It was, she had to admit, a very civilised gathering, bearing out Phereniq's defensive insistence that Augon Hunnamek was no barbarian. Perhaps by the standards of the high Khimizi aristocrats tonight's conversation was banal and the guests' dress and etiquette crude; but there was no doubt that the invaders, inspired by their warlord, were adapting rapidly and gracefully to the ways of their conquered and adopted country.

She wondered about Augon's own land. All she had so far been able to learn of his origins was that he had been born in a rugged and mountainous region far to the east of the Falor desert, and had begun his military career as a mercenary soldier in a wealthy lord's private army. Her knowledge of the world's geography was limited, but she had always viewed the furthest reaches of the eastern continent as backward and disorganised, a region of petty warmongers and strutting, self-appointed princelings. If that was so, then it had spawned a rare son in Augon Hunnamek; one whose ambitions – not to mention abilities – had far outstripped those of his one-time masters, and outgrown anything that his homeland could offer him.

And an ideal host for a demonic power whose only purpose was to bring chaos to the world . . .

People were beginning to move about, she realised suddenly; it seemed that by some unspoken protocol the formalities of the feast were over and the guests were beginning to relax. Phereniq had risen from her couch, and as servants moved to clear away the last of the food dishes she strolled across the terrace to join Indigo.

'Well.' Phereniq smiled. 'Are you enjoying your first experience of court life in Simhara?'

Indigo returned the smile. 'The *new* court life, you mean?'

'Oh, it isn't so very different from the old, I understand. For myself, I'd defy anyone not to be seduced by such gracious opulence.'

Indigo laughed. 'I agree.'

'Do you?' Phereniq's eyes lit with sudden new interest. 'Then this life might hold some appeal for you?'

Indigo hesitated. 'That's a strange question to ask.'

'Perhaps it is. But a lot might depend upon your answer.'

Before Phereniq could say more, however, Augon Hunnamek stood up and clapped his hands together, calling for the attention of the company. The musicians stopped mid-melody, and in the ensuing quiet the warlord rose to speak.

'My friends.' Again, he addressed them in Khimizi. 'At this point in our celebration, I wish to present an especially honoured and esteemed guest.' He gestured towards the arched entrance to the terrace, and, following his direction with the others, Indigo saw someone emerge from the shadows by the arched door. A woman, elegantly dressed but without jewellery, her face veiled: the Khimizi way of conveying that she was a servant, but highly-placed. She carried something in her arms, and Indigo glimpsed a gold-fringed shawl, saw a tiny flicker of movement and heard an infantile gurgle.

She looked quickly back to Phereniq, and though her voice was a whisper it was sharp with surprise. 'The Takhina's child?'

Phereniq inclined her head. 'The Infanta Jessamin, daughter of the *Dowager* Takhina.' The emphasis might have been reproof or warning, Indigo couldn't judge. She watched as Augon stepped forward and took the baby from the nurse's arms. The company gathered about him, and as each in turn was permitted to look at the child, Indigo saw that they had all brought some small gift: a soft shawl, a tiny, tortoise-shell comb, a ball with small bells inside it. It was a peculiar little ceremony, informal yet indefinably charged with significance; but Jessamin remained unperturbed throughout, finally returning to the nurse's charge without protest. The woman bowed to Augon, then withdrew, and Phereniq gazed after her until she and Jessamin had disappeared into the palace.

'Such a good-natured infant.' There was a faintly bleak twist to Phereniq's lips as she smiled. 'She has, you might say, set the final seal upon our triumph.'

Not comprehending, Indigo was about to ask her what she meant when she realised that Augon Hunnamek was approaching them. She inclined her head – foolhardy or not, she couldn't bring herself to bow to the warlord as others did – and Augon smiled down at her. In the softly lit night, his eyes in the dark face looked feral.

'Well, Indigo. Are you enjoying our small gathering?'

'Greatly, sir.' But her voice was stiff.

'I am glad. My only regret is that the Dowager Takhina declined to join us tonight. I had hoped that by now she might have accepted that she may still have an important role to fulfil within the court, but . . . well, we can only pray that with time and kindness she will relent.' He turned, snapping his fingers, and a servant hastened forward with wine. 'You will drink a toast with me, to the little Infanta?'

Indigo didn't like the lazy familiarity of his tone, but could hardly refuse, and Augon pressed a cup into her hand, his fingers brushing lightly across hers. 'To Jessamin,' he said. 'Infanta, and future Takhina of Khimiz.'

'To Jess– ' and the words died on Indigo's tongue as she realised what he had said. She stared at him. 'Future *Takhina*?'

'But of course.' Augon smiled. 'When Jessamin is twelve years old, I intend to make her my wife.' The smile became a soft laugh. 'My dear Indigo, you look like a startled faun! Is the revelation so surprising?'

Indigo couldn't speak. It was such an obvious manoeuvre, yet she had failed to foresee it. A new dynasty, founded on a union between the interloper and the royal bloodline. With the old Takhan's only child enthroned beside him, no one would dare dispute the legitimacy of Augon Hunnamek's claim.

And if Augon was what she believed him to be, the thought of a twelve-year-old girl subjected, through political machination, to his every will and whim made her feel sick to the pit of her stomach. 'The final seal upon our triumph', Phereniq had said. Quickly Indigo glanced at the astrologer, but Phereniq refused to meet her eyes, and instead turned and, with a studiedly careless air, walked away. In the lamplight her face looked haggard and old.

Augon laid a hand on Indigo's shoulder, and she had to exert all the self-control she could muster to stop herself from flinching. Those guests who had been standing close by had also moved out of earshot, perhaps taking their cue from Phereniq, and now Augon steered Indigo gently but implacably away from the centre of the courtyard, until, with the shadows of the walls crowding them, they were effectively alone.

'You appreciate now why the Infanta's wellbeing is of such great concern to me,' Augon said smoothly. 'The child must be nurtured with unstinting care until she is of marriageable age.' He looked down at her, and his pale eyes were suddenly shrewd. 'And that brings me to the matter of your role in Jessamin's development.'

'Mine?' Indigo was nonplussed.

'Indeed. I am not given to prevarication, so I shan't waste words, Jessamin needs a friend and mentor, to guide her through her early years and fit her for her future role. Agnethe, it seems, has determined to turn her back on her own child, which is a matter of great personal regret to me. But we cannot force these matters: until and unless she should relent, I must look for another to fulfil the place that is rightfully hers.' His hand, still resting on her shoulder, squeezed slightly then released her at last. 'I wish you to remain in my household, as companion and teacher to the Infanta.'

Indigo stared at him. When finally she found her voice, she said, 'I'm sorry . . . is this some joke you're playing on me?'

'Not at all.' He smiled, but without levity. 'I quite appreciate your bewilderment, my dear Indigo; I, too, was taken by surprise at first. But I believe you already know that my people, like the Khimizi, set great store by the science of divination in all its forms. The auguries are perfectly clear. They state emphatically that you are the ideal companion for the Infanta – and that is sufficient recommendation for me.'

She couldn't believe what she was hearing. 'But – I am not qualified for such a task; I – '

He interrupted her. 'Oh, but I think you are *eminently* qualified. Whatever fate may have decreed for you in recent years, it's perfectly obvious that you were not born to the life of a common sailor – and there's no need to protest your innocence: I'm interested in the future, not in the past. Now fate has spoken again, through Phereniq's divinations, and I need no further confirmation. The post is yours, if you are willing to accept it.'

So Phereniq – or, more accurately, her astrology – was behind this extraordinary and unexpected development. Suddenly, and with a dreadful sense of irony, Indigo realised that a solution to her greatest problem – that of remaining in close proximity to Augon Hunnamek's household – was being granted to her without her having even to seek it. The knowledge chilled her, for the coincidence was surely too great to be random. Something was manipulating events, apparently to her advantage: but whether that something was friend or foe she didn't dare to speculate.

Augon spoke again. 'If you see fit to refuse my offer, so be it; I will bear no grudge. But I hope you do not refuse. Aside from what the stars have to say in the matter, your departure would give me personal cause for regret.'

Indigo looked up at him, meeting his gaze as an inner shiver went through her like a slow, cold caress. She needed time. And more desperately still, she needed Grimya's advice.

'I . . . am honoured by your invitation, sir,' she replied with careful formality. 'But I will need time to consider it. If I might ask your indulgence for another day . . . '

'Of course: I would expect nothing less.' The hunting carnivore was back in his smile, and he raised his hand as though to touch her again. Involuntarily, Indigo stepped back a pace, and the hand withdrew. 'Though I would like to think, Indigo, that your answer will be favourable, and that we may look forward to a long friendship.' He inclined his head, a gesture that combined punctilious courtesy with something less definable and, she thought, less pleasant. 'I must circulate among my guests, or tongues will begin to wag over my partiality for your company.' He saw her face flush at the teasing implication, and the smile took on a hint of satisfaction. 'Speak with Phereniq tomorrow. Until then, I am delighted to extend my continuing hospitality.'

He walked away, leaving her gazing after him and fighting down a mixture of angry bile and cold unease. She didn't want to remain at the celebration any longer. She wanted to escape to the privacy of her room where Grimya waited, bathe herself and rinse away the taint that, irrationally, she felt was on her in the wake of her encounter with Augon. And she didn't want to speak with Phereniq again; not yet, not until she was able to think more clearly.

A narrow, paved path led around the edge of the courtyard to the arched doorway. Indigo glanced over her shoulder once more to ensure that no one would see her leave, then hurried away, soft-footed, past the heady tangles of flowering vines towards the lamplit quiet of the palace.

Grimya was waiting for her on her return, and when Indigo had bathed and changed from her formal clothes into a loose robe, they talked of Augon Hunnamek's proposal and what it might mean. Grimya readily acknowledged Indigo's suspicion that the events of the evening were more than coincidence, but it wasn't in her nature to delve too deeply: simply and philosophically, she preferred to accept the facts and act according to the dictates of her own common sense.

It is not a matter of 'why', but of 'what', she said, lapsing into telepathic speech to express herself more clearly. *What does your own wisdom say? Listen to that, and it will guide you more surely than anything.*

Indigo fingered the strings of her harp with one hand, damping them with the other to keep the instrument's sound from distracting her. 'You're right, Grimya. I can't fault your logic. But I don't trust the situation.' She got up, pacing across the room towards the window and the balcony beyond. 'I don't *trust* it.'

No one is asking you to trust. We both know better than that. But we have been given a chance, and I do not think it matters where that chance has come from. We have a task to perform, and we must do our utmost to perform it. That is all that counts.

'Then you think that I should accept the usurper's offer?'

Grimya dipped her head uncertainly. *I don't have the right to make such a decision.*

'But I need your advice.' Indigo returned and crouched down, taking the she-wolf's muzzle between her hands and gazing into the golden eyes. 'Sometimes you see matters so much more clearly than I ever can. Help me, Grimya, please.'

Grimya whined softly and licked Indigo's fingers. *Then . . . I think we should stay. I think it is our only chance to confront the demon. But you must make the final choice.*

And the bitter truth was, Indigo told herself later, as she lay on her couch and stared at the room's shadowed ceiling, that she couldn't bring herself to make that choice, for good or for ill.

Beside her, on the floor, Grimya was asleep. There had been nothing left to say after their conversation; Indigo had resolved to think afresh in the morning, but privately she knew that the dilemma wouldn't vanish with the dawn. The truth – which she had been unwilling to admit to Grimya – was that she was afraid. Not afraid to pledge herself to the task that lay ahead, but afraid of staying in Simhara and thus being forced to live with the bitterly painful memories that the city evoked. She was desperately ashamed of the feeling, but shame wasn't enough to banish it. All she wanted was to turn her back on Khimiz and all that it implied, and run away back to the sea where, for a while, she had been able to forget the horrors of the past and be at peace.

The fan creaked monotonously; the sound was an irritant but, she reminded herself, preferable to the sweltering heat of a Simharan summer night. Somewhere in the distance she could hear faint strains of music, intermittent on the sluggish breeze; she tried to concentrate on it, hoping that it might soothe her restlessness and allow her, at last, to relax into sleep. She closed her eyes, but her eyelids itched and one of the couch's cushions was pressing awkwardly against her spine: opening her eyes again she turned her head.

Momentarily, the darkened room seemed to take on an extra dimension. It was a syndrome she knew well; the last conscious hallucination of an exhausted mind before it slipped into dreams. But she was awake. Surely, she was awake?

Then suddenly every trace of colour in the scene drained to grey, and her mother stood in the middle of the room.

Indigo opened her mouth in a ghastly cry, but no sound came from her throat. She tried to sit up, but found herself immobile, her mind detached from her body and unable to control it. Queen Imogen, grey as a statue, grey as ash, gazed down at her daughter's recumbent form, and smiled sweetly. Her lips moved, but Indigo heard nothing.

M . . . mother? She tried to whisper the word but she, too, was voiceless. And then her dream-consciousness froze, as the queen's eyes and tongue turned to glittering silver, and an unhuman laugh, like shards of glass falling on a stone floor, rippled from the phantom's lips. She knew the laugh. Sleeping and waking she had heard it, and it was the sound she hated above all others.

Nemesis.

'Fond greetings, Indigo, my sister.' Imogen's face was now that of the demon; the small, vicious child's mouth smiling, the cat's teeth white and even in the gloom, the silver hair a ghostly nimbus about its head. 'So you have found the serpent's lair at last.'

Her voice – or a semblance of her voice; it wasn't real, Indigo told herself, *it wasn't real* – had returned, and she hissed, 'Go, you filth! You have no place here!'

'Your place is my place, for we are one and the same. Watch for the serpent-eater, Indigo. Do you remember the warning? Or have you already fallen under its spell?'

The fortune-teller in Huon Parita . . . though her

body was remote, she felt the sweat that broke out on her face and torso.

'*Go!*' she shrieked again. 'Leave me in peace – I banish you, I *curse* you! *Leave me be!*'

Nemesis chuckled. 'Curse yourself, sister. Curse yourself, and all of humanity with you. The serpent-eater rises, and you cannot stand in its way.' The obscene blend of her mother and the demon before her warped abruptly, and another face replaced that of Nemesis: an old face, wrinkled, riddled by opiates, canny. The toothless jaws gaped, and a crone's voice shrilled: '*Silver cards for my lady and her fine grey dog?*'

And Indigo woke screaming.

Chapter VIII

If anyone, even Grimya, had questioned her, she wouldn't have been capable of explaining her reasoning, for it made no logical sense. But logic had no part in this: the dream had been the catalyst. Perhaps, Indigo thought bitterly, that was exactly what Nemesis had intended: in which case she was a fool to rise to the challenge. But fool or not, she believed that she had no other choice.

The sun had barely crept above the horizon when she sought out a servant and asked to be directed to Phereniq's rooms. Between the humidity of night and the searing heat of full day, the early morning provided a small oasis of cool relief, but it did nothing to relieve the haunted – or perhaps *hunted* was a better word – sense of oppression she had felt since waking from the nightmare.

If Phereniq was surprised to see her at such an hour, she showed no sign of it, but gravely ushered her visitor into a small antechamber whose walls were covered with astrological charts. The door closed behind them, and for a moment Phereniq studied Indigo's face. She made no comment on what she saw, but said gently, 'What can I do for you?'

'I – ' Indigo hesitated, then realised that she felt too tired and confused for elaborate speeches. Simply, she replied, 'I wish to accept the Takhan's offer.'

Phereniq smiled. 'Yes,' she said. 'I thought that you would. And I'm glad.'

There was silence for a few moments. Indigo wanted to sit down, but could see no chair within easy reach. Then suddenly Phereniq came forward and touched her arm.

'Indigo? You're very pale – are you all right?'

'Yes; I – ' With an effort Indigo shook off the oppressive images of the nightmare and Nemesis's taunts. 'I slept poorly last night. An unpleasant dream – it has left a lingering miasma, I think.' She tried to sound dismissive.

'Would you like to talk about it?' Phereniq asked.

Indigo forced a smile. 'No. Thank you, but . . . it will fade soon enough.'

Phereniq hesitated, then crossed to a table where an ornate silver pot stood on a trivet over a squat candle. 'I think this climate has a bearing on such things,' she said. 'You're not accustomed to the heat, and I too . . . well, never mind; that's probably of no consequence.' Indigo heard the sound of liquid being poured, then the astrologer returned with a small glass cup in her hand. 'I rarely eat breakfast, but I cannot do without my herbal tisane at this hour.' There was a touch of self-mocking levity in her voice: then again she paused. 'And I have something that I could add to it. A cordial of my own devising – it's a great help in calming a troubled mind.'

Indigo accepted gratefully. The nightmare had robbed her of her night's rest, and she would be glad of anything that could give her a respite. She watched as Phereniq took the phial with its amethyst stopper from her reticule, carefully measured six drops into the tisane, then held out the cup. A crisp aroma rose from the brew, and when Indigo sipped it she tasted a rich and pleasant background echo, a little like burnt sugar.

'My cordial has many uses,' Phereniq told her. 'Never hesitate to ask me, if you feel it may be of help to you again.'

Although she doubted if the brew could be affecting her so quickly, there was a sensation of warmth at the back of Indigo's throat, an easing of taut muscles, a calming. She looked up. 'Thank you, Phereniq. You're very kind.'

'Nonsense.' Phereniq made a dismissive gesture, as though embarrassed, and put the phial away. 'Now, you should go back to your room and rest for a while. I think you'll find that you can sleep, if you try, and there

should be no more bad dreams.' She started to lead
Indigo towards the door. 'As to the matter of your new
appointment, send a servant to inform me when you
wake, and in the meantime I will tell the Takhan of your
decision.' She smiled warmly and patted the girl's arm.
'He will be very glad, Indigo. As am I.'

Phereniq's face was thoughtful as she watched Indigo
walk away. Dreams . . . it was a peculiar coincidence,
and one that she wasn't sure how to interpret. She had
stopped short of mentioning her own recent nightmares,
feeling that they might not be relevant; but now she was
less sure. Since her own bad dreams began she had as a
matter of course consulted the auguries; but they had
given her no hints as to a possible cause. That in itself
was strange; and now it seemed that Indigo was afflicted
with the same malaise. The climate? It was true, as she
had asserted, that they were both foreigners, and
unaccustomed to the blistering heat of Khimiz; yet
Phereniq's intuition made her suspect that the real
answer was less simple. Something was amiss, and she
was sorry that Indigo was also affected by it. She hoped
it would pass, for she liked the girl, and her divinations
had made it abundantly clear that her presence at the
Khimizi court would bring only good.

  She shook herself out of her reverie, and realised that
the corridor was empty and Indigo had gone. A stray
breeze had set a small glass mobile in a window tinkling
with the sound of tiny, ethereal bells. Phereniq listened
to the sweet and evocative sound for a moment, then
quietly withdrew into her rooms and closed the door.

High summer in Khimiz was a season of shimmering,
languid days when the sun beat ceaselessly down from a
blue but sultry sky, and breathless nights when there
seemed to be too little air in the entire world to sustain
life. By a seeming miracle, Simhara remained a green
oasis in the parched land, irrigated by a myriad artificial
streams and pools, which were fed by water taken from
the sea and distilled to remove the salt.

In the palace, life had settled into a quietly ordered regime. The new Takhan had not as yet made his presence fully felt, and councillors, officials and servants alike were cautiously but thankfully beginning to relax back into familiar and cherished routines. The only overt signs of change were the presence of many dark-skinned men and women mingling with the honey-haired Khimizi among the palace entourage, and the fact that the court ministers, who customarily had little to do at this time of year, spent many of their waking hours closeted in private session with Augon Hunnamek.

But for Indigo and Grimya, life had altered greatly. A little over a month had passed since they had moved into their elegant new rooms at the heart of the palace. These rooms, which connected by a short corridor to the Takhan's own, were part of the opulent suite allocated to the Infanta and had once been Agnethe's private sanctum, but the Dowager's personal belongings had been transferred to the guarded apartments where she was now housed, and no reminders of her presence were left.

Indigo's duties as the Infanta's companion had so far consisted of little more than supervising the nursemaid and servants who cared for Jessamin, and playing with the child, insofar as it was possible to play with a baby only three months old. For most of the time, she felt, her presence was superfluous, and, omens and auguries notwithstanding, she still suspected a more sinister motive behind Augon Hunnamek's apparently capricious wish to appoint her to this post. In dark moments she couldn't help but wonder if the demon already knew of her mission, and was merely biding its time, playing with her as a cat might play with a wounded bird before making the final kill.

In the early days following her decision to overcome her fears and stay in Simhara, it had been hard to maintain her resolve in the face of that insidious suspicion. And, too, the dark dreams had returned: not dreams of Nemesis this time, but shadowy nightmares in which hints of an elusive evil tangled with distorted

memories of recent events, and which left her drained
and fearful in the wake of their assault.

But Indigo had been determined to fight the effects
of the dreams. And, thanks to Phereniq, she had at
last found the means of putting herself beyond their
reach.

She didn't know the constituents of the cordial which
she kept in a small bottle in an ornate cabinet in her
room, but it proved to be the answer to her fervent
prayers. The astrologer had insisted that she should
have a supply of her own: six drops in a cup of tisane
each evening, she said, and Indigo could rest safe in the
certainty that she would sleep peacefully through the
night. Her prescription had worked: and now, with no
nightmares to plague her, Indigo could turn her mind
more freely to the task which she had come to Simhara
to fulfil.

There, though, lay the worm in the bud. Each night
before she slept, Indigo took the lodestone from its
pouch and gazed for a while at the tiny pinpoint of light
trembling at its centre; and each time the stone's silent
message was the same. *Here*, it said to her. *In Simhara.
In the palace.* In her mind's eye she would picture the
face of Augon Hunnamek, and feel again the shuddering, chilling sensation she'd felt at their earliest meeting,
when she had met the usurper's pale gaze for the first
time. And on the heels of that feeling came a bitter
sense of failure: for as yet she had found not the smallest
clue, not the slightest lead, that might help her to breach
the demon's defences. Wherever she searched, however
hard she strove, there was nothing. Only the testimony
of the stone, and her own inner certainty. And they
weren't enough.

Each morning, on Augon Hunnamek's instructions,
Phereniq brought Jessamin's horoscope to Indigo's
room, so that they might discuss how the Infanta's needs
for the day might best be served. It had become a
pleasant, regular ritual, and on one such morning the
two women were breakfasting together, enjoying the

brief cool respite of the early hour. Hild, Jessamin's newly appointed nurse, was bustling about in the adjoining room, singing cheerfully but off-key in her own language, and in the distance the harbour bells had begun to chime, marking the turning of the morning tide. Indigo listened idly to the bells for a few minutes, then started as a new peal, much closer to the palace, began to ring out.

'Whatever's that?' She frowned, and Phereniq smiled.

'Today is the Dowager Takhina's birth-anniversary,' the astrologer said. 'The Takhan ordered that a paean should be rung in her honour – though I'm sorry to say that she'll probably take little cheer from it.'

Indigo glanced through the window and across the courtyard, to where, some way off on the far side of the palace precincts, a solitary minaret rose against the cloudless sky. At the foot of that tower, though obscured by the jumble of intervening walls, was a two-storey annexe in the palace's northern wing, where Agnethe had been housed since the fall of the old Takhan.

She felt a spasm of guilt as she realised that, during the past month, she had barely given a thought to the woman whose place in Jessamin's life she had effectively taken. She had benefited from Agnethe's misfortune, and though she owed no direct fealty to Khimiz, she found herself wishing suddenly that she could do something to redress the balance.

She said, a little diffidently, 'Has there been no change in the Dowager's attitude?'

'None.' Phereniq's face clouded. 'We have tried to reason with her, but she still refuses to listen to anything we have to say. She won't accept that we wish her no ill, and that there is a place of honour for her in the court. And when we try to give her news of Jessamin, she only turns her head away and says she will not hear it. I think she fears that to show any interest would be taken as an admission of defeat.' She stared at the charts on the table before her for a moment, then shook her head sadly. 'I don't understand how any woman can value her pride more than the love of her own infant. It seems so unnatural.'

Indigo murmured agreement, but privately she believed that she knew what truly motivated Agnethe. The key was hatred. Widowed, cast from her rightful place, her child taken from her, hatred was all that Agnethe had left to cling to; and she would cling to it, nurture it, sacrifice anything to keep its dark fire burning. And the most powerful flame of all must be her desire for vengeance upon the man who had taken her husband's throne and now, gracious in his triumph, offered her the open hand of friendship.

The revelation struck her so suddenly that Indigo had to bite her tongue to stop herself from exclaiming with shock. All this time, all the days of searching for a clue, and she hadn't seen it. She had been a fool – for in all of Khimiz, she could hope to find no better ally in her quest than Agnethe . . .

Phereniq left shortly afterwards, and for a while Indigo sat looking at the chart she had left; Jessamin's horoscope for the day. To her, the network of coloured lines and curves and circles was simply a picture; beautifully executed, but meaningless. Yet to Phereniq, whose religious and superstitious beliefs were as deeply ingrained as any Khimizi's, the chart was a vital part of life, presiding over every aspect of daily activity.

What, she wondered, did Phereniq see when she cast and read the chart of Augon Hunnamek? Though she claimed not to be clairvoyant, her mastery of the science of the stars was undisputed. But could even the most skilled astrologer detect the signs – if, indeed, such signs were visible – of a demon in human guise?

She let the thought slide away. Speculation was pointless: without a level of understanding achieved only through years of study, she couldn't hope to answer such a question. And besides, she had other and more urgent matters to occupy her now.

But, to her intense frustration, Indigo had no opportunity to think further about her embryonic idea concerning Agnethe. Jessamin, with innocent perversity, chose to be fractious for most of the day, and Indigo's conscience wouldn't allow her to leave all the ensuing soothing and rocking and singing of lullabies to Hild alone. By the time evening came she was exhausted, and could do no more than sink on to her couch and pray for sleep. Jessamin, however, continued to wake and cry at intervals throughout the night, and only in the last two hours before dawn did Indigo and Hild finally succeed in settling her. Hild, hollow-eyed and swaying on her feet, went thankfully off to her own quarters, and Indigo was at last able to lie down on her couch and close her eyes.

Sleep, however, wouldn't come. She had passed beyond tiredness into a wakeful, restless limbo, and eventually sat up again with a sigh, aware that she had no real hope of relaxing. At the end of her couch a shadow moved suddenly, and Grimya, who alone had slept undisturbed by Jessamin's crying, stirred and raised her head. Seeing Indigo's silhouette the she-wolf uttered a soft query.

'In-digo? Are you awake?'

Indigo sat up. 'I can't sleep. I don't think I shall now.'

Grimya rose, stretched and shook herself. 'Then come with me on my rr-run. It is good in the first light. We can go to the beach beyond the har-bour and watch the w . . . waves on the shore.'

Grimya couldn't bear to be confined within four walls for any length of time, and had taken to going out before dawn each day. To join her on such an excursion would be both a physical and a mental tonic, Indigo thought; and she smiled, stretching her arms and throwing off the couch's light covering.

'Wait for me,' she said. 'I'll be no more than five minutes.'

The first shafts of sunlight were striking across Simhara from the east when Indigo and Grimya returned to the palace. They had walked through dark, deserted streets to the harbour, then southward to the beach where the gulf tide beat and boomed at the fringe of a vast crescent of sand, and where Grimya could release her pent energy in a race along the shore that reminded Indigo of the few happy days they had spent travelling with Vasi Elder's caravan.

Lamps were beginning to come on in the city as they made their way back in the thin, grey light that heralded sunrise. At the palace gates, the sleepy guards recognised Indigo and let them through with a nod and a smile. They started back through the gardens, breathing in the moist scents of vines and flowers – until suddenly Grimya stopped and raised her head, her ears pricking forward.

'Grimya?' Indigo queried. 'What's wrong?'

Over there – many people. There is some kind of trouble.

Indigo looked up. Ahead, the pale outline of a minaret showed beyond the garden wall, and a cold frisson went through her as she recognised the tower that stood beside Agnethe's prison. With an awful sense of premonition, she turned from the path and ran towards the northerly trellis-gate, Grimya at her heels.

Movement and a susurration of muted but agitated voices greeted them as they emerged on the gate's far side, and they saw that some fifteen or twenty people, mostly servants but also a few palace militiamen, were gathered about the entrance to the annexe. Lamps glowed beyond the open double doors, though their light was superfluous in the strengthening sun, and as Indigo and Grimya approached, a small group emerged from inside. Two veiled women were escorted by more militiamen, and seemed to be weeping; behind them came a steward with two court ministers, and with them was Phereniq. Indigo called out to her; the astrologer raised her head, saw her, and spoke briefly to her companions before hurrying to where Indigo and Grimya stood at the edge of the small crowd.

Indigo took one look at her stricken expression, and felt a surge of cold dread. 'Phereniq, what's happened?' she asked urgently.

'It's the Dowager.' Phereniq's voice was toneless. 'She – ' She covered her face with one hand, and now

98

Indigo could see that she was shaking. 'A steward found her half an hour ago, in the courtyard behind the annexe. She must have slipped out during the night, while her servants were sleeping, and we think she . . . jumped from the top of the minaret.'

'Great Mother . . . ' Indigo whispered.

Tears glittered in Phereniq's eyes. 'I don't think I shall ever forget the sight of that poor, broken, frail body,' she said unsteadily. 'The Takhan is deeply shocked, and deeply grieved. He is with her now: he wanted to pray beside her for a while before she is brought out . . . Oh, Indigo, this is such a *tragedy*!'

Indigo's throat was tight. 'Wasn't she guarded?' she asked softly.

'Yes, she was guarded. And the men who fell asleep at their posts will be severely punished for their negligence. But what's the use of it? No punishment will bring her back to life.' She shook her head helplessly.

Indigo stared numbly at the doorway. More figures were moving in the annexe, and suddenly the crowd parted and Augon Hunnamek, accompanied by his personal steward, came out. He spoke to no one, but walked quickly from the building – then, as he drew level with Indigo and Phereniq, he halted.

'Indigo.' He inclined his head. 'This is a very unhappy day for us all.'

'Yes.' She cast her gaze down, not wanting to meet his pale eyes or see what was in them.

'Such a tragic end to a sad life. And she was so young.'

To Indigo's ears the words sounded glib, and a terrible thought began to take form in her mind. Then she started as Augon laid a hand on her shoulder.

'Would you like to see her, to pay your last respects?'

The terrible thought abruptly crystallised and, stunned, she looked up at him as she realised what it could mean. His gaze was cool, gently querying.

'N– no. Thank you, sir, I – would rather not.'

Augon smiled. 'Indeed. I understand. You would prefer to remember her as she was in life, as would we all.'

Indigo's face was white. 'Yes,' she whispered.

He patted her arm, adding softly, 'And you must be doubly vigilant now, Indigo, in your care of our little Infanta. With her mother gone, she will need a good and loyal friend as never before. Keep her safe for me.'

Before she could reply, he moved on, leaving her staring after him.

'Indigo?' Phereniq spoke with concern as the girl began to shiver. 'Are you all right?'

'Yes, I . . . ' But she wasn't. 'Just – cold,' she said.

'It's shock. Sometimes the effect of it is delayed, but it can be all the worse for that.'

It wasn't shock: or at least, not in the way that Phereniq meant. Only yesterday she had realised that Agnethe might be the ally she so desperately needed, and now Agnethe was dead. It was too great a coincidence. And when Augon had asked, so gently, if she would like to see the Takhina's body, his words had sounded like a subtle taunt . . .

Phereniq took her arm. 'Come back to my room with me. I have something a little stronger than the cordial, which will restore us both. I think we need it.'

Indigo's mind was too frozen to argue. With Grimya trailing disconsolately behind them she let the astrologer lead her away, and they walked slowly through the gardens towards the palace's heart. Augon was some way ahead of them, and once he glanced back. For a moment his gaze and Indigo's met, and she felt something like a sliver of brittle ice stab through her mind in the instant before he smiled thinly and looked away.

Chapter IX

'*A-na! A-na! Tiu, beba-mi – insa houro! Ay?*'

Indigo looked up as Hild scrambled back from the side of the courtyard pool, batting ineffectually at the water-splashes on her skirt.

'*Khimizi* please, Hild. How many times must you be told?'

The nurse gave her a gap-toothed, ingenuous smile. 'Your pardon of me. I learn.'

A gurgle of delighted laughter drew Indigo's attention back to the water. Jessamin had turned away and, plump limbs pumping, was swimming like a little seal towards the far side of the pool, where a small, fair-haired boy watched her approach with solemn interest.

The sun was nearing meridian and the early summer heat becoming too intense for comfort. Grimya had already abandoned the courtyard for the comparative cool of one of her secret shady oases, and Indigo got to her feet, stretching legs stiff from sitting. 'Fetch the Infanta in now, please, Hild,' she said. 'She can return to the pool when the day cools a little.'

Hild bustled around the poolside, and Indigo headed for the palace interior. She hoped there would be no tantrums and troubles today; it was becoming harder and harder to persuade little Jessamin that there must be more to life than constant swimming, but the child was as yet too young to be reasoned with. A day short of her first birth-anniversary – too young even to walk – and yet she had taken to water as though born to it. For six months, since the servants who attended her had reported that she had learned to swim in her bath, Jessamin had spent every permitted moment in or near the pool in her private courtyard. She swam flawlessly, could float, was even beginning to teach herself to dive under like a hunting otter; and her extraordinary prowess was fast becoming legend in the palace.

Entering the outer chamber, Indigo sank down on to a couch. A jug of iced fruit cordial stood on a low table; she filled a glass and sipped from it, while a part of her mind listened to the sounds of splashing and Jessamin's infant protests in the courtyard.

It was hard to believe that she and Grimya had now been in Simhara for almost ten months. Indigo had found it alluringly easy to settle in to her role at the palace; court life had a timeless, idyllic quality, and the days slipped by so calmly that she was only peripherally aware of their passing. But it was a hiatus which, she knew, had lasted too long.

In the turbulent days following Agnethe's death, the court had been in turmoil. There had been an investigation. Indigo had expected it to be nothing but a formality to appease the Khimizi, but she was proved wrong: Augon Hunnamek had been thorough and unstinting. But when all the evidence was collected, there had been a clear and emphatic verdict: the Dowager Takhina Agnethe had taken her own life, and there was no question of any outside involvement or complicity. So, on an achingly perfect evening, the great royal trireme had put out from harbour to commit Agnethe's body to the sea in time-honoured fashion, and the affair was at an end.

But the pronouncement had done nothing to allay Indigo's suspicions. Agnethe had been her first and, so far, only potential ally in her quest to unmask the demon in their midst, and now that she was gone, Indigo was as far from her goal as she had been on the day she first set foot in Simhara.

And as time went by, a further paradox had arisen to cloud the picture: for, however grudgingly, Indigo had to admit that Augon Hunnamek had proved to be a man of honour. She had little direct contact with him – he paid a weekly visit to Jessamin, but that was all; and their only other encounters were at the infrequent formal palace banquets – but he had developed a reputation for scrupulous justice in affairs of state, and, less than a year after coming to power, was proving a more popular ruler than his predecessor.

But respect wasn't the same as liking or trust, and though the Takhan's charismatic popularity was seductive, Indigo knew better than to allow herself to be seduced. If her resolve wavered, she need only turn her head and look out into the courtyard, where a small, naked girl-child was now crawling determinedly across the flagstones, leaving a wet trail in her wake.

She loved the little Infanta. With no experience of young children, she hadn't expected such an emotion to be aroused in her, but over the weeks and months Jessamin's burgeoning personality had captivated her to the point where she now had an emphatic place in Indigo's heart.

And in eleven years' time, that sweetness and innocence, flowering into first womanhood, would be sacrificed to the machinations of a demon in human guise. That was the core of it, the goad that brought back her sense of perspective in times of doubt and reminded her of what she must achieve. For the Infanta's sake, if for nothing else, she *must* discover the weakness in Augon Hunnamek's armour that would enable her to destroy him.

She heard Hild's admonishing voice approaching, and sat up as the nursemaid entered the room with Jessamin crowing in her arms and trying to tug at her dark hair. The small boy trailed silently behind them, and Indigo paused to give him a smile that she hoped was reassuring. Luk was three; too old to be a playmate for Jessamin, yet too young to find any entertainment in the company of adults. Indigo pitied him, aware that his life must be one of unnatural boredom; yet her sympathy was tinged with caution – for Luk, whose mother had died birthing him, was the son of a man whom she had good reason neither to like nor to trust: Leando Copperguild, the Khimizi noble with the scarred face, who had betrayed Agnethe to the invaders.

It had been Augon's decision to place Luk Copperguild in the role of friend to the Infanta. Indigo would have preferred any other child in the palace, but had dared not say so: Leando was firmly established in the Takhan's retinue and apparently determined to see his son well placed in his turn, and Luk had been a blatantly political choice. But to penalise a small child for his father's actions would be grossly unfair, and so, as Hild began to dress Jessamin, Indigo spoke to the boy.

'Would you like some fruit juice, Luk? You must be thirsty.'

Wide, sea-blue eyes looked up at her, and the child lisped, 'Eth, pleathe.' She poured him a glass and he drank carefully, watching her over the rim. When the drink was half gone, he paused and asked hesitantly, 'Ith Grimya here?'

Indigo smiled. Luk had developed a passionate fascination with Grimya, which the she-wolf accepted readily. Sometimes, Indigo suspected that the games they played together afforded Grimya more pleasure than any other aspect of life in the palace.

'I think she's sleeping,' she told Luk. 'She often does, at this time of the day. She doesn't like the heat.'

'Oh.' His disappointment was obvious, and she tried to cheer him a little. 'Did you have your swimming lesson this morning, Luk?'

'No.' An emphatic shake of the honey-blond head. 'I don't like the water very much. Hild thays I thould try, but I don't want to.' He hesitated, then admitted, 'I'm a bit thcared.'

Before Indigo could reply, someone knocked at the door. Hild set Jessamin down and went to open it, and looking up, Indigo saw the familiar hunted eyes and scarred face of Luk's father.

'Leando.' She greeted him with a curt nod; the most she would concede.

'Good morning, Indigo.' Leando Copperguild's response was as wary as hers. Luk ran to him, and he gathered the small boy up in his arms. 'My son has behaved himself?'

'As always.'

'I'm glad.' He ruffled Luk's hair, but the gesture was a distracted reflex; his mind was on something else.

'Indigo, I – ' he saw Hild watching them, and cleared his throat. 'I have the Takhan's permission to excuse Luk from the palace this afternoon.' A quick, forced smile. 'Two of our ships came in on the early tide, and their cargo is much greater than expected. We have arranged a family celebration of the event at my uncle's house, and I wonder if you might accept an invitation to join us?'

Indigo stared at him. For ten months she and this man had coexisted, insofar as their paths had to cross at all, in cold, polite indifference: she made no secret of her contempt for him, and he had never attempted to either justify himself or win her friendship. And now, for no apparent reason, this.

'Thank you, Leando,' she said coolly, 'but I wouldn't wish to intrude on a private occasion.'

'I assure you, it – '

Indigo's eyes narrowed and she cut across what he had been about to say. 'No: thank you. I think instead I would prefer to visit the Temple of Mariners, and say a prayer for the Dowager Takhina.'

Leando's lips whitened. For a moment she thought he would retaliate, but he controlled himself. Then he glanced quickly at Hild and, seeing that she had returned her attention to the Infanta, took three steps across the room. Bending, and making a pretence of gathering up one of Luk's discarded toys from the floor, he whispered harshly,

'Think what you will of me, Indigo, but you have a great deal to learn! I have something to say to you which must be said privately, and it can't wait forever. Turn your face, if it suits you. But don't be blinded!'

And before she could react, he straightened and, bearing Luk on his shoulder, strode to the door and out of the room.

'*A-na!*' Hild turned at the slam of the door, her broad, pleasant face registering disgust. 'Always that one seem so . . . *agitated*.' She beamed at Indigo, pleased to have mastered such a complex word. 'You do not like him, uh?'

Indigo stared at the door, and unthinkingly fingered

105

the lodestone at her neck. 'No, I don't, Hild. But we must be tolerant.'

Jessamin said: 'Ba!', adding her own comment, and laughed. Indigo didn't know whether it was imagination, or the awakening of some intuitive sense within her. But suddenly the sun's heat seemed to drain out of her marrow, leaving her feeling as cold as the southern tundra in winter.

'Indigo?' Phereniq tapped her arm, and she started out of a reverie to focus on the astrologer's slow, warm smile.

'I don't believe you've taken in a word of what I said,' the older woman teased gently. 'What is it? Have you not been sleeping soundly?'

With an effort, Indigo shook off her lethargy and smiled back. 'I'm sorry, Phereniq. I have had a few broken nights lately, and Jessamin has been a little fractious. Please, go on.'

Phereniq gave her an assessing look. For a moment she seemed about to pursue the matter, then thought better of it and turned her attention back to the chart that lay between them on the table. She tapped a diagram that showed two concentric circles, bisected by a single line. 'Tomorrow's conjunction will take place precisely one hour before noon. Of course, it won't be visible – even the most powerful seeing-glasses in Khimiz can't counter the light of the sun, and it would be dangerous even to try; but the knowledge that it is taking place is enough.' She sat back, regarding the chart proprietorially. 'And it is a splendid omen. The Hunter's Star and the Peace-Bringer, coming together in the Serpent constellation at the *exact* anniversary-hour of the Infanta's birth. There could be no better time for the Takhan's inauguration.'

Something in her voice; the slightest catch, no more, but Indigo had grown close enough to her in recent months for it to register. Quite gently, she said, 'And for the betrothal?'

Phereniq frowned. 'Of course.' Her fingers clenched

106

and then suddenly, briskly, she rolled the chart again and set it aside with the others. 'But this really won't do. You must forgive me, Indigo; I have so many things to attend to before morning. And we must all rise early tomorrow, if we're to be at our best.' Her smile was brittle. 'I'll see you at the banquet, when the formal ceremonies are over.'

When they were alone once more, Grimya looked up at Indigo, her eyes troubled.

It is very sad, the wolf observed. *Phereniq feels so much love, and yet it brings her nothing but hurt.*

I know. Aware that Hild might be in earshot, Indigo, too, communicated silently. *I wish we could help her.*

We cannot. And I don't think she would want us to. Not if it meant giving up her dreams.

Indigo poured herself a cup of wine, then after a brief hesitation fetched the little bottle of cordial from its hiding place. She suspected that it was a pointless exercise; she had taken her usual draught last night, but during the past month or so the cordial's soporific effects seemed to have weakened. She was dreaming again; not, thankfully, anything to compare with the nightmare of Nemesis that had plagued her when she first came to Simhara, but dark, formless and disquieting dreams that, on waking, she couldn't recall in any detail. But the cordial was still a calmative, and the thought of its soothing warmth at the back of her throat, the pleasant edge it gave to the wine, appealed. Just a few drops; five or six, no more. It would help her to relax.

The bottle's stopper came out with a faint sound. With great care Indigo measured six drops of the cordial into her cup, then sat back and closed her eyes, sipping at her drink as a sense of peace stole over her in the quiet of the shaded room.

The next morning dawned vivid and hot, with a light north-easterly wind blowing in from the desert. Indigo and Grimya were woken shortly after dawn as bells began to ring throughout the city, and within moments of rising Indigo was caught up in the hectic preparation for the Takhan's inaugural celebrations.

She began to feel unduly tense as she supervised the bathing, dressing and final grooming of Jessamin. The Infanta had woken crying several times during the night, and it took a good deal of patience and the enticement of her favourite toy – Phereniq's little ship – to settle her. But at last, swathed in her gold-embroidered robes and with a tiny, sapphire-studded circlet on her head, she was borne away wide-eyed and uncomplaining to where the highest dignitaries of Simhara waited by the palace's main gates.

Indigo was not to take part in the triumphal procession that would carry the Takhan to the Temple of Mariners for his crowning and confirmation. Instead, she would watch the procession's departure from one of the palace's high minarets, and would be waiting among the thousand guests when Augon Hunnamek returned with the blessing of the Sea Mother to preside over the greatest banquet Simhara had seen in decades and to announce his official betrothal to the Infanta. Indigo viewed the banquet with mixed feelings: she was enough of a sybarite to know that she would thoroughly enjoy the occasion itself, but the underlying implications troubled her. Ten months, she thought, since Augon Hunnamek had wrested power in Khimiz. Ten months, and still she was no closer to the truth . . .

Grimya was not interested in processions and cheering crowds, and didn't like the unnatural view from the high towers, so when the time came to depart, Indigo left her in their apartments, playing with Luk Copper-guild, and joined a party of palace officials who also had no part in the ceremony as they made the long climb to the top of the minaret to watch the Takhan set out. She felt a good deal better than she had done earlier, thanks largely to a small water-pipe which Phereniq had given her some while ago, together with a phial of fine, crystalline powder which, when added to a herbal smoking mixture, produced a pleasant scent and an equally pleasant sense of well-being. She didn't make use of the powder often; but today, she felt – and in the wake of yet another disturbed night – was a special instance. And as she ascended the tower stairs, she found time to be grateful to Phereniq for her kindness.

The processional route was a spectacular sight. The entire way had been decorated with flowers and garlands, turning the normally pale early summer greenery into a riot of colour. Huge glass chimes hung in the trees, joining their shimmering voices to those of the bells, and silk and brocade banners embroidered with sigils of prosperity and good fortune streamed in the hot wind. The broad avenues were thronged with people; as she stepped out on to the minaret's balcony and gazed down at them Indigo could hardly believe that even a city the size of Simhara could contain so many – and these, she knew, were nothing compared to the crowds waiting at the harbour.

A rising wave of sound heralded the appearance of the procession, and the throng surged forward, pressing against the human barrier of militiamen detailed to keep order. Four ranks of warriors came into view first, Augon's own men and Khimizi soldiers mingling in equal numbers; then a great open carriage drawn by six chimelos and bearing the Takhan himself emerged from the palace gates far below.

The cheer that greeted Augon Hunnamek was deafening, and as the carriage cleared the gates several thousand tiny, multicoloured birds were released from ranks of cages behind the walls. They rose like a sandstorm, their iridescent feathers catching the sunlight and shimmering, so that the procession was momentarily eclipsed by what looked like a fountain of jewels. Several of Indigo's companions drew breath in awed delight, and the cheering of the throng grew even louder. Flowers were being thrown at the carriage; as the cloud of birds cleared, Indigo saw Augon reach out and deftly catch a garland, waving an acknowledgement to the woman who had cast it. Resplendent in the blue-green robes of state that symbolised the sea, key to Khimiz's prosperity, he was a magnificent figure, laughing and exuberant and exotic with his dark skin and pale hair; even from the remote height of the minaret his charisma gave him an aura that was almost physical. It was, Indigo thought, as though the citizens of Simhara were recognising and adulating a demi-god in their midst. And beside the demi-god, tiny and vulnerable in the arms of one of Augon's body-servants, the Infanta Jessamin was held up to receive her own share of the crowd's adoration.

Indigo turned away as the procession moved on down the avenue. Her senses had been heightened by the drug, and she was deeply impressed and excited by the spectacle – yet at the same time deeply disturbed. The reaction of the throng had dispelled any last doubts about the new Takhan's acceptance in the eyes of his people. And there was far more to that acceptance than mere pragmatism, for during the ten months of his rule Augon Hunnamek had stinted nothing in his efforts to restore the ravaged city and prove himself a more than generous overlord. He had employed the city's finest architects to repair the damaged buildings, the most skilled botanists to replant the gardens and avenues, the greatest artists and sculptors to replace statuary and murals wrecked by his invading army; and all from the Takhan's private coffers, without raising taxes. He had proved himself a religious man, dedicating four new shrines to the Great Mother at Simhara's cardinal gates, and had personally endowed a charity to support the sons and daughters of impoverished Khimizi who wished to enter temple service. In the great harbour, a scheme was already under way to strengthen and extend some of the oldest piers, thus allowing sea-trade to grow still further. And, like a perfect flower on the vigorous commercial vine of the city, art and music and education and celebration were flourishing anew under Takhan Augon's lavish patronage.

And with every new innovation that was rapturously welcomed by the populace, Indigo's quest grew more ambiguous and seemingly more impossible. How could she hope to destroy the evil that was Augon Hunnamek, when outwardly that evil manifested nothing but good? She had expected him to be a despot and a tyrant, loathed as the warped progenitor of the Charchad cult,

110

her first adversary, had been loathed: instead she was faced with a man beloved of an entire nation, to whom he was a paragon of bounty and goodwill. But beneath that mask lay a horror of which she and Grimya, alone of all the living souls in Khimiz, were aware. And if they failed to find a weakness in his armour, then one day the mask would crumble, and the bright light of Khimiz's new dawn would turn to black despair.

A sudden burst of eager voices about her broke her thrall. Her mind jolted back to earth and she realised that the procession was almost out of sight, and her companions, talking animatedly, were preparing to descend from the tower. She turned to go with them, and a voice spoke at her elbow.

'Indigo?' A plump, beaming little busybody of a man, his almost jet-black skin marking him as a noble of Augon's own race. He was a treasury official, she recalled, and an amateur musician of some talent; they had recently played an impromptu duet at a birth-anniversary party held for another member of the household, but she couldn't remember his name.

'A splendid and auspicious beginning to a great day, don't you think?' He had learned to speak Khimizi like a native.

'Indeed.' Indigo hoped that her smile didn't look too foolish.

He cleared his throat. 'We have several hours now before the Takhan's triumphal return. I – ah – it would be my great pleasure to escort you in the palace gardens for a while. And then perhaps a light luncheon, before we all throw ourselves into the fray once more?'

It was by no means the first such overture she had received since settling in the palace, but, unexpectedly, it crystallised the dark thoughts lurking in her mind. Unbidden, she had the sharp mental image of a stark, white face, grey eyes racked with pain, sweat soaking the dark hair.

Fenran. Her lost and tortured love. And he was at the heart of it. He was the spur, the hope, the reason why she must never give up, never abandon her pledge, never admit defeat . . .

111

Indigo heard her own voice, and it sounded like the voice of a stranger. 'Thank you,' she said bleakly, 'but no.'

The treasury man shrugged, philosophically hiding his disappointment. Suddenly reality swam back into focus and Indigo felt sorry for him. She forced herself to relax a fraction, and tried to soften the refusal. 'The Infanta was restless last night and we were all deprived of sleep. I feel the need to rest for a while before the banquet.'

His face cleared. 'Of course. Then perhaps I might ask you to reserve a dance for me tonight?'

Indigo felt as though she had been immersed suddenly and unexpectedly in icy water. She glanced back over her shoulder as they began to descend the stairs, and heard the crowds still cheering their Takhan. 'I'll be glad to,' she said. That much at least she could do for her would-be suitor, for she owed him a debt, though he'd never know it. For just one moment he had brought back the bittersweet memories that were all she had left of Fenran. And it had provided the catalyst. It was enough.

It was enough.

Chapter X

'It was magnificent!' Phereniq's eyes sparkled in the light of the lanterns that had turned the vast hall into a glittering fantasy, and her hands moved animatedly as she strove, futile though it was, to express her feelings. 'Indigo, you should have seen the throng! They sang – do you know, they *sang* for the Takhan and the Infanta? Such a choir as I've never heard, and all of it without premeditation. It would have touched your heart.'

Indigo glanced towards the dais where the Takhan sat enthroned. Augon was leaning back in the great chair to take a fresh wine-cup from a servant. His smile seemed to encompass everyone about him, and the diadem on his head glittered dazzlingly under the light of a vast, candle-hung glass sphere suspended high over the throne. The feasting was done; now the celebration was getting fully under way, and the dancing and entertainments would continue far into the night. Earlier, Indigo had gone out into the great courtyard to see the spectacle of the entire palace lit by row upon row of many-coloured lamps, illuminating the towers and walls and gardens and fountains, and the sheer, dreamlike beauty of it had stunned her. Westward, the stars in the night sky were eclipsed by the hot orange glow of beacons lit in the harbour, and throughout the city the festivities were continuing as musicians, dancers, acrobats and orators took to the streets in celebration.

Phereniq had described the ceremonies at the Temple of Mariners, where Augon had prostrated himself before the great shrine and received the blessing of the Sea Mother from the hands of Her acolytes. Two of the Three Gifts of Khimiz had been brought from their sanctuary on this rare day: the Trident, age-old symbol of the Takhan's authority, had been ritually and solemnly placed in Augon's hands, thus placing the land, by implication, into his safe keeping; whilst the golden Net – the Takhina's symbol – had been held over the tiny head of Jessamin as the Goddess's blessing was bestowed upon her in her turn. When their newly enthroned lord emerged on to the marble steps, Phereniq said, the crowd had howled in adulation, and when he walked out to the harbour to throw garlands of flowers from the docks before his ritual immersion in the sea, they had burst into an impromptu hymn of praise, not only to the Goddess but also to the man who was, for the Khimizi, Her greatest champion.

'Even the Falorim were moved,' Phereniq said, with a deep sigh at the memory. 'I saw their delegation, and they were singing with the rest. Such an accolade!'

There had been some fifteen or twenty Falorim tribesmen at the banquet. Looking around the hall Indigo saw them again, a small and relatively dour enclave, conspicuous in their austere desert robes. For a moment, recalling the party which had visited Vasi Elder's caravan at the time of the invasion, she felt more than a little sceptical about their professed loyalty; but then she reasoned that the Falorim were no more pragmatic than the dozen or more foreign nations whose ambassadors had also come to heap gifts and congratulations upon Augon and to pledge their friendship.

She was refilling her wine-glass, listening as Phereniq continued to tell her of the inauguration, when a hand touched her arm. Turning, she found herself looking into the face of the treasury official.

'Indigo. The musicians are refreshed and ready to begin again, and you have promised to partner me!'

The first strains of a formal dance were beginning; couples were forming up in the centre of the floor. Indigo rose. 'Phereniq; you'll forgive me . . . ?'

The astrologer smiled fondly. 'Of course.'

The dance began and, concentrating only peripherally on her partner's small talk, Indigo watched the other couples on the floor. One face in particular seemed to move into her field of vision more often than any other. He was partnering a small, dark-haired woman, but every few moments the swirl brought them close together. To all intents and purposes it was no more than happenstance, but when their gazes briefly met for the fifth time, Indigo realised that he was watching her.

Leando Copperguild. Her thoughts returned to the brief but bizarre encounter of the previous day, and she began to feel distinctly uneasy. It was impossible to imagine what could have prompted Leando to speak to her as he had done after ten months of tacit hostility. Though she was aware of the pitfalls in looking for patterns where there might be none, it seemed suspiciously coincidental: Leando had Augon Hunnamek's ear, and seemed anxious to prove himself in his new master's service. And now, this sudden effort to engage her interest.

The dance was coming to an end. Polite applause greeted the musicians' final flourish, and as the treasury official escorted her from the floor Indigo saw Leando apparently engaged in casual conversation with his partner. He was watching her again, and as she turned quickly away she had an unpleasant premonition of what was about to happen.

Another dance struck up; the official cleared his throat nervously and turned towards Indigo, intending to press his advantage and ask her to partner him again. But before he could speak, Leando stepped into his path.

'Indigo.' Leando was smiling. 'You have promised me the second dance of the second set, remember?'

She opened her mouth to protest that she'd done no such thing, then saw the steel determination in his eyes and realised that he was prepared to cause a scene if she refused.

'Very well.' She inclined her head coldly and, with the treasury man looking on in disappointment, allowed Leando to lead her back on to the floor.

For perhaps a minute they danced without speaking. Then Leando said suddenly, 'You look very beautiful tonight, Indigo.'

Her gaze raked him. 'I presume you didn't all but force me to dance with you so that we could exchange glib pleasantries. If you have something serious to say, please say it and don't waste my time.'

'As you wish.' He swung her out of the path of a nearby couple, and she saw that his face had become suddenly set and tense. 'I'm well aware of your opinion of me, and I don't like this subterfuge any more than you do. But I have to speak to you. It concerns the Infanta.'

'Jessamin?' Indigo frowned. 'What of her?'

Leando glanced towards the dais at the far end of the hall. 'Today, our new Takhan, all honour and glory be his own, as the Falorim are so fond of saying, was enthroned as ruler of Khimiz and founder of its new dynasty. And later tonight, he will announce his official betrothal to the Infanta Jessamin, the marriage to take place when she is twelve years old.'

'Thank you,' Indigo said with irony. 'I'm indebted to you for the revelation.'

His eyes, angrily resentful, met hers, then his voice dropped to a whisper. 'And will you be prepared to sit by and watch, on the night that that helpless child goes to his bed and loses all claim to her rightful heritage?'

Indigo halted, staring back at him and hardly able to credit that she hadn't misheard. Leando smiled with no humour.

'Yes; that *was* what I said. Keep dancing, unless you want to draw attention to us.' They began to move again, though for Indigo it was pure reflex.

'You're fond of the Infanta,' Leando continued. 'I've seen you with her, and I've listened to Luk's prattle about you. In fact I owe Luk a debt, for he's opened my eyes to the truth. Whatever our differences may be, we have something in common: a concern for the Infanta's welfare. And her welfare – not to mention that of Khimiz – will be sorely jeopardised by the continuing rule of Augon Hunnamek.'

Indigo was too stunned to speak. Her mouth felt dry, and the air in the hall was suddenly stifling. And one word sprang into her mind. *Trap*.

'Well?' Leando hissed. 'Have you nothing to say?'

Caution! the inner voice warned. She took a deep breath to steady herself. 'No. Not when the words I am hearing are treasonable.'

She gasped as Leando pulled her hard against him. Pressing his mouth close to her ear as he spun her around, he whispered harshly, 'There can be no treason against a usurper!'

Something turned sour and sick within Indigo, and she fired back angrily, 'A usurper? This, from the lips of the man who betrayed the Takhina Agnethe? You hypocrite!'

Leando's face went white but for two patches of burning colour high on his cheeks. 'Damn you, you don't – '

She started to cut across him with a furious retort, but at that moment the music ceased, and she realised the dance was over. Quickly biting back her words, Indigo glared at Leando, pulling herself free from his grasp.

'I have nothing to say to you.' She saw a nearby couple watching the exchange with curious interest, and delivered the whispered words with a smile, as though thanking her partner.

'Oh, but I have more to say to *you*. And you'll hear me.' Leando made a show of bowing, then took her arm in a ferocious grip, steering her forcibly towards the side of the hall. She could have fought him off easily enough, but dared not draw more attention to herself, and so, breathless with anger, went with him.

'We will walk together on the terrace,' Leando said savagely, 'and admire the lights in the gardens. Don't fight me, Indigo. I don't think you want to be at the centre of an unpleasant scene, do you?'

Indigo tried to force her racing heart to calm enough to allow her to breathe freely. Beneath her anger a voice of reason was beginning to assert itself. What had she to lose by hearing what Leando had to say? If, as she suspected, this was part of some devious plan to test her loyalty, she could acquit herself without running any risks.

And if it was not –

She had no chance to allow the wild thought to develop, for Leando was pulling her away. Sound and light faded as they stepped through one of the tall windows and on to a wide, tiered terrace that bordered the garden. They walked down the steps, and Leando led her along one of the paths that ran between the flower-beds. Water glinted nearby, and by a pool whose central fountain made enough noise to prevent any casual eavesdropping he stopped and turned to face her. Away from the artificial glow of the lamps, his face looked angular and dangerous.

'You call me a hypocrite,' he said. 'But perhaps first you should look in your own mirror, and consider what you see there. Tell me, Indigo; do you know how the Takhina died? Or have you shut your eyes to that, as you seem to have done to so much else?'

Indigo's fury welled. 'The Takhina eluded her guards and jumped from a tower,' she retorted. 'Perhaps it was a fitting epitaph for your betrayal!'

'And perhaps it was *murder*!' He grabbed her arm again – then suddenly his eyes narrowed. 'By the Mother, you know, don't you? You know she didn't kill herself!'

Indigo looked away, her heart pounding. 'I know no such thing!'

'Oh, but I think you do! It's in your eyes, Indigo – you've asked yourself the same questions that I've asked so often.' A finger jabbed upwards into the darkness. 'How did the Takhina reach that minaret undetected? How did she evade her guards? And how was it that the sentries slept so conveniently at their posts?'

Indigo felt as though her pulse was about to burst her veins – but she dared not admit to her suspicions. There were too many risks. And one glaring inconsistency. She pulled her arm free from Leando's grasp, and said sharply, 'Your sudden concern for the late Takhina is touching, Leando. But it's a pity you didn't consider such a possibility before you guided Augon Hun-namek's men through the desert to bring her back to such security and safety!'

Leando was silent for a moment. Then, in a voice

charged with bitter feeling, he replied, 'You're quite right. But perhaps if your own son had been held hostage against your co-operation, you too might have found the issue less clear-cut.'

She stared at him. 'Your . . . '

'Luk was kept in one of the palace rooms, guarded by a man under orders to cut his throat if I should fail in my obligation. I understand that he was very frightened and cried a great deal during my absence, but I suppose one can expect no better from a two-year-old child.'

Indigo felt something catch in the back of her throat. 'Leando, I – ' Her aggression collapsed abruptly. 'I'm sorry. I didn't know.'

'Of course you didn't. Few people do. Most believe I betrayed the Takhina from sheer pragmatism, and are pragmatic enough themselves to look on it as an unfortunate necessity in the aftermath of conquest.' He paced along the side of the pool, then turned back to face her again. 'So now perhaps you understand the true nature of my loyalty to Augon Hunnamek.'

Indigo didn't know what to say. Leando's story had shocked her, and given her a new perspective on his character. But, she asked herself, dared she believe him? The facts would be easy enough to verify; but what of the underlying motivations? One thing in particular didn't ring true, and she forced herself to put aside sympathy as she said,

'Leando, why have you told me this?'

'What do you mean?'

'Exactly what I say. I'm no friend of yours. Why tell me – and why now?'

He raised his eyebrows. 'Think, Indigo. Think of your own attitude. You've spent the past ten months hating me because I betrayed the Takhina to her enemies. What does that tell me about your own loyalties?'

'It tells you nothing – except, possibly, that when I see something which I can only interpret as treachery, I don't like it. You forget, Leando, that I have no fealty here. I'm not Khimizi.'

Leando hunched his shoulders, looking out over the garden. 'No,' he said. 'But you do have one cause – your love for and desire to protect the Infanta. Whatever your other feelings may be, I don't believe you'll deny that.' He paused. 'Will you?'

'You seem very certain of it.'

'I'm not; not entirely. But I'm prepared to gamble on your answer.'

She couldn't harm herself by admitting it. Indigo nodded. 'Yes. I do love the child.' She forced herself to relax and smile wryly at him. 'Who could not?'

'Exactly. And that is why we believe you can be trusted.'

'We?' Indigo looked at him. 'Are you saying – '

He interrupted her, making a warning gesture with one hand. Looking up, she saw that several young men were approaching along the path, heads close together, sharing some private joke.

Leando took her arm. 'Let's walk for a little while. This way: it's quieter.'

Their footfalls echoed hollowly on the courtyard's marble slabs as the sounds of the fountain and the whispering youths fell behind. The music from the great hall was faint now, and mingling with less identifiable sounds from the celebrations continuing in the city. Every now and again the sky to the west lit up as a flare shot heavenwards from the harbour, and Indigo thought she could hear distant cheering accompanying each burst. When they had passed by the last of the lanterns and the garden was no more than a dim confusion of shadows, Leando said softly:

'I won't tell you the names of my friends. But believe that they exist, and they oppose the usurper's rule.' His eyes glinted in the dark, feral, reminding her in a bizarre way of Grimya's look when she was distressed or angry. 'Khimiz has no Takhan: it has a *Takhina*. And it is our aim to see her come into her heritage. Not as a dissolute warmonger's property, but alone, in her own right.' He stopped walking, and turned fully to face her. 'I don't think I need to elaborate any further.'

Indigo looked steadily back at him. She was in control of herself now, the fear gone; but her thoughts were moving like a flood-tide. Leando's meaning was perfectly clear. He was telling her that he and some unknown fellow-conspirators planned to assassinate Augon Hunnamek. And if she could believe him, then a door which she had thought tightly closed against her was at last beginning to open.

But she dared not take him on trust. He might be genuine; or this might be some devious and dangerous trial at Augon's behest. To openly accept what he said would be too perilous. She needed more evidence and more time; and yet she didn't want to alienate him. She had to dissemble.

She said: 'You realise, don't you, that if you're wrong about me you could be placing yourself in great danger? If I were to report this conversation to the Takhan, your life would be worth nothing.'

'Indeed. And neither would yours.' He wasn't smiling now. 'You're at a disadvantage, Indigo. You don't know the identities of my friends, nor can you discover them unless they should choose to reveal themselves to you. If you should betray me to Augon Hunnamek, you will die before he has time to thank you for it. That isn't a threat; it's simply a statement of fact. And I think that, like any of us, you consider your own life worth preserving.'

She acknowledged the point with a curt nod, aware that he had effectively cornered her. 'Very well,' she said. 'We understand each other. But you obviously know that I'm at best neutral to your cause. What makes you think that I might be of any value to you?'

'You're the Infanta's companion. No one is better placed to protect her if and when the need arises.'

'Protect her?' Indigo frowned. 'From what?'

Leando shook his head. 'I've said all I'm prepared to say for the time being; the next move is up to you.' He started to walk on slowly, and after a moment's pause Indigo followed.

'You will be invited to a meeting,' Leando continued. 'When and where it will be, I can't yet say: but if you care for the Infanta as I believe you do, I'd strongly advise you to attend.' He looked round at her, and his eyes were cold. 'If you don't you may find it hard in the days to come to live with your conscience.'

Indigo didn't speak. Ahead of them the garden's perimeter wall loomed, pale and ghostly in the dark, and shadowed by the overhanging vines. Leando said: 'I'll leave you now. It might be more prudent for us not to be seen returning from the garden together. And Indigo – '

'Yes?'

'Don't think that I've relied only on mundane observations in judging whether or not to speak to you tonight. There are other ways of delving into someone's true nature.' He hesitated, then suddenly smiled. 'I'm wise enough to know the value of taking that precaution.'

Indigo nodded, wondering uneasily just what Leando and his friends had unearthed through their scryings. 'I'll think on what you've said.'

'I hope so. Goodnight, Indigo. Enjoy the rest of the celebration.'

Indigo retraced her steps towards the palace interior, forcing herself not to look back. She felt queasy and confused, and found herself fighting violently against her mind's efforts to assimilate all she had heard. She didn't want to think about it; she wanted only to return to the celebration and immerse herself in dancing and drinking and laughing. She felt a sudden deep-seated need for one of her potions; the cordial perhaps, or, better still, the water-pipe. *Anything* that would enable her to forget Leando's revelation until she felt able to face it with more equanimity.

A great shout went up suddenly from the hall ahead, drawing her attention. Through the tall windows she could see the glitter of lights, a press of people crowding about some central point. The cheer was given a second time, a third; and as it slowly died away an individual voice, intoxicated with more than wine, rose above the rest.

'*Joy be to the Takhan and the future Takhina!*'

Indigo was immobilised. She stared at the hall, at the

brilliance and festivity and sheer energy that radiated from it, and felt as though something within her was freezing. In the agitation of her encounter with Leando, she had forgotten that the betrothal announcement was to be made tonight.

The tastes of soured wine and food rose suddenly into her throat, and with it came a dull, futile feeling of misery that she couldn't focus. Music struck up; as couples took to the floor to dance, a group of giggling young women spilled out on to the terrace. Indigo watched them as they flitted down the steps like vivid, careless butterflies; then with an effort she turned back to the arched entranceway and walked through. Heat and light and sound met her in a festive wave; a servant came forward proffering a tray of wine-glasses and Indigo took one, drained it, beckoned for another, before moving on into the press of the throng.

Chapter XI

The message was so carefully disguised as a formal invitation to dine at the house of Copperguild that at first Indigo didn't realise its significance.

She and Hild were with Jessamin, encouraging her first stumping, determined efforts to walk, when a palace servant brought the small scroll with its coin-and-ship seal, the Copperguild family emblem, on a crystal tray. Hild, who had no sense of shame, gathered the Infanta on to her lap and leaned blatantly over Indigo's shoulder as she read the invitation, then muttered her disgust at being unable to make head or tail of the Khimizi script.

'What is?' she demanded. 'Is look very important.'

Indigo smiled faintly. 'It's an invitation, Hild. To dine with the Copperguild family this coming neaptide evening.'

'Copperguild, eh?' Hild raised her eyebrows, then suddenly her face broke into a vast smile. 'Little Luk's papa! *I* know what is – he is being admiring to you, isn't it? *I* know!'

Indigo laughed. 'Nonsense, Hild. It's simply – ' and she stopped in mid-sentence as she realised exactly what the invitation meant. She'd forgotten. In the days since the banquet – how many was it? Thirty? Forty? The time had gone so swiftly – she had deliberately put the encounter with Leando as far from her mind as possible, preferring to let it lie until and unless events forced her to face and consider it. Now, it seemed, that time had come.

'You are blush!' Hild accused delightedly.

Her face was hot, skin prickling, but not for the

124

reason Hild assumed. Indigo rolled the parchment and tucked it into a pocket of her gown.

'I am *not* blushing, Hild, and neither is Leando Copperguild "being admiring" to me, as you put it. I imagine it's simply a gesture, to thank me for taking care of Luk.'

Hild wasn't impressed. '*A-na!*' she said. 'You shall go, yes?'

She remembered Leando's strained face before they parted at the banquet, and the way he had urged her – almost pleaded with her, though he'd tried to hide it – to attend the planned meeting. The invitation was to all intents and purposes innocent enough. She could lose nothing by accepting.

'Yes,' she said. 'I think I shall.'

'Lady Indigo.' Mylo Copperguild, Leando's uncle and head of the family, bowed over her hand and smiled warmly into her eyes. 'This is a great pleasure.'

'I'm honoured by the invitation, sir.' Indigo returned the bow, then turned to where Leando waited at the older man's side. Leando simply took her hand and squeezed her fingers briefly.

'Thank you,' he said quietly.

'Our family are gathered upstairs,' Mylo told her. 'It's less formal than our main dining hall, and easier to let in the fresh sea air. May I?'

He took her arm, and they climbed a curving staircase from the reception hall with its domed, mural-covered ceiling, towards the first floor. To Indigo's relief, the miasma that had clouded her senses for most of the day had cleared during the journey from the palace. She had spent the previous evening with Phereniq and had drunk a little too much wine, which had left her feeling leaden and sluggish when morning broke. Aware that she needed an alert mind tonight, she had refused Leando's offer to send a litter, or any other form of escort, and had walked the mile or so to her destination in the relative cool of early evening.

Most of Simhara's wealthier merchant families lived

125

on the city's seaward side, in an enclave of ornate and elegant mansions set back from the great harbour and with a magnificent view of the gulf. The Copperguild house was one of the most impressive, bringing home to her just how prosperous – and influential – the family had become over the years. Mylo, she knew, was not only titular owner of the huge Copperguild mercantile interests, but had also held a high position on the old Takhan's council. Augon Hunnamek had offered him preferment in the new regime, but Mylo had asked that he might be allowed to retire from court life and concentrate on his business interests, in which, he had said, he was better placed to serve the prosperity of Khimiz.

They reached the top of the stairs and entered a large and airy room with balcony doors thrown open to the evening breeze. There were seven others already present, and Mylo introduced Indigo firstly to an elderly woman with a hawkish profile – his mother and Leando's grandmother, matriarch of the household – then to his own wife, and son Elsender, who was perhaps a year or two older than Leando. Next came Leando's married sister with her husband, and another young couple, distant cousins whose names Indigo couldn't later remember.

By the time they sat down to eat, Indigo had come to the conclusion that Leando the courtier and Leando the family man were two utterly disparate individuals. This was the first time she had observed him among his own kin, and the contrast was startling. Though the fact that he spent so much time at the palace had to some degree distanced him from the family, there was an unmistakable warmth between them, a sense of shared comradeship that revealed a new side to Leando's character. His own parents, Indigo knew, were both dead; it was clear that he looked on Mylo as a second father, and Mylo in his turn treated him as well as he treated his own son.

Conversation at dinner was light and informal. They discussed ships, tides and weather: as a one-time mariner Indigo found herself much in demand, and recounted many of her experiences on the *Kara Karai*.

Talk then turned to more social matters; events at court, the progress of the Infanta, the Takhan's patronage of new investments and developments in the city and harbour. Leando's grandmother questioned Indigo closely on the newest court fashions and manners, and when finally the talking was all done, Mylo's wife sat before an ornate musical instrument at the far end of the room, and played some traditional melodies to which the company sang.

Indigo couldn't help but be fascinated by the instrument, which seemed to consist of a glass case filled with crystal chimes which were operated by a system of pedals and levers. The sound it produced was ethereal and spine-tinglingly beautiful; but her enjoyment was clouded by a growing sense of unease. It was near midnight now, and not one word had been said, not the smallest hint dropped, of the true purpose of the evening. To all appearances this was nothing more than a social gathering, and she began to wonder if she'd misjudged the motive behind the invitation.

But then the tide-bells began to ring in the harbour below the house, their sound carrying clearly in at the window. As though this were a signal, Mylo's wife ceased playing and carefully closed the glass instrument before rising to her feet and announcing her intention to retire. The matriarch also rose, and it seemed that Leando's sister and her husband, together with the other young couple, had been waiting for her cue, for they too took their leave. Pleasantries and kisses were exchanged, and Indigo found herself left in the company of Leando, Mylo and Elsender.

When the last footsteps had diminished beyond the closed door, Mylo turned to Indigo with a tight smile.

'My apologies for having detained you so long, Indigo. But, as I think you are aware, tonight's business isn't yet concluded. May we prevail upon you to stay for a while?'

Leando was watching her, his face tense. Indigo glanced quickly at him; then nodded. 'Yes. I – had anticipated this.'

Mylo crossed to the balcony doors and closed them,

drawing the heavy curtains. Leando was already dimming the lamps, so that from outside the room would appear dark. 'We could say nothing until the others had left,' he continued as he turned back. 'No one else in the family knows of our . . . ah . . . concern, and, as I'm sure you appreciate, it's both safer and fairer to them that they remain ignorant. Elsender – perhaps you'll now fetch our other guest, please?'

The young man left the room, and for a few minutes they waited in silence, until the door opened again and Elsender returned. With him was a man who walked a little uncertainly, feeling the way ahead with one hand while holding Elsender's arm with the other. Indigo looked at his face – and drew an involuntary breath as she recognised him. He was the blind pedlar, the carver of little ships, from whom she had bought the bronze net to offer at the Temple of Mariners.

'Karim.' Mylo went forward to take the pedlar's hand and lead him to a couch. 'Welcome to my house. I'm only sorry that we have had to resort to such subterfuge to entertain you. Please, sit, and take a glass of wine.'

The blind man smiled. 'It's a long time since any noble Khimizi family has been able to welcome me openly under their roof, Mylo,' he said. 'I doubt that I would know what to do at a banquet these days.' Elsender pressed a glass into his hand and he sipped appreciatively at it, then turned his head until he was facing Indigo. She had been staring at him, and started guiltily before she remembered that he was sightless.

'I sense an unfamiliar guest, yet not entirely un-familiar,' Karim said. 'Is she here?'

'She is.' Mylo nodded to Indigo, who approached the couch slowly. 'My friend, this is the lady Indigo of the Southern Isles, companion to the Infanta. Indigo: I present to you physician-mage Karim – '

He had been about to give Karim's family name, but the blind man raised a hand, forestalling him. 'No, no, Mylo. Simply Karim. Remember, I have no other name these days; nor any title, for that matter. Greetings, mistress.' He found Indigo's fingers and touched them lightly.

'Sir.' She was shocked, and convinced that she must have made a foolish mistake. *Physician-mage*, Mylo had said. Such men were the most exalted practitioners of medicine in all Khimiz; not only highly skilled healers, but also masters of the arcane and divinatory arts. This man and the temple pedlar couldn't be one and the same.

Karim spoke again. 'So, you are a Southern Islander? A beautiful country, I understand.' A faintly mischievous smile lit his face. 'Whose children have the scent of the sea in their hair, and know what gift will best adorn the Sea Mother's ship.'

Indigo's eyes widened. 'Then you *are* the pedlar – ' The words were out before she could control her tongue; but far from being offended, Karim laughed.

'Indeed, mistress, I am. The pedlar Karim, maker and seller of offerings; no more and no less.' He set his glass down, seeming to sense the proximity and height of the table beside the couch, then turned his head towards Mylo.

'I think we were right, Mylo. But I would like to make certain. With your permission?'

'Of course.' Mylo glanced at Indigo. Leando and Elsender were also watching intently, and Karim leaned forward and beckoned to her.

'Hold out your hands to me, mistress. Look into my eyes, if their blindness doesn't disconcert you, and respond to me with honesty.'

A little hesitantly she reached out towards him. He didn't take her hands, but instead his fingers encircled her wrists: his grasp was firm and steady. She met the sightless gaze, and he said, with no particular inflection, 'Tell me of Augon Hunnamek.'

An image flickered involuntarily across Indigo's mind. She saw Augon as she had first encountered him in the incense-filled room at the palace. Larger than life, charismatic, overwhelming – and loathsome. She felt her flesh crawl, as it crawled whenever Augon touched her hand or her shoulder; she saw the intensity of his pale gaze and wanted to shut her eyes, blot that stare out lest it should latch on to her soul and drag it from her

129

body to leave her empty and desiccated. *Demon*, her mind said. *Demon*.

But she couldn't speak it aloud.

'Augon Hunnamek is Takhan of Khimiz.' Her own voice seemed to come from a vast distance. 'He is – '

'No.' Karim interrupted her, and the spell abruptly broke. Blinking, Indigo found the room swimming back into focus, and its sheer normality disorientated her. Karim smiled.

'I need no careful words, mistress. Speech is rarely a reflection of the absolute truth.'

'But I – '

'Please. Bear with me a little longer.' He fell silent, but continued to gaze at her, and though Indigo wanted to protest, some inner compulsion made her hold her tongue. For a few minutes more Karim held her wrists, sometimes probing the flesh gently, pressing a vein or a bone beneath the skin. His expression didn't change until at last, with a sigh, he released her and sat back.

Behind Indigo, Leando let out pent breath. 'We were right?' he asked.

Karim nodded. 'Yes.'

Indigo was shaking. Her skin tingled, and the fine hairs on her arms were standing upright like Grimya's fur when she was afraid or angry. The hair at the nape of her neck had risen too, and her heart was beating with painful rapidity. Karim had power – *true* power, unlike Phereniq and her ilk – and the thought of what he might have read in her mind appalled her. Fear, coupled with confusion, made her aggressive, and she turned on Leando. 'What do you mean, you were right?' she demanded. 'I don't understand! What are you trying to do?'

'Peace, lady.' Mylo poured a glass of wine and proffered it to her. 'Karim simply safeguards all our interests.' He looked at the blind man, who had sunk back among the cushions. 'What of the other tests, Karim? Do you wish to continue?'

Karim shook his head. 'There's no need: I've seen enough. She *is* the one.'

Indigo appealed to Leando again. 'Leando – you must tell me what this is about! Your uncle speaks of tests, and Karim tells me that I am "the one". In the Mother's name, what does this *mean*?'

Leando and Mylo exchanged a glance, then Mylo nodded almost imperceptibly. Leando sat down beside Indigo.

'I'm sorry if we've alarmed you,' he said, 'but we had to make sure of you before we dared proceed any further, and Karim's judgement was the only one we could trust. Now he has confirmed our belief, I can explain more.

'Last year, shortly after the invasion and overthrow of our Takhan, Karim – in his guise of a pedlar at the Temple of Mariners – encountered a stranger whose presence in Simhara, so his instincts told him, was deeply significant. He divined further into the matter, and what he learned persuaded him to come to us. He and my uncle are old friends, and Karim knew of our disaffection. He told us that this stranger, a woman now living at the palace, was vital to our cause.' He paused, glanced at Mylo again and received another faint nod. 'In short, that she held the key to the overthrow and destruction of the usurper.'

Indigo stared at Karim. She was astonished and chagrined by the thought that he was capable of divining so much from one brief, chance encounter; and it made her wonder again, apprehensively, what else Karim might have discovered about her.

She addressed the blind man, choosing her words carefully. 'Master Karim, I am no expert in arcane matters, or in the arts of divination. Can you explain to me what led you to the conclusion you've made about me?'

The look Karim returned was disconcerting, for it seemed that, despite his blindness, his eyes were humorously challenging her.

'Others rely on the stars and the auguries for their guidance, mistress,' he said. 'But I have followed a path which allows me to see what is in your *true* heart.'

He was being deliberately cryptic, she thought, and

131

that worried her. 'Sir, I – ' she began to persist, but he interrupted.

'No, lady; there is no more I can say to you now, other than that I know you're worthy of trust. For the time being, be content with that.'

Indigo subsided, aware that further argument would be fruitless. Karim turned his head towards the window, and sniffed at the air.

'It's growing late,' he said. 'I smell the tide returning to the harbour. We should conclude our business quickly, Mylo; it wouldn't be wise to send the lady back to the palace at an hour that might arouse too much curiosity.'

'Yes.' Mylo turned towards Indigo. 'Indigo, we've detained you overlong. But before you leave, I have something to say. Karim has told us that we can trust you, and that is all the assurance we need. However, I'm aware that as yet we can't expect you to trust us in your turn. Leando has told me of your doubts, and I appreciate them. I ask only that you'll consider what I am about to tell you, and that what you hear won't be repeated beyond the walls of this room.'

'It won't, sir,' Indigo said quietly. 'Leando knows that I am at least neutral to your cause.' She smiled faintly. 'And he has taken great care to explain the price of betrayal. I have *some* regard for my own life.'

Leando smiled back a little sheepishly, and Mylo nodded. 'My nephew can be unsubtle, but . . . very well; I think we all understand the position. I believe, Indigo, that you know of our intention – to remove the usurper Augon Hunnamek from the throne of Khimiz, and put the Infanta, our country's rightful ruler, in his place.'

Indigo nodded. 'That much Leando told me,' she said. 'You intend, I presume, to assassinate him?'

'Yes.' Mylo smiled drily. 'A man like Augon Hunnamek would never admit defeat if he were merely deposed: it has to be death. Besides, we have more personal reasons for wishing to see him brought down. You're probably not aware of this, but our family is related at only one remove to the royal house of

Khimiz.' An edge crept into Mylo's voice. 'The old Takhan, however imperfect he may have been, was our cousin – and it is therefore our duty, as well as our wish, to avenge him.'

Indigo considered this for a few minutes. She hadn't known of the Copperguilds' link with the royal family, and the revelation lent weight and conviction to what she had heard tonight. But to wish Augon Hunnamek dead was one matter; to kill him was quite another.

She said: 'It won't be an easy task, Mylo. The new Takhan is very well protected in the palace, as both Leando and I know. And he's also proving to be a popular ruler – considerably more popular, from what I hear, than his predecessor was. If you assassinate him, you may well incur the wrath of the whole of Khimiz.'

'That's true enough,' Mylo agreed. 'But if there's one quality that's more deeply ingrained in the Khimizi than superstition, it's pragmatism. The same pragmatism that accepted the usurper's rule without protest will also accept his demise, as long as it poses no threat to the peace and prosperity of Khimiz. And,' his look softened, 'you forget the Infanta herself. Even though she's still a babe, she is greatly loved by the populace. Whatever lip-service our people may pay to the usurper, in their hearts they know that Jessamin is our true Takhina.'

Logically what he said was sound enough, but Indigo was aware of one deadly flaw. Mylo believed that he was dealing with a mortal man; a powerful and shrewd man perhaps, but mortal, and therefore fallible. She knew better. And if the maleficent entity that was the real Augon Hunnamek once suspected a plot against him, then no amount of secrecy or strategy would protect the plotters from the consequences.

Yet she couldn't tell Mylo and Leando the truth. She *dared* not: not until she was certain she could trust them. And even then, she reminded herself grimly, would they believe her? Even Khimizi superstition didn't run that deep, and she had no proof beyond her own intuitive certainty.

She said, her voice just a little unsteady, 'How do you mean to kill him?'

There was a long pause. Elsender cleared his throat nervously, while Leando stared at the floor beneath his feet. Karim simply continued to sip his wine. At last, Mylo answered.

'We have a plan, but there are still many details to be finely honed, and we dare not be hasty. Everything must be right, and we feel . . . forgive me, but we feel it wiser not to reveal more unless we are sure that you're prepared to join us. For your sake as much as for ours.'

She nodded. 'I understand. But in the meantime?'

'In the meantime?'

'You asked me here tonight to do more than test my integrity. You must want something from me.'

'Yes. Simply your pledge to protect the Infanta, until we are ready.'

She stared back at him. 'Are you in any doubt of that?'

Karim shifted on his couch. His blind eyes scanned the room and seemed, unnervingly, to focus on Indigo's face.

'Be in no doubt of it, Mylo, my old friend,' he said quietly. 'The lady speaks the truth. And though she may not dare admit to her innermost feelings, our cause is her cause. Be assured of that, and let it give you peaceful rest tonight.' His smile was for Indigo alone, and she shivered inwardly.

'Yes,' she said. 'I will protect her.'

She made her farewells to Mylo and Elsender – and, a little uneasily, to Karim – and Leando, who was not returning to the palace until morning, escorted her down to the hall. The outer doors stood open, and a litter waited beyond; on the threshold they were briefly alone, and Leando took hold of her hand.

'You'll think on what you've heard tonight, won't you?'

'I will,' she promised gravely. 'But . . . '

'What troubles you?'

She shook her head, not sure if she could explain or even if she wanted to. 'There's so much I still don't understand,' she said. 'You're willing to trust me; willing to take only Karim's word as a safeguard. It doesn't make sense.'

'Karim's word is enough. If you knew him, you wouldn't question that.'

'But who *is* he? Your uncle addressed him as "physician-mage", yet – '

Leando interrupted her, gently, pitching his voice low. 'Indigo, none of us knows Karim's full story. Until a little over a year ago he was as my uncle named him: a mage and physician in the old Takhan's household. Why he chose to leave the court and take up a new identity as a poor pedlar, we don't know; though he lost his sight at about the same time, and we believe that the change may have had some philosophical significance for him. Certainly since his blindness his clairvoyant powers have increased. But he has never wished to explain, and we respect that wish; as we also respect his desire to remain anonymous to all others in Simhara. We trust him, Indigo. And we trust his judgement. That's enough for us.'

There was nothing more she could say, though her doubts were still unassuaged. She silenced the further questions that rose in her mind, knowing they would lead her nowhere, and prepared to leave: but then Leando caught her hand again.

'Indigo.' His face was strained. 'In your care for the Infanta, consider Luk, too.'

She understood his meaning. 'You're afraid for him?'

'I'm afraid for all of us. But especially for Luk. Goodnight, Indigo.' And he kissed her fingers in a way that conveyed something more than mere formality before she stepped out into the night.

The litter-bearers ran quietly and swiftly along Simhara's silent streets and through the deserted bazaars, and Indigo was roused from a doze to realise that they had arrived at the palace gates. The gate-guards, who

135

knew her, smiled with a conspiratorial air as she stepped from the litter; and she made her way through the darkened gardens towards her rooms.

Only a few dimmed lamps burned in the corridors. The wind-chimes at the windows stirred faintly and rang a sweet, harmonic chord as she passed; her weary mind registered the scents of jasmine and honeysuckle on the shifting air. Her door was but a few paces ahead –

And a shadow that was more than a shadow moved from the darkness to fall across her path.

'Indigo.' Pale eyes in the gloom, the smile of a leisurely hunter as Augon Hunnamek touched a light and gentle hand to her shoulder.

Shock made Indigo's heart miss painfully; she recovered enough to bow to him, at the same time stepping back so that his fingers fell away. 'Lord Takhan.'

Augon chuckled softly. 'So you, too, are a creature of the night.' The hand reached out again and this time squeezed her upper arm with delicate precision. 'I promise to keep your guilty secret, if you will promise to keep mine.'

She forced herself to smile at him. 'Of course, sir.'

'*Sir.*' He savoured the word. 'It doesn't come easily from your lips, does it, dear Indigo? I find that so refreshing, surrounded as I am by sycophants and self-seekers. I would like to think that in our rare private moments I am not "sir" to you, nor "lord Takhan", but simply Augon, as I was for all the years of my youth, before ambition got the better of me.'

Heart pounding, Indigo looked away from the intensity of his gaze. 'I think you're playing games with me, sir.'

'Ah. Then let us call this a chance encounter, and retire to our separate dreams. Did Leando Copperguild entertain you well?'

Realisation that he knew where she had been made her queasy; but she told herself that it meant nothing, that there were tattlers aplenty in the palace. She composed her face into an innocent mask. 'He and his family were the perfect hosts, sir. We talked of ships and the sea, and I had the pleasure of recalling many happy memories.'

'I'm gratified to hear it. Perhaps I shall avail myself of Copperguild hospitality one day soon, if it's all you say.' Augon smiled again, but this time it was a private smile, and enigmatic. 'Goodnight, dear Indigo. I'm sure the Sea Mother will send you pleasant dreams.'

She tried to stand rigid as he leaned forward to kiss her brow, but if he felt the inward flinching he gave no sign of it, only turned and walked leisurely, gracefully away. She didn't wait until he was out of sight, but hastened into her apartment, locking the door behind her and leaning against it for a moment as she tried to control her over-rapid heartbeat.

Hints, oblique references, suspicions . . . she couldn't assimilate them, refused to consider the implications. Forcing herself to walk calmly, Indigo crossed the floor to her couch, with only the thin moonlight to guide her. Grimya was a dark shape, sleeping; she didn't want to disturb her, didn't want to face the questions that clamoured in her head. She wanted only to slip into the oblivion of dreamless rest.

She was shaking as she lay down on the couch. For a moment she thought of turning to the small, ornate cabinet where her pipe, Phereniq's gift, lay only waiting to bring her peace. But she was too weary, too drained: already her body and mind were conspiring to drag her down, down into dark, silent relief.

Shuddering, chilled by something that emanated from deep within her psyche, Indigo's eyes closed and she sank into unconsciousness.

Chapter XII

I think that we have no choice. Grimya's unquiet gaze rested on the courtyard beyond the window, where Jessamin splashed happily in her pool under Hild's patient supervision. *We must believe that they are telling the truth.*

Indigo sighed. The she-wolf was right; too much time had already been wasted in fruitless speculation, and she was no nearer to making up her mind than she had been after the meeting at the Copperguild house. Six more days had passed since that encounter, and she'd heard nothing from Leando. For the first three days he had been about in the palace as always, but when he fetched Luk from his play each evening he had – deliberately, she suspected – avoided anything but the most trivial conversation with her. Then on the fourth day Augon Hunnamek had called his council into session, and since then Leando, together with the other advisers, had been closeted with the Takhan through almost all his waking hours.

There was also the mystery of Karim, the mage-turned-pedlar. The little Leando had told her had aroused rather than satisfied her curiosity, and she wondered if perhaps Karim had fallen from grace at some time in the past. Physician-mages were a small and select number, and Thibavor, the court physician, would certainly know of a disgraced member of his brotherhood; but she couldn't question him without drawing unwanted attention to herself. If she was to learn more it must be from Karim himself; and once, on an impulse, she had taken Grimya back to the Temple of Mariners to seek the mage. He was there, in his customary place on the temple steps, but Indigo's courage had failed before she could approach him, and she returned to the palace unsatisfied.

But she couldn't prevaricate for much longer. One way or the other, she had to decide whether to pledge herself to the Copperguilds' cause – and, if she did, whether to tell them the truth about Augon Hunnamek.

On that subject, too, Grimya had been unequivocal. If Indigo was to join with Leando and his uncle, then to let them go unknowing and unprepared against such a demonic power would be like condemning them to death without trial. For her own and Grimya's sake, as much as for theirs, Indigo could only agree. Yet how could she convince them, without breaking the taboo that the Earth Mother's emissary had set upon her, and revealing her own story and purpose?

It was a dilemma that seemed to have no solution, and time was running out. Despite his present silence, Leando would demand an answer before long, and if she continued to evade the issue then the plotters would move against Augon without her. The consequences of that were too hideous to contemplate. Somehow, she had to find an answer.

Her unhappy thoughts were interrupted by a tentative knock at the door, and as she turned, Leando came in. He was heavy-eyed and unkempt, still wearing the crumpled clothes in which she'd last seen him three days ago. And his expression was tight and unreadable.

'Leando.' Indigo rose. 'Is the council session over?'

'We were dismissed ten minutes ago. I had to come here quickly; Phereniq means to visit the Infanta as soon as she has bathed, and there's little time. Indigo, we've had a setback, and it's serious.'

Grimya's ears pricked, and Indigo felt her skin crawl. She glanced over her shoulder to make sure Hild wasn't in earshot, then said urgently, 'What's happened?'

Leando's smile was ironic. 'The one thing none of us had anticipated. My uncle and I are being sent away from Khimiz.'

She was stunned. 'Sent *away*? But – Great Mother, surely the Takhan hasn't – '

He guessed the conclusion she'd jumped to, and

139

shook his head quickly. 'No; it isn't like that, at least not overtly.' He uttered a bitter little laugh. 'We have been appointed as the Takhan's personal ambassadors to the Jewel Islands.'

'*What?*'

'It's a masterstroke, isn't it? The first men to inaugurate an embassy on those isles and to set up a stable and permanent trade between our two countries. A coup for Khimiz, to further her peace and prosperity. And by the Goddess, his reasoning is flawless! Who better than the Copperguilds, foremost of all the merchant families in Simhara, to be his representatives?' Ferociously, unconsciously, Leando had slipped into mimicry of Augon's smooth tones. 'Who better to combine a shrewd knowledge of commerce with the diplomatic skills necessary to break such new ground? We have proved our worth, and we have proved our loyalty. And it's an honour we *dare* not refuse!'

Indigo's mouth was dry. 'Then you think he suspects you?'

Leando shook his head wearily. 'I honestly don't know. It would be so easy to draw that conclusion; but I can't deny that his arguments *are* logical. It may simply be a very unhappy coincidence.' He started to pace across the room like a caged animal. 'Damn him. *Damn* him!'

She asked: 'How many months will you be gone?'

'Months?' Leando stopped, and stared at her. 'We're not talking about mere months, Indigo. It may be *years*.'

She couldn't answer him, couldn't find words. He resumed pacing, now hugging himself as though he were cold.

'All our plans must change,' he said haggardly. 'We daren't try to strike now; we're too unprepared. Though it galls me to say it, we must wait.' He halted again and looked at her, his eyes glittering venomously. 'We have almost eleven years' grace before that filth means to marry our Infanta. If we have to stay our hand right until the eve of the wedding, so be it. It won't come to that, of course; but even if it did, it wouldn't alter our resolve.'

140

He paused. 'But there's one vital question I now have to ask. What of you, Indigo?'

'Me?'

'Augon Hunnamek has forced our hand. We sail in seven days – and we must know your answer before we go. Are you with us, or not?'

It was the moment she had been dreading, but suddenly it had a new and terrible twist. He and Mylo could be gone for years, Leando had said. And that meant years of marking time, of continuing to maintain the charade of her life in Simhara, while she waited for her only allies to return. She couldn't hold back that long. Yet alone, what chance did she have of destroying Augon?

Desperately she said, 'What of Elsender? And Karim? They must surely – '

'Elsender is to accompany us, as is my aunt. Our revered Takhan has been nothing if not thorough. And without the rest of us, Karim can make no move. Indigo, I know I'm asking a great deal of you. But for the Infanta's sake, I beg you to help us.'

Something akin to panic rose in Indigo. 'Leando, I can't make that promise!' she protested. 'I don't even know how long I shall be here in Simhara. If the Takhan should decide that I'm no longer useful – '

'I know, and I understand. But *if* you stay, can we rely on you?' He hesitated, his gaze searching her face. 'I ask no more than that.'

She had to decide, Indigo realised. She couldn't dissemble any longer. And, in all conscience, she couldn't refuse what he asked.

'Yes,' she said. 'While I remain in Simhara, you can rely on me.'

He let out a pent breath. 'Thank you. And as for Luk . . . '

'Surely he'll go with you?'

'Oh, no. He's to stay here. To ensure that his education and development don't suffer from a sojourn in a barbaric country: or at least, that's the official reason. My grandmother is to be his guardian, but Luk will be allocated his own study at the palace, so that he may take full advantage of his privileged position. And again, how can I argue?' Leando shook his head unhappily. 'I fear for him. I fear that he may be a hostage for our good behaviour.'

'I'll care for him,' Indigo promised. 'And I'll protect him in whatever ways I can.'

'Simply keep him free from the machinations of the court,' Leando said. 'Don't let the usurper use him. Because he will. I feel he will.'

'I'll do whatever's possible.' Indigo looked down at the she-wolf, who was watching Leando intently. 'And so will Grimya.'

'Yes. Yes . . . thank you.' Leando forced his shoulders to relax, then stepped forward and placed both hands on her shoulders.

'I love Luk more than my own life,' he said quietly. 'And to know that he's safe in your care will make my leaving bearable. I owe you a great debt, Indigo.' And he kissed her.

His lips were against her cheek and his back to the door, so that he didn't see the door open without warning. Over his shoulder, Indigo found herself looking at Phereniq, who stood on the threshold with an expression of surprise on her face.

'Phereniq!' Hastily Indigo stepped back, and Leando swung round as he realised belatedly what was afoot.

'Indigo, I'm so sorry – I didn't think: I – ' The astrologer made a helpless gesture of apology. 'How rude of me! And Leando – I ask your pardon.'

Indigo pushed back her hair, chagrined that Phereniq had so clearly misconstrued what she'd seen. 'Come in,' she said tautly. 'Please; I – '

'I was just leaving.' Leando gave Phereniq a look of undisguised dislike, then turned to Indigo once more. 'I'll collect Luk in a little while. Don't tell him yet, please. It will be easier for him if I break the news myself.'

'Of course.' She went with him to the door, and at the threshold he made a pretence of bending to kiss her once more.

'Don't, Leando!' she whispered urgently. 'Phereniq must already think we – '

'Let her think it,' he interrupted. 'It will allay any suspicions she might have. We must talk again – I'll see you tomorrow, early.'

'Very well.' His hand was gripping hers and she squeezed his fingers briefly. 'Have a care.'

He hastened away down the corridor, and as Indigo closed the door, Phereniq approached her.

'Indigo, I'm mortified! Whatever must you think of me?'

'You weren't intruding, Phereniq.' Indigo took care not to let the astrologer see the expression on her face. 'It was nothing important.'

'No, no.' Phereniq followed her across the room, halting her with a hand on her arm. 'My dear, don't feel that you have to hide your feelings. Leando's news must have been a great shock.'

Indigo was about to explain to Phereniq that her sympathy was misplaced, but Grimya's mental voice sounded in her mind.

Let her think it. Leando is right: she might otherwise become suspicious.

The warning came just in time: Indigo swallowed back her words and put a hand to her face, affecting suppressed distress and hoping that the gesture wasn't theatrical. 'I'll be all right, Phereniq,' she said. 'As you say, it was something of a shock . . . but I mustn't be selfish. It's a great honour for Leando.'

'Yes.' Phereniq sounded wry. 'And men's priorities are not the same as ours, are they? We value peace and stability, but they have a thirst for adventure and new horizons which is hard for them to resist, even if it means leaving their loved ones behind.'

The sheer, unwitting irony of her assertion brought a bitter laugh to Indigo's throat, but she quelled it. Still taking care not to let Phereniq see her face, she walked towards the open doors that led into the court-yard.

'I'll grow used to the idea soon enough,' she said, pushing her hair back and deliberately adopting a lighter tone. 'After all, there will be much to occupy me in Leando's absence.'

Phereniq patted her arm. 'I'm glad to hear you sound so positive. The time will pass quickly for both of you, I'm sure of it. And if you ever need someone to tell your troubles to, you'll always know where to find me.'

'Thank you.'

The astrologer came to join Indigo on the threshold, and for a minute or two they watched Jessamin, who was still in her pool and oblivious to their presence.

'A true child of the Sea Mother,' Phereniq observed. 'She'll outgrow this pool soon, and we will need to make new arrangements to indulge her pleasure.' She paused. 'Do you know, Indigo, it's strange, but her birth-chart shows no indication of this talent for swimming. I can't imagine what can have gone wrong with my calculations.'

'It's not necessarily a reflection on your skills. After all, no system of divination can ever be perfect.'

'You mean that perhaps this is a special gift of the Goddess that even the stars couldn't foresee?' Phereniq smiled wryly. 'You're very kind, and I'd like to think you're right; but it's more likely that I'm simply growing careless in my old age.' She stepped out into the courtyard, stretching her arms and flexing her fingers. 'Such a beautiful day! It's good to be away from that overheated council-chamber at long last.' Her look suddenly became mischievous as her full good humour returned. 'Let us find a shady spot in the courtyard where we can enjoy the fresh air, and I'll call for some wine. I think we deserve a little indulgence, don't you?'

Seven days later, the *Agantine Lady* sailed from Simhara on the morning tide, with Leando, Mylo and Elsender on board. Indigo didn't go to the harbour to see the ship leave. The final parting was a private family affair; she had said her own farewells to Leando, and her presence at the quay would have been an intrusion.

It was, by all accounts, a splendid departure. The previous evening Augon Hunnamek had honoured his new ambassadors with a private banquet in the palace, and from the servants' gossip Indigo gathered that he had been fulsome both in his praise and in his generosity: Mylo and Leando set sail with a full royal escort, and with the Takhan's personal gift of enough wealth to keep them in the height of luxury during their stay in the Jewel Islands.

Luk was brought back at noon, his eyes red-rimmed but his expression stoical, and Grimya, taking pity on him, led him off to one of her favourite private haunts, to play with him and see if she could cheer him a little. Despite his tender years, Luk understood all too well that his father would be away for a long time; watching him as he trailed in Grimya's wake, Indigo's heart went out to him for the loss that he couldn't quite take in yet felt with all the keen agony of childhood. As yet, she was powerless to help him; until he had come to terms with this frightening new situation in his own way, all she could do was wait in the background, and be there if and when he needed her.

And Luk's plight highlighted her own dilemma, for of one thing Indigo was now certain: with his father gone, she couldn't abandon the little boy to the capricious tides of fate. At their last meeting before his departure, Leando's reserve had deserted him and he had pleaded with her to keep Luk safe. Moved by his brimming, barely-controlled emotion, Indigo had on impulse made a promise that now terrified her, for she had sworn on her own life and integrity that, until Leando could return to claim his son again, she would be the mother that Luk had never known, and would protect him as fiercely as though he were her own. In Khimiz, it was rare for a man – especially a high-born man – to cry: but Leando had wept when she made that oath. And, with a fatalistic certainty that turned her blood cold when she thought on its implications, Indigo knew that no power in the world would induce her to break her promise.

She was trapped: and it was a trap of her own making, to which she had given herself as a willing sacrifice. But in the burgeoning personality of little Luk she had seen echoes of her own younger brother, Kirra, dead now these fourteen years yet still so dearly recalled. Luk had the same exuberance, the same eager curiosity and lively imagination. He was, she often thought, what Kirra's own son might have been, had Kirra lived to father children. Or – and the thought stung her with savage pain – the son she herself might have born to her own love, Fenran. But Fenran and Kirra were lost, victims of her tragic folly. There was only Luk. And he and Jessamin were the essence of the invisible but unbreakable chains that bound her to Simhara.

She felt the weight of those chains as she watched Luk and Grimya disappear into the depths of the palace garden. Jessamin, for once not clamouring to swim, was playing on the floor, pushing her toy ship back and forth along a rug and crowing with delight as the little banks of oars went up and down. Suddenly a thump followed by a childish giggle drew Indigo's attention, and she looked up to see that the ship had overturned. The Infanta gleefully clapped her chubby hands above the little vessel, then suddenly announced: '*Sivva!*'

A sensation like the thrust of a cold knife stabbed at Indigo's stomach. Jessamin was only just beginning to talk, and little that she uttered was as yet intelligible. But Indigo thought she recognised the word.

She leaned forward, holding out one hand to attract the child's attention. 'Jessamin? What did you say?'

The Infanta beamed at her, showing three milk teeth. 'Sivva!' she said again, emphatically.

To Indigo's ears, it seemed that she was trying to say, *silver.* And the cold knife seemed suddenly to twist, as though it were biting through her flesh and beyond it, to the core of her frightened soul.

Chapter XIII

' . . . And so, dear Indigo, our sojourn seems set to
continue for some while yet. It is hard to believe that near
on three years have passed since we sailed from Simhara,
and our home is constantly in all our thoughts. Thank
you for your continuing kindness and diligence towards
Luk. He forms his letters very well now, and I was greatly
moved by the message in his own hand which came with
your last letter. I have written to my grandmother asking
her to commission a portrait of him, to be sent to me on
the next cargo ship. I look forward greatly to seeing it.

The Sea Mother bless you for all you have done. Keep
faith – as do I.
Your friend, in gratitude,
Leando Copperguild'

Indigo folded the letter and slipped it into her reticule,
trying to push back a sense of sick despondency. Still no
respite, no prospect that Leando and Mylo would return
in the foreseeable future. This morning, hearing that a
cargo from the Jewel Islands was putting in to shore,
she'd prayed fervently that this time there would be
good news; but yet again she'd been disappointed.
Though, as always, Leando took great care to reveal no
sign of dissent in his letter, she sensed his frustration and
disquiet; and the occasional hint that only she would
understand – such as the cryptic phrase, *keep faith, as do
I* – was emphatic confirmation.

Three years since Leando had left Khimiz, and still
she waited, biding her time, making no move. She, too,
felt the frustration keenly; yet in her heart she was
honest enough to acknowledge that a part of her didn't
want the respite to end. Life in Simhara was peaceful
and pleasurable, and the city had become a safe haven

where she could feel sheltered from threat and travail. She could, Indigo acknowledged, be happy here, and only Leando's letters brought home again the poison in the bloom, which was otherwise so easy to forget.

There was, perhaps, a faint irony in the timing of the latest cargo ship's arrival from the Jewel Islands, for today was Jessamin's fourth birthday. At this moment servents were busy in the courtyard outside, completing the preparations for a celebration party, and soon the guests – children of noble families deemed suitable companions for the Infanta, together with the customary scattering of favoured courtiers – would begin to arrive. In the adjoining room Indigo could hear Hild entertaining Jessamin with some of her simple but, to a young child, magical conjuring tricks; the nurse's voice was punctuated by shouts of delight from the Infanta, who was excited and eager to make the most of her day. All morning gifts and messages of greeting had been arriving at the palace; the whole city was celebrating, and the occasion promised to be one of joy and delight and merriment, with nothing to cloud it. Nothing but Leando's letter, and its timely, discomforting reminder.

The sound of scampering footsteps in the corridor outside snatched Indigo's thoughts back to the immediate moment, and seconds later Luk, flushed and breathless, came running into the room.

'Indigo!' The small boy's face lit as he saw her, and he waved a piece of parchment. 'Papa sent me a letter! All of my own! And I read it, by myself!'

He scrambled on to the couch beside her and spread his letter out on her lap. As he proudly read aloud, stumbling sometimes over the harder words but stoically refusing to let her help him unless he floundered badly, Indigo looked down at his bowed blond head and felt a familiar blend of fondness and sympathy fill her. Life for Luk hadn't been easy since Leando's departure. He missed his father greatly, and missed, too, a father's influence, which normally would have been the pivot of a six-year-old boy's existence. With no close friends of his own age, he looked increasingly to her and to Grimya to find that elusive combination of mentor and playmate that Leando would otherwise have been. It was a heavy responsibility, but one that, for reasons beyond her promise to Leando, Indigo was anxious not to shirk.

Luk came to the end of his letter, and looked up. 'Indigo, is Papa coming home soon?'

She couldn't bring herself to lie to him, and sighed.

'I honestly don't know, Luk. He hopes it won't be long, but we must wait and see.'

Luk nodded, biting his lip. 'I wish he was here *now*,' he said. 'I wish he could come with me to Jessamin's party.'

'I know; and I wish it, too. But you'll be able to write to him, won't you, and tell him all about it?'

Luk's face brightened just a little. 'Ye-es . . . ' Then abruptly his expression cleared. 'Will there be jugglers? And storytellers? And games?'

'Indeed there will. And,' she added mischievously, knowing Luk's appetite, 'more food than even *you* can eat.'

Luk shouted with laughter. 'I could eat a whole chimelo. I could! If I wanted to.'

'I don't doubt that for a moment!' Indigo laughed with him, aware that the cloud was passing and thankful for the youthful resilience that enabled him to shrug off his disappointments so quickly. She ruffled his blond hair, then turned as the door that connected her room with Jessamin's opened, and saw Hild ushering the Infanta in.

Jessamin was an almost preternaturally beautiful child, with hair as gold as her mother's had been curling abundantly around a small, delicate face. In a blue silk dress embroidered with gold thread and with a tiny gold shawl draped over her chubby arms, she looked like an exquisite little doll. Her expression broke into a sunny smile as she saw Indigo and Luk, and she ran forward.

'Luk-y! It's my birthday!'

Luk jumped down from the couch and, with very adult solemnity, bowed formally to her. 'Happy birthday, Jessamin.'

Jessamin's eyes, which were the colour of dark honey,

149

widened. Then she held out her skirt and returned him an equally formal curtsey before covering her hand with her mouth and succumbing to a fit of giggling.

'Silly!' she said. '*Silly!*'

Luk grinned back at her, then held out his precious sheet of parchment. 'Papa sent me a letter,' he said. 'Would you like to see it?'

Jessamin blinked up at Indigo. 'Luk-y got a letter,' she informed her, then: 'Yes. Show me!'

As the two children pored together over the parchment, Hild moved round to where Indigo stood and, with sidelong movements of her eyes, indicated for her to withdraw out of Jessamin's earshot. By the window, the nurse said in a low voice,

'All is good now, it seems. But last night, she had the bad dreams again.'

Indigo's pulse quickened. 'The same nightmare?'

'Yes. Clerri was her night-servant, and this morning she told me of it. The Infanta woke two – no, three times, each time crying, each time saying of something dark was chasing her.' Hild hissed softly through her teeth, and shook her head. 'I do not like it. It is not good.'

'What does physician-mage Thibavor say?'

The nurse shrugged. 'He don't know. First he tried one medicine, then another, but nothing has worked. The dreams keep coming back.' She paused, gazing sympathetically at Jessamin. '*A-na!* Poor *beba-mi*. This cannot go on, Indigo.'

'No; indeed it can't,' Indigo agreed emphatically. 'If only she were old enough to tell us more clearly what troubles her . . . '

Hild nodded. 'But we cannot wait for that to be. Something must be done, whatever.'

Something must be done . . . Hild's words haunted Indigo as Jessamin's party progressed through the hot afternoon. The Infanta was happy enough now, and, as always, it seemed that the dawning of a new day had banished the nightmares altogether; for when subtly and gently questioned, Jessamin never seemed to be aware that she had dreamed at all.

In fact, for the past few months the dreams had been at a low ebb. Only recently had they begun to return: and that followed a disturbing pattern, for each year the Infanta's nightmares seemed to reach a peak during the time surrounding her birth-anniversary. When the dreams recurred, they were always the same – a darkness, something vast and shapeless and black, pursuing the helpless child through endless corridors of echoing terror that twisted and turned without end, and intent on eating her alive. That, at least, was the clearest interpretation that Indigo had been able to piece together from the sobbing and incoherent pleas for help which were all that, at her tender age, Jessamin could express. Grimya had attempted to use her telepathic abilities to probe deeper, but had failed; there was, the she-wolf said, a barrier in the little girl's mind beyond which she was unable to pass.

And moreover, not only Jessamin's dreams but Indigo's too had begun to follow that same peculiar cycle, starting in the early spring, reaching their greatest intensity about the Infanta's birthday, then fading as summer grew on. She wondered if her years of close contact with Jessamin might have generated an empathy between them that spilled over into the dream-world, but even if that were true it gave her no useful clues as to the essence or cause of the nightmares.

A surge of laughter and applause distracted her suddenly, and she saw that the storyteller – a man of Augon's own race, who had developed an unparalleled reputation in his trade – had finished his tale of a sea-captain who set out to fetch a fabled jewel from a magical island. The story was an old Khimizi favourite, and the adult guests as well as the children had been enthralled by the rendition. The children threw flowers and sweetmeats to the storyteller, who gathered up the offerings and, with a flourishing gesture, presented them to the Infanta. Music struck up, and amid the cheerful chaos Indigo saw Augon Hunnamek rise to his

feet and approach Jessamin. He said something to her –
those near enough to overhear laughed and nodded
encouragement – and with great dignity Jessamin stood
up, curtseyed and began to dance with the Takhan. The
sight of Augon's giant figure solemnly partnering the
tiny girl brought more laughter, but it was affectionate,
approving. Only three people didn't join in the merriment: Indigo, to whom the spectacle, so close on the
heels of Jessamin's dream, had a chilling undertone of
ill-omen; Luk, who simply stared, expressionless; and
Phereniq. As others, young and old alike, took their cue
from Augon and also began to dance, the astrologer
withdrew from the main body of spectators and came
across the courtyard to where Indigo stood by the open
casement. For a few moments they watched the Infanta,
who was dancing gravely and with great concentration,
then Phereniq said affectionately,

'Look at her: each step is little short of perfect. Such
grace and poise, and she's so young still. I envy her
youth, Indigo; truly I do.' She shifted her posture, then
grimaced and pressed the knuckles of one hand to the
small of her back.

'Have you hurt yourself?' Indigo asked solicitously.

'No; no. Just my old bones protesting, as they do all
too often these days. It's the price we must pay for the
wisdom that supposedly comes with age.' Phereniq
laughed, though the laughter had a brittle edge underlying its gaiety, 'Do you know, I am reaching a stage in
life where I quite *dread* being asked to dance, for fear
that my body might betray me with a spasm just when
I'm demonstrating my best steps!'

'You've been overworking of late,' Indigo said. 'The
council taxes you, Phereniq; you're too conscientious
for your own good.'

'You may well be right. But until this current spate of
problems is over, I have little choice in the matter.'

Indigo looked at her. 'Then there's no sign of an end
to the troubles in the city?'

'None. And the Takhan is very worried. The people
look to him for help, but so far he has been able to find
no solutions.' Phereniq shifted her position again to

ease her aching back. 'The snakes are the worst of the problems, I think. Most of them don't appear to be venomous, but a few are – some people have already died of their bite.' She sighed. 'And their sheer *numbers* are so disturbing. We think they must come from the sea – they're only plagueing the area about the harbour so far – but we can't be certain. Then there's the fever. No one has died of that yet, but again, it's virulent in the harbour district, and shows no sign of abating. The physicians are baffled as to its cause, and so can't suggest a cure.'

Indigo considered this in silence for a few moments. In the otherworldly comfort of the palace she had been isolated from the troubles in Simhara's western quarter; anxious that the Infanta should run no risk of infection, Augon had placed the area out of bounds to all palace inhabitants who had no essential business there. Grimya was forbidden her customary morning runs along the beach, and even Luk couldn't return to his grand-mother's house, but had been given temporary quarters adjoining Indigo's. But there were no barriers to news, and Indigo was well aware of the inexplicable twin plagues that were causing increasing chaos along the coastal strip. An apparently sourceless fever, and an infestation of small, green snakes that found their way into homes, offices, storehouses . . .

'What of the auguries?' she asked.

The astrologer shook her head. 'That's just it. We can find no clue to this mystery, though we strive day and night to unravel it. I confess to you, Indigo, my faith in my own skills has been sorely tested during these last seven days. The answer is there – it *must* be – but it eludes me.'

There was applause as the dance ended, and then children's voices began to clamour for games. Phereniq walked slowly along the terrace towards Jessamin's pool, and Indigo followed, absently watching the cele-bration while she considered what she had heard. Not for the first time since these inexplicable troubles had begun in the city, she recalled the words of the old fortune-teller in Huon Parita. *Watch for the serpent-*

eater. There was no logical connection, yet the significance of that warning, she felt, couldn't be ignored.

By the pool edge Phereniq stopped, and said, 'One of the harbourmasters has advanced a theory that these unpleasant events may be connected. It's possible, he says, that abnormal winds and tides out beyond the Gulf could have brought in freak currents from the far west; maybe as far as the Dark Isles. The Mother alone knows what manner of things dwell in those seas – they must be a breeding-ground for sicknesses the like of which we've never seen. If that's where the serpents come from, they could be fever-carriers.'

'It's a plausible idea,' Indigo agreed. 'But I suspect it doesn't convince you.'

'No, it doesn't; for one simple reason. Not one of the captains we've questioned has encountered anything untoward in the sea-lanes this past year. Even the Davakotian escorts report nothing, and they above all others would surely – '

'Phrenny!' A shrill, excited voice interrupted her, and Jessamin, skirt held up and dignity forgotten, came running towards them.

'*Beba-mi.*' Phereniq's face broke into a smile and she held out her arms to the little girl. Jessamin took her hands and jumped up and down.

'Phrenny!' It was the closest approximation she could manage to 'Phereniq'. 'Did you see me dance? *Did* you?'

'Of course I did, little Infanta. You were splendid.'

Jessamin tugged at her hand. 'We're going to play seek-a-mouse. I'm mouse, I'm going to hide! Come and play, Phrenny!'

Phereniq looked helplessly over her shoulder at Indigo. 'I am summoned,' she said with a wry but warm smile as Jessamin pulled her away. 'Indigo, we'll talk later.'

'Indigo, you come too!' Jessamin demanded.

Indigo laughed, capitulating, and started to follow them along the poolside. Ahead, a breath of wind disturbed the pool's surface suddenly, sending a ripple out from the edge; she glanced at it reflexively, though it didn't consciously register in her mind.

And realised abruptly that it wasn't a ripple.

'Phereniq.' Indigo's voice cut harshly across the pleasant background of laughing, chattering voices. 'Phereniq, stop. Keep still. Exactly where you are. In the name of the Mother, *don't move!*'

Talk ceased suddenly; heads turned in their direction. Then a woman screamed.

Phereniq saw it as it slid sinuously over the raised edge of the pool not three paces ahead of her, and with a strangled cry she snatched the Infanta back against her skirt. Scaled, shimmering wetly, its body as thick as a man's arm, the snake barred her path, coiling like a living rope as more and yet more of its length appeared from the water. It raised its head, tongue darting, until the tiny, malevolent eyes were on a level with Jessamin's own.

An awful, whimpering sound came from the Infanta's throat. She clung to Phereniq, and for a moment it seemed that Phereniq would try to drag her back, out of range.

'No!' Indigo cried. 'If you move, it'll strike! *Keep still!*'

Phereniq glanced over her shoulder, a wild, desperate plea in her eyes. Beyond her, in the impossible sanctuary of the main courtyard, children were screaming, women sobbing, men calling out, cries and pleas mingling in a rising hubbub.

'Great Mother, help us!'

'The Infanta – '

'Save her – someone, do something!'

The reptilian head began to sway from side to side. Jessamin moaned. And Indigo's mind and body were frozen rigid, beyond her control, as the snake's colour registered on her brain.

Silver.

'BE STILL!' A new voice roared from the confusion, and Augon Hunnamek shouldered his way to the front of the crowd. The babble subsided, and over Phereniq's head as she clutched the Infanta to her, Augon's eyes met Indigo's.

155

'Do as Indigo says.' There was terrible calm in his voice now, an iron control; but Indigo could see sweat gleaming on his dark skin. 'If you love the Infanta, don't move, don't speak. Phereniq: do you understand?'

An almost imperceptible nod. Phereniq was beginning to tremble, and utter silence had fallen in the courtyard. Even Jessamin was too terrified to wail. The snake continued to watch her, motionless now, implacably patient, waiting. It wouldn't strike, not yet; not unless some untoward movement triggered its instincts and provoked it. But it would take very little to spring the trap.

'Indigo,' Augon said softly.

She looked back at him. His intervention had broken her paralysis, but she knew that the barrier between self-control and panic was still perilously flimsy. Her mouth dust-dry, she whispered, 'Sir?'

'Move back slowly, until you're well clear, then run for my bodyguard. Tell them – ' And as he faltered, Indigo realised that he didn't know what to say, for he didn't know what to do. No human ability could match the speed of a striking serpent. One slip, one false move, and Jessamin would be beyond help. They dared not take such a risk.

There was a flurry of movement by the open doors of the palace, and suddenly Indigo felt a presence in her mind.

Indigo? I sense fear! What –

Grimya! Alarm filled her as she glimpsed the she-wolf's grey form from the corner of her eye. *Stay there – stay still!* She had left Grimya sleeping, knowing that she disliked crowds and noise: now though, the turmoil had woken the wolf and brought her to investigate. Swiftly Indigo opened her mind, showing Grimya the nature of the danger. She felt a mental bristling, anger vying with alarm as Grimya understood – then Augon's voice, thick with fear, hissed, 'Indigo, your dog! Keep her back!'

No, Grimya! Indigo projected urgently, but Grimya ignored her. Dropping to a crouch, she was slinking slowly and cautiously across the terrace. The snake's head moved a fraction; Grimya froze.

Grimya! It will kill you!

It will not. Hatred burned in Grimya's mind; the instinctive hatred of a warm-blooded mammal for an alien, mindless and deadly adversary. She wanted to kill, to protect her territory and her pack, and Indigo knew that nothing she could say would turn the wolf from her intention.

Augon's face was haggard, muscles standing out in his neck. 'Indigo, in the Sea Mother's name, *stop that animal!*'

Indigo, too, was sweating, and the sickness of helpless terror burned in her throat. 'Sir, she – won't heed me.' She met the Takhan's gaze again, starkly. 'She knows what she's doing. It may be the only chance . . . '

Grimya was now no more than five feet from the snake, and had dropped to the ground, tense and motionless. If the reptile was aware of her it showed no sign, but continued to stare fixedly at Jessamin. Indigo knew when the moment was coming, for she felt the first surge of intent in Grimya's mind – then, faster than she'd thought possible, so fast that all she saw was a stunning grey blur, Grimya sprang.

There was a hiss and a whiplash of movement. Taken unawares, the snake was forced to abandon its desired prey, and reared high, whipping round to meet the she-wolf's onslaught. As its coiling length turned, Indigo launched herself at Phereniq, spinning her round, dragging her back and Jessamin with her, and as the three of them crashed to the ground together she glimpsed Augon charging forward into the fray. Metal glinted in his hand, Grimya was snarling rabidly, the snake's body writhing, smashing against the paving. Then suddenly the focus of chaos changed and guests began to scream, the crowd parting like water, falling over each other to get out of the way as something shot through their ranks. At the far side of the courtyard the vines on the wall rustled violently as their leaves were forced aside; silver flickered briefly in the sunlight on the wall's coping, then vanished.

Gradually, the pandemonium died down. Children, many of whom didn't understand what had happened, were still crying loudly. A few feet away from Indigo, who had struck her head as she fell to the ground, Phereniq had raised herself on her elbows and was vomiting; Jessamin, sobbing now, clung to Augon Hunnamek as he crouched beside the pool, her small body wrapped and all but invisible in his powerful arms. And Grimya –

'Grimya . . . ' Indigo's voice was high-pitched and distorted. 'Where's Grimya? Earth Mother, is she hurt?'

'She's unharmed.' It was Augon's voice. Picking Jessamin up, he rose and walked unsteadily towards her, then dropped to a crouch again. 'She's safe, Indigo. And she saved our Infanta.'

Indigo tried to sit up, but the scene tilted and wavered before her blurred eyes. 'The snake – '

'It got away. But it harmed no one. Thanks to your dog.'

Indigo heard a soft whine beside her, and Grimya pushed her muzzle against her face, licking her cheek. *I am all right*, the she-wolf communicated. *But you –*

'I – hit my head on the pool edge.' Indigo laughed at the absurdity of it, then found that she wanted to cry instead. 'When I fell, I – ' She stopped, wondering if she was going to be sick.

Servants were scurrying from all directions now, and Augon snapped a finger to an anxious steward. 'You! Get the lady Indigo inside, and make her comfortable.' And to Jessamin, 'It's all right now, *chera-mi*; it's all right. *Chero* Takhan will take care of you.'

Through a daze of nausea and disorientation Indigo heard him, and her mind tried to protest. It was all wrong. Augon comforting Jessamin, holding her, embracing her, while she clung to him as her rock and her protector . . . it was all *wrong*. The snake – silver, colour of demons – and the stark terror in this other demon's eyes when the Infanta was threatened . . . It didn't fit. It made no sense. It was –

The courtyard swelled in and out of focus, then went

dark, as though heavy dusk had suddenly fallen. She made a protesting sound, felt hands solicitously lifting her, helping her, but couldn't find her feet. Someone said the word *concussion*, and Grimya was whining anxiously, trying to communicate, but the message couldn't get through the fog that was thickening in her brain –

'She's fainted.' Augon signed urgently to a servant. 'Fetch physician-mage Thibavor. When he's seen the Infanta, have him tend to Indigo, too. And as for Grimya . . .' He looked down at the she-wolf, who blinked back uncertainly. 'I don't know how best to reward a dog, but it will be done. Simhara has two new heroines today. And I owe them both my lifelong gratitude.'

Chapter XIV

Phereniq rose from her place at the long table and pulled her shoulders back, pressing practised fingers against her spine to ease its aching. The only sound in the room was the uneven sputtering of the lamps, which were burning low and needed refilling; beyond the room the palace, too, was quiet, and the sandclock in the table's centre had long ago run through its cycle with no hand to turn it. The hour must be very late; for her health's sake she should have been abed long ago, but there was so much to catch up on, so many small matters demanding her personal attention in the wake of today's council session. She would, she promised herself, sleep late into the morning as compensation.

She began to gather up her charts and calculations, meticulously sorting them into order – then started at the sound of a footfall behind her. Turning, she saw that Augon had entered the chamber, silently as was his way, and now stood gazing at her with a faint smile on his face.

'Ah, Phereniq. So you are the mystery conspirator who works long into the night, while the rest of us lie in the comfort of our beds.'

She looked away. 'I have much work to do, my lord, as you know. And as our recent efforts have been dedicated to scourging the city of these plagues, there are many other matters that have been neglected.'

'Indeed; and as always, I'm indebted to you.' He came across the room and lightly touched the nape of her neck, where her hair was bound up. She felt his fingers tangle in a stray strand, and tensed at the ambiguity the sensation aroused in her.

'We have done well,' Augon said matter-of-factly.

'The fever and the wretched harbour-serpents both banished, and all in the space of less than two months.'

She grasped the shift of mood gratefully; it put her on firmer ground. 'It was your scheme that accomplished it, my lord. To bring in those desert animals to hunt and kill the serpents was a masterly stroke, for which all of Simhara praises you.'

'And it was your auguries that led me to the solution. That, and the example set by our four-legged heroine.'

'Grimya is a creature of many talents.'

'Like her mistress. Do you know, dear seer, that the ballad-singers have made a song about them? I understand it's taking the western quarter by storm.'

She could smell perfume on his skin. The heady flower-essence used by the current favourite of his seraglio . . . it brought an inner tingling sensation, a stab of quick, jealous pain.

'When Indigo's services are no longer required here, I think I shall reward her further,' Augon continued. 'Some land; perhaps a title. Think of it: a woman granted such honours in her own right. It will outrage the Khimizi sense of propriety and storm the walls of a few outdated traditions, and that will be no bad thing. Although of course by then the notion may be redundant.'

'Redundant?' Phereniq frowned.

'I mean, my dear, that when Leando Copperguild returns, Indigo may have other plans of her own.'

'You know of their liaison?' She was surprised, but only for a moment before she reminded herself that little in the palace escaped his notice for long.

'Indeed I do. It is most touching.'

Phereniq hesitated, wondering whether or not to ask the question that hovered in her mind. Then she decided that she had nothing to lose by frankness.

She turned to face Augon, and drew breath. 'My lord, will you not recall Leando Copperguild to Simhara? He and his uncle have been your ambassadors now for more than three years, and they have proved themselves in your service – '

'Which is why they were chosen.'

161

'Yes. But when there are other ties . . . . Leando is young still, with his life before him. And Indigo – she says nothing, but I know she longs for his return. If you want to reward her, my lord, I can think of no greater gift you could give her.'

Augon smiled down at her. 'Ah, Phereniq. Your plea touches me, and I only wish that I could oblige you by agreeing to it. But you know that I cannot. As you said, Leando and his uncle have proved themselves in my service; so much so, in fact, that I would be acting against the best interests of Khimiz were I to recall either of them before their work is completed.'

Phereniq's hopes withered. Casting her gaze down, she nodded. 'Of course, my lord. I understand.'

'I'm sure that a woman of Indigo's many accomplishments will be able to find enough diversions to make the waiting bearable. Besides, she has the Infanta to occupy her.' He paused, walking slowly to the table and staring down at Phereniq's gathered charts. 'That child grows more beautiful every day. I understand she is now learning to write, and that the first word she wrote unaided was "Takhan". I find that very gratifying.'

Phereniq looked away.

'I also gather that her nightmares have lessened. Apart from that one odd incident last month, when she proved to be so frightened of the snake-killing animals and dreamed about them, she has suffered no more terrors. That, too, pleases me. I feared that the ugly affair of her birth-anniversary might have had some lasting effect.'

Phereniq made no comment. She, too, was relieved that the Infanta's nightmares had abated; but while Jessamin now seemed to be free of that particular torment, she was not. She had told no one of the dreams, which had begun a month before that fateful celebration, and her efforts to analyse them or even find their cause had so far failed. The pattern was similar to that of the spate of nightmares she had experienced a few years ago; and she suspected that, as before, she wasn't alone in her suffering. Hild had told her privately

162

that Indigo had begun to shout out in her sleep at night, as though challenging or fighting some dreadful adversary. And just lately Indigo had begun to ask more often for supplies of the powder which she used in her water-pipe. It was not, Phereniq thought, a healthy omen.

Wrapped in her own thoughts, she didn't see Augon return to her, and started as his hand fell on her shoulder.

'You're very quiet, dear seer. Does something trouble you?'

'No.' She shook her head in quick denial. 'I am simply tired, my lord.'

'Then I shan't detain you any longer. Go to your bed, and take one of your nostrums to ensure your rest. I want nothing more from you tonight.'

'Nothing . . . ?' It was out before she could stop herself, and she felt shamed.

'Nothing.' He smiled, and she hated him for the pitying, amused affection that his voice conveyed. 'Give those wise old bones a few hours' respite.'

The barb – though not deliberate – stung her, and she turned her head aside, not wanting to look at him again as he went to the door. A voice within her asked: *why? Why did I –* and then she cut it off, forcing it out of her mind. There were tears on her eyelashes, though she hated herself for it, and she brushed them away with an angry gesture. In her room, she had a black resin that could ensure complete and dreamless sleep. She rarely used it, and knew it would leave her fit for nothing in the morning, but she didn't care. She would take Augon at his word, she thought bitterly, obey his injunction to rest as she obeyed him in everything else. It was a childish response and small consolation, but it was all she had.

She snuffed the lamps, and walked slowly, stiffly out of the room.

In the following year there was fever in the harbour district again, though mild this time, and with few

163

fatalities. Again, too, the dreams started to invade sleeping minds as spring burgeoned, and only waned with the coming of full summer. In the palace, secret sighs of relief were breathed, and private potions and soporifics were quietly and gratefully abandoned as the nightmares – each peculiar to the individual dreamer – gradually relinquished their hold. No one knew of that small epidemic, for, oddly in portent-conscious Khimiz, the dreams' victims felt reluctant to reveal their experiences to a seer, or even to discuss them with their closest friends.

In her heavily-curtained room with its myriad charts, Phereniq burned incense to the Sea Mother in gratitude for her release from the night-borne horrors, put away the black resin that she had used more and more frequently, and drank a purgative draught that would clear its narcotic miasms from her blood and reduce the danger of addiction. Jessamin began to sleep soundly again, bringing further heartfelt thanks from physician-mage Thibavor, who five days earlier had taken a gift to the Temple of Mariners in the hope that this would succeed where all his nostrums had failed. Hild, too, found that her broken sleep was no longer racked by monstrous images; and in the opulence of the Takhan's private apartments, Augon Hunnamek dismissed the procession of women exhausted by the demands that were his only relief from the oppressions of nightmare, and spent his first untrammelled night alone. While in his grandmother's house, Luk Copperguild didn't dream, but often lay wakeful through the windless, overheated hours of the dark, staring beyond his window to the sea, where the moon hung remote and unreachable in a slate-dark sky, and thought of the father he barely remembered, and of golden hair and a smile like sunlight, and felt a sense of uneasy yearning that he was too young to comprehend, yet which was like the fire of achievement and the ice of failure and the starless black of disappointment all at once.

And in the rooms that abutted those of the sleeping Infanta, Indigo no longer shrieked like a banshee in her sleep, and no longer woke shivering and racked with nameless horrors that even Grimya couldn't soothe. Like Phereniq, like Hild, like so many others who kept their own counsel, she recalled nothing of her dreams when each morning broke. All she felt was a dull, inexorable sense of dread that wouldn't be shaken off, and an awareness that something was appallingly wrong. But the storm wasn't ready to break yet. And while the lull held, she relied on the twin solaces of her peaceable day-to-day life and her growing collection of herbs and powders and cordials, to keep the fears and speculations at bay.

Time passed, and Jessamin continued to grow and to bloom. At six, she still had the doll-like look of her babyhood, but beneath it were the first signs – as yet no more than promise – of a more adult beauty, and with it a rare innate serenity. A sweet, diligent and obedient child, she was already showing an early talent for music, and spent hours on end poring over Indigo's harp, frowning with determined concentration as she plucked simple tunes from the strings. Many activities were proscribed by the restrictions of her rank; she couldn't roam about the city, couldn't mingle freely with other children, and the few friends she had were carefully chosen for her. But despite so many caveats, the Infanta never seemed anything but content. She loved Indigo, who was both companion and teacher. She loved Luk, who was in effect the brother she had never had. And she loved the man she called '*chero* Takhan', who gave her presents and indulged her wishes and, more and more often now, came to play with her and laugh with her and admire her accomplishments. On her fifth birthday, *chero* Takhan had given her a new swimming pool, far larger than the little courtyard oasis which she had outgrown. Jessamin's passion for swimming was unabated: when the gift was presented to her she had covered her benefactor's face with kisses, declaring him the finest, dearest and kindest man who had ever lived. Indigo had been present at the occasion, and had turned quickly away, not wanting the look upon Augon Hunnamek's face to register in her mind and set the old, dark thoughts in motion.

And then, on her sixth birthday, *chero* Takhan had given the Infanta a ring. A ring made of five precious metals plaited intricately together, and set with five precious stones that reflected the changing moods of the sea: an emerald, a sapphire, a zircon, an opal, a moonstone. Gravely, he put the ring on the third finger of Jessamin's left hand, and told her that from this day she must wear it always.

Whether Jessamin understood the ring's significance, Indigo didn't know. The Infanta was aware that she was betrothed to Augon Hunnamek, but had only a child's simple concept of marriage as some special game which one day she would be allowed to play. She was too young to know better.

That night, Indigo took the black resin that Phereniq had given to her, and slept dreamlessly. But even without nightmares to plague her, she couldn't escape from the cold fact that, though the day of Jessamin's marriage was still far in the future, time was passing. And eventually, in its slow, quiet, inexorable way, time would run out.

'*My dear Leando,*

This is the first letter I have been able to write to you for some time, for it is only now that cargoes can sail from Simhara again since the fever epidemic that struck us three months ago and confined us all to quarantine.

You may have heard news of the epidemic and its aftermath from visiting traders. Before I tell you more of it, let me reassure you that Luk is safe and well; neither he nor the Infanta took the sickness, thanks be to the Mother, though many of us in the palace were ill. Your grandmother also escaped, I understand, although I have not seen her.

But there have been many deaths here, and, as with the lesser fever that scoured the western quarter four years ago, the physician-mages have been unable to do anything but stand by helplessly and let it run its course. We

166

are all resigned to the small epidemics that afflict Simhara each spring, but this sickness, which struck, as always, in the month before the Infanta's birthday, has been far worse than anyone had expected. We can only give thanks that it is over at last and we are now free of the infection.

The Takhan has ordered nine days of mourning for the dead, with ceremonies at all the temples. I probably will not be able to attend them, for I am but a short time from my own sickbed, and Thibavor warns me that I must rest a while yet.

Please forgive me if I am brief in this letter. I will write again with further news when I am stronger. Meanwhile, Luk is also writing to you, and will reassure you of his good health if there are any doubts in your mind.

We long for your return, and the flame of faith still burns.

> *With kindest thoughts,*
> *Indigo.'*

Recuperation was a slow process. She had no stamina, and at first did little but sleep; even when this stage was past, her spirits seemed reluctant to rally, the will to improve lacking. And in addition to her physical weakness, another matter had arisen that gave her cause for concern.

Karim, the mage-turned-pedlar, had disappeared. Since the city was officially pronounced free of fever and life had begun to return to normal, Grimya had taken to visiting the harbour each day to look for the blind man at his customary place on the steps of the Temple of Mariners, and each day she reported that he was nowhere to be seen. Knowing the appalling toll that the sickness had taken, Indigo feared the worst; and when a month had gone by and still he didn't reappear, she was forced to face the likelihood that Karim was dead. It made her feel that a vital link with her only allies had been broken. The feeling was irrational, for she had had no contact with the pedlar since Leando's departure; but none the less she couldn't shake off the frightening sense of being suddenly adrift and utterly alone. Karim's seer's skills had in many ways made him the backbone of the conspirators; without him, they would be like men fishing in dark and dangerous waters, never knowing what manner of horror might be biting at their line.

Despite her own misgivings, Grimya tried her best to be reassuring.

'He may be alive, Indigo,' she said, when thirty-three days had gone by without word of the mage. 'We do not know for sure. I w-ill go again tomorrow.'

'What's the point?' Indigo was lying on her couch, staring through the open casement to the sunlit courtyard. She had poured herself a glass of wine, heavily laced with the cordial, but could barely summon the energy to lift the cup to her lips. Weariness was still a constant companion in the wake of the fever, and she seemed to have lost the will, both physical and mental, to rally what strength she had.

'What real difference can it make to us whether Karim is dead or alive?' she continued sombrely. 'Without Leando and Mylo, he's powerless anyway. And even if they were to return tomorrow, would it make any difference?'

'Wh-at do you mean?'

There was a long silence. Then Indigo said: 'You and I can't harm Augon Hunnamek, either in his true form or in human guise. We have no allies like Jasker to summon power for us; we haven't even the physical strengths of Leando and Mylo. But even if Leando and Mylo were here, what could we do?' She picked up her drink at last and sipped at it. 'What could *any* of us do, against a power like that?'

Even as she spoke, she knew the answer to her own bitter question. With or without Leando and Karim, there was only one choice that she and Grimya could make. They must wait in Simhara, until a way could be found to unmask the demon. If it took a lifetime, that was of no consequence; for they would neither age nor change. And if Karim was dead, and if – she shrank from the thought, but couldn't entirely dismiss it –

Leando failed to return to Khimiz, then she and Grimya must stand alone against that evil power, for until it was destroyed they could travel on no other road.

She turned away, pressing her face against the soft pillows that cushioned her head. She didn't want to think any more of demons and obligations; she wanted only to turn her back on harsh reality, lock thoughts of the uncertain future securely away and escape into the sanctuary of the drug-induced rest which since her illness had been her only comfort.

'Let's not talk about it now,' she said. 'I'm tired, Grimya. I just need to sleep for a while.'

Grimya watched her for a few moments, then turned and padded disconsolately out into the courtyard. Though she tried to understand the lethargy and depression that had afflicted her friend since the fever, she felt out of her depth: and she was worried that the miasm seemed to have continued for so long. But it seemed that nothing she could say or do was of any help to Indigo.

The sun was hot, and reflected with aching brilliance from the surface of the pool. Grimya paused, gazing at the still water and thinking of the question that Indigo had asked. How could they hope to triumph against Augon Hunnamek, with nothing but their mortal strength to help them? It seemed as futile as trying to hunt and kill the wind, and Grimya had no answers.

She raised her muzzle suddenly, feeling the urge to howl her unhappy confusion to the sky. Her throat and chest quivered; but then the sound died stillborn. She couldn't give free voice to her feelings, not in this crowded, civilised land where high walls closed her in and human presences constricted her: and the howl became instead a soft whine.

She looked back at the open window, but couldn't see Indigo. For a moment she hesitated: then, head drooping, padded slowly away towards the shrubbery at the courtyard's edge, where the leaves were cool and damp and she could pretend, for a little while, that she had come home to her beloved forests.

Chapter XV

'Indigo! Oh, Indigo, come and look! Come and *see*!'

The high, clear voice was vibrant with excitement, and Jessamin was away, running across the dunes towards the beach that stretched in a vast, smooth-washed crescent under the morning sun. More sedately, her companions climbed out of the two closed litters that had brought them, and Hild, who was far too stout to run after her young charge, shrilled, '*Beba-mi!* Not to the water, or I shall scold!'

'Oh, let her be, Hild.' Phereniq smiled as she slipped off her shoes and curled her toes appreciatively in the warm sand. 'She so rarely has such freedom, and she can come to no harm.'

Luk fidgeted and looked up at Indigo. 'I can go with her,' he suggested hopefully. 'I'll look after her.'

Indigo smiled. 'Go, then, Luk. See if you can outrace Grimya.'

The boy grinned broadly. 'That I shall *never* do!'

As Luk and the she-wolf ran off after Jessamin, the three women stood watching them, enjoying the sunlight and the sea breeze and the magnificent vista spread out before them. Though autumn weather in Khimiz was hot by many standards, the heat was far kinder than the searing furnace of high summer, and the day had a delightfully mellow edge. Far away across the smooth sand the Gulf glittered dazzlingly; breakers boomed on the distant low tideline, and the horizons were bathed in a dusty, bronzed haze. Indigo found it hard to believe that only a single headland separated them from Sim-hara's harbour; and harder still to credit how long it had been since she last set foot on the beach. Grimya still visited it regularly, more often than not with Luk, whose love of the outdoor life showed no signs of diminishing with dawning adolescence, but since the epidemic of two years ago Indigo had lacked both the energy and the inclination to join the wolf on her walks. Now though, as she gazed at the three diminishing figures racing across the sand, she felt a sense of physical and mental renewal. The changing season, too, was a great relief, for the feverish dreams she had yet again been suffering had diminished, and she was able now to rely less heavily on the narcotics that were her only means of keeping the nightmares at bay. For the first time in many months, she felt cleansed – and felt, too, the tug of her old empathy with the sea returning after a long absence.

'They are so carefree at that age, aren't they?' Phereniq had moved to stand beside Indigo, and smiled, adjusting her sun-veil slightly. 'We should indulge them while we can. The Mother knows they'll have enough of duty and convention when they're older.'

Indigo glanced over her shoulder. Beyond the dunes' edge she could see the palace guardsmen who had been detailed to keep onlookers away. They had needed to exercise a good deal of subterfuge in arranging this outing; if word had got out in Simhara that the Infanta was to visit the beach today, the dunes would have collapsed under the weight of adoring citizens anxious for even the smallest glimpse of her.

'She was so disappointed to have her birth-anniversary spoiled, when she took that sickness,' Phereniq continued. 'This will be some recompense for her. Poor child; yet another birthday marred. It seemed only yesterday that she was learning to walk, learning to talk, and now she's ten and almost a grown woman.' She paused, then laughed. 'Well . . . not by the standards of us aged folk, perhaps, but certainly in the eyes of Khimizi law. It sobers me to think that in two years' time she will no longer be Infanta, but Takhina.' Something intangible as a breath of air yet charged with a sharply emotional edge clouded her eyes momentarily. 'Time passes, Indigo. For all of us.'

Behind them, the servants were bringing out baskets

171

of food and drink. Embroidered cloths were spread out on the sand; fine china and silverware clinked faintly. Far out across the beach, Jessamin and Luk and Grimya were tiny, indistinct figures on the sand's vast expanse.

'And you.' The astrologer took Indigo's arm and led her down the dunes' gentle slope, taking them out of Hild's earshot. 'You seem content now, my dear. Has the sadness faded at last?'

'Sadness?' Indigo didn't understand.

'At the loss of Leando.' Phereniq smiled with gentle sympathy. 'It must be nine years now since he went away.'

'Ah . . . ' A discomfiting sensation bit deep and hard in the core of Indigo's mind. She pushed it down, and returned the smile. 'Yes. We still write to each other, but . . . well, it has been a long time, and time heals. I'm content enough.'

'I'm thankful to hear it. Few souls have it in them to be so philosophical.' The arm linked with hers squeezed tightly. 'But you shouldn't give up all hope, Indigo. You're young enough yet. And when Leando *does* return, who knows what the future might hold?'

Her words, kindly meant, were unwittingly laced with terrible irony. Indigo didn't know what to say; but before she was forced to reply they were hailed by a distant cry from across the beach. Looking up, Indigo saw Jessamin running back towards them.

'Indigo! Phrenny!' Jessamin still used her old pet name for the astrologer; she slithered to a halt in a fine spray of sand and stood before them, breathless and flushed with pleasure. The hem of her skirt was soaked. 'The waves are *wonderful*! You must come and look at them!'

Phereniq laughed. 'I'm much too old and dignified to cavort on beaches, *chera-mi*,' she said with mock severity, then smiled. 'Take Indigo to look at the waves, and Hild and I shall sit and watch you.'

Jessamin was already tugging at Indigo's hand, and she capitulated with a wry grin. Phereniq watched them set off towards the tideline, then turned and made her way back to the dunes.

172

'It is good to see the *beba* so happy.' Hild munched on a candied fruit and gestured towards the faraway figures on the beach. 'She get little enough play time now, and whatever anyone say, she isn't grown up yet.'

She echoed Phereniq's own earlier thoughts, and the astrologer nodded. They were sitting beside the prepared picnic, shielded from the sun by parasols and enjoying the warmth soaking through their skin and into their bones.

'Is a pity Indigo don't come here more often,' Hild added. 'It would do her good, too. She don't get the exercise like she should.'

'Ah,' Phereniq plucked a stem of marram-grass and twirled it. 'I wanted to ask you about that, Hild. Since this last spate of fever I've been so busy that I've seen less of Indigo than I would have liked. Does she seem a little better in herself, do you think?'

The nurse shrugged. 'Maybe; is hard to say. She still sleep too much, more than is healthy. And drink, a lot of wine but she don't get drunk. And the other things. Herbs, powders, all the time. Mind, she been taking less of them this last month or so. But earlier, she seem to need them just to keep normal.'

Phereniq cast the grass stem away, her face troubled. 'That is not a healthy sign. Tell me, do you think she might have been suffering from bad dreams?'

Hild snorted. 'Don't say to me about bad dreams! That's why she was having so much of the powders, trying to stop them. Every year they come back just the same – and it's not just Indigo. I get them, the Infanta get them – '

Phereniq stared at her. 'But I thought the Infanta's nightmares stopped years ago.'

'*A-na*. Much they didn't! Every year, like I said, she get them again. Start in spring, don't go away till summer's nearly over.'

'And it's the same for you and Indigo?'

'Yes. Indigo don't say nothing, but I've heard her, shouting out while she sleep, and Grimya trying to wake her up and not getting nowhere. *Every* year.'

'What – ' Phereniq's voice sounded peculiar; she

swallowed and tried again. 'What do you dream about, Hild? What kind of nightmares?'

Hild frowned. 'I don't know. Can't never remember them the morning after. But *bad*. And the Infanta, just the same thing happen to her.'

'You mean she can't remember her dreams either?'

'Uh, that's right.' The frown deepened. 'I never thought about that before. Is strange, isn't it?'

'Very strange.' In her mind, Phereniq was calculating, and what Hild had told her tallied precisely with her own experiences, for she, too, had never been able to shake off the yearly bout of terrible nightmares that had plagued her for . . . well, it must be almost a decade now.

Hild had taken another candied fruit, but her enthusiasm for the sweets seemed lessened. 'Another thing,' she said slowly. 'These dreams, always they come about the time of the *beba-mi*'s birth-anniversary. And so do the fevers.'

'The fevers?' Phereniq looked up, realising what she was driving at. 'No; I don't think the two things are connected, Hild. You and I have both escaped the fever for the past two years, but that hasn't put a stop to the dreams. Besides, the fever's just a regular Khimizi malaise. A hazard of this climate, if you like.'

To her surprise, Hild shook her head vigorously. 'No,' she said. 'It isn't.' And as Phereniq opened her mouth to argue, 'This isn't the right climate for fever. Too dry. You ask old Thibavor – he tell you that there weren't no fevers here till we came to Khimiz.'

The astrologer stared at her. 'Are you *sure*?'

Hild shrugged. 'I don't know, do I? I weren't here before, no more than you. But it's what Thibavor say.'

She hadn't realised, and suddenly it opened a new and unnerving avenue of thought. The coincidence was too bizarre to be dismissed.

'You want to ask Indigo, too,' Hild added. 'She must know plenty about Khimiz, from all that history she got to teach the Infanta.'

Khimizi history . . . yes, Phereniq thought, it might be worth pursuing; for she had an instinctive feeling that

174

what Hild had told her could have some link with a mystery which she had been trying, so far unsuccessfully, to unravel.

'Thank you, Hild,' she said thoughtfully. 'I shall most certainly mention it to her.'

The afternoon was half done when at last the remains of the picnic were cleared away and the small party settled into the litters to begin the journey back to the palace. All in all the day had been a great success; Jessamin, Grimya and Luk had spent hours at the water's edge, hunting for the small shellfish that burrowed in the sand along the tideline, and after the repast they all sat watching the incoming tide while Hild and Indigo told stories turn by turn. Jessamin's head was nodding with weariness by the time they left, and as they were borne away from the beach Phereniq, too, fell asleep almost immediately. Indigo could faintly hear Hild's voice from the other litter, talking to the children, and she let her head rest back against the embroidered cushions, lulled into a doze by the heat and the litter's swaying rhythm.

They were passing the Temple of Mariners when Grimya's voice cut abruptly into a semi-dream. The wolf was trotting alongside – she found being carried unnerving – and Indigo woke with a jolt as she heard the excitement in the mental message.

Indigo! He is there!

Indigo sat up, startled, but before she could project any response, Grimya added, *On the temple steps – it is Karim!*

Indigo jerked forward, pulling back the litter's heavy curtain. And there, in his old place among the pedlars and pilgrims thronging the great marble stairs, sat the blind mage.

She only just prevented herself from shouting to the litter-bearers to stop. That would have been unthinkable: she dared not provoke unwanted questions. But as they were borne away and the temple fell behind, her heart pounded suffocatingly. *He wasn't dead.* She'd given up hope, certain that Karim had succumbed to the fever and was gone forever. And now –

Grimya, she said silently, *we must come back tomorrow. We must speak to him!*

Yes! Grimya replied eagerly. Then: *Indigo . . . do you think it is a sign?*

Indigo shut her eyes, trying to steady her erratic breathing. *Pray it is*, she said.

Indigo and Grimya had intended to slip away from the palace early the next day, but their plan was thwarted by the unexpected arrival of Phereniq. The astrologer looked as though she had slept badly or not at all: she must speak to Indigo, she said, and the matter was important.

'Sit down, and take a glass of tisane.' Her errand would have to wait a while, Indigo decided; there was an underlying agitation in Phereniq's manner that her obvious weariness couldn't disguise. She gestured towards the couch and forced a smile. 'Something important? It sounds a little ominous.'

Phereniq didn't return the smile, but only said: 'I hope not.' She sat silent until the refreshments were brought, then as the servant left them she looked over her shoulder to ensure that the door had been firmly closed before saying,

'I know that Jessamin has an early lesson with her tutor today, and I wanted to speak with you while we shan't be interrupted.' She picked up her tisane, sipped it. 'It began with something Hild said to me yesterday – a chance remark, no more; but it set me thinking. Indigo, does it not seem strange to you that each year, at the time of Jessamin's birth-anniversary, Simhara is stricken by fever, and certain individuals among us in the palace experience a spate of bad dreams?'

Indigo was about to feign ignorance – the dreams weren't something she wanted to admit to – when she realised suddenly what Phereniq implied. 'You, too, have had them?' she asked in surprise.

'Every year, like the Infanta, like Hild, like you –

Hild told me about your nightmares. It was indiscreet of her, but we may well all thank her for it in the long run.' She folded her hands together and stared at them. 'Nightmares which we can't later remember, but which seem to strike at a very deep level of our minds. And always at the same season.'

Indigo frowned. 'I'm sorry, Phereniq, but I don't quite understand. If, as you say, these dreams coincide each year with the fevers, then surely the connection's obvious?'

'That was what I had always thought,' Phereniq said. 'But it isn't quite that simple.' And she recounted her conversation with Hild at the beach the previous day concerning the peculiar anomaly of the fevers and the nightmares, and the nurse's assertion that there had been no summer infections in Khimiz until the coming of the invaders.

'I asked Thibavor about that,' she said, 'And I also checked the palace records. Hild is quite right: fever was almost unknown in Khimiz until ten years ago.' She got up and walked across the room, restless. 'My first thought, of course, was to consult my astrological charts. And I found something that I suspect has a bearing on this matter. Each year, at about the same time, two negative influences form a conjunction with Khimiz's natal star. It's highly unusual for other heavenly bodies to match the yearly cycle of our own world so closely; in fact I've only ever encountered such a phenomenon once before, and it was an aspect of no significance. But this is a very different matter.'

Indigo frowned. 'Forgive me, Phereniq, but I don't quite understand,' she said. 'I know nothing of astrology, but you seem to be saying that this – conjunction could be the link you've been seeking between the fevers and the spates of dreams. If that's so, then surely the mystery is solved?'

Phereniq turned to look at her. Her face was grave. 'You've forgotten one small point, Indigo. These conjunctions have been taking place regularly for hundreds, perhaps thousands, of years. But the dreams and the fevers began only a decade ago.'

177

Indigo was silent as she realised suddenly what Phereniq was implying. The astrologer continued to regard her for a few moments longer, then resumed her pacing.

'Two momentous events took place in this country at about that time,' she said. 'One: we – my people – came to Khimiz. And two: Jessamin was born. I know it makes no apparent sense, but I can't rid myself of the conviction that somewhere, somehow, there must be a link between one of those events and the awakening of this malign influence. The coincidence is too great, Indigo. There *has* to be a connection!'

Indigo's mouth had become very dry. She picked up her cup and drank, though the taste of the tisane didn't register. 'And which of the two,' she said carefully, 'do you think is the more likely cause?'

'I believe I know,' Phereniq replied sombrely. 'I can't be certain, not yet; but I believe that it has something to do with Jessamin. You see, there's more I haven't yet told you.' She came back to the table, twisting her hands together, and sat down again. 'I need your help, Indigo. I didn't sleep last night, and I'm too tired and too confused to be objective any more. Please, listen to what I have to say, and tell me whether or not you think I may be right.'

'Go on,' Indigo prompted quietly.

There was a pause while Phereniq seemed to be marshalling her thoughts. Then she said:

'This malign conjunction takes place, as I said, every year at about the same time. Normally, its influence is relatively weak: it might provoke minor outbreaks of sickness such as we have been suffering each spring, or it might manifest as small disturbances in the minds of those who are psychically sensitive.'

'In the form of dreams, for instance?'

'Exactly. But twice in the past ten years it has coincided with a dark moon – or a new moon, as my own people call it; which means that the moon's beneficent influence is at its weakest.' She looked up, her eyes troubled. 'Think back. Remember what happened at the time of the Infanta's fourth birthday, and at the time of her eighth. Do you recall the plague of sea-snakes,

178

and the serpent in the pool? And do you recall the epidemic that claimed so many lives?'

Indigo began to understand. 'You mean that on both occasions, this influence was strengthened by a dark moon?'

'Yes. And now I come to the worst of it.' Phereniq picked up her cup again and drank; the tisane was almost cold but she seemed not to notice. 'Next year, in the spring, the conjunction will take place as usual. But this time it will coincide with something else – not a new moon, but an eclipse.' She set the cup down again. 'To say that this is not a happy omen would be a great understatement. To an astrologer, the moon is one of the most powerful forces for good; it is the strongest symbol of the Goddess's beneficence, especially in a land like Khimiz where so much depends upon the sea's tides. The moon also rules the constellation of the Serpent, which is Jessamin's own natal sign, and therefore it has great significance in her life. So when the moon is eclipsed during the same hour that the conjunction takes place . . . ' She paused, regarding Indigo sombrely. 'Do you begin to understand what I am saying? Do you see the nature of the augury for that hour?'

Indigo did. Very quietly, she said, 'And when – precisely when – will the conjunction and the eclipse occur?'

Phereniq's face was haggard as she replied, 'One hour before dawn, on the night following the Infanta's eleventh birthday. And I am too afraid even to think about what the consequences might be this time.'

Indigo stood up and walked slowly towards the window. Her mind was in turmoil, but she forced herself to be calm, trying to counter Phereniq's fear with cooler reason.

She said: 'Let me understand you clearly, Phereniq. You're saying that something momentous – and malevolent – will take place at that hour, and that you feel the Infanta might be threatened by it?'

Phereniq nodded unhappily. 'She *must* be the link. I have searched and searched for another possible

179

answer, but each time I come back to the same conclusion. The influence of the moon in her natal sign, the plagues and dreams that have beset Simhara at the time of her birth-anniversary each year . . . the evidence is too strong to be ignored. And there's one more thing. A small thing, but it turns my flesh cold when I think of it.'

'What is it?'

'The malign conjunction has a name. I don't know where it originated or even why it came about, but the Khimizi mages call it the Serpent-Eater.'

The blood in Indigo's veins seemed to slow to a sluggish crawl, and icy sweat broke out on her face and torso. 'The . . . Serpent-Eater?' she whispered.

'Yes. And Jessamin was born under the sign of the Serpent.' Phereniq hugged herself, shutting her eyes. 'What will happen to the child of the Serpent when the Serpent-Eater dominates the skies with no moon to counter its influence? That's what I can't stop asking myself. What evil will strike our Infanta on that night?'

From arctic coldness, Indigo's skin had now turned clammily hot. Striving to keep her feelings from showing in her expression, she said urgently, 'Phereniq – if this is true, then surely you would have seen it in Jessamin's charts? You've drawn her horoscope almost every day of her life, and yet this has never come to light before!'

'I know,' Phereniq said miserably. 'And at first I told myself that my theory must be wrong. But now I think I know the answer. I've made a mistake, Indigo: a grave mistake.' She clenched her hands tightly together until the skin stretched taut over her knuckles. 'I found some documents among the palace archives; minor domestic records only, and of no practical use, which is why they were overlooked for so long. But they date from a little over ten years ago. And they lead me to believe that the natal horoscope from which I have been drawing my charts all these years may be wrong.'

Indigo stared at her, astonished. '*Wrong?*'

Phereniq nodded. 'When a royal Khimizi child is born, the attending physician-mage certifies personally the exact time and circumstances of the birth. I thought to check in case I had made some error – and there is no such record for Jessamin. There is only the midwife's testimony that Agnethe bore her child safely after a long confinement; that, and the seal of some minor official. The only record of the exact time of the Infanta's birth is in the later proclamation made by the Takhan and Takhina.'

'You mean that . . . the information on which you've always based your charts might be wrong?'

'Yes.' Phereniq looked up at her and managed a bleak smile. 'How often have I joked with you about losing my touch, because I failed to predict some major event in Jessamin's life? I *know* my skills aren't slipping, Indigo. And this could be the answer to that conundrum. If the hour of Jessamin's nativity was wrongly recorded, it could explain a great many anomalies. But if I am to help her, I *must* find out when she truly was born.'

Indigo frowned. A picture was beginning to take shape in her mind, but still there were parts of the jigsaw that didn't fit. She said:

'But does this mean that there was no mage attending Agnethe at the time? Surely Thibavor would know?'

'Oh, he does. I spoke to him this morning, but the information he gave me is of little use now. There was a mage, but he is no longer in the royal household. In fact it seems that he left the old Takhan's employ only two days after Jessamin was born, and Thibavor thinks he must have moved away from Simhara altogether, for the mages have heard no more of him since that time.'

'And the midwife?' Indigo asked.

'Dead. I gather from the records that she took her own life a short time later, after a lovers' quarrel.' She paused, then: 'An odd coincidence, to say the least, don't you think? As if there was some reason why the old Takhan didn't want the time of Jessamin's birth made known.'

An unpleasant thought was rapidly taking form in Indigo's mind. 'You think, then, that the midwife's death and the mage's disappearance might not have been as innocent as they appear?'

'It isn't a pleasant theory to consider; but yes, I do.'

'The mage.' Indigo felt as though red-hot wires were in her stomach. 'Do you know his name?'

Phereniq nodded. 'Thibavor told me, though, as I said, it's of no real value. His name was Karim Silkfleet.'

Karim. The hot wires released their grip, and Indigo felt a peculiar kind of relief. She'd known it. A physician-mage fallen from grace, hiding his true identity . . . It could only be Karim the pedlar. And he must be the only living soul who knew the true time of Jessamin's birth, and – if Phereniq's theory was right – the reason why her parents had been anxious that it should remain a secret.

She said, thinking uneasily of her own mission: 'Have you spoken to the Takhan about this?'

'Not yet,' Phereniq told her. 'I needed to talk to someone else first, to clarify it all in my own mind.' She smiled pallidly. 'Forgive me; that must sound as though I've used you as a foil for my theories – '

'Not at all,' Indigo reassured her gently. 'On the contrary, I'm greatly flattered that you felt able to confide in me.'

'You above all others, I think.' Phereniq put a hand up to her face, and sighed. 'But now that I have talked to you, and have been able to put my fears and suspicions into perspective, I think that I must delay no longer.' She glanced towards the open casement. 'I'm afraid for the Infanta – and I'm afraid for the Takhan, too. I must tell him, Indigo. Even if I have no final proof of anything, I must tell him.'

'The conjunction is surely proof enough,' Indigo said soberly.

'I believe so. But if only I could get to the root of this mystery concerning the Infanta's birth . . . I feel in my bones that it's significant, but unless this missing mage can be traced there's little hope of learning the truth.' She shivered slightly, then rose to her feet. 'I feel that we're faced with something beyond our understanding. Whatever happens, Jessamin must be protected. She *must*. Or I daren't think of the possible consequences.'

182

When Phereniq had gone, Indigo stood stock-still for a few moments. Then, abruptly, she turned and snatched up her broad-brimmed straw hat.

Grimya? She projected the urgent call, and the she-wolf appeared from the courtyard.

I heard it all. Grimya's eyes were amber with disquiet. *It seems that the man Karim is more important than we thought.*

Yes. And we must be cautious in our search for him. There was every chance, Indigo knew, that when he heard what his astrologer had to say, Augon would institute his own hunt for the mage. She didn't want Karim to be found by the Takhan's forces. He must be warned.

As they went out into the corridor, Grimya said, *What do you think this might mean? Could the Infanta be in danger from this meeting of the stars that Phereniq spoke of?*

I don't know, Grimya. But I have an intuition that the truth doesn't lie quite in the direction that she believes. She said, if you recall, that two events happened at the time these fevers began – Jessamin's birth, and the coming of the invaders.

Grimya understood. *Then you think that these events might have something to do with the demon rather than with the Infanta?*

That was precisely what Indigo thought. And if she was right, then Phereniq, by telling Augon Hunnamek of her suspicions, might inadvertently provide the catalyst for which they had been waiting for so long.

And that, she realised, would place not only her and Grimya but the whole of Khimiz in the gravest danger.

He isn't there.

Grimya turned in dismay towards Indigo as she conveyed the message. Indigo stopped, and stared at the sweeping stairs that led up to the Temple of Mariners, glittering dazzlingly in the brilliant sun. And there in the midst of the ever-present crowd, were the pedlars and fortune-tellers and sellers of offerings, and Karim wasn't among them.

She started towards the steps, then stopped again as she realised that the gesture was useless; closer proximity wouldn't make the blind mage miraculously appear from nowhere. Grimya, trotting at her side, said, *He may not have come yet. Yesterday, when we saw him, the sun was lower in the sky*.

'He must come.' Heads turned curiously, and she realised that she'd spoken aloud. Hastily she switched to telepathy. *He must, Grimya!* She began to climb the stairs, pausing to stare hard at each pedlar as she passed, receiving uneasy looks in return, seeing nothing familiar. At the top of the flight, on the wide, paved terrace before the temple, a troupe of jugglers were showing off their skills to an appreciative audience; Indigo hurried past them towards the ornate building looming ahead, feeling a drift of spray from the gigantic water-curtains prickle her face and arms. She was ferociously repeating Karim's name in her mind, only just stopping herself from shouting it aloud in frustration. But he wasn't there.

Then abruptly every sense snapped into focus as she saw a face at the door of the temple. The figure was shadowed by the great portal, and watery reflections from the pool at the entrance played across the features, distorting them. But the eyes were laughing at her, and the hair above the eyes glinted silver in a stray shaft of light. And the mouth was smiling, revealing the small, savage, pearly teeth of a vicious little cat.

Indigo! Grimya's mental call was articulated as a yelp that startled people nearby, and she ran in pursuit as Indigo raced towards the temple. Reflex, no more, made Indigo kick off her shoes just before she splashed into the pool; then she was through the water and had emerged into the huge, cool and peaceful interior.

The temple's atmosphere struck her like a hammer-blow and brought her up short. Figures moved in the quiet gloom, pilgrims and attendants mingling; breathing hard, she looked about, but the silver-haired figure had vanished. Yet she had no doubts, no doubts at all, as to its identity.

Nemesis. Her *alter ego*, her personal demon, the evil creature which, so many years ago, had faced her in the crumbling Tower of Regrets and laughed its pleasure at her folly. Blind hatred boiled in Indigo. She had kept Nemesis and its influence at bay for so long, only to find it suddenly rising like some filthy grave revenant to taunt her. She would not be taunted, she would *not* be mocked; least of all in this holy place.

Grimya hadn't entered the temple, but stood on the far side of the pool, trying to make mental contact. Indigo ignored her, and regaining a measure of self-control, started slowly towards the great ship-shrine that towered phantasmically overhead. Her initial shock had worn off now, and the hate was crystallising into a cold, implacable force. She would find the demon. If she had to take the temple apart with her bare hands, she would *find* it. And when she did –

'Might I be of assistance to you, madam?'

The voice jerked her back to reality. Turning, Indigo saw a pleasant-faced, middle-aged man in the sea-green robe of a temple attendant. He was smiling kindly, reaching out a hand to steady her as it looked as though she might lose her balance. She stared blankly at him.

'You are visiting the temple for the first time?' His voice was soothing, peaceful. 'The shrine can often have a disquieting effect on those who've not seen it before. We like to feel that the breath of the Sea Mother can be felt even in a house built by the hands of men.'

In the face of his kindly sincerity Indigo's rage crumbled into fragments that she could no longer grasp. 'Thank you,' she said, her voice shaking, 'but I shall be well enough in a moment. The sun, I think; the contrast. It – '

On the edge of her field of vision, she saw silver flicker by the temple entrance.

The excuse died in her throat. Startled, the attendant stared after her as she ran for the doors.

Grimya, where is it? Where did it go?

It was all Indigo could do not to yell the question

aloud as she stumbled to a halt before the pool. Grimya's ears were back, the fur along her spine bristling, her fangs bared as she, too, stared out at the brilliant day where the unperturbed throng continued about its business.

I saw it! Helpless fury blazed up in Indigo. *It was here, and then –*

I saw nothing, the she-wolf told her dismally, *but I felt it pass. A coldness, like the winter wind of my homeland, but I couldn't catch it, couldn't follow it. It's gone, Indigo. And I don't know where.*

In her head Indigo imagined she could hear an echo of Nemesis's mocking laughter. She looked away from the bright scene and stared down at the temple pool. After-images from the sunlight danced before her eyes; she rubbed them fiercely –

And saw, distorted by the shadows of flowers on the water's surface, an incongruously angular shape glimmering on the pool floor.

Logic said it was nothing more than some small item dropped by a careless pilgrim, but instinctively Indigo knew better. She reached down, her arm plunging elbow-deep into the pool, and snatched the shining thing out: then as water streamed from its flat surface she held it wordlessly for Grimya to see.

It was a fortune-telling card. The back was unadorned, but coated with silver that glinted in the sun. The card's face depicted the sea at night: the glaring, eldritch corona of an eclipsed full moon shone down on a sullen, dark swell – and from the swell a living nightmare was rising, undulating, breaking the waves around it into tumbling chaos.

A silver serpent.

Indigo wasn't consciously aware of wading through the pool, retrieving her shoes, slipping them on to wet feet. Only when she and Grimya stood at the top of the temple steps and gazed down at the bustle of the harbour did her eyes re-focus on the real world. And when they did, they were suddenly bright with feverish understanding.

'A gift from Nemesis.' She spoke aloud, but so softly

that Grimya alone could hear her. 'A sign of its presence, to disconcert us. And I believe, Grimya, that the gift may be more valuable than the demon intended.'

The she-wolf looked up at her. *I don't understand.*

Indigo smiled. There was something feral in her expression. 'But I think I do,' she said. 'There *is* something afoot, and Nemesis knows it – why else would it have chosen to show itself again now, after so many years in hiding? It's trying to mock us with its knowledge, but it has underestimated our ability to see what really lies behind its games.' She looked at the fortune-telling card again. 'The Serpent-Eater and the eclipsed moon . . . Phereniq's right to fear the evil that conjunction heralds, but its source doesn't lie where she believes.' Suddenly Indigo crushed the card with a violent gesture. 'This is the confirmation we've been waiting for, Grimya. The demon is stirring at last.'

Chapter XVI

Augon Hunnamek sat back in his chair, steepling his fingers before his face and frowning at them, while Phereniq watched him intently but uneasily. As the years passed she was finding his moods harder to read, and she couldn't yet judge how he would react to what she had told him. In her mind she screamed for him to say something, but she didn't want to be the first to break the silence.

At last he raised his head, and his pale eyes met hers levelly.

'I am in your debt, Phereniq. Yet again it seems that you have done me a great service.'

Relief flooded her, and she allowed herself to let out a pent breath. 'Thank you, my lord. I was . . . ' Her voice caught; she cleared her throat quickly. 'I was afraid that you might find my report a little too speculative.'

'Not at all.' Augon let his hands fall back to the table, and flicked the topmost page of the records she had unearthed. 'This is more than mere speculation, my dear seer. The epidemics and the infestations – I'm astonished that it's taken us so long to see the pattern, although I can see why it was so easily overlooked. And as for the questions you've raised concerning the circumstances of our Infanta's birth . . . '

'I have no proof of anything, sir. But – '

Augon held up a hand, silencing her. 'No proof, no. But enough evidence to suggest very strongly that all was not as it should have been.' He had returned his gaze to the documents as he spoke; now he looked up again. 'You said that the midwife who testified to the birth died shortly afterwards?'

Phereniq nodded. 'Apparently she took poison nine

days later. It's officially documented that she killed herself through grief after her lover abandoned her.'

'Ah; woman's folly. And how very convenient for those who wanted her safely out of the way. So, Phereniq. You're my adviser: what conclusion do you draw from this pretty parcel?'

'My lord, until and unless I can discover the true hour of the Infanta's nativity, I can make no further progress in assessing the threat that this next conjunction might pose to her,' Phereniq replied.

'But – with or without that knowledge – you are certain that the threat exists?'

'I am certain, my lord. And I am very afraid for her.'

Augon got to his feet and walked towards the window. This small audience room looked out over his private courtyard; a heavy, semi-opaque curtain cut down a good deal of the light from outside, and his figure as he stood before the glass was little more than a silhouette.

'I too have experienced these dreams,' he said, quite suddenly. 'Every year, at the same season.' He turned to face her again and saw the expression on her face. 'That surprises you?'

'You have never told me of it, my lord.'

'No, I haven't. Thibavor knows, of course; but Thibavor also knows what's good for him, and so has kept his own counsel.' He moved towards her. 'Dreams of pursuit, Phereniq. Dreams of something dark and nameless following me through the endless corridors of the palace, and refusing to be shaken off no matter what I do. Always at my back, relentless, getting closer.' He reached her, put both hands on her shoulders. 'Is that *your* dream, too?'

'Yes.' She shivered, remembering. 'And the Infanta's. And Indigo's, and Hild's – '

'And doubtless a long list of other names, if we only knew it.' Augon swung away, pacing back to his chair where he sat down. For a moment he stared at the pile of records, then said thoughtfully: 'The mage, Karim. I believe it would be as well to instigate a search for him.'

189

Phereniq was surprised. 'Surely, my lord, he must be long dead?'

'Perhaps. But I have my doubts. I know these Khimizi wise men – they take care of their own, whatever they might protest to the contrary; and I'll wager that Karim didn't share the midwife's fate. There's a chance – though a slender one, I grant – that he may still be living in Simhara. And if he is, I will find him.'

There was silence then for a few moments. Augon continued to gaze at the documents, though Phereniq had the impression that his mind wasn't taking in what his eyes registered. Then he spoke again.

'With or without the missing mage, however, we have the matter of the conjunction to consider. I do not appreciate threats, Phereniq, be they from men or from auguries. And I will not allow myself to be intimidated by them.' He tapped one finger on the table, a random, staccato pattern; then abruptly his expression cleared and a slow, predatory smile began to spread across his face. 'In fact, dear Phereniq, I like nothing better than a challenge, and I shall take great pleasure in meeting this one. The Infanta is in need of protection from malign influences: very well; then I mean to protect her.' He raised his head, and his eyes were vivid and animated beneath the heavy lids. 'I want you to go back to your charts and manuscripts, my seer, and I want you to prepare for me three auguries – mine, the Infanta's, and that of the city of Simhara.'

Phereniq frowned slightly. 'For what day, my lord?'

'For Jessamin's eleventh birthday.' There was amusement in the smile now, and something in his gaze that she didn't want to interpret. 'I am not afraid of the Serpent-Eater, Phereniq. And when it rises again it may find that, this time, it is faced with a little more than it can devour.'

The message from Augon Hunnamek, ordering that Jessamin should be made ready to attend a banquet that evening, took both Indigo and Hild by surprise. This was an impromptu affair, with, it seemed, a guest list that comprised only the members of Augon's council and a few of the highest-ranking nobles. Indigo was not summoned to attend; but Luk, to his own surprise and chagrin, was.

'He's head of the family with his Papa gone,' Hild pointed out as she helped Indigo to choose Jessamin's gown for the occasion. 'And now he's grown up, almost a man. Stands to reason he start to have to do these things, even if he don't like it.'

'But this is so sudden,' Indigo said. 'I don't understand it.'

Hild tapped the side of her nose. 'Mark me, is something afoot. Else why would the Takhan call so many councillors and nobles in such a rush, eh? Why not wait till tomorrow, or day after? Something is happened. You wait and see!'

She could do little else, for the palace servants, who usually had wind of the latest news long before official announcements were made, knew nothing of the reason for this abrupt and unexpected development. When Jessamin had left, accompanied by a full royal escort, Indigo spent an uncomfortable evening playing card-games with Hild and trying not to speculate on what might be brewing. From her window she could glimpse the reflected lights from the banqueting hall; by midnight they were still blazing, and Hild, muttering admonishments about the Infanta's bedtime, admitted defeat and retired to her own room. Grimya was asleep; and Indigo too dozed in her chair, until the sound of the door opening behind her startled her awake.

Jessamin came in. She paused uncertainly on the threshold, then, seeing Indigo sit up, came running towards her.

'Indigo!' Her face was flushed, and beautiful in a disconcertingly adult way. 'Oh, I have had a *wonderful* time!'

'*Chera!*' Indigo hugged her. 'What's the hour? It must be very late!'

'It is, and it's so exciting!' Jessamin ran to the window and looked out. 'They're putting out the lanterns now. I

191

didn't leave until the very end of the feast! And I danced – I danced every dance there was with *chero* Takhan! And Indigo, do you know what has happened?'

Premonition like a cold, heavy stone lodged in Indigo's gut. 'No,' she said. 'What is it, dear one?'

The Infanta turned back to face her, her honey-gold eyes brimming with excitement. 'I won't have to wait until I am twelve to become Takhina!' she announced delightedly. 'I am to marry *chero* Takhan next year, on my eleventh birthday! Oh, Indigo – isn't that *wonderful*?'

Augon Hunnamek stood at the window of his private apartment. For once the curtains were open, and he gazed out across his courtyard to the great hall, where servants scurried like quiet ants as they dismantled the last trappings of the celebration. Other servants, his personal maids and valets, bustled about in the room behind him, preparing his bed, laying out his night-robes, fetching cakes and wine in case he should wake from sleep and want refreshment. The bed itself was pristine and empty; tonight he wanted no concubine to warm his sheets and arouse his instincts, but was content to be alone.

He savoured his thoughts of the decision he had made in the wake of Phereniq's revelation. The auguries for the great day could not be better. Phereniq had completed her calculations and brought them to him earlier in the day; and he had found them intensely gratifying. A day of great triumph, so the stars said; for himself, for the Infanta and for Khimiz. A day of strength, of the awakening of new power – power enough to counter the malignancy of the conjunction that threatened to blight the Infanta's young life. By the hour of the Serpent-Eater's rising, Jessamin and her new lord would be united, and his strength would be more than sufficient to keep her safe from harm.

Without turning, he snapped his fingers, a signal for the servants to leave. He could sense them bowing their way out, and knew instinctively when the last of them had gone. Then he returned his full concentration to the dark, peaceful scene outside.

Jessamin had kissed him before she left with her escort to return to her apartments. A child's kiss, but as spontaneous and adoring as that of the most ardent lover; and Augon felt a glow of satisfied triumph spread through him like the warming effect of good wine. She was so young and malleable, a fresh new canvas awaiting the first touch of the skilled artist. With his artistry he would teach her, mould her to his ways and his desires; in learning to pleasure him she would restore his jaded palate. And more than that. Far more. For, slowly but surely, she was awakening something else in him; something he had long ago buried and tried to forget, believing that it was beyond his reach.

Jessamin. She was almost woman enough for him now. And soon – far sooner than at first he had hoped – he would possess her . . .

This time there was nothing to hinder Indigo and Grimya when they left the palace early the next morning. And as they hastened through the quiet streets, Indigo's thoughts were churning like a sick tide within her.

Six months. That was all the time left to her before Jessamin would be wed to Augon Hunnamek. Six months: and she was bereft of allies, bereft of clues. Leando and Mylo were still on the Jewel Islands, and Karim – Karim's future was now far from assured. Augon's decision to change the marriage date could only have been prompted by Phereniq's revelations; he must therefore know of the missing mage, and there was every chance that a search would be set in train for him. She *had* to make contact with Karim; urgency had become deadly imperative. If it meant waiting at the Temple of Mariners from dawn to dusk every day until Karim appeared, Indigo had to find him.

They hastened through the bazaars, ignoring the blandishments of the traders, hucksters and fortune-tellers who were already abroad in the hope of catching early trade, and emerged into the dazzling openness of the harbour front. By the time the Temple of Mariners came in view Indigo was having to force herself not to run – then as the plaza opened before them, she stopped.

Karim was there, on the temple steps. For a moment she hardly dared believe it, fearing that it must be a mistake, an illusion. But Grimya's excited yip, and the telepathic surge of eager recognition from the she-wolf's mind, were confirmation enough. They ran across the paved promenade and up the stairs, and halted before the blind man.

'Karim – ' Indigo's voice was tight with tension and relief together.

Karim raised his head. Though he couldn't see her, she had the unnerving impression – not for the first time – that he knew her instantly. He looked surprised, but not startled.

'Lady Indigo?'

She dropped to a crouch before him: there was no time for preamble. 'Karim, I have to talk to you. There have been changes at the palace – Augon Hunnamek has announced that he intends to marry the Infanta next year, on her eleventh birthday.'

'*Next* year?' Karim's thin frame tensed. 'But – why? What has prompted this?'

Tersely, Indigo told him of Phereniq's discovery concerning the conjunction, and of her fear that evil might befall Jessamin on the night of the eclipse. When she finished, there was a long pause; then Karim said:

'So; the usurper means to thwart the Serpent-Eater by laying an earlier claim upon its prey.' He clasped his hands together. 'This is not happy news.'

'No. It means that we have only six months before the marriage ceremony is due to take place. And Mylo and Leando are still in the Jewel Islands.' She hesitated, watching him carefully, then added: 'But there's more.' She leaned forward, speaking close by his ear. 'Augon has also discovered a mystery concerning a physician named Karim Silkfleet, who attended the Takhina

194

Agnethe when Jessamin was born, and who disappeared shortly afterwards.'

'Ah.' Karim wasn't quite able to conceal his reaction. She saw the quick tightening of his facial muscles and decided to gamble on her intuition. 'You are that physician, aren't you, Karim? And there's something you're aware of, which the rest of us aren't privy to. Something that happened when the Infanta was born, and which the old Takhan wanted no one else to know.'

Karim didn't answer her at first; and Grimya, who had also been watching him intently, observed:

There is great turmoil in his mind. I think he is afraid, but not of Augon Hunnamek. And I also think he will not be willing to tell you the whole truth.

'Karim.' Indigo reached out and covered the mage's hands with her own. 'If there is a secret concerning Jessamin, I beg you to tell me of it. *Why* were the palace records destroyed? And you – why did you disappear from court life? In the name of the Mother, please, you *must* tell me!'

Karim sighed and, quite gently, removed his hands from her frantic clasp. 'Lady,' he said quietly, 'I attended the Takhina Agnethe when her daughter was born, and the old Takhan rewarded my service by having my eyes put out. But for two good friends at court, who helped me to escape from my prison cell, I would have been quietly but swiftly killed, as was the midwife who assisted me. My friends both died with the Takhan in the invasion battle: the Takhina, too, is dead; and so I am the only witness to the Infanta's birth still left alive.'

'Then there *was* something – '

'There were omens,' the mage said, and from his tone Indigo knew that he was telling her only a part of the truth. 'But my knowledge is incomplete. I am – or rather, I was – a physician and a clairvoyant, not an interpreter of auguries.'

'But you must know why the old Takhan acted as he did,' Indigo persisted. 'The deaths, the destruction of the records – what was the secret they were trying to conceal?'

Karim's face was haggard. 'I know what it was,' he said softly, after a pause. 'But I do not know what it means.' He looked up, the sightless eyes focusing on nothing. 'The science of the stars is a closed book to me, lady. But if matters are as you say, then it may well be that the Infanta is in mortal danger. And I sense – I *feel*, though I cannot state it more clearly, that her marriage will increase the peril rather than lessen it.' Suddenly he caught Indigo's fingers again with a quick, sure movement that belied his blindness. 'For her sake, and for the sake of all Khimiz, the marriage must not take place; yet we haven't the strength to do what must be done to stop it. We need the others – Mylo and Leando and Elsender. Until they return to Simhara, we dare not make a move. You must send them a message, call them back – '

'That's impossible!' Indigo protested. 'Any letter I send might be read by a dozen of Augon Hunnamek's loyal servants before it reaches their hands!' Her voice was rising with frustration; she took a grip on herself and continued with soft urgency. 'Karim, listen to me. We can't depend on being able to warn Mylo and the others in time. You know there's something evil afoot, and you know its nature, if not its source. How can I hope to combat this thing, or protect Jessamin against it, if I don't know what it is I'm fighting? In the Mother's name, you *must* tell me everything you know!'

'No,' Karim said emphatically. 'There is nothing more I can tell you; not until the five of us are together again. That must be our first imperative.'

Indigo drew back a little and regarded him with narrowed eyes. 'Why?' she demanded. 'What are you afraid of?'

'Lady, I can't answer that question, because I don't know. But I sense something in my blood, in my marrow; and it threatens us all. You and I alone are too weak to combat it – we *must* have the strengths of the others at our side before we dare to act. Brand me a coward if you will, but I will not risk stirring up what is best left to lie until they return!'

196

Indigo felt that she was on the point of exploding with frustration: but she also knew that no amount of arguing or pleading would sway Karim. He was afraid, not only for himself but for her, and nothing could break down that barrier.

She opened her mouth to make a further protest and plea, but before she could speak, Grimya suddenly gave a warning growl.

Palace soldiers! They are coming this way!

Indigo swore aloud and looked over her shoulder. Two men in the distinctive colours of Augon's personal guard were moving through the busy throng, already climbing the steps and heading in their direction. Their presence here might be coincidence; but she dared not take the risk.

Quickly making a pretence of examining the trinkets on the mat, she addressed the mage in a rapid whisper. 'The palace guards are abroad; they may be searching for you. I must go – if they see me talking to you, they might suspect something amiss.' Again, frustration surged: there was so much more she needed to say. 'I must talk to you again!' she added urgently.

Karim nodded. 'Yes. I will be here.'

Indigo, the men have seen you! Grimya interjected. *They are turning towards us.*

'The guards are coming.' Indigo started to get to her feet.

'Wait.' Karim's fingers fumbled quickly on the mat before him, and he held out a small pewter ornament fashioned in the shape of a crab. 'Take this, and go into the temple,' he whispered. 'It will allay their curiosity, for it will appear that you were simply buying an offering. And Indigo – I beg you, send a message to Mylo. It is *vital*.'

She had no time to argue with him, but took the trinket, and abruptly raised her voice so that it carried through the crowd.

'It's a worthy piece, pedlar. I will recommend your work.'

'The honour is mine, lady.' Karim bowed his head,

then added, barely audibly, 'Have a care. And the Sea Mother protect you.'

The militiamen had stopped a few paces away and were watching the exchange, though only, it seemed, with idle curiosity. They recognised Indigo, and as she straightened and caught their glances, both saluted her. She returned their acknowledgement with a nod and a pleasant smile, and walked away up the remaining steps to the temple entrance. Only when the vast, dimly-lit peace of the interior closed about her and Grimya did she allow herself to breathe freely again.

They didn't speak as they crossed the temple floor. Several small bands of pilgrims were gazing up at the shrine while the ever-present attendants hovered unobtrusively in the background; they moved past them, and finally halted in the shadow of the great ship's stern, where they had sufficient privacy.

'Great Goddess . . . ' Indigo needed to articulate the words, to relieve a little of her tension. She switched then to telepathic speech. *What are we to do now, Grimya? Karim has brought us so close to the truth, but it still isn't enough.*

However hard you try, he will not be persuaded to tell us what he knows, Grimya said sombrely. *He is too afraid. I think his instincts know, even if his mind doesn't, what it is we are fighting.*

Yes: but he doesn't understand its true nature. Indigo paced slowly across the floor, staring at the patterns in the marble without seeing them. *If only he would trust us, so that we could combine our knowledge, and* – She broke off and shook her head, realising that there was nothing to be gained from railing. *I don't know what to think, Grimya, let alone how to act for the best.*

I believe we should do as he asked of us, and try to get a message to Leando, Grimya replied. *It will be hard to do. But it may be our only choice.*

You're right. Indigo saw a party of visitors about to intercept her path; she turned and began to pace back into the shrine's shadow. *But how to alert Leando without alerting others — that's the problem I can't resolve. If I had to sail to the Jewel Islands myself I'd do*

198

it, but that's as impossible as sending a letter that gave a clear enough message. Great Mother, I don't know what to do!

Grimya said: *Indigo . . .*

She was preoccupied, and the sudden change in the wolf's tone didn't register. But then she called again, and Indigo stopped and turned. Grimya hadn't followed her, but was standing motionless, staring across to the far side of the temple.

'Grimya?' Indigo asked, aloud. 'What is it?'

Just now you spoke of the Great Mother, Grimya said. *I think that She has heard you.*

She was watching a small group of people who had just entered the temple. They had come in laughing and talking a little raucously; a nervous reaction often provoked in those who were seeing the shrine for the first time: but as they crossed the floor their voices dropped away to awed whispers. From their garb, Indigo recognised them as Davakotian sailors; probably the crew of a hunter-escort making their first call in Simhara.

And then she saw that they were nearly all female, and that in their midst was a stocky, tough-looking little woman with cropped black hair and a diamond embedded in either cheek.

She had changed, she had aged: but there could be no mistake. It was Macce – Indigo's old friend, and captain of the *Kara Karai*.

Chapter XVII

'I still don't believe it!' Macce thumped her cup down on the table, setting knives and plates dancing and turning heads in the crowded tavern-room. 'Ten years, and you look *exactly* the same!' She chuckled, and tugged at a strand of Indigo's hair. 'Where's the new grey, eh? Not like me – I'll be white in another five seasons, and I've got lines that'd give a mapmaker bad dreams!' She pulled the skin of her own face down with two fingertips, twisting her expression comically. 'Look at that! So come on, what's the secret? Where's the fountain of eternal youth that you haven't told old Macce about?'

Indigo drained her own cup, and didn't argue when Macce refilled them both. They'd both had a good deal of wine, but Macce's capacity for drinking was legendary, while Indigo, as always seemed to be the case these days, had remained utterly sober.

There had as yet been no chance to discuss the matter that begged urgently for attention. Davakotian hospitality was never lightly offered and never wisely refused; so when, after the initial incredulous greeting, Macce had insisted on celebrating their reunion at one of the harbour's best inns, Indigo hadn't hesitated to accept. The rest of *Kara Karai*'s crew had joined them for the first hour, but had then returned to their sightseeing, leaving the two old friends alone. Macce wanted to know everything about Indigo's life in Simhara, and there was a great deal of good-natured teasing about wealth and softness and easy options. But the old spark of comradeship was still there, and Indigo felt optimistic about the chances of enlisting her help.

She only wished that Macce wouldn't keep referring to the fact that she hadn't aged. It was obvious that the little woman was disconcerted; every now and again she'd slip in a subtle but probing question, and the constant references were making Indigo nervous.

'Mind, there's no flesh on you,' Macce observed, having swallowed half the contents of her replenished cup in one draught. 'What do they feed you on at that palace – sugared chimelo's brains?' She cackled at the idea. 'I can't see Grimya taking kindly to that. Where's she gone, by the way?'

Indigo had seen the she-wolf slip unobtrusively out of the door a few minutes earlier; the noise and smells and confinement of the tavern were not at all to her taste. 'She'll be back in her own time,' she said.

The innkeeper approached their table at that moment, slate in hand, to ask if they wanted anything to eat. After some consideration Macce ordered enough food to satisfy half a ship's crew, and when it was brought she began to eat lustily, exhorting Indigo to follow suit. Indigo wasn't hungry – Macce had been right when she said she was thin, for these days she rarely had any appetite worth speaking of – but did her best, and for a while there was silence between them.

At last Macce sat back, wiping her mouth and uttering a gusty, satisfied sigh. 'I needed that.' She grinned across the table at Indigo. 'Three months at sea, and you start to forget what real food tastes like. Or real wine.' She picked up the flagon, found it empty, and set it down again with a philosophical shrug. 'So, old friend: I won't be able to persuade you to leave your sinecure and set sail on the *Kara Karai* again, for old times' sake?'

Indigo smiled, but her pulse quickened. This could be her opportunity to broach the subject.

'I don't think so,' she replied. 'But if we're talking about old times, Macce, there *is* something I wanted to ask you.'

'Ask.' Macce crammed a last piece of bread into her mouth and chewed it appreciatively. 'Good,' she added with her mouth full. 'Very good food. And this Simharan wine's some of the finest I've ever tasted. D'you know, I was beginning to think I'd go to the Sea Mother without ever getting to see this city with my own eyes. And the Temple of Mariners . . . ' She shook her head wonderingly. 'It's all they said it would be, and more. But then I don't need to tell you that, do I?' Suddenly her smile became mischievous. 'Did you ever say that prayer for me at the shrine?'

Indigo smiled back. 'Indeed I did. On my first visit.'

The Davakotian chuckled. 'I shouldn't have asked. Always knew I could trust you.'

'Then would you trust me again now?' Indigo asked.

Macce caught the change in her tone, the underlying tension. She paused, and a slight frown replaced her cheerful expression. 'You said you wanted to ask me something, for old times' sake. You mean it's something serious?'

'Yes.' Indigo met her frank gaze for a moment, then looked down at the barely-touched food on her own plate. 'I'm sorry, Macce. This isn't the ideal moment; we've just met again after all these years, and I don't want to cast a cloud on the celebration. But I'm desperate.'

'Go on,' Macce said quietly.

Indigo nodded, unable to voice the gratitude she felt for the little woman's swift appraisal and reaction. 'I need your help,' she said, lowering her voice. 'I have to get a message to the Jewel Islands, and I daren't send it by the normal means. It's vital, Macce; a matter of life and death – ' She stopped, realising how foolishly melodramatic the last words sounded; but Macce was still watching her intently.

'Your life?' she asked.

'No.' Indigo wasn't going to lie about it. 'Not mine. I can't tell you the details; but – there's a man in the Jewel Islands, a Khimizi; he's the Takhan's personal ambassador. It's imperative that he and two others should return to Simhara immediately, but it's also imperative that no one must know they're coming back. If the Takhan were to discover – '

'Stay.' Macce suddenly raised both hands, palms outward. 'If this is some political plot, then I don't want to hear any more. Politics and my trade don't mix, and I wouldn't touch any such schemings with a harpoon twice my own height!'

'It isn't that.' Indigo shook her head emphatically.

'What, then? Something personal?'

Indigo bit her lip. It was as close to the truth as she dared admit; as close as hard-headed Macce would be willing to believe.

'Yes,' she said. 'But I can't tell you any more than that. Macce – '

'Indigo?'

The new voice startled her, and she turned quickly, almost upsetting the remains of her wine.

Luk stood by their table, with Grimya at his side. His gaze slid uncertainly to Macce then back to Indigo, and he made a formal, slightly awkward bow. 'I'm sorry. I didn't realise that you were in company.'

'Luk, what are you doing here?' Indigo asked.

The boy shrugged, diffident. 'I came down to the harbour to . . . ' he couldn't bring himself to say, *to find you*, so dissembled. 'To look at the ships. Then I saw Grimya.'

I couldn't avoid him, Grimya communicated. *I'm sorry, Indigo.*

No matter. Macce was staring at Luk, Indigo saw, and there was a peculiar expression on her face. She couldn't explain, not now; and so said to the boy,

'Luk, I am a little busy at the moment. Will you wait for me outside?'

He looked hurt. 'But – '

'Please, Luk. For me?'

I will go with him, Grimya said. *But Indigo –*

I'll tell you everything later, love. But I don't want Luk to overhear.

The boy went, though clearly unhappy at the dismissal. When he and Grimya had disappeared, Macce turned to Indigo.

'Who is that child?'

There was a pause. Then Macce said: 'He's not – *your* son?'

'No.'

The little woman visibly relaxed, and laughed with a

203

self-conscious edge. 'Forgive me; that was foolish. I may not know much about children, but even I should have realised that he's too old.' Then her face sobered. 'But he's involved in this, isn't he? Call it intuition; I just sense it.'

Indigo hesitated a bare moment, then nodded. 'Yes. His father is one of the men I need to reach.'

Again, silence for a few moments. Macce was toying with a knife, her expression thoughtful but beyond that unreadable. At last she looked up again and said,

'Indigo, I have my crew to think of. We're scheduled to escort a convoy to Scorva in three days' time, and – '

'I can pay you,' Indigo interjected. 'Not what you'd earn from that commission, but – '

Macce uttered a Davakotian obscenity. 'I'm not talking about money, sprat-brain. You know me better than that. I'm talking about reputation. Listen.' She drew her bench up more closely to the table and leaned forward. 'I want you to look me in the eye, and tell me that if I agree to what you're asking, I won't find myself embroiled in something illegal, dishonourable or likely to bring me and my ship up against the Simharan authorities. That means no plots, no smuggling, no dirty work. Well?'

Indigo gazed steadily into the little woman's bright eyes and said, 'I promise it. There's no need for any subterfuge. All I ask is that you tell no one of the letter that I want you to carry.'

'And there'll be nothing in the letter that goes against the interests of Khimiz or any other country?'

'Nothing,' Indigo confirmed emphatically. 'In fact . . . it could be vital to Khimiz, and a good deal more besides.'

Macce considered this for a few moments. Then, abruptly, she nodded and slapped her hand down on the table. 'All right. You've made yourself a bargain.'

Relief flooded Indigo like a tide; she felt her whole body begin to shake with the sheer sense of release. 'Macce, I don't know how to thank you – ' she began.

'Don't thank me: I never know where to put my face when people start expressing gratitude. And don't ask

204

me why I've agreed to this: maybe it *is* for old times' sake, or maybe it's something else.' She glanced briefly towards the inn door. 'That boy; Luk did you call him? I get the feeling that this is very important to him as well as to you . . . ah, I'm getting soft. Must be my dotage coming on early. I don't pretend to know what all this is about, Indigo, but I'm prepared to trust you. And because of that, I'm willing to do more than simply be a messenger. You want these friends of yours to return to Simhara, right?'

'Yes.'

'Then if it's that urgent, and if they're willing to put themselves in my care on a sea-voyage, I'll bring 'em back myself.'

Indigo could hardly believe her good fortune. She wouldn't have dared ask such a thing of Macce – one imposition was enough – but this offer was the answer to her prayers. Only the attention she might have drawn from the tavern's other customers stopped her from flinging her arms about the little Davakotian and hugging her.

'Right!' Macce thumped the table again. 'Then I've got things to do. There's another Davakotian ship in port and idle; I'll reassign the convoy commission to her – at a percentage, of course.' She grinned, sharklike. '*Kara Karai* will sail on tomorrow morning's tide. So you'd best get back to your cushioned couches and your servants, and see about writing that letter, eh?'

Indigo tried again to thank her, but Macce swept her gratitude aside, though she was obviously touched by it. She also tried to persuade the small woman to dine with her that evening at the palace, but Macce firmly declined. Royalty and sea-captains didn't mix, she said, adding slyly that if she once had a taste of the high life, she might follow Indigo's example and turn into a landfish. Instead, she'd meet Indigo at the quay early on the following morning.

They parted at the inn door, and before she strode away to round up her crew, Macce stood on tiptoe and kissed Indigo soundly on both cheeks, at the same time pulling her hair affectionately. Indigo watched her go, then turned – and found Luk and Grimya waiting for her.

Luk came forward slowly, and the taut unhappiness in his eyes gave her a twinge of guilt. She put an arm round his shoulders. 'Luk, I'm sorry. I didn't mean to be so abrupt with you earlier.'

He smiled, but uncertainly. 'It doesn't matter. It was my fault, anyway: I shouldn't have interrupted your business.'

'Well, my business is completed now. Shall we all return to the palace?'

They began to walk back through the city. Luk seemed disinclined to talk, and so Indigo took the opportunity to relay to Grimya the details of her talk with Macce. When she heard what had been agreed, the she-wolf's tail wagged eagerly.

That is very good news, she communicated. *We should tell Karim, as soon as we can. He will be greatly relieved.*

'Indigo,' Luk, who was unaware of the exchange between the two of them, spoke up suddenly. 'Who *was* the lady you were with? She looked like a seafarer.'

Indigo quickly adjusted her consciousness. 'She is,' she told the boy. 'Her name's Macce, and she's captain of a Davakotian hunter ship.'

'Macce?' Luk brightened, remembering the stories she had told him. 'Of the *Kara Karai*, the ship you sailed on before you came to Khimiz?'

'The very same. We met purely by chance, in the Temple of Mariners. This is her first visit to Simhara.'

For a few moments Luk said no more. Then: 'Indigo . . . '

'Yes?'

His face was flushed, then suddenly the words came out in a rush. 'Macce isn't sailing to the Jewel Islands, is she? Because – I wanted to ask you to write to my father, because he'd be more likely to pay heed to you, and you could explain properly, and . . . ' He stopped, swallowed. 'I so much want him to come home.'

Indigo stopped and gazed at him. He could be trusted, she thought. He was old enough, and wise enough, to share this secret and not inadvertently give it away. And she hated seeing him so unhappy. It was only fair that he should know.

She turned fully to face him, and said, 'Luk – if I tell you something, will you promise me that you won't breathe a word of it to anyone? Not to Jessamin or Hild, or even to your great-grandmother?'

He nodded, baffled but with dawning interest. 'I promise.'

'Then I have some good news for you. Macce *is* sailing to the Jewel Islands. She leaves tomorrow. And she's going to bring your father back to Simhara.'

Luk froze, and his eyes widened. 'Indigo – ' He could hardly get the word out. 'Indigo, is – is that really true? Is Papa coming back?'

'Yes, love. He's coming back.'

'Then – oh, Great Mother!' And Luk flung his arms around Indigo's waist and hugged her with all his strength. 'He's coming back, he's coming *back*!' He released her, looking into her face with vivid excitement. 'He'll stop it, won't he? He'll stop the Takhan from marrying Jessamin?'

Indigo stared at him, stunned. '*What* did you say?'

But he was racing on, oblivious to her astonishment. 'And then she'll be free. And Papa and Uncle Mylo will give us their blessing, and – '

'Luk, wait!' Indigo grabbed his shoulders. 'What do you mean, their blessing? What are you saying?'

The boy smiled radiantly back at her, and in that moment she realised the truth that had been clear before her for so long, had she only had the wit to see it. Luk had adored Jessamin since his early childhood; and now that he was, as he saw it, nearly a man, that adoration had flowered into something greater and deeper. And his eager words, as he clasped her hands, were the final confirmation of what she, in her blindness, had failed to anticipate.

Luk said: 'If Jessamin doesn't have to marry the Takhan, then everything will be all right, won't it? And *I'll* be able to marry her instead, just as I've always wanted to do!'

Chapter XVIII

Kara Karai put out on the mid-morning tide the next day, with Indigo's letter safely secreted in her captain's personal cabin-chest.

The letter was brief and to the point. The main, urgent message spoke for itself, and Indigo had stressed that Macce's integrity could be utterly trusted: it would be enough to ensure that, whatever the risk, Leando and his uncle and cousin would waste no time but set sail for Simhara immediately. Macce estimated that the outward voyage would take anywhere between thirty and fifty days to complete at this time of year; returning, the autumn currents and winds would be with them and should enable them to make faster time. So within three months, barring twists of fate, Leando should be home.

Indigo hadn't intended to take the black powder that evening, but events had overtaken her. To begin with, Augon Hunnamek's proclamation concerning his marriage date had been made public, and Simhara was rejoicing in its customary way. Even in the seclusion of the palace it was impossible to be unaware of the cheering celebrants who thronged the streets, the ringing of the bells, the flicker of flares in the sky as evening fell; and the festivities were an unwelcome reminder to Indigo of the urgency of her predicament.

There had, too, been further developments within the palace walls.

The search for Karim had been set in train, and Augon had also ordered a thorough investigation of the palace records, lest any vital clue had been overlooked. Indigo, trying to cope with the demands of Jessamin's lessons and Luk's tense excitement and a social visit from Phereniq – who was herself in a strange mood – was constantly haunted by thoughts of what might befall if the searchers were to find the mage and bring him before Augon for questioning. So when night fell, and finally Jessamin was abed and Phereniq was gone and peace reigned, she turned to the water-pipe, gratefully inhaling the resinous smoke that would banish the churning fears from her mind at long last.

She fell asleep on her couch, and almost immediately began to dream.

It wasn't one of the seasonal nightmares that followed the yearly cycle, though at first it seemed to Indigo's sleeping mind that the pattern had slipped out of kilter and was resurging before its time. There was the same sense of density, colourlessness; a feeling that she was, in fact, awake, and that the faintly distorted contours of the familiar room were part of the real world and not the realm of nightmare. On the rug by her couch, Grimya slept, her even breathing a soft counterpoint to the incessant mutter of the fan. The lamps were out, though she knew she hadn't doused them. The curtains were closed, though she had left them open. The palace was silent.

And something sat in an ornate chair by the door, a silhouette more solid than shadow, forestalling any impulse she might have had to run from the room.

Lithe limbs uncurled in the darkness as Indigo sat up, and a radiant glimmer that had no apparent source abruptly lit a small, feral face, and eyes that glinted silver.

'Sister,' Nemesis said with sweet venom, 'you have made a foolish mistake.'

Indigo flung off the light shawl with which she'd covered herself, hearing it slide to the floor in the sudden acute silence.

'*You* – ' In her shock she could think of no other word with which to greet the demon-child.

Nacre reflected on the small cat's teeth as Nemesis

209

smiled. 'Are you content with your little triumph, Indigo?' it asked. 'Do you feel strong now? Strong enough to face what you have unleashed?'

She had snatched up one of the darkened lamps, ready to throw it at the demon before she realised the utter futility of the gesture. The lamp hit the floor with a dull rattle of brass filigree. 'Your taunts mean nothing to me,' she said harshly. '*You* are nothing. This is merely a dream.'

'Perhaps.' Nemesis shrugged carelessly; then the smile became more predatory. 'And yet . . . how does Macce's little ship fare tonight, my sister? Do her crew sleep soundly in their hammocks? Or do they, too, dream of what might await them at the end of their voyage?'

'Damn you!' Indigo hissed. 'Get out of my mind!'

Nemesis ignored her. 'And Augon Hunnamek – what does he dream tonight?' it taunted. 'Does he dream of his child-bride? While she, in untainted innocence, sleeps the sleep of the righteous?' Soft, unhuman laughter shimmered in the air. 'Poor Jessamin. What will become of her, Indigo? Who will be her champion now?'

Indigo opened her mouth to scream an obscenity. But the sound wouldn't come, wouldn't take form in her throat. Nemesis rose sinuously to its feet, its body surrounded now by an aura that shone with unholy phosphorescence. It raised one arm in a brief gesture: and something fell, flickering and spinning, from its outstretched hand. Indigo didn't have to look at it to know what it was. A card. A fortune-telling card, silver-backed. She didn't need to see its face.

'Omens, sister.' Nemesis spoke softly, sibilantly. 'But can you interpret them truly? Or are your eyes blinded by reason?' Again, the quiet, cruel laughter. 'You have set wheels in motion, but now that they are spinning you can't stop them, and you can't control them. It is beginning at last, Indigo. Your adversary is awake and aware. The Serpent-Eater is coming, and you haven't the power or the wisdom to turn it back. Remember that, in the days to come. And remember that, in my affection for you, I gave you timely warning!'

The demon's image shivered suddenly, dragging Indigo's seething perceptions into a momentary but chilling warp. Her mind came back with a violent shock; she felt the hard, *real* contours of the couch beneath her, and something within her snapped.

'*Get out of this place!*' Her voice rose in a demented shriek. 'Damn you and curse you a thousand times, *be gone! Go! GO!!*'

And she woke, screaming the words into a dark and empty room, as Grimya leaped across the floor to hurl her warm, comforting body into Indigo's flailing arms.

The shrieking panic that brought Indigo out of her nightmare had also brought Hild and one of the serving-girls running from adjoining rooms, and though she told them that it was merely a dream Hild had all but forced her to take a strong draught of her own preparing, which put her back to sleep – though dreamlessly this time – until mid-morning. When she finally woke, feeling heavy-limbed and disorientated from the combined after-effects of the draught and the water-pipe, Hild insisted fiercely that Luk and the Infanta could do without her ministrations for a while and that she was to rest.

Indigo felt too drained to do anything other than obey; but though her body was enervated, her mind was in turmoil, for she knew that Nemesis's visitation had been no dream and no coincidence. In its cryptic mockery, the silver-eyed being had confirmed Karim's fear that any attempt to intervene directly in events – which, by enlisting Macce's help, she had effectively done – would stir up something beyond her control, and place her and her allies in peril. Indigo knew she had had no choice, but none the less she felt a deep sense of dread. Leando, Luk, Karim, even Jessamin – there was no way of predicting where the demon would choose to strike, or when; and she and Grimya had pitifully few resources with which to fight it.

Her unpleasant reverie was interrupted at noon by

Luk, who, defying Hild's orders that Indigo shouldn't be disturbed, slipped into her room while the nurse was taking Jessamin to be fitted for a new gown. He paused on the threshold, calling Indigo's name softly, then closed the door with oddly furtive care. His face was flushed and he was breathless, as though he'd been running fast.

'Indigo?' Luk tiptoed across the room. 'How are you feeling?'

'A good deal better, thank you, Luk.'

'I'm glad. Indigo, I must speak to you. It's urgent – and private.'

Something in his tone . . . she sat up, her pulse quickening. 'What is it?'

'I have a message for you.' Luk glanced quickly first at the closed door and then out to the courtyard before crouching down beside her. 'I had no lessons this morning, so I went to the Temple of Mariners to ask the Sea Mother to keep Father safe on his voyage home. I wanted to take an offering; there was a pedlar on the temple steps, a blind man – '

Indigo's heart lurched.

' – and when I stopped to look at his wares, he suddenly took hold of my arm and said, "You know the Lady Indigo". So I said yes, I did, and he said that I must bring you a message, and that I must tell no one else of it. Indigo, does this make any sense to you?'

Indigo nodded tensely. 'Yes, Luk. What was the message?'

'He said you must meet him at the customary place – he didn't say where that was – tonight, when the tide-bells ring. He said it's vitally important, and you would understand.'

Indigo swore softly under her breath. She'd under-estimated Karim. How had he known Luk, and known, too, that the boy could be trusted? His clairvoyant skills must be far greater than she'd ever realised.

Luk was waiting for her to say something; and when she didn't speak he couldn't contain his curiosity any longer.

'Indigo, who *is* that pedlar? How do you know him – and what could he possibly want?'

Indigo was on the point of dissembling when she thought: Karim had seen fit to trust Luk, and Karim's judgement was sound. She could do no less than he had done.

Softly, she said: 'I can't tell you everything, Luk; not yet. But the pedlar is a good friend of your father, and he wants to help us.'

Luk's eyes lit. 'Does he know that Father is coming back to Simhara?'

'Not yet; though he may have guessed it, for he's a seer. But Luk, it's *vital* that no one else should know that I'm meeting him tonight. Whatever happens, the secret must be kept. Do you understand that?'

'Of course.' Luk nodded emphatically. Then: 'Indigo, may I come with you?'

'No, Luk. I'm sorry; but I don't want to involve you. It's safer if I go alone; and besides, I'm not sure that Ka– that the man would want you there. Please, don't argue with me,' as she saw him open his mouth to protest. 'I'll tell you everything as soon as I'm able to, but until then you *must* trust me.'

Luk hesitated, then shrugged reluctantly. 'Very well. I'm sorry.'

'Don't be.' She kissed his forehead. 'And I *will* tell you about it in good time. I promise.'

The tide was due to turn an hour after midnight, and Indigo and Grimya set out for their rendezvous with plenty of time in hand. The night was oddly quiet in the wake of the previous evening's celebrations; a warm, languid peace had settled on the city, and the moon, just beginning to wane from the full, drenched the streets in dreamlike luminescence.

They left the palace by one of the lesser gates, where there were no guards to see them, and emerged into the shadowy avenue that would lead them down towards the harbour district. Grimya's claws, clicking softly on the paving, were the only sound to break the silence as

213

they began to walk away from the vine-hung palace wall –

And a shadow detached itself from the shelter of a spreading tree, stepping into their path.

'I'm sorry, Indigo.' In the darkness Luk's eyes were unfathomable wells in the paler frame of his face. 'But I had to come. I *had* to.' Mischief glinted suddenly, and he made a formal bow, drawing a short sword from a scabbard at his belt and displaying it in a salute. 'A lady alone after dark must have a proper escort.'

'Luk – '

'I won't be in the way. I'll stay back, out of sight.' The courtier became the child again. '*Please*, Indigo – '

He must have slipped away without his great-grandmother's knowledge, risking all manner of punishments if the stern old lady were to discover his absence. In the face of such stubborn determination, Indigo couldn't help but relent. To turn him away would have been the act of a hypocrite.

'Oh, Luk!' her voice was affectionate. 'Come, then. Champion me through the city. And . . . ' She paused, then decided to say what was in her heart. 'And thank you.'

Simhara's great harbour had an enigmatic and tranquil atmosphere far removed from the bright bustle of the daylight hours. Lamps on tall iron posts burned along the broad promenade that flanked the quay, augmented by a few dimmer lanterns in the windows of the imposing harbour office that never closed its doors. The sky was clear, and the autumnal moon hung swollen and golden above the city, etching phosphorescent patterns on the sea where it lapped quietly at the quayside walls. The occasional cat from the harbour's thriving population went about its scavenging business, but human presence was almost completely absent; the tide was at a low ebb and the ships that rocked and dipped at anchor were silent, their crews either asleep or carousing in one of the taverns behind the harbour front.

They saw the dome of the Temple of Mariners long before they reached it, and paused to stand and gaze for a few minutes at the huge, glowing hemisphere that reflected the moonlight like a shimmering jewel. The Sea Mother's beacon, shining out across the water to speed Her children on their way or to call them home . . . Indigo felt a twisting, clutching sensation that made her want to laugh and cry together as she thought of the *Kara Karai* and her mission. And then they were moving on, and the great flight of carved stairs was before them at last, gleaming like bone, rising towards the temple and the silent, shining dome.

Grimya said very gently in Indigo's mind: *The hour has not come yet. He will be here soon.*

She gazed at the empty stairs, and felt something move within her consciousness. A worm of disquiet . . .

'It must be almost time.' Luk's voice was a whisper, an instinctive reverence for the night's unsullied quiet. 'Will he come, Indigo? Or – '

She held up a hand to silence him, listening to the small and barely discernible sounds of the darkness. A faint hiss from the nearby lamp that threw their shadows into stark relief. The thoughtful murmur of the sea, moving against the stone walls of the docks. The creak of seasoned timber as a trireme shifted at her moorings. Nothing else.

Then . . .

Grimya, with senses far more acute than those of any human, heard it first, and her hackles rose stiffly along her spine as her head came sharply up. Luk, too, caught something, and tensed.

It was no more than a breath of sound, barely audible among the softer noises of the night, but it clashed in a shivering discord. And it came from a human throat.

Indigo felt the alarm in the she-wolf's mind an instant before Grimya sprang away up the steps. She and Luk followed, unable to match Grimya's speed – and reached the top of the flight to see the wolf standing over a dark, shapeless pool of shadow that lay huddled only five paces from the darkened but ever-open entrance of the temple building.

Indigo's involuntary cry cut the darkness like a knife and was swallowed in the harbour's huge silence.

'Karim!' She knew, she *knew*, even before her muscles powered her instinctively to Grimya's side and she fell to her knees on the unyielding marble, her hands, ghastly in the moonlight, reaching out to the huddled, shrivelled husk of a man who lay as lifeless as the stone in the temple's shadow.

He wasn't long dead. His flesh was warm – but the skin that covered the flesh was cold, slick, *wet*, as though the sea had disgorged him only moments ago. Slime, like the echoes of rotting weed, lay across his arms and his face, which was plastered with sodden hair. The blind eyes stared sightlessly into nothing. One arm was flung out from the huddled frame in a last, dramatic, futile gesture. And his lips were drawn back from his teeth in a rictus of utter insanity.

A distant part of Indigo's mind, shrieking rationality, heard Luk's ghastly intake of breath, the scrabble of his footsteps as he stumbled away, the sound of him retching: but the rest of her, the instinct, the current that ran deepest of all through her consciousness, had already focused on the telltale sign that intuition had told her would be there, that could *only* be there. Karim's corpse was white as the skin of a fish under the impassive moon. Bloodless: as though something had fastened on to him and sucked him dry even as he gasped and pleaded and withered and died; draining him, leeching him, drawing the stuff of life from his limbs and his torso and finally from his pulsating heart . . .

The marks were clear and dark beneath his jaw; the stigmata that told of the manner of Karim's death. Blood had flowed unchecked from the twin, ragged wounds; it was smeared across the marble, mingling with salt water, with the slithering tracks of the thing that had come out of the sea to coil and twist and crush and, finally, to power its deadly venom through Karim's veins and to sever the fragile cord of his life.

Serpent. *Serpent.*

Indigo . . . Grimya's telepathic voice sliced through her mind, shocking, unreal. *Before he died, he tried* to write something. On the stone. His blood . . . look!

Her eyes were glazed but her gaze swung involuntarily to the plaza's marble surface, only inches from the dead man's rigid, distorted face. Symbols – her mind registered them but they meant nothing to her. They were like the meaningless, futile scrawls of a young child: and already the bloody marks were fading and dissolving as they mingled with the water that pooled beneath Karim's corpse.

The serpent from the sea. And *Kara Karai* was on that sea tonight, unwitting, unknowing, and vulnerable . . .

Suddenly, from their squat tower down on the harbour front, the tide-bells began to ring, clanging across the night and shattering the silence as they marked the lowest ebb. Indigo raised her face to the vast indifference of the sky; to the remote, shimmering moon that stared down on the grisly scene, and her voice cracked as harshly as those of the bells.

'Great Mother, what have I done?'

Chapter XIX

'It's no use.' Indigo crushed a clenched fist down on to the scrawled notes on the table before her. 'If he was trying to tell us something, then I can't even begin to fathom it. It could be a code, a formula, it could have word correspondences – or it could all be a grisly coincidence; nothing more than random marks made by his hand when he . . . ' Her voice tailed off at the ugly thought and she shook her head.

Luk was still staring over her shoulder at the copy of Karim's last, cryptic message. 'It isn't that,' he said sombrely. 'This does mean something, I'm *sure* it does. But there are so many possibilities, aren't there? Seers use all kinds of secret symbols that ordinary people don't know about.'

And physician-mages use a good many more, Indigo added silently to Grimya, who sat on the floor between them. She hadn't told Luk of Karim's history, feeling that the less he knew, the safer he would be.

Luk traced the symbols, frowning. 'Indigo, couldn't we ask Phereniq if it means anything? After all, we wouldn't need to tell her why we wanted to know.'

Indigo shook her head. 'It's too great a risk, Luk. We'd have to offer some explanation, and for all we know, the symbols may contain some meaning that would give our secret away.' She shivered inwardly, remembering how, with guilty reluctance, she had hurried Luk and Grimya away from the macabre scene on the temple steps, aware that it was imperative no one should know of their presence and telling herself that Karim would not lie unshriven for long. In that, at least, she had been right; by first light the body was discovered, and there was uproar in the harbour district when the cause of the pedlar's death became apparent. News of the killing had been brought to the Takhan's ears as a matter of course, but there was nothing to link the slaughter, however bizarre and disturbing, of a blind artisan with the search for a disgraced mage. Karim was a common Khimizi name, and Augon Hunnamek had no cause to suspect a connection. So the dead man had been given to the sea in time-honoured fashion, and his fellow pedlars had reverently placed his store of unsold wares on the great ship-shrine and said their own prayers for his spirit on its journey to the Mother's arms.

And Karim's only legacy was a single brief and arcane message, to which no one save Indigo and her friends was privy. On that basis, Luk's suggestion made sense; but still Indigo was unwilling to take the gamble. It would need only one slip, one chance remark, one small hint of an interest in the pedlar's death, and Phereniq's suspicions would be aroused. They must find the key without outside help.

But that begged a simple question: how? And Luk, with the uncomplicated frankness of youth, voiced it first.

'Then what *are* we to do, Indigo? We can't simply forget about the message.'

Voices from the courtyard outside intruded suddenly: Jessamin had been swimming, and was returning from her pool with two serving-girls in attendance. In the few seconds left to her before the Infanta's arrival, Indigo leaned forward and whispered urgently, 'Luk, I don't know what we can do. Your father might understand what Karim was trying to tell us – '

'But it could be three months before he returns!'

'Believe me, I'm aware of that. But we may have no other choice than to wait. Whatever happens, we mustn't speak of this to *anyone* else.' She took his hands in a fierce grip. 'Promise me, Luk!'

He nodded. 'I promise.' For an instant his gaze met hers and his eyes were trusting but uncertain. Then, hastily, he thrust the sheets of parchment with their scrawled figures under a book and out of sight as

Jessamin came into the room and ran laughing to greet him.

Winter in Simhara was a far cry from the long months of ice and snow and ferocious gales with which Indigo had grown up in the Southern Isles. Here, the change in the seasons was subtle and understated; much of the city's lush greenery took on a gold patina and shed its worn-out leaves, but even the shortest days were pleasantly mild with no more than the occasional hint of a chill from the prevailing southerly winds. And by the time of the midwinter solstice, when even at noon Carn Caille would be lit only by dim and eerie reflections from the sun below the horizon, new shoots were appearing on Simhara's trees and bushes, and the palace gardens were starred with flowers.

To the Khimizi, the celebration of the turning of the year was a great event, and though the festivities were very different to the Southern Isles customs of her childhood, Indigo always enjoyed the seasonal merriment; the ceremonial baking and eating of festive foods, the adorning of rooms and city streets, the songs and dances and plays performed in honour of the Mother of Earth and Sea. But this year, it seemed that her pleasure must be soured by the knowledge that the Mother's gift of the reborn sun was dawning on the final resolution of her greatest hope and her deepest dread.

There had been no news yet of *Kara Karai*. Indigo had tried not to count the days since Macce had left on her mission, but in the back of her mind was a constant awareness that time was passing and the lease growing shorter. Preparations for the Takhan's marriage were well advanced, and barely a day went by in the palace without some reference to the nuptials; a new delicacy invented for the banquet, a new entertainment devised for the celebrations. Jessamin herself was eager, excited, innocent and ignorant of what she faced. And Indigo, often accompanied by an ever more tense and taciturn Luk, went now to the great temple on the harbour at every opportunity, to pray silently and fervently for Leando's return.

At last the midwinter feasting was over. Despite her early doubts, Indigo had been caught up in the gaiety and roistering, which had enabled her to forget for a while the fear and frustration that lurked at the back of her mind. But now that distraction was gone. And with each day that dawned, she had to face the increasingly obvious fact that *Kara Karai*'s return was overdue.

It had been easy at first to dismiss the nagging worry. Winds and currents were capricious; not even the world's greatest sea-captains could make more than a vague estimate of the duration of any voyage. And there were further considerations, equally valid: Macce might have had trouble contacting Leando; and – even allowing for the time it would take her to convince them of the urgency of her message – Leando and Mylo couldn't simply leave their posts and sail on the next tide. There would be formalities, stories to concoct to allay suspicions, arrangements to be made. They needed time.

But when nearly five months had passed and still there was no sign of the Davakotian ship, all the reasoned logic in the world wasn't enough to counter Indigo's dreadful certainty that something had gone wrong.

Spring was coming to Khimiz, and with it the first of the big equinoctial tides that swept through the Agantine Gulf like a fearsome but benevolent scour, cleansing the sea-lanes of the quiet season's detritus and bringing fresher, stronger winds and currents to the shores. The fervour of the new season was rife throughout Simhara, and underlying it was a current of new excitement as the day of the greatest event since Augon Hunnamek's enthronement drew nearer and nearer. There was little more than one month now to wait; and it seemed that the auguries, too, were taking a hand in the general air of anticipatory rejoicing; for, against the pattern of the past, there had so far been no resurgence of the nightmares that usually began at this time, and no sign of the fevers and small plagues which had accompanied them. The pattern, so it appeared, had been broken.

And then, as though something had been waiting, laughing behind its hand, for the lull, *Kara Karai* – or what was left of her – came back to Simhara.

News of the disaster spread up from the harbour in the wake of a night of buffeting windstorms and a particularly heavy tide. Hild, as always, was one of the first at the palace to hear of it, and, with a look of gloomy relish on her face, came into Indigo's room as she was breakfasting. Indigo was heavy-eyed, not yet fully awake, and it took a few moments, as Hild began the tale, for the implications to register. But when they did, she abruptly put down her cup of tisane as she felt her hand begin to shake.

'Hild – what ship was this? What are you saying?'

Hild bridled. 'I am trying to tell, but you don't listen!' Shipwrecks were blessedly rare in the Agantine Gulf and the nurse was determined to make the most of this dramatic event. 'Like I say, the ship wasn't sank, but it was next thing to sinking, and how it got home to port wasn't nothing but a miracle of the Sea Mother.'

'But *what* ship?' Indigo started to feel queasy. 'What was her name?'

Hild, disregarding, went on, 'And you know what? They say it was fish done it, big fish, in the bay.' She leaned forward conspiratorially. 'Whales, or things even worse!'

Indigo stared at the nurse as queasiness flowered into nausea. 'Whales aren't fish,' she heard herself say. 'And they don't attack ships.' And thought: *but other things could* . . .

'Well, if it was fish or if it wasn't, it came out of the sea. I hear the Takhan's steward say so with his own voice!'

It couldn't be *Kara Karai*, Indigo thought: it couldn't, it *mustn't* –

'Hild, *please*!' She clenched her fists, trying to contain her frustration. 'What was the ship's *name*?'

Hild shrugged. 'How should I know? But is all right – it wasn't from Simhara, so not so much need to fret. One of them little boats, the ones that go with the big convoys.'

'Great Goddess . . . ' Indigo pushed the table back, almost knocking the tisane flying as she scrambled to her feet. Grimya bounded up after her, ears back.

'*A-na!* What is it with you, Indigo?' Hild called as the girl headed for the door with the she-wolf at her heels. 'What you doing?'

The slam of the door at Indigo's back was her only answer.

Like penetrating a maze, more and more snippets of information came as they hastened on their way towards the harbour. Pirates, one rumour said; a hurricane, another advised. Two Southern Isles Cat class war-boats, of which only one had limped into port to tell the tale. A convoy escort separated from her sister-ships in fog and foundered on uncharted rocks. But gradually a firm thread began to run through the conflicting tales, a true picture emerging. One ship. A Davakotian. Great loss of life. And attacked by something that came out of the sea.

The harbour was in turmoil. Crowds, drawn like bees to honey by the alarm, were milling on the quays, watching, speculating, gossiping. Indigo stopped people at random, and her frantic questions brought more information. There had been a rescue attempt, it seemed. Another Davakotian vessel had put out in response to the stricken ship's distress flare, and, thanks to the efforts of the captain and crew, there were some survivors from the wreck. Indigo and Grimya battled their way through the throng, and when finally they emerged, dishevelled, on to the gusty harbour front, Indigo saw the black-and-yellow hull and pugnacious snout of a Davakotian hunter-escort, dipping and swaying at her mooring on the heavy swell.

The *Sivake*. She must be the one . . . Indigo ran towards the quay and halted by the ship's gangplank, feet sliding on the wet stone, then looked wildly from one end of the ship to the other. There was no one on deck: she cupped a hand to her mouth, shouted, in the Davakotian tongue Macce had taught her, for the captain, the bo'sun, anyone. People turned, curious; from the body of the crowd a man in the bright sash of a customs official emerged and hastened along the hard towards her. As he approached, a head appeared from the *Sivake*'s companion hatch, and a stocky, swarthy man in early middle age, his black hair cropped and stiffly upstanding, emerged on deck. A small emerald was embedded in each cheek, just below the eyes, and his look was mistrustful and unwelcoming.

'What do you want?' he called in accented Khimizi. 'I've said all there is to say five times over, damn it! There's nothing more I can tell you people!'

The customs official was bearing down on her, gesticulating angrily and waving her back. Quickly and desperately, Indigo addressed the captain in his own tongue, and as soon as she mentioned Macce's name and told him of their connection, his expression immediately changed.

'You were with Macce?' He looked swiftly towards the official and made a cancelling gesture with both arms. 'It's all right, custom man. Leave the lady be!'

The official veered away, shaking his head in weary exasperation, and the Davakotian ran lightly down the plank and dropped to the hard in front of Indigo.

'Amyxl, captain of the *Sivake*.' He inclined his head in a curtly formal greeting. 'You've heard about *Kara Karai*?'

It was final confirmation. She nodded, swallowing back bile. 'Macce – is she – '

'Macce's alive. But she's one of the few. They've taken the survivors to some place behind the Temple of Mariners, where they've got physicians.'

The Seafarers' Sanctuary. Indigo knew it; it was a part of the temple precinct – another of Augon Hunnamek's endowments. Macce could have no better care. But the others . . .

'You went to her aid,' she said urgently. 'Please: I *have* to know what happened. There were passengers on

224

the ship; two, or perhaps three. It – wasn't a normal run for *Kara Karai*.'

'Ah.' Amyxl frowned. 'That explains why she wasn't in convoy.' His eyes grew shrewd yet sympathetic. 'More friends of yours?'

Indigo nodded.

'And you've seen the wreck?'

'No. I've only just heard the news.'

Amyxl hissed through his teeth. 'Then you'd best look at what's left of *Kara Karai* for yourself. She's in the bay, south of here; that's where she came ashore last night, Mother help her.'

Indigo glanced involuntarily in that direction, though the great beach was invisible from this distance. 'I've heard that . . . that she was attacked. Not by pirates, but by something which . . . ' She couldn't finish, and turned back to him in silent appeal that he would deny it.

The Davakotian stared at his own feet. At first she thought he wasn't going to answer her, but after a few moments he seemed to make a decision.

'Look, lady,' he said, 'If it's of any help to you, I'll take you to the bay myself, and you can see the truth with your own eyes.' He raised his gaze to meet hers again. 'I'll also tell you what I saw last night, and you can make of it what you will. But I'll say this now. I don't know what hit the *Kara Karai*, but in all my years at sea I've never seen anything capable of doing that to a ship.'

'That . . . ?' Indigo said uneasily.

The captain grimaced. 'Best see for yourself.'

A greater crowd than that at the harbour had gathered on the dunes that fringed the beach. The tide was receding, and a short way beyond the first angry lines of the surf *Kara Karai* lay broadside to the shore, her back broken and the waves booming and surging over her. There was a good deal of jetsam strewn above the tideline; spars, rigging, smashed fragments of the hunter ship's ballista. Militiamen were patrolling the dunes, keeping back onlookers and – ghoulish, but inevitable even in Simhara's civilised society – souvenir-

225

hunters. And further along the beach, two men stood rigidly, guarding something that lay motionless on the sand.

Amyxl nodded towards the distant tableau of the guards. 'If you want an inkling of what happened to the *Kara Karai*,' he said sombrely, 'go and look at that.'

Indigo frowned, querying, but he'd turned his head away, and so, with Grimya silent but uneasy at her heels, she started through the crowd and out on to the sand. A militiaman intercepted her, then, recognising her, hesitated.

'Lady, I'm not sure if I should allow – '

The lie came quickly to Indigo's lip. 'Armsman, I'm here on behalf of the Lady Phereniq, the Takhan's astrologer. There was no time to prepare the proper documentation; Lady Phereniq deemed the matter too urgent to wait.'

'Very well, madam.' He clearly didn't have enough faith in his own authority to argue. 'But I wouldn't advise you to go too close.'

'Why not?'

The militiaman looked helplessly at Amyxl, who had caught up. Amyxl shrugged non-committally, and the man gave way.

'It's as you wish, lady.' He turned, and led the way across the beach.

Even as they drew close to the shapeless lump, it was hard to discern any detail. The object was surrounded by a thin film of water that had gathered in the depression made by its weight, and to Indigo's eyes it looked like just another piece of jetsam from the wreck, a fragment of mast timber perhaps, partly obscured by a tangle of seaweed. But as the small party halted beside it and the guards backed away, she realised it wasn't jetsam – and suddenly she swung aside, clapping a hand to her mouth in an effort to stop herself from retching as her brain took in the truth.

The man couldn't have been dead for more than a few hours, but even so the sea would by now have begun to bloat his corpse – if there had been anything but the skin and skeleton left. It was like looking at a slimy, empty

226

sack, a nightmarish parody of the human form, complete, but flaccid, deflated, all but two-dimensional. A grotesque mockery of a face stared up at her, eye-sockets empty, nose and lips flattened – the lower jawbone protruded through one torn cheek, the teeth still intact – and here and there another bone shaped the skin envelope into a tortured semblance of solidity. In the worst of her dreams, Indigo could never have imagined anything so gruesome.

A hand grasped her upper arm, and Captain Amyxl pulled her back. 'You see?' he said, and his voice was ice cold.

She stumbled round. Grimya had started forward to look for herself, but Indigo recovered enough to hold a hand out, forestalling her. 'No, Grimya! Don't!' She wiped her mouth and shook her head violently before meeting the unhappy gaze of the militiaman. 'Who . . . was he?'

'We don't yet know, lady. It hasn't been possible to . . . ' He cleared his throat, looked away.

'I can tell you one thing,' Amyxl put in. 'There's enough left of his clothes to prove he wasn't a crewman.'

Something within Indigo squirmed suddenly, like an icy worm in her gut. She didn't want to, but she had to look again; and, steeling herself, she turned to face the monstrosity on the sand. A voice inside her head said *no, you can't judge, you can't be sure.* But she was. For there was a familiar echo in the grisly parody of a human face; and the few ragged strands of hair that still clung to the shattered skull were honey-gold streaked with grey.

'Oh, Great Mother!' Indigo stumbled away and vomited violently on to the sand. The beach was turning, twisting; she dropped to her knees, unable to maintain her balance, knowing the truth but incapable, even as she accepted it, of also accepting what it meant.

For the weed-draped horror lying on the sodden beach with its flesh and its organs sucked out of it, was the corpse of Mylo Copperguild.

Amyxl took her to one of the taverns on the north side

227

of the harbour. She needed a drink, he said, after what she'd seen at the beach, and his second sight of the corpse hadn't diminished his revulsion; he wanted to cleanse the bile from his own throat. And as they sat at a quiet table and the shock began to recede from Indigo's mind, the captain told his story.

Kara Karai, it seemed, had approached Simhara shortly after midnight. The storm had made the incoming tide mountainous, and a sailor on watch aboard *Sivake* had been alerted by the distant glimmer of fore-and-aft lanterns out to sea. She'd woken Amyxl – the entire ship's crew was sleeping on board, only waiting for the storm to abate before setting homeward to Davakos – and he'd watched the intermittent shimmering, silently cursing the unknown ship's captain for a thousand fools for attempting to make harbour in such weather. Then the sulphur distress flare went up, and Amyxl had immediately ordered all hands to the oars. They had come upon the *Kara Karai* to find her heeling broadside into the waves and near sinking, her mainmast smashed and her terrified crew abandoning their posts and jumping – or falling – into the heaving sea. *Sivake*'s crew manoeuvred as close to the foundering ship as they dared, trying to pick up survivors: and then, Amyxl said, he had seen something that he would not forget until the day the Sea Mother took him to her own. A vast, phosphorescent silver-grey shape, that emerged from the trough between two rising waves to tower over the stricken ship. Something like a tail, but titanically massive, came smashing down across the *Kara Karai*'s bow, spinning *Sivake* helplessly in the huge backwash as the monstrosity plunged below the surface again.

'One glimpse,' Amyxl said, staring at his cup and seeming to see into a world beyond the tavern's dusty quiet. 'That was all we had of it. But we ran. We got *Sivake* under control again, and the rowers pulled for harbour with all the strength they had in them.' He pinched the bridge of his nose, shutting his eyes tightly for a moment. 'We couldn't even take it in; it happened so quickly, and we were more concerned with holding our course and looking for survivors. Seven. That was

how many we picked up. Seven. The rest . . . I can only
pray that it was the sea took them, and not . . . *that*.'

Indigo said softly: 'Could it have been a serpent?'

'Perhaps.' Amyxl's voice was bitter and wary. 'But
whatever it was, the Sea Mother didn't create such an
abomination.' He looked up and met her gaze. 'All I
know is that I saw something that shouldn't rightly exist
in this world. And may I die on land if I tell a lie: I am
afraid!'

Chapter XX

It was nearly noon by the time Indigo and Grimya returned to the palace. Amyxl was leaving on the next tide; he feared that the unknown horror of last night might still be lurking in the bay, but had no choice; he and his crew must work or starve. Indigo wished she could have told him the truth: that *Sivake* was in no danger. The monstrous serpent – she had no doubt now of its identity – had done its work, and wouldn't strike again.

At least, not in that way.

Parting from Amyxl, she had gone then to the Sea-farers' Sanctuary, but her request to see Macce had met with a gentle but implacable refusal. The survivors from the wreck were not to be disturbed or questioned until they had recovered: there could be no exception. Even the Takhan himself, said the pleasant-faced temple brother who heard her entreaty, would be turned away in the greater interests of the patients' wellbeing.

He did, however, relent enough to give her a little more information. Macce's injuries were minor; with good care she would recover soon enough. There had been seven survivors all told; the captain, five of her crew, and one passenger. No, the passenger's name wasn't known to the Sanctuary, for he wasn't in their care. A Khimizi merchant, so the brother understood, who had been taken to his own home in the city.

Indigo was torn between horror and thankfulness. Two dead – but one still alive. Leando, or Elsender? She forced the question from her mind, thanked the brother, asked that word might be sent to her at the palace when Macce was fit to receive visitors, and turned bleakly away as the door of the Sanctuary closed.

She should go to the Copperguild mansion. She should ask for news, learn who had lived and who had died – but she couldn't face the prospect of what she might hear. Cowardly, perhaps, but she found the gnawing uncertainty easier to bear; for with uncertainty there was also room for hope.

And so, numbed beyond any feeling but the dull, leaden pains of grief and guilt, she slipped through the wicket gate, smiling reflexively but without heart at the guards, and entered the Infanta's apartments – to find Phereniq and Augon Hunnamek with Jessamin in the courtyard garden.

'Indigo.' Phereniq rose at sight of her, coming forward with her arms held out. 'Oh, my dear, I am so grieved by this news! When Hild said you had heard of it I tried to find you, but you'd already left.'

Augon was watching her, his dark face solemn, his eyes filled with sympathy. *Hypocrite*, a silent voice within Indigo said savagely. *Hypocrite – and murderer –* she turned away from his steady gaze and passively let Phereniq embrace her.

'Have they allowed you to see Leando?' the astrologer asked.

'No; I –' Then she took the words in fully. 'Leando . . .?'

'You didn't know he was on board?' Phereniq looked shocked, then horrified. 'Of course – how could you have done! I didn't think –'

Hope, an agonising flare in the dark miasm, constricted Indigo's throat. 'I – I saw the wreck. And I went to the Sanctuary; but they couldn't tell me anything.'

'Oh, my dear . . .' Phereniq stood back. 'I'm so sorry: I shouldn't have broken it to you in such a way. They were all on board, Indigo – Leando, Mylo and Mylo's son. Not his wife, thank the Sea Mother; she was to follow them later . . . But Leando's alive, Indigo. He was one of the few saved from the sea – he's injured, but he'll recover.'

Indigo nodded, barely able to take in the news. 'Luk,' she said. 'Has he been told?'

'He's being taken home now. He was very brave,

though he's greatly upset. Poor child: to lose his uncle and cousin in such a way . . . ' She shook her head, unable to express what she felt.

Indigo's mind was beginning to function more clearly in the wake of the shock, and the significance of that struck her sharply. How could anyone know that the three Copperguilds had been on board *Kara Karai*? It was impossible: the voyage had been a secret –

The panic-stricken thought was interrupted by Augon Hunnamek.

'Indigo, I blame myself for this tragedy,' he said gravely. Indigo quickly looked up, to see him approaching with Jessamin following a pace behind. 'Their recall was intended to be a happy surprise for Luk, and also for you. I can't begin to express my sorrow.'

'Their recall?' She didn't understand.

Augon shook his head sadly. 'You were not told of my decision. Call it a romantic impulse; a wish to share my happiness at my forthcoming marriage with those who have been my loyal friends . . . I sent word to the Jewel Islands two months ago, releasing Mylo from his duties and summoning him and his kinsmen back to Simhara with all honour. Their return was to be my gift to them, and to you and Luk.'

Indigo continued to stare at him.

'No one could have foreseen this dreadful event, but I feel the responsibility keenly,' Augon went on. 'Such a terrible, *terrible* loss.'

Indigo was fighting for breath. 'You're telling me that – '

'That Mylo and his son Elsender lost their lives in the wreck.' He mistook her meaning, taking her sudden trembling for shock at further bad news; an error for which, when she had time to consider it later, she was thankful. 'Yes. We have no confirmation yet, but we believe that it must be so.' He laid a hand on her shoulder; a gesture with which she was long familiar, and loathed. 'That such a tragedy should result from my action grieves me more deeply than I can say. I shall pray with all my heart for their souls' safe passage to the Mother's rest.'

Indigo's shivering threatened to flower into full-scale, uncontrollable shudders as the Takhan stepped back, and her entire inner being was screaming outrage at the sheer blatant hypocrisy of his speech. This creature, this *monster*, by whose unhuman hand so many innocent victims had died, spoke smoothly of grief and sorrow and responsibility . . . like a red-hot knife her fury communicated itself to Grimya in a silent, ferocious protest: *What manner of fool does he take me for?*

But she couldn't say it aloud; couldn't express her blazing revulsion. All she could do, though the effort was almost beyond her capability, was turn aside, staring blindly across the greening garden, and whisper through clenched teeth:

'Thank you, my lord.'

'Indigo . . . ' It was Jessamin, her honey-gold eyes wide and emotional as she came diffidently up and slipped a small hand into Indigo's own. The contact dragged Indigo back from the brink: she swallowed, looked at the Infanta and saw that she had been crying.

'Indigo, do you think Luk-y will be all right? His face was so *white*.' Her hand clenched. 'Oh, *why* did such an awful thing have to happen?'

Ask your chero Takhan, you poor, innocent child, Indigo thought with renewed savagery. But she said nothing, only kissed Jessamin's troubled brow, and added a silent promise to the hatred churning inside her.

He will die for this. One way or another, he will die.

The anticipated message from the Seafarers' Sanctuary didn't come until four days later. Indigo had tried to contain her nervous impatience, immersing herself as best she could in everyday matters; but it was hard, especially as, for the Infanta, almost every waking hour was directed towards thoughts of the approaching marriage.

Luk hadn't returned to the palace; nor had there been any word from the Copperguild house save for the final confirmation Indigo had dreaded; that Mylo and Elsender had perished in the wreck. Leando was out of danger, but there was no further news of him; and so by the time the brief note from the Sanctuary was delivered to her, Indigo was at a pitch of tension, and desperately thankful for something to break the hiatus.

She and Grimya found Macce in the Sanctuary court-yard, sitting in a rattan chair and swathed, despite the day's warmth, in a blanket. Her face was white and pinched; there were heavy crescents of shadow beneath her eyes. When she saw Indigo approaching she tried to smile, but the effort was too great.

'Macce.' Indigo crouched down beside the chair. 'They wouldn't let me see you before today. I . . . don't know what I can say to you.'

'I'm glad you came.' Macce's voice was like stone; lifeless, inert. She clasped her own upper arms briefly, as though cold. 'They told you what happened, did they?'

'Amyxl did. I saw him the day afterwards.'

'Ah, yes. I wanted to see Amyxl, too, but they said he'd sailed.' She shut her eyes. 'Sea Mother protect him. *Sivake* pulled six of us out of the sea, d'you know that? Six. And one of your friends, too.'

'I know.'

'I should be dead, by rights All of us should. After what happened . . . '

'Macce.' Indigo took the small woman's hands. What she wanted to say came hard, but the question had to be asked. 'Amyxl told me that – *Kara Karai* was attacked. He saw something – he couldn't truly describe it, but – '

Macce interrupted her. 'A serpent,' she said flatly. 'It was a serpent. And if anyone tells you different, they're lying.' Suddenly her expression became fierce. 'People are saying it was my fault. They're saying the storm made us founder, and I was to blame for trying to bring her in to shore. But it isn't *true*! If we'd stood off from land, we'd have gone down with all hands and there'd have been no bones for those human vultures to pick over! Amyxl knows that – but even he doesn't know a tenth of what happened, a *hundredth* of it!'

Indigo's grip on her hands tightened. 'What do you mean?'

A huge shudder racked Macce's frame. 'We had everything on that return voyage. Currents where there shouldn't have been; gales; fog; becalming. And then that. Within sight of harbour, and that abomination came out of the sea and struck my ship, and *smashed* her, like so much firewood.' She wrenched her hands free of Indigo's and crashed clenched fists down on the arms of the chair. 'It wasn't *possible*! Such things don't *exist*! It was like – like something conjured by sorcery. Or worse – as if it was a *demon*.'

Indigo turned away. 'Oh, Great Mother . . . ' The choked words came out before she could stop them. 'I should have known: I should have – '

'*What?*' Macce's voice cut across her like a honed knife.

Indigo looked up again and their gazes met. Her face gave her away; there was guilty understanding in her eyes, and Macce realised instantly what it could only mean. For a moment there was a tense, palpable silence. Then Macce said, in a changed voice,

'A demon . . . I'm right, aren't I? That's exactly what it was. And you – you knew about it all along. You *knew*!'

'Macce, I – ' A quick lie came to Indigo's lips, but her conscience rebelled. 'Oh, dear Goddess, I didn't think you'd be in danger! I didn't think it could touch you – I only realised after you'd sailed, and then it was too late. And I thought – '

'You *thought*!' Macce's voice shook with bitter contempt. 'You're telling me now that there *was* something evil, and you knew it – you knew what might happen to my crew and my ship. Yet you let me go, without even *warning* me . . . '

'How could I?' Indigo pleaded. 'You wouldn't have believed me!'

'You didn't give me the *chance* to believe you! What d'you think I am; *stupid*? I may not be a superstitious Khimizi, but I know enough to realise that demons exist!' With a violent gesture Macce flung the blanket off and got up. Limping, she started to move away, then stopped and turned back to face Indigo again.

'But oh, no; you weren't about to let me in on that part of your little secret, were you? Because you knew damn' well that if you did, I'd no more have risked my crew and my ship on that accursed voyage than grown gills and *swum* there!'

'Macce – '

'Don't "Macce" me, you bitch!' Breath sawed in the small woman's throat. 'Do you realise what you've done? Do you realise that, but for you, my crew might still be alive, and your yellow-haired merchant friends with them? Honesty, Indigo. *Honesty*. That was all I asked of you. But no; you *lied* to me, you *deceived* me, you let me lead my crew into danger without even having the humanity to tell me that the danger existed!' Her shoulders shook with a deep, racking spasm. 'If I live to be a hundred, I hope I'll never again come face to face with such selfish, craven *cowardice*!'

Indigo felt tears well in her eyes, and with them the suffocating knowledge that, though she might argue, grovel, plead her case, when the veneer was stripped away she couldn't deny that what Macce had said was the truth. *Kara Karai* had sailed blind and unwitting into disaster, and responsibility for the tragedy lay solely at Indigo's door.

She rose to her feet, pushing away Grimya's anxiously questing muzzle as the she-wolf sought to comfort her. She could take no comfort, and deserved none. If nothing else, Macce had opened her eyes.

'I'll go now, Macce,' she said quietly. 'I don't think there's anything more I can say.'

'Words won't bring back the dead.' Macce watched her, emotionless.

'I know. If I could make amends – '

'You can't. And don't ask me to forgive you, because I won't. But I've one last thing to say.' She stood unmoving, her face set like granite and old, suddenly old. The gulf between them was immeasurable, all friendship shattered, all trust betrayed. Then Macce said quietly: 'If you were the person I once believed you to be, you'd realise that making amends means more than sobbing into your wine and saying prayers for lost

236

souls. But I don't think you are that person, not any more. And I don't want to know the creature you've become. Goodbye, Indigo.'

Indigo thought long and hard about Macce's last words as she walked slowly away from the Sanctuary with Grimya trailing at her heels. *Making amends means more than sobbing into your wine and saying prayers for lost souls.* The parting shot was vicious, but it was true. As a result of her inaction, people had died. Karim, Mylo, Elsender, most of Macce's crew. She might have prevented their deaths. But she'd done nothing; and now she had lost almost all of her allies, while Augon Hunnamek's triumph was nearly complete.

She stopped suddenly as she realised that, without having made a conscious decision, her footsteps were leading her towards the Temple of Mariners and the very act that Macce had so contemptuously condemned. She couldn't pray to the Sea Mother for the souls of the dead; she wasn't *fit* to pray for them. Macce was right: if amends could be made, the path lay in *doing* something, not in piously repenting all that she had failed to do.

Well then, she would take that path. Self-recrimination was a luxury she could no longer afford; the time for languishing in guilt was past. She must *act*.

Grimya, sensing her friend's abrupt shift of mood, raised her head. There was no one in earshot, so the she-wolf spoke aloud.

'In-digo? Your thoughts are s . . . uddenly clearer.'

Indigo looked down at her. Dear, loyal Grimya – she never condemned, never turned her face away. 'Yes,' she said. 'I think I've realised just what Macce meant when she said what she did, and I mean to take heed of it.'

Grimya's tail began to wag. 'That is *good*! We have s-spent so much time w . . . aiting, unable to do anything.'

'Too much time.' And she would begin, Indigo thought, by telling Leando the whole truth. How he would react to the knowledge she didn't know; but she owed it to him, and to Karim and Macce and all the others.

And, perhaps most of all, to herself.

The next ten days tested Indigo almost beyond bearing. Goaded by her new-found resolve, she tried every means she could find to see Leando, and at every turn she found the way closed to her. Letters sent to the Copperguild mansion went unanswered; three visits met only with the solemn face of a servant telling her that, by strict order of Leando's grandmother, the house was closed to all callers and all messages until the period of mourning for Mylo and Elsender was over and the young master had regained his strength. Indigo railed and pleaded, but to no avail; as befitted a noble Khimizi family, the Copperguilds were observing all the proper ritual traditions of bereavement, and nothing could break the barrier before the proper time.

But time was in desperately short supply. There were fifteen days to go now before the marriage ceremony, and almost every hour that passed brought more reminders that the sands were running out. Dignitaries from all over the world were arriving for the celebrations, and the palace played host to a constant stream of visitors paying their respects to the Takhan and his bride. Every quarter of the city was being decked out with flowers and pennants and streamers; brilliant new murals had appeared on walls in the bazaars, coloured lanterns were strung through the trees and between buildings, and the broad streets were strewn with aromatic herbs. It was all sharply reminiscent of the bustle and excitement that had surrounded Augon's coronation a decade ago, and for Indigo that was bitter wine, for it brought home to her the enormity of her failure. She had been in Simhara for nearly eleven years, and the demon still lived and flourished. In a mere few days, he would take first the hand and then the body and the soul of Jessamin: and on the night that followed the ceremony, the Serpent-Eater would rise under the eclipsed moon to devour its prey – and that would be the beginning of the end for them all.

Jessamin herself was blissfully unaware of Indigo's fears. She was immersed, day and night, in the excitement of the great day to come, and her life was a whirl of formal receptions and seemingly endless rehearsals for the ceremony. Her schooling was, effectively, at an end, and so Indigo found herself with a good deal of free time, which only served to increase her frustration.

And then, ten days before the wedding, she was alone in her room when someone knocked at the door. Turning, she saw the door open – and Leando stood on the threshold.

Indigo's mouth opened, but sound wouldn't come. He had *changed* so – his build was heavier, the honey-coloured hair shorter and showing early signs of receding at the temples, and there were faint lines on his face: youth was gracefully giving way to the approach of middle age. But his eyes had the same intensity, and his voice, when he spoke her name, was the voice she remembered so well.

'Indigo . . . ?'

She couldn't say anything, not even one word with which to greet him after ten years of separation. But suddenly she was running across the room towards him, arms outflung to embrace him, hug him, hold him tightly against her as though he were a living talisman.

'Indigo, Indigo.' He all but crushed the breath out of her, then suddenly stood back and held her at arms' length, gazing into her face. 'But . . . you're exactly the same! Not a hair changed, not a line, *nothing*! I can't believe it . . . '

She found her voice at last. '*You* can't believe it!' Tears threatened to choke her as relief swamped her mind and mingled with a surge of affection she hadn't realised was in her. 'I'd begun to think I'd never see you, that your being home was a dream, that it hadn't happened – '

'I couldn't come before today. Our family has been in mourning.' Involuntarily he glanced at the grey band that he wore tied about one arm; the token of the bereaved.

Indigo put a hand up to her face. 'Oh, Leando, whatever can I say to you? When I heard – '

'There's so much to say, and I too don't know where to begin. The terrible, bitter *irony* of it, Indigo – that's

239

what hurts so much. When we received Augon Hunnamek's message, summoning us back – '

'What?' Indigo's eyes widened. 'You mean – he *did* recall you?'

'Oh, yes. His timing was perfect. The summons arrived the day before *Kara Karai* put in to port. We were already making preparations; but when we read your letter, we thought it best to make speed rather than wait for the packet boat . . . . ' The words tailed off and he shook his head miserably. 'Even now, the sweet Mother knows, I can't even begin to assimilate what happened! But Indigo, there's something else, something it's vital I must tell you about that voyage – '

Sounds of running feet interrupted him before he could say any more, and Luk burst in, Grimya only a pace behind him.

'Indigo, did you – ' And the boy stopped, his eyes lighting. 'Papa; you found her!'

'Indeed.' Leando held out an arm towards his son, pride suffusing his face. Then he hesitated, staring beyond Luk to the she-wolf, and his expression altered. 'That surely isn't – '

'It's Grimya,' Luk said happily. 'I told you, didn't I, Papa, that she was still alive and well? Now you can see for yourself.'

Leando looked quickly from Grimya to Indigo and back again. 'But . . . Indigo, how *old* is she?'

Indigo knew what he was thinking. Leando had returned after a ten-year absence to find his son grown almost to manhood, all his friends and acquaintances changed. It was natural, as was the fact that he, too, had aged with the passing of time – and yet in Indigo and Grimya he saw no sign of alteration: they both looked exactly as they had done on the day he had sailed from Simhara.

She remembered Macce's angry challenge, and knew she must tell him the truth.

'Leando.' Taking his hand she drew him towards her. 'I have a great deal to explain to you, and part of it involves the conundrum of Grimya and me. But the telling will take time.' She glanced at Luk, not wanting

240

to say too much whilst he could overhear. 'If, tonight, we can – '

'Tonight I'm bidden to dine with the Takhan.' Then Leando smiled bitterly. 'You see how easily the title comes to my lips now? I've spent ten years respectfully referring to the usurper as "Takhan" in my dealings with the Jewel Islanders, and the habit's become ingrained. But I can't decline the invitation; Luk must come with me, and I believe you are also to be included among the guests.'

'To complete the happy picture of friends re-united?'

'Doubtless. He always did have a well-honed sense of irony. But when that ordeal's over, we could return here and talk.'

It meant delaying longer than Indigo would have liked, but there was no other choice. She nodded.

'But Indigo, before then I *must* tell you about the voyage; warn you – '

'No, Leando.' Again her gaze slid briefly, obliquely, to Luk. 'Not here; not now. Besides, I – think I know what you want to say.' She hesitated, then: 'You want to tell me that we are in danger, and that there is sorcery involved.'

He stared at her. 'How did you discover that?'

'I've known it for a long time; and a good deal else besides. And Karim – '

'Karim?' Leando hissed eagerly. 'You've seen him?'

Of course: he didn't know of the mage's death, for Luk had promised to say nothing. Indigo held up both hands, palms outward.

'Please, Leando. Tonight I'll tell you everything, but I daren't begin now. We must both be patient, for a few hours longer.'

'But you're *aware* of the danger – '

'Yes. And I won't do anything to court it, have no fear of that.' She turned away, looking back across the room. Its warm opulence made her feel suddenly claustrophobic, as though other, invisible but palpable walls were closing in and threatening to suffocate them all in a deadly embrace. 'This evening we must play our parts,

241

and laugh or cry as the moment demands. We must do *nothing* to arouse suspicion.'

There were faint voices in the passage beyond the door, sounds of sandalled feet and the chiming of the glass mobiles as servants went about their work. They could say no more to each other; the risk of eaves-droppers was too great. Leando took both Indigo's hands and raised them to his lips, kissing her fingers.

'Till tonight, then. And Indigo – ' He paused, smiled. 'No: it'll wait.' He kissed her again, on the brow this time, and shepherded Luk out of the room.

Chapter XXI

Leando stared down at his own tightly-clasped hands and said, in a voice charged with emotion:

'I can't take it in, Indigo. It's too . . . ' Words failed him.

'Incredible?' Indigo prompted softly. She was sitting on her couch, legs curled beneath her and Grimya's warm presence at her side, watching Leando across the table. On another couch Luk sat propped by cushions; he had striven to keep awake but it was a losing battle, and his head was drooping.

'No.' Leando had considered, and now shook his head emphatically. 'That's one of the things that un-nerves me – I believe you. Rationally I know I shouldn't; but I can't ignore the evidence, especially in the light of my own experience. And Karim's story – we knew that he left the court suddenly, and that he wanted his old identity to be forgotten: our family had known his for many years, and that was why he trusted us to keep his secret. But he would never tell us *why* he left, or the cause of his blindness. We thought – assumed – that it was a personal decision; we didn't know about the palace records. Now, I'm beginning to understand a great deal more.

'But as for what you've told me about yourself . . . ' He forced a quick, pallid smile. 'I believe that, too. Call it instinct if you like; I know no better word. But . . . Great Sea Mother, I hadn't anticipated *this*.'

She said nothing more, aware that he needed time to let the facts settle in his churning mind. A long and serious talk with Grimya earlier in the day had reinforced her decision to tell Leando everything – including the truth about her own quest. That, she suspected, had shocked him above all else: for a long time after the story was done he had sat staring at her, his face expressionless but his eyes silently struggling to equate what they saw with the terrible revelation. Unageing, unchanging, undying, until her search was over and the evil she sought rooted out and destroyed – it was the stuff of legend, of tales told by candlelight to sleepy children. But he believed it. The instinct he'd spoken of told him that he had no choice.

In the far distance Indigo could hear the harbour tide-bells ringing. It must be very late; but she doubted that there would be any sleep for her or Leando tonight. They had dined in the Takhan's private reception room, a rare honour; and the party had been small and select. Herself and Leando, Jessamin demure and beautiful at Augon's side, Luk, and Phereniq. It was, Augon had said gravely to Leando, both a thanksgiving for his safe return and a personal memorial for Mylo and Elsender; and Indigo had had to admire, however cynically, his seemingly genuine show of sorrow as, without ostentation or theatrics, he had spoken quietly of his respect for Mylo and his sense of indebtedness to the Copperguild family. Leando had borne the small oration with rigid composure and had thanked his host with the utmost courtesy. Only Indigo – and, she surmised, Luk – had seen the glitter of loathing in his eyes as he took his place at the table.

The gathering had passed off well enough; though Phereniq was conspicuous by her silence. The astrologer looked ill; her eyes were glazed and she had no co-ordination; her hand shook as she picked at her food, and once she knocked over a cup of wine, sending a crimson stain spreading across the damask cloth. Knowing her of old, Indigo realised that she had drugged herself almost to insensibility, and pitied her. She and Grimya and the Copperguilds were not, it seemed, the only souls in Khimiz who didn't want to see Augon Hunnamek wed; and this was Phereniq's only solace.

And then, when at last the small feast was over and

they were making their farewells, Augon took Indigo's hands and, with Leando standing only a pace away, said:

'I hope, my dear Indigo, that rejoicing may yet arise from tragedy. It would content me greatly to know that my happiness with the Infanta might be reflected before long in your own.'

Hot colour flared in Indigo's cheeks, and she hadn't dared to meet Leando's gaze. Neither of them spoke a word as they walked back to her room with Luk; and she had assumed that Leando's tense silence stemmed, like her own, from embarrassment and anger. But now, as she watched him and saw the inner battle to take in and accept what she had told him, she realised that she had made a fundamental mistake.

He looked up suddenly and met her gaze, and her face must have given her away.

'Oh, dear Goddess.' He stood up, made as though to move towards her and then thought better of it. 'What am I to do, Indigo? I'd rehearsed what I'd say to you, down to the last syllable. All these years in the Jewel Islands it's been growing, and it seemed so *right*. All your letters, and the things Luk has told me . . . ' He glanced swiftly, apologetically at his son, but Luk had fallen asleep. 'I'd spent so much time planning our future together.' A sharp, self-mocking laugh escaped him before he could stop it. 'You must find that hard to believe of me. But – '

'Please, Leando.' Her throat was constricted. 'Don't say any more.'

He sucked in a deep breath. 'No. You're right; I should have said nothing. But you'd guessed, hadn't you?'

'Yes,' she told him gently. 'I'd guessed.'

'And you . . . ' He was struggling for words now, wanting to save his own face and yet at the same time groping for some reassurance. 'If things had been different, Indigo, do you think it might have been possible that . . . ?'

Indigo closed her eyes. She didn't want to lie; but there were times when truth could only hurt to no good purpose. And perhaps, she thought, if circumstances *had* been otherwise . . .

'I think it might have been possible,' she said.

For what seemed like a very long time there was silence and stillness in the room. Leando was gazing out at the dark garden, his stance tense. Then, so abruptly that both Indigo and Grimya started, he clapped his hands together. It was a ritualistic gesture, the closing of a book, the slamming of a shutter; and when he turned back to her his expression was calm once more.

'It's a favourite maxim of my grandmother's that the past, being done and therefore unchangeable, is best not dwelt upon.' He returned to his chair, sat down and poured himself a fresh cup of wine. 'And we have the future to think of; even if it isn't quite the future I had in mind.' He smiled faintly, wryly, and Indigo knew intuitively that he wouldn't speak of his dashed hopes again, but from now on would be simply Leando her fellow-conspirator and friend; nothing more. He was waiting only for her final confirmation: she returned the smile, and with it a barely perceptible nod.

Leando sighed, a mingling of regret and relief, and when he spoke again his tone was brisk and businesslike.

'We have suffered a great setback,' he said. 'It seems inhuman to look at it in such a way, and to be so hard-headed when we should be mourning the loss of our kin and friends. But time won't wait on our finer feelings. And I don't think that Karim and Mylo and Elsender would have wanted us to waste what little we have left. Indigo, we have only eleven days in which to strike against the usurper. We *must* find a way to kill him, before it's too late.'

It was what Indigo had feared he would say, and she shook her head in emphatic denial. 'Leando, that isn't feasible. If he is what I believe him to be, then what weapons do we have that would be of any use? Poison or a sword wouldn't harm him – they might hurt his human body, but they'd be worthless against what lies beneath it. We're dealing with a *demon*, not a mortal man! Do you – forgive me, but do you have any true idea of what that means?'

246

He looked at her unhappily, unsure of himself, and with a bitter pang Indigo recalled the first demon she had encountered, years ago in the Charchad vale, and the appalling power that had been needed to bring about its downfall.

'I know of only one way to fight such an evil,' she said quietly. 'Fire with fire – sorcery must be defeated with sorcery. But you and I aren't magicians, Leando. And if we try to move against Augon Hunnamek without help, the only thing we'll succeed in destroying is ourselves.'

'But what alternative do we have?' Leando countered. 'Karim had some skill in sorcery, and that would have aided us, but – '

'But Karim is dead,' Indigo interrupted. 'Doesn't that in itself tell you more than enough? Karim's skills couldn't save him when he was attacked. How could he have hoped to prevail in a full confrontation?'

Leando acknowledged the point with a slumping of his shoulders. 'Very well. I accept that – and I'm not such a fool that I'd throw my life away to no good purpose. But if we can't kill Augon Hunnamek, who can?'

'I don't know.' Indigo felt frustration welling as the all too familiar circular argument began again in her mind. Without a strong enough weapon, they dared not strike at their quarry. Yet if they didn't strike, the demonic power would come to full manifestation in just eleven days' time, and then all hope would be gone. They were, it seemed, at an impasse.

Leando was frowning into his cup, twisting its stem between his hands and watching the wine shift like a small tide in the bowl. Suddenly he said:

'There is one possibility. Years ago, when Mylo and Karim and I made our original plans, there was a contingency. We didn't think we'd ever need it – and now, with only the two of us to carry it out, it won't be easy – but it might at least buy us some time.'

Indigo leaned forward eagerly. 'Tell me.'

He looked up at her. 'There can be no wedding without a bride. If the Infanta were to disappear, what could the usurper do then?'

247

'You mean – abduct her?'

'Exactly.'

Indigo considered the idea. 'It would be dangerous, Leando. We know what's already happened to those who tried to thwart the demon's will.'

'True. But which would be the greater risk? That, or standing by and watching the marriage take place?'

Indigo looked at Grimya, who lay with her muzzle on her friend's lap. The she-wolf's eyes glowed amber in the dimly-lit room, and she said silently,

I think it may be the only way. And he is right: to do nothing would be worse.

'I don't know how we'd achieve it, or where we would take her,' Leando continued, lowering his voice though there was no one who could possibly overhear them. 'But they're not insurmountable problems; we could flee to the sea or the desert. And though Augon might pursue us physically, I think he'd stay his hand from anything else for fear of harming the Infanta. Then, once the conjunction is past, we can decide what to do for the best.'

It was an insane scheme, but none the less Indigo felt excitement growing within her. Leando was right when he said that Augon wouldn't risk endangering Jessamin: and if they could get her away, *far* away from Simhara, they would at least have a breathing space. As yet she couldn't think beyond that point, but no matter: they would have averted the imminent disaster. And with seemingly no other avenues open to them, it was a chance they couldn't afford to lose.

She said: 'We'd need to plan every step with the utmost care. But . . . I think we can do it.'

Leando's eyes lit. 'I *know* we can, Indigo!' Then he hesitated. 'There's just one stipulation I must make.' He glanced towards the other couch, where Luk was still sleeping. 'I don't want Luk involved in this. He's too young and too vulnerable. I'll risk my own safety, but I won't risk his.'

'He may have to be involved,' Indigo pointed out. 'We daren't leave him in Simhara; that would put him in far greater danger.'

'I know; but for the time being he must know nothing of our plans. I'll leave him with my grandmother, and once we have Jessamin safely away from the city I'll send for him.'

'There is a complication,' Indigo said.

'What do you mean?'

'You haven't realised? Luk's said nothing?'

Leando's face was blankly uncomprehending. Indigo sighed.

'Leando, Luk is in love with Jessamin. Months ago, when he first learned that you were coming home, he told me that everything would be all right, because you would stop the wedding and give him your blessing to marry Jessamin in Augon Hunnamek's place.'

Leando stared at her, stunned. 'Sea Mother . . . ' he said at last, and looked quickly again at the couch and his sleeping son. 'But he's only a child – '

'He's thirteen,' Indigo reminded him. 'Old enough to think of himself as almost a man.' And gently she added, 'You've been away for a very long time.'

'Yes.' Leando's brow creased. 'Yes; I have . . . and it's so easy to forget. Poor Luk . . . ' He drew breath through clenched teeth. 'This isn't going to be a simple task, Indigo. But I still think it's the only choice we have.'

Indigo rose to her feet. 'Perhaps we should say no more at this stage,' she said. 'We'll meet again as soon as we can, and in the meantime I'll study the programme of the Infanta's activities for the next few days and see if I can find the most auspicious time for us. When – ' And she stopped in mid-sentence as Grimya suddenly projected a soundless, wordless warning. There was a movement on the periphery of her vision – her head whipped round, and she saw Jessamin standing in the doorway that connected her apartment with Indigo's.

'*Chera!*' Indigo felt her cheeks flush hotly with shock and chagrin. How long had the child been standing there, unnoticed? She surely couldn't have overheard . . .

Jessamin rubbed her eyes. 'I woke up, and heard your voices,' she said, then transferred one hand to her mouth to stifle a yawn. 'I'm sorry. I didn't mean to be in the way.' Shyly she looked at Leando and smiled, then glanced beyond him to the couch. 'Is Luk asleep?'

Relieved, for it seemed that there was no harm done, Indigo put an arm about the Infanta's shoulders, smoothing back her tousled hair. 'Yes, dear one, and so should you be. What was it that woke you?'

'I don't know. I don't think I was dreaming. Indigo, might I have some fruit cordial?'

'Of course.' She turned to the table. Leando touched her arm.

'We'll go now, Indigo. I'll call on you tomorrow, if I may?'

'Yes . . . please.' She watched as he gathered Luk into his arms – the boy didn't stir – and moved to the outer door. On the threshold he saw Jessamin looking at them over the rim of her cup, and made a show of kissing Indigo's brow. 'Until tomorrow.'

The door closed behind him. Jessamin finished her cordial and set the cup down, then allowed Indigo to shepherd her back into her bedchamber. As she climbed between the silk sheets, she said,

'I'm very happy for you, Indigo.'

'Happy for me?'

'Now that Luk's papa is home. *Chero* Takhan told me that you're going to marry him one day soon.'

'I – ' No, she thought; best say nothing. 'Thank you, *chera*.' Her voice was a little strained.

'I shall be Takhina then, so I shan't be able to walk behind you and throw the Sea Mother's net over your hair. But I shall give you a very special gift. Anything I wish, *chero* Takhan says. I'll think very hard about it.'

Indigo felt as though her heart was tearing inside her. Such sweetness, such innocent joy. They *must* succeed in what they had set out to do, she told herself fiercely. The alternative was unthinkable.

'You're very dear and very kind, Jessamin,' she said, trying not to let emotion get the better of her. 'And I shall love you always.'

'I love you, too, Indigo.' Jessamin reached up and hugged her. As Indigo went softly out of the room she lay down again, only her contented, honey-dark eyes visible like dimly shining lamps in the darkness.

They were ready. Though she was constantly racked by uncertainty, plagued with fears that something would go wrong at the last moment, Indigo knew that there was nothing more to be done save pray to the Earth Mother that the plan could and would succeed.

It had been easy to contrive frequent meetings with Leando in the four days that followed their first evening together. With few palace duties to constrain her she had been free to do almost entirely as she pleased, and though Augon's smiling approval disgusted her, it was none the less a welcome smokescreen for the true purpose of their trysts.

Choosing the right moment for Jessamin's abduction had been, thankfully, a simple matter. Two nights before the wedding, Augon Hunnamek planned to observe a Khimizi tradition by which the bride and groom both celebrated, separately, their imminent transition from single to wedded status. The two festivities were to be strictly segregated, the men gathering together in one of the palace gardens while the women gathered in another; and everyone from the highest council to the most menial servant was to be present. By midnight or thereabouts almost all the revellers would be riotously drunk – that, too, was a part of the tradition – and there would be no better opportunity to spirit Jessamin away.

Indigo's part in the plan was relatively simple. She had only to ensure Jessamin's compliance, and that she could easily do. One dose of a certain powder in the watered wine that the Infanta was allowed to drink on special occasions, and Jessamin would sleep soundly until the following day. She would administer the drug during the festivity, and the Infanta's weariness would be seen as nothing more than over-excitement; Indigo would bear her back to her apartments, away from the revellers, and there Leando would be waiting. Luk was safely installed at his great-grandmother's house; in the

251

quiet outer gardens, Grimya would be keeping watch; the palace gates would be all but unguarded, and they should be able to slip away with no one the wiser until Jessamin was sought in the morning.

On the day of the prenuptial celebration, Indigo's nerve was close to breaking point. Outwardly she went about her tasks calmly enough, but her mind was raging, stomach churning. She started at the slightest disturbance, found herself unable to concentrate on anything for more than five minutes at a time, and again and again she returned to her ornate cabinet to look at the powder she'd prepared and check yet again that the constituents and the dose were right.

But at last the sun began to set, and the lanterns were lit and the musicians struck up and the first cups of wine were poured; and with Hild at her side Indigo led Jessamin along the paved path and into the women's garden to greet her guests.

The Infanta was radiant. In keeping with the celebration's significance – her last public appearance as a maiden – she wore a simple sky-blue gown, and her only jewellery was her betrothal ring and a plain circlet of sea-pearls set upon her head. Her hair was unbound, cascading over her small shoulders, and she carried herself with grave dignity as, with her chaperones, she moved among the throng.

Indigo allowed herself to be distracted for a while by Hild, who was brimming with the latest palace gossip. She was grateful for the respite, and nodded and laughed and expressed shock as required while Hild recounted new scandals and anecdotes. But all the while a part of her attention was on Jessamin, and her mind was waiting, calculating the right moment . . .

When the moment came it was almost too easy; almost as though Jessamin herself were conniving at the conspiracy. She came to Indigo smiling and asking for another drink: could she have just a *little* unwatered wine, as this was such a special night? Indigo made a show of relenting, hardly able to credit her good fortune: unwatered wine would better disguise any lingering taste from the powder, and she poured

Jessamin a cup of the palace's best vintage. The drug went in unnoticed by anyone, swiftly dissolving in the ruby liquid, and the Infanta sipped appreciatively, rolling her eyes sidelong at Indigo with the shared, illicit pleasure of this venture into adult status.

The powder didn't take long to work. Within fifteen minutes Jessamin had found a chair and sat down, and though she resisted determinedly, Indigo saw the yawns she was trying to hide. Hild noticed, too, and frowned.

'*A-na*. The little *chera* is tired, I think. Too much excitement – they forget she is only a child!'

'I gave her a little unwatered wine,' Indigo confided. 'I know I shouldn't have done it, but she so wanted to feel like a grown woman . . . ' She shrugged with a pretence of helpless guilt, and Hild grinned.

'Probably a good thing for her. She got another rehearsal for the ceremony tomorrow, and then the day after – well, we all know about that. Maybe better she should get some sleep.'

Indigo silently thanked the Earth Mother. 'Yes; I agree.' She smiled. 'I'll take her back to her room. She won't be too disappointed.'

'Ah; good thing. Do you want help?'

'No, no; I can manage.'

Jessamin was tottering as Indigo helped her away, out of the garden and back along the path. Few noted their departure; as she'd anticipated, the wine was doing its work and the women were cheerfully giving way to its effects. By the time they reached the quiet sanctuary of the apartments the Infanta's head was lolling against Indigo's arm; Indigo didn't undress her, but simply settled her on her sleeping couch, pulling the light covering up over her small body and then watching until she was certain that the child was soundly asleep.

Thus far, all was well. Returning to her own rooms she looked at the timepiece on a side table. An hour to go before Leando was due; they'd given themselves a wide margin for the sake of safety. All she now had to do was return to the gathering, and await the prearranged moment.

By the time it came, the dancing had begun. Freed

from the restraints of more formal occasions, some of the women had persuaded the musicians to conjure some of the old fishermen's dance tunes out of their memory, and a lively hornpipe was in full swing when Indigo looked up and saw that the lower edge of the rising moon was just touching the top of the vine-hung east wall. She rose, setting down her cup – she'd drunk nothing but fruit juice and water all evening, though no one had noticed – and, easing behind a small knot of servant girls who were clapping in time to the dance, slipped beyond the lamplight, and away to her rooms.

Leando was waiting for her. The room was lit only by one lamp; but even in the gloom she could see the tension in his face.

'They're dancing.' She kept her voice pitched low. 'And I doubt if there's a sober head among them.'

'It's the same with the men. Even Augon Hunnamek's the worse for drink, thank the Great Goddess. And Jessamin?'

'Sleeping, for the past hour. She won't wake.'

'Good.' Leando glanced about him. 'Have you gathered everything you want to take with you?'

'I only need travelling clothes for myself and Jessamin, and my harp. They're ready.'

'Then we'd best waste no time.'

They moved together in the direction of Jessamin's apartments. The distant sounds of the revels carried faintly through the open window, though there was barely a breeze to stir the night air. Indigo took a final, lingering look at the room that had been her home for more than a decade. She felt no wrench, no regret; only a sense of emptiness as the gulf of an unknown future yawned before her. She forced it back; opened Jessamin's door, and stepped through.

There was no light in the Infanta's bedroom, but a thin moonglow was filtering in at the window, casting a metallic patina on the rich wall-hangings and on the sleeping couch. It was enough to reveal that the couch was empty.

'*Leando!*' Indigo's frantic hiss brought him hastening to the door. She started to turn towards him in agitation.

And behind the bed, a shape moved with a convulsive twist.

Intuition shrieked a warning, but Indigo's conscious mind was slower to react. For a crucial instant the warning didn't register – and in that split second the silver serpent smashed up from the shadows, over-turning the couch, a table, a child-sized chair, as its huge, uncoiling length whiplashed out of a darkness beyond the physical planes and burst across the room at her throat.

Chapter XXII

Leando's yell of horror clashed with the maddened, insensate hissing of the massive snake as it launched itself towards them. Indigo glimpsed the twin, venomous fangs flashing at her face, and flung herself aside, slamming against the door-jamb and ricocheting off-balance to the floor. The serpent reared above her, its head almost touching the high ceiling, and as it hissed again she saw water showering from its sinuous scales, droplets glittering like hurled gems. To her horror, she realised that this was no mortal creature but a manifestation of a demonic force, its existence straddling the physical and astral worlds. She started to scrabble to her feet, one arm coming up in an instinctive move to shield herself –

And suddenly Leando's figure was interposed between her and the serpent. The blade of a long knife glinted in his right hand, he was raising it, muscles bunching to strike –

'Leando, no!' Indigo screamed. 'It isn't mortal – you can't kill it that way!'

Her last words were eclipsed by a noise that seemed to explode out of nowhere, battering her senses in a massive concussion of sound. It was the roar of water, a cataract, a tidal wave, thundering through the room and bowling her frantic cry into oblivion. Blue-green light flared, and with it came a sense of twisting distortion – the walls were bending, familiar shapes warping, rippling as though a furious sea had burst violently in and drowned the world. Gasping – she knew she breathed air, but had to fight the illusion that tried to tell her her lungs were filling with water – Indigo attempted to launch herself towards Leando, meaning to push him out of the way before the monstrous snake could bear down on him. But she felt as if she was pushing against a huge wall of water that pressed her back, bore her down, slowed every movement to drifting, dreamlike fragments. She couldn't co-ordinate her limbs; her arms seemed to be floating, and everything was happening so slowly, so *slowly* –

'Leando!' she cried again. The word broke into boom-ing, drawn-out syllables, and their pitch fell, distorting, vanishing far below the audible spectrum before they could reach their goal. Treacherous, deep-water light rippled across Leando's face as he turned agonisingly slowly towards her, arms outstretched like a floundering swimmer, eyes wide with shocked in-comprehension. Indigo pushed with all her strength against the air's huge resistance, flailing, struggling towards him, trying to make ground before it was too late –

The snake struck. Unhampered by the illusion that snared Indigo and Leando, it seemed to move with the speed of lightning, blurring into a silver-grey streak of energy as it speared down. Indigo twisted about in an involuntary reflex – and as she did so, the image of the room burst into ten thousand shards, collapsing in on her like imploding glass. The illusion shattered, time meshed back into place, and she heard Leando's yell of pain and terror as the snake's sinuous body whipped around his, pinning his arms, sending the knife spinning uselessly from his trapped hand. He fell back, the demon crashing with him to the floor; then his cry rose to a hideous, strangulated pitch as the silver coils tightened, driving the breath from his lungs as it sought to crush him.

Indigo's nerves and muscles blazed like fire as the shock of release from the spell's thrall hit her. Un-balanced, she careered across the floor, collided with a couch, spun back, tripped over a rug and fell full length, her limbs unable to adjust fast enough to the change. She saw Leando and the serpent writhing together on the floor, the reptile's huge head darting, jaws wide as it sought to close in for the final death-strike; heard the snap of bone –

257

She propelled herself across the floor, striving to reach the fallen knife which had skidded under a chair. Her fingers closed round the hilt; she tried to scream mentally for Grimya, but there was no time to rally her mind behind the alarm. She didn't pause to think, but jack-knifed to her feet and launched herself at the thrashing chaos of human limbs and serpentine coils. The knife sheared down and plunged through silver scales into pulsing flesh; foul liquid, neither blood nor sea-water but with elements of both, and stinking like decaying seaweed, spurted from the wound and spattered her face and arms. The snake hissed and the hiss became a snarl that sounded appallingly human: its great head swung round and for a split second Indigo was staring straight into the tiny, mindlessly vicious eyes. Then, so fast that she couldn't have hoped to evade it, the silver tail lashed out, slamming into her with tremendous force. She was hurled back across the room as though she weighed nothing, landing on a table and smashing it to splinters as the flagon, wine-cups and ornaments that had stood on it flew in all directions. The back of her skull struck something that didn't yield, and Indigo sprawled, stunned, among broken wood and glass and spilled wine.

Concussion turned the world crimson. Her mouth opened but no words would come; her senses were running amok, sights and sounds rushing at her in mad confusion. She saw the snake, bleeding still but seemingly unhindered by the wound she'd inflicted; it writhed anew and Leando's torso was momentarily revealed, twisted into an impossible contortion between the crushing coils. His head jerked, turning towards her; she saw his tongue, black and swollen, protruding between lips flecked with bloody foam, and his eyes bulged insanely from their sockets. Again came the sickening sound of bone breaking, and a ghastly rattling rasped from Leando's throat as his agony redoubled. Then the snake's head came up again, poised, the jaws opening wider, wider –

Indigo's paralysis broke in an inchoate howl of protest, a desperate plea to any benevolent power that might hear her. She reached out, hands clawing towards Leando as though to tear him bodily away from the monstrosity that was squeezing the last of his life – but nauseous dizziness rose like a wave, the room swelled and bulged at her, she couldn't reach him –

The serpent's head speared down, and the most hideous sound that Indigo had ever heard in her life broke through to her reeling senses as the snake ripped out Leando's throat, breaking his spine, shattering the bones of his neck and jaw and all but tearing his head from his shoulders. A crimson fountain erupted over the squirming bodies and Indigo's last, appalling vision was of the demon serpent twisting about and lurching towards her before red changed to black and then to nothing as she lost consciousness.

For one moment in the wake of mayhem the room was utterly still. Indigo lay motionless; Leando – torn almost in two and barely recognisable as human – was crumpled flotsam in a sea of his own blood. And between them the great serpent hung like a poised, supernatural sword, head swaying from side to side, eyes glittering as hard and cold and insensate as diamonds as their gaze flickered from one to the other. It hissed once more, the sound chilling against the sudden silence. Then, slowly, slowly, it began to curve over, the evil stare fastening now on Indigo's still figure, the jaws starting to gape, poising, anticipating . . .

Sound in the corridor outside. Not audible to the human ear, but the flat reptilian skull came up sharply, the body swivelling towards the source of the disturbance. Unnatural senses probed beyond the door, encountered heat, movement, mammalian consciousness –

The serpent vented another hiss and this time there was frustrated anger in the sound. Abandoning its new prey it whipped around, wrapping its sinuous body again about Leando's broken corpse. The man's limbs jerked in a spasmodic, horrible mockery of life as the coils took a tighter hold: then the outlines of both snake and man shivered like a desert mirage. For an instant the outlines of the room shimmered through their

259

solidity; then came a sound that was not sound, an inrushing of air, and, taking with it Leando's remains, his blood, all traces of his physical existence, the demon vanished from the world just as Grimya hurled herself against the far side of the door.

Indigo! Indigo! The she-wolf projected her frantic cry again and again as she scrabbled at the door of the apartments. The wood bore deep gouges from her claws, but the door stayed obdurately closed; the latch was down on the far side, and nothing Grimya could do would force it to open. She squirmed about, turning this way and that in her distress as she realised that her efforts were useless, and fought down the urge to howl aloud.

Indigo's cry of horror as the serpent slaughtered Leando had reached the wolf where she waited by the darkened side gate in the palace gardens, knifing into her mind in silent telepathic agony. It had taken her less than a minute to streak through the shrubbery and into the palace to her friend's aid: but now she was stymied at this last moment, and Indigo wouldn't or couldn't answer her desperate attempts to communicate.

She prepared to launch her full weight at the door in the hope that she would prove stronger than the latch; but even as she backed away in readiness, she heard voices and footsteps behind her, and then someone called, 'Grimya?'

Panting, the she-wolf spun round, and saw Hild with two of the Infanta's servant girls approaching along the corridor. Eagerly Grimya wagged her tail, then whined and scratched at the door.

'What is matter? Your mistress not back from the revels yet, and you can't get in?' Hild came forward and laid her hand on the small round knob that worked the latch from the outside, and which Grimya hadn't been able to manipulate. The door swung open; Grimya wriggled past into the room, almost upsetting the nurse – and saw the smashed table, the spilled wine, and a dark, limp form lying among the debris.

Hild had been turning away, but the she-wolf's strangulated howl startled her back to the door. In the poor light it took a few moments for the scene to register, but when it did she gasped in dismay.

'*A-na!*' She hastened towards Indigo's limp form as her companions crowded in the doorway, then her hand gestured frantically. 'Light some more lamps! Is too dark to see proper!'

Sobered, they hastened to obey, and as the room lifted from gloom to relative brilliance Hild crouched beside Indigo, running practised hands over her scalp, neck and limbs. Then she looked up and gazed about the room. Nothing was out of place; nothing but the table which Indigo had broken as she fell.

'She must have drank too much.' There was wry humour in her voice. 'Come back here, falled over and hit her head. Clerri,' she flapped a hand at one of the goggling women, 'go and find a physician, yes? I don't think Indigo is much hurt, but is better to be sure.' Then, as the girl ran away, Hild paused. 'Grimya? Eh, what is?'

Grimya was standing in the middle of the room, staring at a spot on the floor. There was nothing visible there, no debris, no spillage, but the she-wolf's hackles had risen and her nostrils were quivering. A low growl rumbled in her throat.

'Grimya!' Hild said again. 'Is all right – don't be foolish!'

Amber eyes flicked uncertainly to her, and Grimya licked her own muzzle. The woman was right; there was nothing to see, no danger, no threat. Yet she had scented something, sensed it . . . her nostrils flared again and she realised that the aberration was gone. Yet there had been *something*.

She whined, and turned back to Indigo. Hild climbed heavily to her feet, pausing to rub the wolf's ruff. 'There now; is all right. I better see for the Infanta.' She picked up a lantern and, crossing the room, eased the adjoining door open. The lamplight fell on a tranquil scene; furniture undisturbed, the coverings of the couch barely rumpled; a glint of honey-gold showed Jessamin's curled, sleeping form under the silk sheet. Hild smiled and withdrew, quietly closing the door behind her.

'All is well,' she said. 'I think no harm done.'

The remaining women sighed with relief. Only Grimya, crouched now like an alert guardian beside Indigo's unconscious form, felt an inward shudder that told her Hild didn't know even a part of the whole truth.

'Calm, Grimya; calm.' Augon Hunnamek raised placating hands as the she-wolf rose uneasily, ears back and eyes glittering with protective zeal. She subsided, though a little reluctantly; and physician-mage Thibavor pursed his plump lips in a smile.

'She is a remarkable animal, my lord. She has sat vigil beside her mistress through the night and all day; she refuses food and even water unless it's brought directly to her.'

As the physician bent to examine Indigo, Augon continued to look at Grimya. His pale eyes looked sympathetic, which puzzled the wolf.

'Your mistress isn't seriously hurt, Grimya,' he said. 'It's simply concussion, and my good physician here has administered a potion to ensure that she sleeps comfortably.' He hesitated, then laughed self-consciously. 'Listen to me, Thibavor: I'm talking to the creature as though she could understand what I say. Last night's excesses have addled my brain.'

'If I may say so, my lord, your powers of recuperation have proven stronger than those of the rest of us,' Thibavor replied with a touch of dry humour. 'My apprentices have been called to attend many aching heads in the palace today – even the Infanta woke only with the greatest reluctance this morning.'

Augon chuckled softly. 'Then you'd best instruct them to replenish their supplies of nostrums. I suspect there'll be a few hundred more sufferers to contend with after tomorrow.'

'Indeed, my lord.' The physician straightened, satisfied. 'I detect no signs of complication. With quiet and rest, she should recover quickly enough.'

262

'I'm glad to hear it.' The pale gaze slid sidelong to the older man. 'Thank you, Thibavor.'

Aware that he was being dismissed, Thibavor bowed and left. Augon made as if to follow him, then paused and turned back to the couch where Indigo lay. Grimya tensed, but made no further move, only watched intently as the Takhan took Indigo's limp hand and chafed it gently between his own.

'Poor Indigo.' He spoke reflectively and – again, Grimya was disconcerted – with what sounded like genuine affection. 'What lies behind this little mystery, eh? Drunk? No, I don't think so. You can hold your wine as well as any man I've ever encountered. And what of your lover Leando? Missing from the revels for most of last night, and now no sign of him in the palace or at his home.' He sighed, and released her hand at last, shaking his head slowly. 'Ah, Indigo, I had such hopes for you and Leando Copperguild; and now this. You have been a good friend to me, and it saddens me to see my friends suffer when my own happiness is complete. We shall find a way of making amends, my bride and I. We shall find a way.'

Grimya stared after him as he quietly left the room, and her mind was racing. *Leando?* Surely he hadn't been responsible for Indigo's accident? And, more shocking still, it seemed to her that Augon Hunnamek's concern for Indigo was genuine. His small speech had been reinforced in the shallow levels of his mind that her telepathy enabled her to probe. Grimya knew nothing of what had happened last night, save that somehow Indigo and Leando's plan had gone drastically wrong; and until Indigo woke she couldn't find out the truth. She'd jumped to the conclusion that it had some connection with the demon: but it seemed she'd been wrong.

Baffled, Grimya uttered a small, uncertain whine. Whatever the risk, however great the urgency, there was nothing she could do until she could communicate with Indigo. Until then, she had no choice but to wait.

Due to the powerful soporifics administered by Thibavor, who had deemed it wise that she should be kept sedated as long as possible, Indigo didn't regain consciousness until very early the following morning; the day of the Takhan's planned marriage. Although dawn was only just breaking the palace was already a hive of frenetic activity, and as the sun's first rays cleared the early sea mist, portending a brilliant day, the first celebratory bells began to ring out through the city.

The return to wakefulness was slow and lethargic as she reluctantly dragged her mind and body up through the heavy layers of the drug's after-effects. When at last she opened her eyes, wincing even though there was little light in the room, the first thing she saw was Grimya's anxious face looking over the edge of the couch at her.

'In-digo – you are awake at ll . . . ast!' There was intense relief in the she-wolf's voice. 'You slept for so long, I was w-*worried*!'

'How . . . ' Her voice cracked and she swallowed convulsively, trying to ease the dryness in her throat. 'How long have I been here?'

'Two nights and a day,' Grimya told her.

For a moment Indigo didn't realise what that implied; then her eyes widened. 'Great Mother, *what day is it*?'

'The day of the w . . . edding.'

'It *can't* be! Oh, sweet Goddess, where is – ' And the words cut off as the memory that Thibavor's drugs had suppressed suddenly awoke. 'Oh, no,' she whispered. 'Leando . . . '

'He is m . . . *issing*,' Grimya interjected. 'I heard them say so. In-digo, what happened to you that night? What went wrr . . . wrong?'

Indigo didn't answer her. She was staring across the room, but blindly, and her eyes reflected stark horror. The wolf repeated her question more urgently, and at last awareness seemed to return.

'Leando's dead,' Indigo said hollowly. 'The demon killed him.' She covered her face with her hands.

Grimya whimpered, her hackles bristling. '*How?* What h-*appened*?'

There were starkly clear images in Indigo's mind. She

264

remembered every gruesome moment; but remotely, as though it had happened not to her but to someone else. And in that terrible, detached way she found she could describe all that had taken place: the serpent's appearance, the attack, Leando's grisly death. Yet as the story came out, Grimya grew more agitated with every moment, and at last she could contain herself no longer.

But, Indigo, there is something wrong! She switched to telepathic speech, aware of her vocal limitations. *When I found you, there was no Leando and no blood. Only the table you must have broken when you fell. And the Infanta was in her room, soundly asleep!*

Indigo started to shiver. 'That monstrosity was more than physical, Grimya. Somehow it managed to exist in the demon world and in our own at the same time.' And to what ghastly dimension, she wondered, had it taken Leando's broken corpse? The shivering culminated in a racking shudder as she realised how narrow her own escape had been.

'We've got to stop him,' she said harshly. The blanket that covered her slid to the floor as she got unsteadily to her feet. 'Now that we know for certain what he is, now I've *seen* what he's capable of – '

Grimya interrupted her. 'He?' she said aloud.

'What do you think that serpent was? It was the usurper's doing; it was Augon Hunnamek!'

'No,' Grimya said. 'I d . . . do not think it was.'

Indigo stopped and stared at her. 'Grimya, what do you mean?'

Grimya bristled. 'He was *here*, Indigo. While you slept, he came to see you. There was no one else in the rr . . . oom but me.' And she recounted what had happened, what Augon had said as he looked down at Indigo and stroked her hand. Indigo listened in taut silence, and when the wolf finished she didn't react for a long time; only a small frown appeared on her face, deepening as she thought.

At last she spoke. 'But . . . if he didn't send that creature . . . '

'He had no reason to pretend,' Grimya told her. 'He c . . . ould not have known that I would understand.'

Slowly, Indigo sat down again, Grimya's point was valid: why *should* Augon have lied when, as far as he was concerned, there had been no one to overhear him? It made no sense at all. Unless there was another factor involved; something she hadn't even begun to guess at.

Karim's last message. It was the only avenue left unexplored. There *had* to be a clue there . . .

She got to her feet again, then swayed as giddiness overtook her. The cabinet: she had secreted the copy she had made of Karim's sigils in a small drawer. She must find it –

'Indigo, wh-at is it?' Grimya asked anxiously as Indigo stumbled to the small cupboard. 'You are n . . . not well, you shouldn't exert yourself!'

'I have to find it!' Indigo slumped on to an ornate chair, and, with hands that didn't seem to want to co-ordinate, pulled the drawer open and rummaged through its contents. She felt sick, dizzy; her fingers found the parchment, fumbled it out –

And a silver-backed card came with the parchment, and fell on to her knee.

Her vision blurred as she stared at the card, but she didn't need clear focus to know what it was. And it confirmed her rising fear.

'Oh, Goddess . . . ' She struggled to her feet, catching the chair-back to steady herself as the dizziness redoubled. 'Grimya, this is the key. It *is*, it's – '

Before she could finish, the door opened.

'Indigo!' Physician-mage Thibavor's eyebrows lifted in shock. 'What is this? You should be abed!'

'I have to find – ' Indigo lurched suddenly. The mage crossed the room in a few rapid strides and caught her before she could lose her balance altogether.

'Woman, you're in no condition to do anything save return to your couch! Here now; lean on me.' He began to lead her away from the chair.

'You don't understand,' Indigo mumbled. 'It's urgent, it's *vital* – '

'Nothing is more urgent than preserving your own health.' Another, younger man – his apprentice – had followed Thibavor into the room and stood hovering by the door. The mage snapped his fingers imperiously. 'Merim, the blue phial from my satchel if you please. I fear the lady has not recovered as quickly as I'd hoped.'

Indigo felt too disorientated to argue as she was lowered gently but firmly back on to her couch. Her head ached fiercely, and the room seemed to be revolving slowly around her; she tried to focus on Thibavor's face and failed.

'Please,' she said indistinctly. 'I – ' But the words wouldn't come; she couldn't think with any clarity.

Thibavor clicked his tongue. 'Lie back. That's better. Now; look at my hand, and tell me how many fingers – ' And he stopped, frowning as he saw what Indigo was clutching.

'What's this?' He plucked the parchment from her, not noticing the card as it fluttered to the floor. For a moment he studied the sigils, then the frown deepened. 'How did you come by this paper?'

Indigo shut her eyes. 'I . . . found it . . . '

'A piece of script in the private cryptography of the mages? Someone has been most careless!' He stared at the parchment again. 'Still, it's nothing of any import. Merely a date. Now, then.' He took the phial that his apprentice held out, poured a few drops from it into a cup and filled the cup with water. 'Drink this, my dear. It will take away the sickness and allow you to sleep. Sleep is the best healer of all.'

From its slow spinning, the room seemed now to be pulsing, the walls swelling in and out; and when Indigo tried to open her eyes again, light glared painfully and set her head pounding afresh. She couldn't have risen if she'd tried; she felt too ill, and it was all she could do to swallow the sedative without retching.

Grimya whimpered in confusion as Indigo's head lolled and her consciousness faded into the stupor of deep sleep; as the mage stepped back she looked up helplessly at him, her tail between her hind legs.

'Good dog.' Thibavor bent down and, cautiously but not unkindly, stroked the top of her head. 'See now; your mistress is sleeping.' And, turning to his assistant: 'I'd thought the concussion less severe, but one can never predict how long the effects of a blow to the skull might last.' He sighed. 'And rather unfortunate, today of all days; not to mention inconvenient for all concerned.'

'Will she sleep for long, sir?' the apprentice asked.

'Oh, a good few hours at least.' Thibavor smoothed down his dark green robe, fussily settling the folds back into place. 'And when she wakes again the miasm should be considerably lessened. Now, Merim, you'd best carry on without me; I must bathe and prepare myself, or I shall be late for the procession. Oh, and you'd best inform the palace stewards that one of the Takhan's favoured guests is indisposed, and will be unable to attend the marriage ceremony.'

Chapter XXIII

'And thus in the beloved name and beneath the shining
light of the Great Goddess, Queen of the bountiful sea,
Progenitor of the good earth, Mistress of the beneficent
sky, do we call all joy and blessing upon these most
devoted servants of Her choosing, and count ourselves
blessed in our turn that they shall nurture and guide and
rule over us fruitfully and blissfully in the wisdom and
the enlightenment of the Mother of us all.'

A cascade of sound from a hundred tiny bells shimmered down through the temple's vast dome as thirteen
young girls, all dressed in the iridescent colours of the
sea, lifted up the ancient golden Net that was, of the
Three Gifts of Khimiz, the Takhina's own symbol, and,
spreading out in a wide half-circle, stood on tiptoe to
hold it over the bowed head of the small but composed
figure who stood in their midst. Light from a multitude
of lamps shone down on the figure's loosed honey-gold
hair, which seemed to catch fire like a waterfall of flame;
the thousands upon thousands of tiny gems that
encrusted her gown and the long cloak streaming behind
it also blazed with brilliance, so that for one breath-
taking moment Jessamin's entire frame shone like an
earthbound star. Slowly, the Net was lowered; as it
touched her hair the Infanta turned with grave dignity to
face her new husband, magnificent in viridian green and
cobalt blue silk, a sea-king personified, who held out to
her the golden Trident in which his power and authority
were vested. Their hands touched, clasped; then Augon
Hunnamek kissed his bride, first on the mouth, then at
each budding breast, then at her stomach, and finally on
her bare, gold-ringed feet. A hushing, emotional
whisper of pent breath released susurrated through the

temple as the rapt onlookers softly voiced their approval, and high above, where the ship shrine loomed aglow with lanterns, the huge white sails belled gently outward as though breathing their own blessing on the scene.

In the midst of the congregation, behind the foreign nobles but taking precedence over most Khimizi guests, Luk Copperguild stood rigidly at his great-grandmother's side and felt tears trickling down his cheeks as sheer misery washed over him. This was the final abandonment. His father, so lately restored to him, was gone again and no one would or could tell him where. Indigo, his trusted friend, was not here. And Jessamin, his beloved Jessamin, was turning her adoring face to the man she had pledged to love and serve for the rest of her life, and was utterly lost to him. So many promises broken, so many hopes dashed; and all Luk felt was bitter, bitter hurt at the magnitude of the betrayal that ate down to the core of his soul.

He bowed his head, trying to stem the tears but truthfully not caring if anyone should notice. He was empty, a husk, all love and all trust dead within him. As hollow as the spaces where his father should have been, where Indigo was to have stood, where Phereniq was missing from this great and momentous gathering. He didn't care about disguising his grief and being manly and stoical. It didn't matter any more. *Nothing* mattered any more. He only wished that he could die.

When Indigo woke for the second time, the room was dark. At first the dimness disorientated her; but after a few moments she realised that many hours must have passed since she sank into the enforced sleep. Night had fallen – and panic gripped her as she realised what that meant.

'Grimya!' She sat up with a violent start. 'Grimya, where are you?'

'I am here!' A warm muzzle pressed against her groping hand. 'Indigo, are you all r . . . right?'

She hesitated. There was a residue of queasiness and

her limbs felt weak; but her head no longer ached, and her vision was normal. It seemed that Thibavor's drugs had done their work well and she was recovered. But her sleep had been plagued with dreams which were only now returning to her mind in disjointed fragments. She had dreamed she was back in the desert, with Agnethe and baby Jessamin, and again Agnethe had been pleading with her to flee . . .

And, so suddenly that it was like a physical shock, an old memory slipped into place as the last words Thibavor had said to her before she fell asleep meshed with the dream of Agnethe.

'Grimya, what's the hour?' Panic made her voice shrill. 'How long have I slept?'

The she-wolf's eyes gleamed unhappily. 'It is too l . . . late,' she said, her tone dismal. 'It is all over.'

'Oh, dear Goddess . . . ' Indigo stumbled to her feet. 'Is the celebration still going on?'

'I th . . . *ink* so,' Grimya said. 'There are lights in the grr-eat hall, and I have heard mu-sic.'

Phereniq. She had to find Phereniq. But she would be at the festivities, she couldn't reach her –

'She is not.' Grimya picked up the thought from her mind. 'I hh-eard a servant say that she would not go, and that she is in her rr . . . oom.'

For a frozen second Indigo stared at her, hope and fear fighting for precedence. Then she turned for the door.

'Quickly, Grimya.' She cursed the sedative's after-effects that made her movements so slow and clumsy. 'We must find her – oh, I've been such a *fool*!'

Grimya hastened after her as she stumbled out of the room. The palace corridors were lit but empty: everyone from the highest minister to the lowest servant had some part to play in the wedding festivities, and there was no one to see and wonder at Indigo's unsteady progress as she and Grimya headed towards Phereniq's rooms. Distant strains of music floated in at open windows; their goad, together with the fresher air of the passages, cleared the last of Indigo's stupor, and reaching the astrologer's door, she knocked loudly and urgently. There was light spilling under the door; a shadow moved across it but the knock wasn't answered. Indigo turned the handle and pushed, but the door wouldn't open; the bar on the far side was down and the wood moved only an inch before resisting.

'Phereniq!' Indigo hissed sharply through the crack. 'Phereniq, it's Indigo – I must see you. Open the door!'

Grimya's ears pricked alertly, *She is there*, she communicated. *I heard a footfall.*

'Phereniq . . . ' Indigo bit down hard on her lower lip, then decided to throw caution aside. 'Phereniq, I know you're there, and I have to talk to you. If you don't open the door, I'll break it down!' To emphasise her point, she shoved her shoulder forcibly against the unyielding panel.

Wait, Grimya said. *I think she –*

Before she could finish there came a sliding sound from the far side, followed by a click. Indigo drew breath, glancing quickly along the passage, then pushed. The door opened, revealing a room in chaos. Cups had been overturned, cushions and ornaments thrown about, and the floor was littered with the charts that were Phereniq's pride, torn and trampled.

Phereniq was walking slowly and stiffly back to the chair where she had been sitting. She didn't look at Indigo, and when she spoke her voice was slurred and barely recognisable.

'What do you want?'

Indigo stepped into the room, quietly closing the door at her back. 'Phereniq, I have to talk to you. It's very urgent.'

'I don't want to see you. I don't want to see anyone.' Phereniq reached the chair and slumped down, keeping her face averted. 'Go away, and leave me alone.'

On a nearby table stood a water-pipe and a collection of phials, some tipped over and spilling their contents across the table's polished surface. Indigo crossed the room in three rapid strides, forcibly turned Phereniq's head around – she offered no resistance – and stared into her eyes. They were glazed, the pupils grotesquely dilated, and filled with a terrible blend of venom and grief. Indigo's heart sank. The Earth Mother alone knew what mixture of drink and drugs Phereniq had taken in an effort to shut out the reality of what was happening elsewhere in the palace. She must have been closeted alone in this room all day, with only her wine and her potions to console her . . .

She started to say, 'You *fool!*' then stopped as anger was replaced by pity. 'Oh, Phereniq . . . ' she finished despairingly.

Phereniq's eyes glittered and she twisted her head away. 'I don't want your sympathy. I don't want *anything*. Just leave me *alone.*' She pressed her face to the chair-back, one arm dropping limply over the side.

Indigo stared at her. She didn't want to be cruel, but need had to take precedence over pity. Turning to the table, she rummaged through the chaos until she found what she wanted among the piles of herbs and concoctions. A strong purgative: whatever Phereniq had used to bring herself to this pass, it should be a sure antidote. She measured a triple dose into a hastily-poured cup of water and held it to the older woman's lips. 'Phereniq, drink this.'

Phereniq swatted at her with a petulant hand. 'No,' she said mulishly.

'*Drink* it!' Indigo was the stronger of the two; twisting Phereniq's head round again she held her jaw forcibly until she was certain the draught had been swallowed. Then as the astrologer sagged back once more she set the cup down and crossed to the window, dragging back the heavy curtain and flinging the window open to the courtyard and the cooler night air.

From the chair came a protesting mumble. 'Oh, sweet Mother – ' Phereniq was trying to struggle to her feet. Indigo went back to help her, guiding her to the window. She let her stumble out into the night unaided, then listened to the pathetic sounds of her vomiting among the bushes. Afterwards there was silence for a few minutes: then, unsteady but upright, her hand trembling as she gripped the window-frame to support herself, Phereniq came slowly back into the room. Her gaze met Indigo's, sweat beading her forehead and trickling down the sides of her jaw.

'Sea Mother . . . ' she whispered. 'My head *hurts* so . . . '

There were two more jugs on the table, miraculously not overturned. Indigo found fruit juice in one and poured a generous measure. As she helped Phereniq to her feet she felt shamed by her single-mindedness, which left her no room to express the sympathy she felt. But to reverse the effect of the drugs was vital: Phereniq *had* to be sober.

The astrologer slumped on to the nearest couch. This time when Indigo held the cup to her lips she didn't try to argue but drank gratefully, easing the constriction in her throat. Then, her voice blurred still but a little stronger, she mumbled, 'Why did you do that to me? Why couldn't . . . couldn't you leave me be?'

Indigo set the cup down and took hold of her shoulders. 'Phereniq, I'm sorry. I didn't want to hurt you, but I have to ask you something, and I must have an answer *now*.'

Phereniq shook her head slowly. 'I can't tell you anything. I can't tell anyone anything, not any more.' A long, unsteady sniff. 'I can't help you.'

'You can – you're the only one who can!' Indigo insisted. 'Phereniq, *please* – '

'For the Goddess's sake, will you stop *plagueing* me!' Phereniq wrenched free the arm which Indigo had gripped in her agitation. 'Isn't it enough that you've come in here when I want to be left alone, that you've . . . ' Her voice tailed off, and suddenly she sighed miserably. 'Damn you. Damn *all* of you! All right, all right: I shall have no peace, shall I, until I've given you what you want.' She wiped the back of one hand across her mouth, then added savagely, 'Ask.'

Pushing down a fresh stab of guilt, Indigo fumbled in her reticule and brought out a small piece of parchment. She unrolled it and held it out to Phereniq. 'Can you tell me what these symbols mean?'

Phereniq peered at the parchment. She was still having difficulty focusing, and she swayed back and forth, trying to adjust her vision. At last she looked blearily up into Indigo's face.

'It is a date, written in the script of the mages. What of it?'

'You can read the script?'

'Of course I can!' Phereniq struck the parchment with an unco-ordinated hand, almost knocking it out of Indigo's grasp. 'Is that the question that's so urgent, that makes you come here pestering me?'

'Yes.' Indigo told her implacably. Her heartbeat had quickened: Phereniq had confirmed what Thibavor had inadvertently told her, and suspicion flared into certainty. 'But there's more, Phereniq. Please – I want you to construct an astrological chart from these sigils.' She paused, touching her tongue to her lips and wondering if she could risk being brutally honest. Surely, she told herself, she had nothing to lose. 'I know you love Augon,' she continued. 'I know what his marriage means to you, and how you grieve. But if you do truly love him, you *have* to help me now, because if you don't, you may lose him – not just to his new wife, but irredeemably and forever!'

A flicker of uneasy intelligence, like a dim candle, returned to Phereniq's eyes as she looked up again. 'Wh . . . what do you mean?'

'I don't know; not for certain. But . . . ' Far away she could still hear the music from the palace's great banqueting hall. Another hour, perhaps even less, and the Takhan and his new Takhina would be walking through the long arch of linked and upraised arms as the wedding guests sang them to their nuptial chamber. And then –

'Phereniq.' Indigo made one last, desperate effort to break through the fog of misery and intoxication that ensnared the older woman. 'I might be wrong; in fact I pray that I am. But it could be that Augon Hunnamek is in terrible danger.'

Acute silence followed her words. Phereniq continued to stare at her, still confused; but something was struggling towards the surface of her mind. An alarm; unformed as yet, but growing. Instinct, intuition . . .

'Give me that.' Abruptly Phereniq reached out and snatched the parchment from Indigo's hand. Her expression rigid, she rose unsteadily to her feet – Indigo moved to help her, but was waved petulantly away – and stumbled across the room to where her worktable stood against one wall. A plain, uncushioned chair stood before the table; Phereniq slid on to the seat and began to pull charts and books from a recessed shelf above the table-top.

Indigo felt hope rise within her. 'Phereniq, do you – '

'Be quiet,' Phereniq interrupted harshly. 'I want *quiet*.'

Indigo and Grimya exchanged a look, and silence fell as Phereniq began to work. How much time passed before she raised her head again, Indigo couldn't tell; there was no timepiece in the room, and from here she couldn't see the slow transit of the moon. She longed for a cup of wine, but fiercely resisted the temptation, forcing herself to drink fruit juice instead. Thibavor's sedative was still lurking in her veins, and above all she needed a clear head.

At last Phereniq was done. She sat back, pushing away the chart she had drawn: and when she turned to look at Indigo her face was haggard.

'Where – ' Her voice cracked. The silence was like an electric charge of lightning. '*Whose natal hour is this?*'

Very slowly, Indigo stood up. 'What is it?' she breathed.

The astrologer also rose, and for a moment they faced each other like adversaries across an unasssailable gulf. Then Phereniq spoke again. Her voice had changed: the drugged miasma was gone, replaced by strength – and harsh fear. 'This chart . . . it is the most hideous augury that I have ever seen.'

Grimya's ears pricked alertly, and Indigo began to feel queasy. 'Tell me about it,' she said tensely.

Phereniq glanced down at the chart she had drawn, and Indigo saw a shiver of revulsion run through her body. 'Whatever was born at this hour on this day was not human,' she said, and now there was a peculiar, chilly catch to her voice. 'The Sea Mother Herself would

276

turn in revulsion from such a monstrosity, for it portends something soullessly, implacably maleficent. The sixth hour of the fourteenth day under the constellation of the Serpent . . . it's not a happy augury at the best of times. But in the year that this nativity refers to, the year of Blue . . . ' she shivered again, then looked up at Indigo. 'At that hour, a conjunction occurred that was almost a twin to the conjunction that will come tonight. There was an eclipse of the moon. And the Serpent-Eater had risen . . . '

'You said *almost* a twin . . . ' Indigo's voice was tense.

'Yes.' Reluctantly, Phereniq's gaze slid back to her chart and her hand hovered over it, as though reluctant to make contact with the paper. 'Indigo, this was worse. *Infinitely* worse. There was a third malign aspect which entered the conjunction, and it was in retrograde. I can't explain it fully to you; it's too complex – but if any child had been born at that hour, that child would be the quintessence of evil!'

'Wait,' Indigo said, wishing fervently that she'd been a more attentive pupil. 'The year of Blue – what do you mean by that?'

'It's a way the Khimizi mages have of numbering the years; a cycle of colours, though it's rarely used now. The last Blue year was . . . ' she consulted her chart again, ' . . . eleven years ago.' And suddenly Phereniq's face froze as she realised what she had said.

'Eleven years,' Indigo repeated hollowly. Certainty was growing, though she fought it, telling herself it couldn't, *couldn't* be true.

'No,' Phereniq said. 'Not that – it isn't what you're thinking, Indigo. The Infanta was born on the *thirteenth* day, and in the eleventh hour, not – '

Indigo cut across her. 'Was she?'

Phereniq's eyes widened. 'Oh, sweet Goddess, the palace records . . . ' She swung round, staring down at the chart again. 'No!' she said vehemently. 'It isn't possible! They wouldn't have let such a creature live; they would have *known*, they would have *slain* it – '

Indigo thought again of Agnethe in the Falor desert;

277

a helpless, frightened woman striving to protect her baby, caring for nothing but that her little one should be saved. In her drugged sleep, she had relived that moment with terrible clarity. And she knew now that it had been far more than a dream.

They will kill her. They will kill my child . . . It had lain dormant in her memory, long dismissed and forgotten. But now she knew what the Takhina had been trying to tell her.

'Indigo?' Phereniq was looking at her, suddenly tense as she saw the stark horror on Indigo's face. 'What is it?'

'Agnethe,' Indigo said.

'What of her? Indigo – '

'When I encountered her in the desert, years ago – ' Indigo began to breathe rapidly, stumbling over the words, 'she told me – I'd forgotten, all this time I'd *forgotten* – she begged me to abandon her and get Jessamin away. She told me that they would kill her child, because she'd been born on the *fourteenth* day of the Serpent, in the hour before dawn!' She met Phereniq's stunned gaze, her face white and haggard. 'Oh, Phereniq . . . ' And the truth, the hideous, unassailable truth that made mockery of more than ten years of searching and striving, surged into her mind like a tidal wave. '*Jessamin is a demon!*'

They ran, Phereniq straining every muscle in her ageing body, gasping with the pain of exertion but driven by a fear and horror that eclipsed all other considerations. Through the twisting corridors, down marble steps – once Phereniq tripped and fell; Indigo dragged her to her feet and, with no breath for thanks, the astrologer stumbled on again – towards the banqueting hall, from which the strains of joyful music, an obscenity now, seemed to taunt them. They reached the long, wide entrance hall, the double doors now only yards ahead of them – and with an ululating wail of despair Phereniq slid to a halt.

Indigo too slewed and stopped, looking back at the older woman. 'Phereniq! What's wrong?'

Phereniq only moaned again, pointing to the floor. Indigo looked, and understood. The veined marble was covered with flower petals. In her frantic race she hadn't noticed them, but she instantly recognised their significance. Traditionally, a newly wedded couple were showered with such petals as they left their nuptial celebrations. She and Phereniq were too late – the triumphal procession to the bridal chamber had already taken place.

She ran to where Phereniq was standing paralysed. 'Where is the bedchamber? Tell me, quickly!'

Phereniq raised an unsteady hand, pointing. 'At – at the end of that passage. But it will – '

Indigo didn't wait to hear the rest, but ran back the way they had come, Grimya racing beside her. They rounded a corner – and she stopped as she saw the gold-chased door ahead of her, with the Takhan's seal in its centre and two liveried militiamen standing guard at a discreet distance from the portal.

Seeing her, one of the guards hastened forward, holding out one hand in a forbidding gesture. 'No further, madam! This corridor is barred to all but – '

'Please,' Indigo gasped, 'let me pass! The Takhan is in danger!'

The guards exchanged a look, and one grinned wryly, pressing two fingers to his own skull in a signal that meant, *drunk*. The other turned back to Indigo. 'Why don't you return to the celebrations, madam? There's enough fun to be had there without risking the Takhan's wrath in the morning!'

'You don't understand!' she pleaded. 'This isn't a jest – the Takhan's life may be imperilled!' Footsteps sounded behind her, and she turned to see Phereniq hurrying towards her. Relief swept through her. 'The lady Phereniq will tell you; she has seen the portent – Phereniq, they won't listen to me! Tell them; for the Mother's sake, *tell* them!'

The guards began to look worried. Phereniq was not under any circumstances a practical joker, and the look on her face seemed to support Indigo's entreaty. The astrologer had regained her composure; she cast one terrible look at the closed door, then grasped the nearer guard's arm.

'How long ago did the Takhan and his bride retire?'

The man hesitated. 'An hour, lady; maybe a little more.'

Phereniq tensed. 'Open the door,' she said.

'Madam, that's not possible! Not on – '

'I said, *open* it. I take full responsibility – *in the Sea Mother's name, do as I say!*'

Torn between duty and fear, the guard was about to dissemble further when another sound silenced them all. Grimya, unnoticed in the argument, had slipped past the two men and run to the nuptial chamber. She had lowered her head to sniff at the foot of the door: and suddenly, shockingly, she uttered a howl that stabbed through to her human listeners' marrow.

'Grimya!' Indigo pushed the militiamen aside and raced towards the she-wolf. 'What is it, what – oh, no, *no! Phereniq!'*

Water was seeping under the door from the room beyond. It was no more than a trickle, pooling in a slight dip in the marble; but it was brackish, edged with yellowish scum. Like the water at the edge of a tide-pool that the sea had left behind . . .

She heard the guards curse as they, too, saw it. One of the men elbowed her out of the way, hurling his weight against the door; there came the small sound of the latch snapping, and the door swung open.

Soft light, tinted amber and crimson by the coloured glass chimneys of low-burning lamps, met their eyes, highlighting the huge and magnificent sleeping couch with its domed canopy and cloth-of-gold drapings. Gold and silver plates containing a feast of delicacies glinted untouched on a side table. Over a chair, Jessamin's wonderful bridal gown lay pristinely folded.

And the sleeping couch was empty.

Or so, in those first seconds, it seemed.

Indigo was the first to recognise the dissonant note in the room's opulent comfort. A shapeless mass, discordant with the rich draperies, trailing down from the couch's edge . . . and a sharp, acrid and familiar smell

280

assaulted her nostrils. *Seaweed*. There were strands of it caught up in the curtains, a tangled, slimy web wrapped around one of the canopy's posts. The embroidered coverings, rumpled from recent use, looked dark. Wet. Crimson and wet. And in the deepest shadows, where the drapings hung low over the silk pillows, was a motionless, formless *something* . . .

An unhuman screech shattered the silence then, and a figure plunged past Indigo. The guards tried to stop Phereniq, but their reactions were too slow; she evaded them and flung herself over the threshold, sprawling on the thick carpet, her hands clawing, struggling, reaching out for something that lay on the floor. She snatched it up, and her cries rose shriller and louder still, demented, howling like a wolf herself, as she rocked wildly back and forth with her prize cradled in her arms and her face twisted beyond recognition. Instinctively Indigo stumbled forward, thinking to pull her away – but then the guards' moans, the ugly but painfully human sound of someone retching, and Grimya's horrified yelp assailed her senses all at once. She stopped – and then stared, eyes widening, mouth working, gasping uselessly like a landed fish, as she saw that Phereniq's bare arms were smeared from wrist to elbow with crimson, and that what she cradled, like a beloved child, in her embrace was the gore-soaked, eyeless and partially devoured head of Augon Hunnamek.

Chapter XXIV

'I loved him. I loved him so much, though he never wanted me, not in that way. But I loved him. And now he's *dead* and I've *lost* him, and I might have saved him, and – and – oh, Indigo, what am I going to *do*?'

In Indigo's room, sheltered from the uproar and confusion that had turned the palace into a madhouse, Phereniq clung tightly to Indigo and sobbed like an abandoned child. The room was an oasis in the midst of chaos. Around them, lights blazed in every corridor and crevice and throughout the nightbound gardens; armed men ran back and forth, shouting conflicting orders while women wailed and lamented – and almost every able-bodied soul in the palace had been swept up in the search for their beloved, abducted Infanta.

Indigo had striven to make them understand, but her pleas and protests were useless. To those who witnessed the carnage in the bridal chamber there was only one possibility – some unknown assassin, human or otherwise, had murdered the Takhan as he lay with his new bride, and the bride herself – of whom there was, of course, no trace to be found – had been carried off by her husband's slayer. The assassin must be found, and, if she had not already shared her lord's fate, Jessamin must be saved. Hampered by the screaming Phereniq, her own shouts and arguments lost in the uproar, Indigo had finally despaired and, unable to make anyone listen to the truth, had taken Phereniq away to sanctuary.

Now, alone with the weeping astrologer but unable to help her other than by trying to soothe her desperate outpouring of grief, Indigo felt her own misery like a leaden weight within her as again and again she cursed herself for her blindness, her failure to realise the demon's real identity. Deep down a small voice argued that she shouldn't blame herself; she had known only that the demon was in Simhara, and with no other clues to guide her the assumption that Augon Hunnamek was the source of the evil had been all too alluring. But that was no comfort now, either to her or to Phereniq. There *had* been clues, if she'd only had the wit to see them. But she had been so certain of her path that she'd ignored the evidence before her eyes, and now it was far too late to put right the terrible mistake she had made. Leando was dead, as were Karim, Mylo, Elsender, Macce's crew – and, by a terrible irony, the man she had spent ten years plotting to kill, yet who would, had she known it, have been her most valuable and powerful ally. She had not loved Augon Hunnamek as Phereniq had done, far from it: but now that the veil had lifted from her eyes she could see him as he truly had been: painfully human, flawed, but no worse a man than most.

For the hundredth time, Macce's accusing shade rose in her mind. *Sobbing into your wine and saying prayers for lost souls.* But she couldn't even do that; couldn't express her shocked and overloaded emotions in any way that had any meaning. She felt drained, empty; a useless, hopeless failure.

Phereniq's weeping was at last beginning to subside, fading firstly to hiccuping sobs and then to an empty silence. At last, with dignity, she sat up, detaching herself from Indigo's supporting arms, and turned to a side table where one jug of wine and another of water stood. Her hand touched the wine, hesitated, then moved on and she unsteadily poured herself a cup of water. Indigo had prepared a mild calmative; wordlessly she offered it, and with a small, grateful smile Phereniq added a little to her cup.

'Forgive me,' she said in a small, quiet voice. 'I should . . . should have had greater control of myself. I should have learned that much in all these years – ' she choked the words off, shutting her eyes against a fresh wave of pain.

Indigo squeezed her arm gently, aware that she was in

shock and anxious not to provoke a fresh breakdown. 'Don't, Phereniq. Don't be afraid to grieve.'

Phereniq shook her head. 'It isn't that. I just feel – so *desolate*.' She sipped at the water, trying to calm herself. 'He was . . . everything to me. But you know that, don't you? I've tried to hide it, but you've seen the truth.' A long pause. 'There weren't so many years between us, did you realise? Between Augon and me. Not so many. Less than you'd think, to look at my grey hair and raddled body. But our paths were different: so very different.'

'Phereniq – '

'No – no, please; let me say it. It helps, a little.' She sniffed. 'I loved him. Ever since the first day I saw him, and that was more years ago than either of us would have cared to remember. But he . . . well, it was different, you see. In those days he was a warrior; it was all he knew. And as warriors do, he grew stronger with age; almost more youthful. But I . . . ' A shudder ran the length of her spine, then she turned to look at Indigo's face. Her eyes pleaded. 'I was very handsome once. Can you believe that?'

'Yes,' Indigo told her softly.

She smiled, a quirk without mirth. 'A lot of men – among my own people – found me beautiful. But he wanted me in other ways: he wanted my skills, my powers. He *needed* them, to help him in his ambition, and I gave them gladly. I sacrificed my youth to the demands of my studies and to further my abilities, because I loved him. And he . . . ' Another, longer hesitation. 'He was grateful to me. He knew what I'd done for his sake, and he was always grateful. But I didn't want his *gratitude*. I wanted . . . ' She shook her head, mutely protesting the futility of her own words. 'What does it matter now? What does *anything* matter? He's dead. I keep trying to tell myself it isn't true, but it is. He's . . . *dead*.'

Indigo stood up and walked slowly towards the open door that led to the courtyard. Grimya sat by the threshold, tail twitching restlessly as she stared out into the darkness: at Indigo's approach she looked up, but there was no communication from her mind. Like Indigo, she didn't know what to say or what to do; Phereniq's grief served only to increase her sense of helplessness.

And yet, Indigo thought, there must be something they could do. Macce again: the little Davakotian's bitter taunt about making amends had gone deep. There must be *something*.

She started to turn back to Phereniq, who had lapsed into tight, miserable silence, but before she could speak the inner door opened. Indigo looked up – and saw Luk on the threshold.

The boy's face was deadly pale, and he'd obviously been crying. He came in, shutting the door behind him, then hesitated as he saw Phereniq, who was hunched over on the couch and hadn't reacted to his arrival. Indigo made a quick signal, indicating that Phereniq didn't wish to be troubled, and Luk hastened across the room to her. His voice was a tense whisper.

'Indigo – have you heard anything? Is there any news? I've been helping the search in the south gardens, and no one would tell me anything!'

He, like all the others, knew nothing of what had really taken place, Indigo remembered with a feeling of cold dread. He wasn't even aware of what had happened to his father, and she didn't know how to break the truth to him.

'Luk.' She drew him away from the couch and Phereniq. 'Luk, there's something I have to tell you, and you must be brave – '

His expression froze. 'Jessamin? Have they – '

'It isn't that, Luk. They haven't found her. And – I don't think they will, because . . . ' She drew a deep breath. 'There's something about Jessamin's past that you don't know. She – she isn't the person that we've always believed her to be.'

'I don't understand. What are you talking about?' Luk's tone was abruptly tinged with aggression.

She couldn't couch it gently: there was nothing for it but to be cruelly honest. 'Please, Luk,' she said, 'listen to me. The Takhan has been murdered. Everyone thinks – '

Indigo!

Grimya's warning erupted in her mind before she could say any more, and with it came a violent jolt of fear. Indigo whirled round – then froze.

Under the lintel of the garden door, framed between the gently shifting curtains was Jessamin.

She wore a sky-blue silk nightgown that left her smooth-skinned arms bare. The garment was soaking wet, water pooling on the floor beneath the hem, and traces of seaweed clung to the skirt. By an obscene irony the shimmering Net, the Gift of Khimiz, was still draped over her hair, which curled beneath it in soft wisps about her face. Her eyes, huge and dark, were wells of undiluted innocence. And sweetly, a little shyly, she was smiling.

'Jessamin! Oh, Jessamin!' Luk's face lit with love and relief. He started towards the window, reaching out to the Infanta – then stopped in mid-stride as relief changed to chagrin and then, suddenly, to horror.

Jessamin continued to smile. But she too was now holding out her arms, and the palms, upturned, were slick and crimson and dripping. And her lips were parting, her jaw widening impossibly to a gaping, unhuman maw, exposing two needle-thin, curving fangs, and a black, forked tongue that flickered and flickered and flickered.

Luk leaped back, slamming against Indigo with such force that he almost knocked her over. His body heaved violently as he struggled for breath, tried to speak, tried to deny what his eyes and ears were telling him; but he could only utter a wordless mewl. On the periphery of vision Indigo saw Phereniq, every muscle paralysed, staring with insane eyes at the smiling child; while Grimya, belly to the floor and ears laid flat, was backing away, snarling her fear. And the thing that was Jessamin was metamorphosing. The sodden nightgown shimmered and fell away, and beneath it was the body not of a child, but of a huge, undulating, silver-scaled snake. Only the arms and bloodstained hands remained, and the golden curls – though the head beneath them was that of a serpent. And from the flattened skull, above the grinning jaw, Jessamin's honey-dark eyes gazed out with ghastly tranquillity. Those eyes swivelled in their sockets, until they focused on Indigo's face. And a voice that hissed and rustled like water, alien, reptilian, cruel, said:

'Ah, my friend and nurturer. I have come back to give you my thanks, and to bid you farewell at last.'

Indigo stared back at the monstrosity that the Infanta had become, feeling sick with loathing. She couldn't answer: the demon was taunting her, mocking her foolishness and failure. And there was nothing, *nothing* she could do against it.

'I have a parting gift for you,' the Jessamin-serpent continued. 'A token by which it may please you to remember me in the times to come. For you will have a great deal of time to regret your mistakes, will you not? Here, Indigo. A memento of me. And of the man you so sadly misjudged, whose foolish and misplaced love was the catalyst that set me free from my mortal chrysalis. Cast this upon Augon Hunnamek's sea grave, for his bride has no further need of it.' It raised one of its child's hands to the Net that covered its golden hair. The Net came free, its jewelled fish glinting brightly in the lamplight. And carelessly, contemptuously, the demon screwed the precious relic into a crumpled ball before throwing it down at Indigo's feet.

'I am almost complete now,' the susurrating voice said with sweet, malignant triumph. 'Tonight I go to lie in darkness and in silence, so that my strength may gather and my power reach its zenith. But I shall return. In the cold hour before dawn, the Serpent-Eater will rise – not the devourer of serpents as you believed for so long, but the Serpent who Devours. And in that hour, you will see me again. For in that hour a new reign will begin – and then all Khimiz shall know my true name!'

An appalling, barely human sound came from Phereniq's throat, but the demon ignored her. The evil head turned, slowly, sinuously, making one final, contemptuous sweep of the room. Then the golden hair shrivelled, falling like dead leaves from its skull, and

287

the dark eyes shrank and paled to tiny, unhumanly expressionless pinpoints. The child's arms withered, flesh puckering, desiccating, until all that remained was bare, white bone which in its turn browned, blackened, and crumbled to dust that blew away on the night breeze. Hideous in its entirety the serpent rose, uncoiling, shimmering with a nacreous aura. The light around it blazed brighter – Indigo saw the scene distort violently, as though she had been suddenly plunged deep underwater, and the sound of a vast wave breaking boomed in her ears. She cried out –

And the serpent was gone.

She was on the floor, swept back and bowled over by the huge but silent concussion that had accompanied the demon's vanishing. She saw Grimya struggling to her feet, Phereniq on her knees and clinging to the side of the couch, Luk –

Luk was getting up. His eyes were wildly dilated, their stare fixed immovably on the open window where the thing that was Jessamin had swayed and mocked them all. Indigo reached out towards him; the movement alerted him and his head snapped round. For one moment their gazes met, locked. Then Luk gave a terrible, inarticulate cry of grief and agony, and ran, as though a thousand more demons pursued him, out of the room and away down the corridor beyond.

Slowly, Indigo rose to her feet. Grimya, the fur along her spine still bristling, crept towards her. The wolf's voice in her mind was filled with fear.

Indigo, what are we to do?

The sibilant, unhuman whisper of the demon still echoed in Indigo's head. *In the cold hour before dawn, you will see me again.* The monstrosity had returned to the sea, to await the deadly conjunction that would complete its transformation and realise its full potential. They had no more than a few short hours before it would return. And when it did, nothing and no one could prevail against it. As the demon serpent had sneeringly predicted, a new reign would begin – and Indigo knew that it would spell the end of all hope in Khimiz, and the ruination of her quest.

But what could she do? She had no powers, no weapons, nothing with which to combat such an evil. Yet every part of Indigo's being was screaming at her to act, to do something, *anything*. She couldn't accept defeat. There *had* to be a way –

A sudden movement alerted her, and she turned to see Phereniq, still on her knees, crawling towards the crumpled bundle of the Net that the demon had thrown mockingly into the room. Reaching it, the astrologer caught it up and began, with shaking but determined hands, to unravel it, smoothing out the crushed folds, reverently untangling the tiny gem-fish. Her tears sparkled like jewels themselves as they fell among the shining mesh.

'Phereniq.' Indigo moved to her side and crouched down, laying a hand over her feverishly working fingers.

Phereniq looked up, abject misery on her face.

'Phereniq, listen to me,' Indigo said urgently. 'There's very little time left to us. We have to find a way to fight this demon!'

Phereniq turned her head away. 'There's nothing we can do,' she said desolately. 'Let it come. Let it destroy us all, if that's what it intends. I don't care any more.'

'You *have* to care! We can't give in now – we have to do something to stop this!'

'Why?' Phereniq asked bleakly. 'What does any of it matter, Indigo? It's all gone; it's all over.'

Indigo's lips narrowed. She didn't want to be cruel, but Phereniq had to be jolted out of her apathy. She had few enough allies as it was: she couldn't afford to lose another.

She said: 'Is that what Augon would have said? Or what he'd have expected to hear from you? I thought you were his champion, Phereniq, but it seems your loyalty doesn't extend as far as you've always pretended!'

Phereniq's head jerked round and her fists clenched in the tangles of the ancient Net, almost tearing it. 'You know nothing about it!'

'Oh, but I think I do. Enough, anyway, to realise that

whatever else he might have been, Augon Hunnamek wasn't a coward!'

Anger flashed in the astrologer's eyes. 'How *dare* you – '

'Revenge, Phereniq,' Indigo interrupted, ignoring her. 'Revenge for what happened to him. Don't you want that? Wouldn't it be a final tribute, if you loved him as much as you say?' She smiled grimly. 'And if your own life doesn't matter to you any more, then surely the risk is worth it?'

The goad had gone home; she saw it, saw the flicker of uncertainty, then of hope. But the hope quickly died.

'How?' Phereniq said hollowly. 'How can I avenge him? I'm neither a sorceress nor a mage. And even if I were, what use would that be? Do you think even the greatest sorcerer in the world could prevail against that – that *thing*? It's beyond the power of any human being. Only the Sea Mother Herself could stop it now.'

She was worrying at the Net again, distractedly, unaware of what she was doing – and suddenly something slipped into place in Indigo's mind. She went rigid as Phereniq's last words sank home. Only the Sea Mother . . .

'Phereniq,' she said in a tight, peculiar voice. 'The Net – it's one of the Three Gifts, isn't it: the gifts given to Khimiz by the Sea Mother, centuries ago?' She paused, then 'Don't you remember the legend?'

Phereniq's hands stopped their restless movements and she stared at the folds of mesh, letting them slip through her fingers in shimmering handfuls. 'The legend . . . ?'

'Yes! The Three Gifts are more than symbols – they were given by the Goddess's own hand, and they're the foundation on which Khimiz was built! Don't you see what that means? They have power – *true* power!' Her heart was pounding suffocatingly with excitement, fear, hope. 'Couldn't those gifts be called upon to help us now?'

Phereniq's expression began to change. 'Dear Goddess . . . but *how*?'

'I don't know: but there *has* to be a chance! Phereniq,

the other two Gifts – do you know where they are?'

'The Trident is in the palace,' Phereniq said breathlessly. She was rapidly becoming infected with Indigo's excitement. 'It was carried back from the temple in the procession, and displayed in the great hall.'

'And the Anchor? What of the Anchor?'

The astrologer shook her head. 'According to all the records, it is – or was – kept somewhere in the temple, but I don't know where. I've never seen it, nor do I know anyone who has.'

'The ship-shrine has an anchor,' Indigo said eagerly. 'Could it be – '

'No, no. Like the Net and the Trident, the Anchor is made of solid gold. The one on the shrine's merely a wooden model; it isn't the Gift. But the real Anchor *is* in the temple.'

'Then we must find it!'

'Yes.' Phereniq looked out into the courtyard, where the moon was tracking slowly across the sky, and shivered. 'There's so little time left . . . Indigo, you must go ahead to the temple. Take the Net; begin the search for the Anchor. I'll fetch the Trident, and follow you as quickly as I can.'

Indigo was half way to the door when abruptly the astrologer spoke again.

'Indigo – '

She stopped, looked back.

'Even if we find the Anchor,' Phereniq said tautly, 'I don't know how to awaken any power the relics contain. But I feel in my bones that this is the only thing we can do. And we must at least *try*.' A ghost of a sad smile touched her lips. 'You made me realise that. And you also made me realise that I do want vengeance for Augon. I like to think that he . . . he would have appreciated that.' Her voice faltered: she put a hand up to her face, then shook her head emphatically. 'No; this isn't the time or the place for more grief. Go, Indigo – hurry. And pray that the Sea Mother will look kindly on us tonight!'

291

Chapter XXV

The vast dome of the Temple of Mariners shone like an eerie, earthbound moon, reflecting pallid light on to the marble steps as Indigo and Grimya ran up the sweeping flight. The real moon hung high and remote, its light drowning the stars and giving the sky the intensity of black velvet; the eclipse hadn't yet begun, but it was all too easy to imagine the first edge of shadow beginning to move across the cold, glowing disc. Behind them the sea muttered restlessly: tonight its voice sounded menacing, portentous; and Indigo had to fight an urge to keep looking back over her shoulder. Images of Karim's huddled, drained carcass assailed her mind, and it was all too easy to imagine that one of the long, distorted shadows stretching across the plaza might not be a shadow at all, but would suddenly move and come gliding, slithering noiselessly over the flagstones to intercept their path. She was thankful when, without incident, they finally reached the sanctuary of the temple entrance.

The Temple of Mariners never closed its doors. After dark there were few if any attendants present, but the lamps within burned constantly, and at almost any hour of day or night at least one pilgrim could be found engrossed in private contemplation before the huge, silent shrine. Wading through the pool and emerging into the temple's dim interior, Indigo was chagrined to see two figures by the prow of the great ship, standing under the shadow of the carved and unnervingly lifelike figurehead. She hadn't bargained for this . . . but as she stared at the two in frustration, Grimya's ears pricked up – then suddenly the wolf started forward, and Indigo heard the relief in her mental exclamation.

Indigo, it is Luk!

Startled by the sound of her claws on the mosaic floor, the two figures raised their heads. Luk's face was a deadly pale oval; from this distance Indigo couldn't see his expression in the gloom, but his stance was tense. The other figure had also stiffened, and Indigo's steps abruptly faltered as she recognised the boy's companion.

'Macce . . . ' Her voice echoed oddly in the emptiness; it sounded as though someone else had spoken.

'I found him here.' Macce put an arm about Luk's shoulders, as though to protect him from some imagined threat. 'He's . . . told me about it. Everything.' A pause. 'Is it true?'

'It's true,' Indigo said.

'All of it? About the Infanta, the demon? And the Takhan being murdered?'

'Every word.'

Grimya, aware of the tension, drew back and whined softly, but her thoughts weren't clear. For a few moments there was silence, while Macce and Indigo watched each other warily and Luk stared at the floor. Then, brusquely, Macce said:

'I think we'd better talk, Indigo. I know what I said last time we met, but things have changed, haven't they?' She made an attempt at a smile, but it didn't reach her eyes. 'Don't think I'm retracting anything I said then; I'm not. But I understand more of the story, and if I can't sympathise with what you did in the past, at least I can see the dilemma you're faced with now.' She gave Luk's shoulders a gentle and reassuring little shake, then released him and walked slowly to where Indigo stood. Lowering her voice, she added, 'And I'm sorry for the boy. I want to help him, if I can. If anything can.'

Despite the fact that Macce's approach was at best reserved, Indigo felt warmed by the simple fact of having another human soul who knew the truth and, to however small a degree, understood. It gave at least the illusion of greater strength.

'I don't know if anything can be done now,' she said,

'we've so little time. But there's just one hope, though it's a slender one.' And she told Macce of how she had discovered the demon's true nature; of the grisly deaths of Leando and Augon Hunnamek, and of the legend of the Shrine and her desperate need to find the Anchor that would complete the triad of the Sea Mother's three gifts. When she finished, the little Davakotian hunched her shoulders, staring around her at the quiet, dim temple.

'Even three days ago I'd probably have said you were mad,' she replied. 'Even after what I saw on that voyage, I'd . . . no; never mind that.' Her hard gaze met Indigo's again. 'But after what the boy told me – '

'He doesn't know yet that his father's dead,' Indigo said sombrely. 'I . . . don't know how to break it to him.'

'Ah. Sweet Sea Mother, that's a task I don't envy.' Macce suppressed a shudder. 'And the Takhan dying like that . . . well, I'd better believe what you've told me, hadn't I? And it seems to me that you need all the help you can get. Better safe than sorry, eh?'

Indigo looked away. 'Macce, I – '

'No. There isn't time for that; and as I said before, your remorse isn't any use to me. If the Anchor's here, we'd best start looking for it. And Indigo – talk to Luk. Don't tell him about his father; but see if you can reassure him. He's been badly frightened, and a lot of the things he believed in have been swept from under his feet. But he still trusts you, and if you can give him something to hope for now, it might help.'

Indigo nodded. 'I understand. And – thank you.'

Macce made a disgusted noise. 'Thank me if I'm the one who finds the Anchor, Indigo. Without that, it looks as though we're all going to be lost.'

By the time Phereniq arrived at the temple, they had found no clue to the whereabouts of the missing third Gift. Indigo, nearest to the entrance, saw the astrologer as she picked her way carefully through the pool, and went to meet her. Phereniq was perspiring with exertion, and in her arms she carried a carefully wrapped bundle which she gratefully handed over.

'Forgive me for taking so long,' she said breathlessly. 'It's a longer walk than I remembered, especially with such a burden. And the light outside is growing tricky.' She shivered. 'The eclipse is beginning: we have very little time left. Have you – ' And she stopped as, for the first time, she saw Indigo's companions. 'Luk!' Astonishment and relief mingled. 'You found him – I'm so thankful. But who is the woman?'

Quickly Indigo explained Macce's presence and belief in their cause, though without telling the full story. Macce and Luk had seen them now and were approaching; Luk hesitated for a moment as he stood before Phereniq, then wordlessly ran forward and hugged her, trying to express what he couldn't bring himself to say. Phereniq was visibly moved, as Indigo had been when, following Macce's advice, she had spoken quietly and privately to the boy before the search began. Now that the initial shock of learning Jessamin's true nature had abated a little, Luk was striving with all his will to face and accept the cruel revelation, and – though a part of him still protested miserably against the inevitable – to help in the desperate quest to destroy the monster that his beloved Infanta had become.

Indigo briefly introduced Phereniq and Macce, and the Davakotian reported the results, so far fruitless, of her search.

'There's nothing on the east side that looks even remotely promising,' she said unhappily. 'Carvings and decorations by the score, but not an anchor among them. In fact, I'm beginning to suspect that the only anchor in the whole temple is that wooden one on the Shrine, and that's peculiar in itself.'

Indigo looked again at the carved anchor. Supported by a slim chain slung from the side of the huge ship, its flukes rested on the floor beneath the keel, creating the illusion that it alone moored the Shrine within the temple hall. It was nearly as tall as she was, and unlike most of the Shrine's artefacts its surface was plain, though years of diligent polishing had given the old wood a warm, burnished sheen that made it glow like bronze. Her curiosity aroused by Macce's strange observation, Indigo walked back towards the anchor, carefully sidestepping the Net which she had left folded beside it, and laid a hand on the hard, shining surface.

At her throat, the lodestone on its thong pulsed as though a live coal had momentarily touched her skin.

The others looked up in alarm at Indigo's cry of shock, and Grimya came running. *Indigo! What is the matter?* The she-wolf's anxious query was echoed aloud by Phereniq.

'I – don't know.' Indigo stepped back, clutching at the lodestone, which still felt hot though the burning sensation had gone. 'I touched the anchor, and . . . ' She reached out again, tentatively, then drew her hand back, afraid to repeat the experiment. It was as if the lodestone had tried to tell her something.

Then she looked down, and saw that the golden net's folds had been disturbed. Her foot must have brushed against them as she stepped up to the anchor . . .

'Phereniq!' Her voice was hoarse with excitement. 'Bring the Trident over here, *quickly*!'

The astrologer hastened towards her, Macce and Luk on her heels. The Trident was still wrapped; Indigo took the bundle and pulled away the cloth, lifting the relic out, and Macce let out a soft whistle of admiration.

'What a beautiful thing!' Reverently she reached out and touched it. 'Such craftsmanship – is it really as old as the legends say?'

'No one knows for sure.' Indigo, too, was gazing at the Trident, turning it slowly in her hand so that the dim light caught it. It was, as Macce said, beautiful. The slim shaft was of solid gold, tapering into the form of a stylised golden fish from whose mouth sprang three barbs tipped with diamonds fine-cut to arrow points. Green and blue gems girdled the haft and the fish's tail, where they formed the shape of a curling wave.

But there was more than beauty in this ancient artefact. Indigo felt it now, surely and instinctively; the Trident seemed to be quivering in her hands – or perhaps her hands were trembling – and the lodestone pulsed again like a tiny, living heart. She turned back towards the wooden anchor and reached out to touch it again, her excitement growing.

'It's here,' she said. 'Somehow, this anchor and the one we're seeking are connected. But I don't know – ' And she gasped as, under her palm, she felt the anchor shift.

'It moved!' Macce hissed. 'I saw it; it *moved*!'

And she was holding the Trident, as before she'd been touching the Net . . .

'Phereniq – ' Indigo gestured frantically towards the astrologer. 'The Net – '

Hope and a glimmer of understanding dawned in Phereniq's eyes. She gathered up an armful of the shimmering mesh, moving forward and almost tripping over the Net's tangles in her haste. Indigo caught hold of her flailing hand, meaning to steady her –

And the wooden anchor rocked as though something had struck it a massive physical blow.

'*Great Mother!*' Phereniq froze.

'Touch it!' Indigo cried. Suddenly, gloriously, she *knew* what was about to happen. 'Touch the anchor – complete the link!'

Still clutching the Net, Phereniq stumbled forward. Her fingers made contact with the polished wood, and light flared suddenly in the temple, making Macce and Luk jump back and Grimya yip in alarm. The brilliance lasted only a moment before winking out – and as her eyes struggled to readjust, Indigo felt the wood beneath her hand splitting, crumbling. She heard Phereniq gasp and realised that she, too, was experiencing the same phenomenon. Then, with a snapping sound, the entire frame of the carved anchor splintered and collapsed.

And, shining softly in the gloom, the third golden Gift of Khimiz, preserved for so long within its wooden casing, rocked gently at the end of the quivering chain.

Macce whispered a Davakotian oath, then smothered it, remembering where she was. Luk and Grimya could only stare, dumbfounded; while Indigo and Phereniq both felt the thrill of achievement and vindication course through them like heady wine.

'It was here,' Phereniq whispered. 'It was *here*, yet no one knew. And you . . . ' She looked quickly at Indigo. 'How did you – ' she couldn't finish the question.

Indigo didn't even try to answer her. Their hands were still linked, she grasping the Trident, Phereniq clutching the Net; and she thought: the Three Gifts are together. But what now? Goddess help me, *what must we do now?*

High above their heads a soft sound intruded on the quiet, but no one paid it any heed. Indigo shut her eyes, trying desperately to cudgel her mind's turmoil into clear thought. They had the Gifts, the Sea Mother's protective talismans. But how to use them? Power was awakening in the temple. She felt it like chained lightning in the air; already it had broken through the dormancy of long years to bring the Anchor from its age-old hiding place. But something still held it back. Something was *missing*.

The sound she had heard before but ignored came again. A sighing, as though something huge had exhaled gently far overhead. Involuntarily Indigo looked up, past the lowering bulk of the ship-shrine's hull to where the white sails towered ghostly into the dome. There was a light at the mainmast; not the glow of the temple lanterns but dimmer, colder; a diffused and remote shimmer. Faint reflections played across the fabric of the sails and she realised that they were moving a little, shifting, though there was not even the slightest breeze to disturb them.

And without forewarning, a voice spoke in her head. A vast voice, gentle yet ferocious, and awesomely powerful, that uttered one word.

'*UP.*'

Indigo's involuntary cry clashed with an inarticulate yell from somewhere behind her. Shocked, she spun round, and she saw that the entire temple seemed to be shimmering with the same chilly, diffused radiance she had glimpsed among the ship's sails. Standing rigid by the prow, her figure ghastly in the nacreous glow, Macce stared back at her with wild, dilated eyes.

'*It spoke!*' There was naked terror in the small woman's voice. 'Indigo, it *spoke*! I couldn't hear, but I saw it, I saw the mouth move!' And, seeing that Indigo didn't comprehend, she stumbled towards her, pointing back over her shoulder. 'The figurehead! The image of the Sea Mother – oh, Goddess help me, *I saw her lips moving!*'

In her panic she had abandoned Khimizi for her native tongue, and neither Phereniq nor Luk knew what she was saying. But Indigo understood. Her stomach seemed to turn over within her, and again she looked swiftly at the white sails towering overhead. They were belling, the light that shimmered through them growing stronger – and as though in final confirmation of the wild, impossible thought that smashed into her mind, there came a groaning creak from one of the age-old timbers under its crust of gems.

'*Run!*' she shouted with all the power her lungs could muster. '*The steps – run!*' And without waiting to see if the others were following, she raced towards the flight of wooden stairs that led up to the ship-shrine's deck. As she ran she felt the air growing thicker, charged with static energy as the power latent within the Temple of Mariners began to agitate. Everything was haloed in cold, blue-green radiance; sparks crackled in her own hair and in Grimya's fur as she raced beside her; and the Trident in Indigo's hand glowed with a searing light, as though it were white-hot.

They reached the steps and Grimya leaped ahead of her, looking more like a blue-grey ghost than a living animal as she streaked up to the deck. Gaining the rail, which shimmered with a corona of agitating colours, Indigo looked back to see Luk coming after her and helping Phereniq with the Net. Only Macce hung back, gazing up white-faced and frightened and suddenly vulnerable from the floor below. Indigo felt a flood of sympathy and warm affection fill her, and called down, holding out one arm as though she could take Macce's hand and reassure her.

'Macce, don't you see it? Don't you see what the Sea Mother has granted us, and what She wants us to do? We need you, Macce – we need your skills now as never before!'

For a moment the little woman hesitated; but a stronger and deeper emotion was taking over from the fear in her eyes. Then the ship creaked again – and Macce moved, darting forward and taking the steps three at a time, to fling herself on to the deck and into Indigo's welcoming arms. Indigo hugged her as though she were a long-lost sister, then found herself pushed fondly but forcibly aside as Macce swung round and surveyed the deck in a single glance. Her look was still wild, but with excitement now.

'Get to the sheets!' she yelled, pointing to the ropes that secured the sails' lower edges amidships. 'Indigo, you know what to do – show the boy, and – '

The rest of her words were drowned out as wind came roaring through the temple out of nowhere and the massive sails above them filled and bellowed with the noise of it, cracking like titanic whips. Lightning speared across the ship's bows, and with it came the sound of stone splitting as the huge pylons on which the shrine rested collapsed. The deck lurched beneath Indigo's feet; clutching the rail, her hair streaming in the wild wind, she stumbled to obey Macce's command, calling to Luk to help her. Macce, her body shockingly lit by the blue-green radiance that now streamed out of the temple walls, seemed to be everywhere at once, bawling orders, shouting encouragement – even Phereniq, her skirts flapping madly in the gale, was on her feet and turning deft hands to the ropes with a strength she hadn't known she possessed. And the ship itself was starting to change. The masts were losing their polished, pristine sheen, taking on the look of timbers saturated and all but petrified by years of weathering at sea; the ropes and rigging were thickening, becoming rough and tarred and immensely powerful; the sails were no longer silk but heavy canvas, salt-stained and straining with a thunderous noise against their moorings. Everywhere, gems and precious metals and fine, carved woods were turning to brass and bronze and iron and seasoned timber, as the shrine and the countless thousands of offerings that adorned it metamorphosised, a slumbering beast awakening at last, into a true ship. And filling

Indigo's ears above the shouting of the wind and the ramp and rattle of the billowing sails came a new sound – the ceaseless, exhilarating roar of the sea.

Macce, hearing it too, ran to the rail. The steps at the ship's side were falling away, shattering on the floor far below, and even as the Davakotian looked down, the floor seemed to heave as though it were turning from marble to water.

'WEIGH ANCHOR!' Her stentorian bellow ripped across the rising din and Indigo saw her start to haul on the chain to which the golden Anchor was secured. She raced to Macce's side, adding her own strength to the exertions; moments later Luk joined them and laid hands on the chain, and the three of them hauled together, feet braced against the drag of the Anchor's weight as slowly, slowly, it began to rise. Macce, sweating, biceps straining with effort, started to chant a Davakotian work-song; her gaze caught Indigo's and Indigo grinned and joined in the shanty, her body unconsciously falling into the steady, hypnotic rhythm as she pulled. Heady memories surged through her mind, of the old days aboard *Kara Karai*, with the deck pitching beneath her and the sea and the wind and the waves singing in her blood – and then the Anchor was appearing, rising over the ship's side, and it was no longer thin and golden but a huge, iron weight, encrusted with barnacles and streaming with water –

'ALL HANDS TO THE ROPES!' Macce roared as a violent shudder rocked the shrine from bow to stern. 'SHE'S MOVING!'

Suddenly the ship gave a tremendous lurch, throwing Luk and Phereniq off their feet. And from the bows another new sound rose, shivering, thrilling through the quaking temple. Indigo looked forward, and grabbed Macce's arm with an inchoate cry as she saw the outflung arms of the great figurehead begin to rise, the hands opening, the hair no longer carved and motionless but real, whipping back from the serene face. The wild siren-song that poured from the image's laughing mouth swelled, vibrating with the tide of energy that surged through the temple as the walls seemed to fall away, melting, tumbling into chaotic darkness, and the ship began to move. Ahead of them the doors were stretching wide, and as the ship gained momentum they shattered open to the night. The harbour was gone, Simhara was gone; instead, through the gaping chasm where the doors had been, the sea thundered and boiled towards them – and over the sea, eldritch and phantasmic, hung not the familiar white eye of the full moon, but a black, malevolent disc, surrounded by a halo of ghastly silver. Indigo had one last glimpse of the temple's true form shimmering away into the distance like a broken dream, and then they smashed through dimensions, through the unknowable barriers between worlds, and the shining ship, a huge, ghostly avatar, sailed out on to the tide that came surging to embrace her.

Macce's triumphant yell was torn away on the wind as the ship cleaved the first wave and spray fountained over the prow. Indigo too was shouting with exhilaration, the flying spume stinging her skin and soaking her hair, while Luk and Phereniq clung to the rail, huddled against the spray's assault yet catching the fever of excitement. Grimya, legs splayed to brace herself, stood on the foredeck with her muzzle lifted to the gale. Indigo sensed her thoughts, eager with memories rekindled – the sea's booming, the moan of the wind in the sails, the creak of timber and tackle – as the ship sheared on with no human hand needed to guide or urge her and the great figurehead still singing her challenge to the night.

And then above the noise came Macce's voice.

'*Ah-hey-ya!*' It was the Davakotian sailors' warning cry, delivered at the full pitch of her lungs. '*Starboard, fifteen north!*'

Turning, throwing aside the sodden weight of hair that slapped across her face as the wind snatched it, Indigo narrowed her eyes and stared into the darkness beyond the plunging deckrail. White water – it was close, though impossible to tell how close; ragged, broken crests in a long line, contrasting starkly with the

302

black swell all about them, and Indigo's seafaring instincts sent the adrenalin of fear coursing through her blood. Rocks – a reef – she started towards Macce, then suddenly yelled aloud as, with no warning, the ship heeled violently. Timbers groaned in protest, the sails snapped and cracked as though in outrage as they fought the changing course, and the beat of the sea beneath the keel collapsed into churning chaos as the prow began to turn inexorably to starboard.

'She's veering towards it!' Macce bawled. 'Bring her round! Bring her round!'

Indigo darted across the deck, dodging an unsecured and wildly swinging rope that ricocheted past her head, and dived for the halyards. But before she could do anything Phereniq shrieked at the top of her voice,

'Ah, look! LOOK!'

Indigo and Macce both froze in mid-movement as they, too, took in what Phereniq had already seen. The white water was breaking up, as something that was neither a reef nor an isolated rock broke surface. A huge, undulating mass, slickly phosphorescent, rose out of the sea; it cleared the swell, looping, twisting – and the monstrous head of a titanic silver serpent reared from the water in an eruption of spray.

The wash of its rising hit the ship in a turbulent broadside, setting her pitching and bucking. Indigo was flung across the deck, crashing into Grimya, who had also been thrown off her feet; staggering upright she saw Macce's face demented in the eerie light, saw her mouth contorting as she shouted – but an instant later all other sound was eclipsed by an ululating, bone-jarring scream that rose from the lips of the living figurehead, a cry of hatred and wild challenge. The sea-serpent towered sky-wards, water cascading from it like burning silver nacre – and suddenly, superimposed in her mind's eye, Indigo saw again the fortune-telling card that she had found in the temple and which had been Nemesis's own mocking challenge to her. That same scene was coming to life before her, complete in every hideous detail – and as the serpent reared higher, higher against the grim ghost of the eclipsed moon, inspiration hit her like a hammerblow.

303

'Macce!' She bellowed the little woman's name. 'Phereniq, Luk – the Net! *Help me!*'

Phereniq grasped her meaning before the others did, and stumbled to where the Net and the Trident lay, miraculously undisturbed in the chaos, by the larboard rail. Indigo and Grimya reached it seconds later, and between them they began to pull at the Net. More and yet more folds of mesh paid out as they worked and, stunned, Indigo realised that the Net was growing, becoming denser, heavier – and the jewelled fish too were altering, changing into the glass spheres that weighted a traditional fisherman's net. The rich, acrid smell of old tar stung their nostrils, and there was tar on Indigo's hands, the rough feel of the finest and strongest hemp between her fingers though the Net still shone gold. She scrambled to her feet again, dragging one edge of the weighty mass with her: Phereniq took the other edge with Grimya between them in the centre, and they began to struggle towards the prow.

'Indigo, *no*!' A shape detached itself from beside the foremast, intercepting them and clutching at Indigo's arm. She stopped, and stared into Luk's contorted face. Tears were streaming down the boy's cheeks and he shook his head in frantic negation. 'No, Indigo, you can't! It's still Jessamin! *Please –* there must be another way!'

'There's no other way!' Indigo shouted back over the sea's roar and the shrilling scream of the ship's own voice. 'Help us, Luk, or keep out of the way – don't try to interfere!'

'But it's *Jessamin*!' He flung himself at her, arms flailing, and a clenched fist slammed into her left eye. Indigo reeled back dizzily; then suddenly another figure was in the fray, and Luk yelled in furious protest as Macce's brawny arms hauled him away from his quarry.

'Get BACK, boy!' the little Davakotian bellowed. 'What are you, *mad*? Damn your thick hide, *we're trying to avenge your own father!*'

Luk's eyes widened and his jaw dropped. 'No! You – '

304

'*Yes!*' Macce roared. 'Your father is dead, and that thing slaughtered him, just as it slaughtered his uncle and cousin and my crew, may the Mother save their souls! Now, will you get out of the way!'

Indigo had time for nothing more than a momentary, desperate glance in Luk's direction as, her eye still throbbing, she regained her feet and stumbled on with Phereniq and Grimya. The demon serpent towered above the ship now, blocking out the moon and casting a massive shadow on the straining sails. It was impossibly gigantic, and in an instant despair overcame her. They couldn't hope to snare it; even the Net in its transformed state wouldn't be enough. The demon was too powerful now, there was nothing they could do, they were lost –

'INDIGO!' It was Macce's voice; and suddenly in her mind she was thrown back to her earliest days aboard *Kara Karai*, as the crew battled to keep headway in the teeth of a rampaging storm. She had made a mistake, one small mistake, the result of inexperience; and her captain's furious onslaught had been worse than the onslaught of the gale, shaking her out of her panic and into the blind, unquestioning obedience that was their only hope of survival.

That same instinctive reaction powered her now, jolting her from paralysis to action. They were in the prow, the sea creaming vertiginously beneath them, and the Jessamin-serpent-demon was a living, shining wall dead ahead. Indigo hauled the Net upwards, felt Phereniq respond, and then Grimya darted to safety and Macce had taken her place, and together they hefted the huge, shining mass. Their arms reached to full stretch, muscles bunching to throw – and suddenly there were other hands, huge and powerful, catching the golden Net and drawing it up, up, as the arms of the giant figurehead rose to join with theirs in a vast surge of raw and furious power. Indigo felt new energy flood through her muscles, her arteries, her bones, heard her companions shout in unison and shouted with them – and then the Net was flying over the bows and skywards, out and up like a glittering bird, spreading and turning and

305

shearing down again to engulf the serpent's writhing head and body.

An ear-splitting, whistling shriek filled the night, obliterating even the howling song of the figurehead. The serpent flailed as the mesh caught and entangled it, and vast silver-grey coils humped out of the sea, twisting, threshing, smashing the water and fountaining it skywards. Through the chaos of golden mesh and silver scales Indigo glimpsed the serpent's vast mouth gaping wide as though in rage or agony or both, and saw, too, that where the Net touched it, the demon's skin seemed to be burning. An instant later the image was wiped out along with all other vision as what felt like a solid wall of water thundered down on the ship. Indigo was bowled over and back as the huge back-wave from the serpent's flailing crashed on to the deck; her frantic, windmilling hand caught a lanyard, bringing her to a painful halt, and she staggered up, soaked through and spitting water, to see the others safe, clinging with hands or teeth to ropes, rails, the mast, as the wave boiled away over the stern. But her relief lasted only a moment. Macce, still in the prow, was struggling to her feet, but suddenly froze, looking up. Then she let out a warning shriek, audible even through the cacophony.

"Ware above!" She signalled frantically. *'Look OUT!!'*

Maddened by pain and fury, the demon serpent was rearing higher into the black sky, the monstrous head threatening to tear through the entangling Net and break free. Its body, now so close to the ship that Indigo had the appalling feeling that she could have reached out and touched it, lifted from the water, a vast blur of sickly phosophorescence that filled her vision as it towered heavenwards – and then with a heaving twist that sent fresh waves battering against the oncoming ship, the gigantic head curved over and down towards them.

'Indigo! Indigo!' It was Phereniq's voice, shrill with terror and augmented by a howl from Grimya. 'The Trident! *Where is the Trident?'*

The words were like a sword-thrust in Indigo's mind, breaking the thrall of horror that for one precious, vital moment had paralysed her. Turning, she raced towards the larboard rail, but before she could reach it she heard the racket of splintering wood as the serpent struck the ship. The mainmast snapped, and an avalanche of broken spars came crashing down towards the deck. The ship heeled with an agonised groan, hurling Indigo in a skidding slide to her goal, and she groped and clawed desperately among the chaos of shattered timber and smashed tackle. She couldn't find it – the Trident was gone, it was lost –

'Here, Indigo!' The shout came from a few feet away, and she saw someone fighting their way towards her, clambering through the fallen spars and sails. It was Luk – and he was clutching the Trident. Indigo had time for one glimpse of his haggard, agonised but resolute expression before another juddering crash rocked the ship, and the mainsail, still attached to its boom, thundered down. Indigo screamed at Luk to get back, and the vast acreage of canvas smashed on to the deck between them, cutting them off from one another.

A shrilling, insensate scream split the air, and she looked up. Where the mainsail had been there was only gaping blackness – and against the sky she saw the serpent's head rearing back, tossing aside the tattered remains of sails and timbers that its jaws had ripped from their lashings before the huge maw opened again, a black, shrieking cave with fangs like murderous stalactites, and plunged down on the stricken ship for the final strike.

'*Luk!*' Indigo yelled. She could see him, but couldn't reach him; he was staring up, mesmerised, and his face was twisted with terrible emotions. She threw herself towards the barrier that separated them, tearing at the spars which blocked her way, yet knowing despairingly that there was no time –

The demon's head struck the remaining mast, shattered it, plunged through the flying tatters of the last sails and came spearing down – and the Trident in Luk's hand glowed suddenly as though it had burst into flame.

Golden light flickered along the shaft, and the diamond-tipped barbs burned like savage magnesium flares. Luk drew his arm back – and as the silver monster hurtled towards him, he flung the Trident with all his strength straight into the yawning chasm of its jaws.

The Trident became a fireball, an earthbound meteor, white-hot flame streaming in its wake as it smashed into the demon's maw and erupted. An explosion of light seared the ship from end to end, and the serpent shrieked on an ear-shattering note. The monstrous head sheared up and away, and the sea heaved titanically as the coils of the creature's body thrashed out of the water, whipping, flailing, twisting. The shriek changed to a howl, and against the black sky Indigo saw fire belching from the demon's mouth and blazing in its eye-sockets as it writhed high above the ship. The deck was pitching as the vessel bucked wildly; she heard Macce yelling, Grimya howling, and clung desperately to the rail as wave after wave swamped the deck. The serpent had become a towering phantasm, and as Indigo struggled to stop herself from being swept overboard she saw lines of gold fire appear among the silver scales on the monster's head, a fine network of striations. They spread, blazing through its entire body, as though some massive force were cracking it open; and the demon shrieked in mortal terror. One last time it tried to hurl itself up and out of the sea – then the vast, reptilian form split, like an eggshell shattering, and a bolt of blinding, blue-white light erupted upwards from the writhing form with a sound that blasted the night apart. The ship reared like a wild horse; Indigo saw Grimya hurtling towards her, saw Macce flung against the broken stump of the mainmast, saw the energy-bolt spearing into the sky, challenging the moon herself as gouts of blue fire that were all the demon's mortal remains came down on the water, on the deck, on the tatters of the ruined sails. Then the sea heaved, like a giant shrugging continent-wide shoulders, and she felt the ship being lifted on a colossal wave and swept upwards in the wake of the light, higher, higher, through shouting colours and roaring vortices and shattering dimensions and –

Chapter XXVI

The night had imploded. Later, that was the only way in which Indigo could define what had happened even to herself, though it fell grievously short of the reality. It was as though sea and sky had smashed together, crushing the ship and its terrified passengers between two massive walls of utter blackness. Sound and vision were obliterated – and then she found herself lying face down on the deck with water pooling all about her, in a world that was utterly silent and still.

For a few moments she dared not raise her head. She was too afraid of what she might see, where she might find herself. What had happened to the sea? And the others – did they live? How much time had passed? Involuntarily she moaned -- and then started as something snuffled by her left ear, and a warm and rasping tongue licked her wet hair.

Indigo! Grimya's eager mental voice was punctuated by a blend of relief and wonderment. *Indigo, it's all right. You can look. I think . . . I think we are back!*

Giddily, she pulled herself up on her elbows, blinking at the unaccustomed light that radiated softly from all directions. Something huge and white moved sluggishly nearby, making her start in alarm; but it was no demon, no threat. Merely a huge, tattered bundle of silk billowing gently as the air moved it. Silk . . . her heart lurched and she looked up.

Above her head, the broken masts stood stark against the few remaining rags of sail that still clung to them. And higher still, beyond the jagged spars, was a soft, diffused glow that she realised with a shock was the dome of the Temple of Mariners.

They had returned. All around them, the walls of the

309

temple shone with the gentle light of its eternal lanterns. Before them, the doors stood open to a soft, charcoal darkness relieved by a scattering of stars and the faint glow of lamps on the quay. She could hear the sea's voice, deep and fierce yet somehow reassuring. And the ship –

She turned full circle, very slowly, as her stunned mind gradually assimilated what her eyes took in. The ship had changed yet again. Back on its marble pylons, it was once more the shrine that had graced the Temple of Mariners for centuries past. Filigree inlays sparkled on the deck. A crusting of gems glittered on the rail. A halyard, hanging loose and tapping with a quiet rhythm against the remains of the foremast, was threaded with bright ribbons and adorned with carvings, trinkets, countless tiny offerings. Battered, ravaged, her sails ripped, her masts broken and her deck holed in several places, the ship-shrine stood in her old, familiar place, her work done and her promise fulfilled.

And the demon . . .

Indigo looked again towards the doors and the harbour beyond, and knew the answer to her own question. The sky was starting to pale, stars fading as the first hint of daylight crept in from the east. The conjunction was past, the eclipse was over, and the demon had not returned; for it was dead. The years of waiting, of searching, of trial, were over; and the thing that had been born of the darkness under a black moon was finally destroyed.

She turned to Grimya, who sat watching her with eyes that spoke their understanding without the need for words. Silently she embraced the she-wolf, pressing her face into the dense, wet fur, hugging as tightly as her drained strength would allow. Though the flame of triumph burned, there was still an emptiness behind it, the knowledge that, for them, this was only one more step on a long, long road. And she felt so tired.

A soft footfall made her look up at last, and she saw Phereniq standing a few paces away. Like Indigo and Grimya, the astrologer's hair and clothes were soaked with sea-water; but her face was serene and her dark eyes warm.

'Indigo . . . ' She seemed unable to find more words to express what she felt. Then a tiny, sad smile touched her lips. 'He is avenged,' she added very quietly.

Indigo rose to her feet. She wanted to embrace Phereniq as she had embraced Grimya, but as she stepped forward Phereniq drew back a little, and she realised that this was not the right moment.

'The others are safe,' Phereniq said. Her voice was tremulous, but then as she turned to more mundane matters her self-control returned. 'Macce was hurt – I think her arm is broken – but I've found her a makeshift splint and she should do well enough. Luk is uninjured, but . . . I suspect he would prefer to be alone for a little while.' Her gaze met Indigo's again. 'You know what he did?'

'Yes. It must have taken more courage than . . . ' She stopped, shook her head, then added softly, almost to herself:

'Leando would have been proud of him.'

Some while later, Indigo and Grimya climbed down the steps, restored now and returned to their old place at the ship's side. Phereniq was tending to Macce, making her as comfortable as possible until men could be fetched to help carry her down, and Luk, for the moment, was better without company.

Indigo and Macce had exchanged no more than a few words, but they were enough. The little Davakotian's broad grin, accompanied by a muffled curse as she injudiciously tried to move her broken arm, had wiped away past enmities, and there would be no more talk of remorse or forgiveness. Macce had had just one request, which Indigo was now about to fulfil.

'Go and thank Her for me,' she had said, and her eyes crinkled with their familiar mischief. 'You know the proper words to say; I'm just a common mariner and no use at rituals. Thank Her. And tell Her She's the best crew member I ever had!'

The ship's giant figurehead was just that now and nothing more; an exquisite but motionless and lifeless wooden carving. But as she moved into the shadow of the prow and looked up, Indigo gasped in shock. The figurehead's lovely head and flying mane of hair were unchanged – but only inches below the figure's shoulders the wood was smashed and splintered, nothing but ragged stumps remaining where the graceful, outspread hands and arms had been.

She started forward, every instinct protesting this desecration – then stopped, as memory came flooding back. Again in her mind she heard the figurehead's eerie, thrilling song, and recalled the huge, unhuman hands that had caught up the golden Net as she and Phereniq and Macce had struggled with its heavy mass, and with power and strength far beyond their puny mortality had hurled it up and out to ensnare the demon serpent.

And then, for the first time, she saw the figurehead's face.

The Sea Goddess no longer sang. The full, beautiful lips, carved so lovingly by a long-dead craftsman of an earlier age, weren't fixed in their familiar open-mouthed cry, but instead smiled a serene and knowing smile of beatitude. For a long, long moment Indigo gazed up at that magnificent countenance, and a sense of incredible peace stole over her. Unconsciously her own arms reached out to where the figurehead's arms should have been, and she felt as though she touched a warm, flowing current of water, healing, loving, promising a future without pain. Her eyes closed and she felt tears streaming down her cheeks, a tumbling chaos of emotions, yet a release, a certitude, something to which she could hold and cling and which would never deny her.

'Indigo . . .'

The quiet, tentative speaking of her name brought her consciousness surging back to the surface of reality. Blinking, she turned her head and saw Luk. He had stolen down from the ship's deck and stood before her, shoulders set, face expressionless, eyes –

Everything was in his eyes. All the pain, all the grief,

312

all the betrayal. And yet under the burden of his emotions huddled a spark that kindled a like flame in Indigo. There was *hope*.

'Oh, Indigo!' And suddenly the grown young man was a child again, as he flung himself into her arms and sobbed his misery and his release with his face buried in her soaked and salt-stiffened hair.

The atmosphere in the palace anteroom was tense, but without the chilly edge that so often accompanied formal occasions. Macce, who hated farewells, fidgeted restlessly on her ornate chair, catching Indigo's eye every now and then and grinning self-consciously. Her arm, though still in a sling, was healing well according to physician-mage Thibavor, and she would have no trouble on the voyage ahead; indeed, she was anxious to feel a moving deck under her feet again. Indigo knew that her impatient thoughts were constantly straying to the newly-commissioned *Pride of Simhara* that waited at her mooring in the harbour with a full complement of crew. The ship was a gift of gratitude from Khimiz's new Takhan, and at the small acceptance ceremony six days earlier Indigo had seen Macce, for almost the first time in her life, at a loss for words.

For herself, there had been no gifts. The Takhan had argued, as had Phereniq; but Indigo had been resolute. She wanted nothing: no lands, no title, no wealth. What would a simple mariner, she had asked with a gentle smile, do with such bounty? And though they had cajoled her, pleaded with her, begged her, she had told them that she could not stay in Simhara, but must travel on.

She wished she could have explained to them. She wished that the pangs of hurt might be soothed away by understanding. But the secret that she shared only with Grimya was already calling her; the tiny, shimmering pinpoint of the lodestone showing the westward journey they must take, across the sea, to a new land and a new danger. This farewell, she knew in her heart, would be forever.

Macce's voice broke into her sad reverie.

'D'you know, Indigo, it gladdens me to see you set for the sea again after all these years.' The small woman was smiling broadly. 'Just like old times, eh?'

'Yes.' Indigo returned the smile. 'Just like old times.'

'And a new ship beneath us, and a good north-easter to speed us on our way,' Macce added. 'There'll be some tales to tell when we get to Davakos!' She gazed about her at the room, and at the summer-blooming garden beyond the open windows, and her eyes took on a faraway look. 'I'm going to come back next year, to see the Shrine again when the restorations are finished. I promised Her that. And I'll bring Her an offering the like of which Simhara's never seen, you mark my words I will. And I'll see all our friends again, and tell them you made landfall safely – I promised that, too. And I'll . . . ' She faltered, and put an impatient hand up to her diamond-studded cheeks. 'Oh, *damn*.' She sniffed.

Her further embarrassment was saved as the inlaid doors at the end of the room opened and a small group of people came in. All were formally dressed, and the Takhan, in their midst, was resplendent in viridian robes, with a ceremonial cloak of gold thread edged with emeralds cast over one shoulder. At his side was Phereniq, the gold torque of the Regent of Khimiz vivid against the quiet dark blue of her gown. Indigo and Macce rose – and Luk Copperguild threw aside his dignity and ran forward to embrace them both in a hug that owed nothing to protocol and everything to love.

'I don't know what to say to you!' he confessed as at last he let them go. 'I'd prepared a speech, but I can't stand here and say goodbye so formally; it feels all wrong. I just – I just wish you didn't have to go!'

Macce withdrew a little, aware that the young Takhan's words were for Indigo more than for herself, and Indigo and Luk stood with clasped hands, both trying to smile.

'I'll never forget you, Indigo,' Luk said. 'All of Khimiz will never forget what you did.'

She gazed back at him, proud of his youthful fervour and deeply moved by the inner strength she saw beneath the uncertainty in his eyes. She knew that Luk had been reluctant to take on the mantle of his new position; but she also knew that the court council had made a wise choice. As first cousin to the old Takhan whom Augon Hunnamek had deposed, and the eldest surviving male member of the Copperguild family, the throne of Khimiz was Luk's by birthright. And though time wouldn't entirely wipe away his unhappy memories, he would put them aside for the sake of his great responsibility. He would be a good ruler. And Phereniq would help his wounds to heal.

Luk said: 'You'll try to come back, won't you? One day?'

'I hope so, Luk.' She meant it. 'There's nothing I'd like more.'

'I'll remember you in all my prayers to the Sea Mother. Oh, Indigo – may She keep you safe always!' And he flung his arms around her again, tears sparkling on his lashes.

She had said her private farewells to Phereniq earlier in the day, so as they embraced for the last time neither could find more words to express their feelings. As she kissed the astrologer's lined cheek, Indigo said softly, 'Take care of him, Phereniq.'

'I shall, as if he were my own.' A pause. 'We can do much to comfort each other, Luk and I; for we both know what it is to lose the one we loved. He will cease to grieve for Jessamin in time.'

'And you . . . ?'

'I? Oh, I shall live out my days as the Great Mother wills it. What more can any of us ask? But I think there will be good times as well as sad ones.' She smiled, blinking over-rapidly, and squeezed Indigo's upper arms. 'You'd best go, my dear friend, or you'll miss the tide. Farewell. And the Goddess bless you.'

In the closed litter that bore them to the harbour, no one had a word to say. Even Grimya, who lay beside Indigo with her head resting on her friend's lap, was lost in her own thoughts, remembering the last hug she had

315

received from both Luk and Phereniq, and wishing that she could have spoken her own goodbyes rather than simply licking their hands and their faces. Macce had flatly refused to cry but had come dangerously close; while Indigo, who had been prepared for tears, found that instead she felt a sense of poignant warmth, albeit tinged with deep regret, that kept them at bay.

A large number of people had gathered at the quay-side. Macce had hoped to get away without a crowd to see them off, but word had got about that the three heroines of Khimiz were leaving on the afternoon tide, and as they stepped down from the litter, blinking in the brilliant sunlight, they were cheered rapturously. Some of the crowd threw flowers, and Macce gathered up a posy of honeysuckle and buried her nose in it to cover her embarrassment as they walked the few yards to the quay's edge and the gangplank that awaited them. *Pride of Simhara*, magnificent in new paint and sails and with her name emblazoned at her bows in both Khimizi and Davakotian, rocked on the swell as though eager to be under way, and her crew – mostly Davakotian, half of them female, and all hand-picked by Macce from among Simhara's itinerant seafaring population – yelled and waved at their captain from the deck.

As she padded on to the plank, Grimya raised her head and sniffed the mingled scents of tar and brine and wood and paint that were the familiar brew on board any ship. Then she gave a pleased little whine, and shook herself before looking up at Indigo.

I like the sea, she said, and there was a new note in her mental voice, a touch of eagerness. *It will be good to be sailing again.*

Indigo smiled. *Yes,* she replied. *I think perhaps it will.* And there would be time enough on the voyage to find that elusive peace she had once known, even if only for a little while. As for the future . . . well, she wouldn't think of the future as yet; not until the past was truly behind her.

As Macce began to shout orders to the ship's crew and the sails went rattling up the masts, Indigo looked for the last time on the great harbour of Simhara, on the

316

sunlight reflecting off the tall, gracious buildings, on the distant shimmer of the great dome atop the Temple of Mariners. The phantom images of Leando, Karim, Augon Hunnamek, even Jessamin in her human guise, rose in her mind, and she felt an aching sadness. But the bane was broken: the dark clouds were gone from Khimiz, and in the wake of tragedy there could be a new beginning.

A stentorian yell from amidships made her look round, and she heard Macce cry, 'Up anchor!' The great chain rattled as it was hauled in, and then came the call, 'Anchor aweigh! Cast off and let her go!'

The deck dipped and swayed beneath Indigo's feet; the sails cracked and filled, and a fresh cheer went up from the harbour as *Pride of Simhara* began to swing round and set her prow to the open sea. Hands were waving, people shouting farewells and blessings – and at the back of the crowd Indigo's eye was suddenly caught by a flicker of brilliance that seemed at odds with the colourful scene. A hint of silver – she tensed, narrowing her eyes; and then as a section of the throng shifted she saw it more clearly.

A small figure, solitary beyond the fringe of the massed faces. She couldn't see its features clearly from such a distance, but it was no taller than a child. And the silver hair that shone like a nimbus in the sun was final confirmation.

Outcast from the well-wishers on the quayside, who were not even aware of its presence, Nemesis stared towards the departing ship, and Indigo felt the anger and hatred that radiated from its mind, like a chilly breath of wind flicking across the widening gap between ship and shore. Then the baleful figure was gone, as though it had been no more than a momentary hallucination, and the sun shone down on an empty space where it had stood.

She looked at Grimya, and knew that the she-wolf, too, had seen what she had seen.

It does not like to be defeated, Grimya said soberly. *Next time, we must be even more on our guard.*

Indigo reached into her pouch, drawing out a

crumpled, silver-tinted square. She had kept the fortune-telling card, Nemesis's mockery and its mistake, but now she had no further use for it. Briefly, curiously, she opened the crushed ball out. The silver backing was beginning to flake. She turned it over –

The card's face was blank. Indigo smiled.

'Yes,' she said to Grimya. 'We must indeed be on our guard. But I think that, for a while, we shall have a respite.'

The crumpled card spun up and out as she threw it, glinting briefly before it struck the water. For a few moments they saw it bobbing on the swell, then *Pride of Simhara*'s bow-wave caught and washed over it, and it was lost in the ship's churning wake.

Forthcoming in July . . .

NOCTURNE
Indigo, Book 4
Louise Cooper

AND THEN THERE WAS A MORNING WHEN
THE SUN DIDN'T RISE . . .

The arrival of the Brabazon Fairplayers at the Autumn
Revels should have been a joyous occasion . . .

Indigo, cursed to find and slay the seven demons she
released, is travelling with the players, now almost a
part of the ramshackle family she has come to love.

But the crops are blighted. There are tales of near
zombies wandering the countryside. And of a forest that
moves.

Indigo's lodestone flickers wildly. The demon seems to
be all around her. But if she is to fight it, what will be the
consequences for her friends, and for Grimya, the
she-wolf who is inexorably bound to her quest?

Slowly, life is being leached from the land and its
people. Must Indigo face the challenge alone, to protect
those she loves? Fate may have other plans . . .

INFERNO
Indigo Book 2
Louise Cooper

'ANGHARA KALIGSDAUGHTER,
WHAT MAKES YOU THINK YOU HAVE A
RIGHT TO DIE?

Stripped of her family, her home and her title, Princess
Anghara is condemned to wander the Earth. Her only
      name now is Indigo, and even in her deepest
grief she may not rest, nor may she hope for death.
Remorse is not enough: there can be no respite for her
until the seven evils released by her hand are conquered
and destroyed.

Now, in a land where sullen, volcanic fires simmer deep
within the earth, Indigo must face an alien power that
warps the minds and bodies of all who fall under its
baleful spell.

Only by calling on a fire as dark yet more hideously
ancient can she hope to eradicate its corruption. But fire
burns. Can Indigo control the flames? Or will the wrath
that blazes within her prove more deadly than the
demon she is pledged to defeat?

THE INITIATE
Book 1 of the Time Master Trilogy
Louise Cooper

The Seven Gods of Order had ruled unchallenged for an aeon, served by the Adepts of the Circle in their bleak Northern stronghold. But for Tarod – the most enigmatic and formidable sorcerer in the Circle's ranks – a darker affinity had begun to call. Threatening his beliefs, even his sanity, it rose unbidden from beyond Time; an ancient and deadly adversary that could plunge the world into madness and chaos – and whose power rivalled that even of the Gods themselves. But though Tarod's mind and heart were pledged to Order, his soul was another matter . . .

THE OUTCAST
Book 2 of the Time Master Trilogy
Louise Cooper

Denounced by his fellow Adepts as a demon, betrayed even by those he loved, Tarod had unleashed a power that twisted the fabric of time. It seemed that nothing could break through the barrier he had created until Cyllan and Drachea – victims of the Warp – stumbled unwittingly into his castle. The terrible choice Tarod has to make as a result has far-reaching consequences . . .

THE MASTER
Book 3 of the Time Master Trilogy
Louise Cooper

Tarod had won his freedom – and lost the soul stone, key to his sorcerous power. Cyllan, the woman he loved, had been taken from him in a supernatural storm. With a price on both their heads, Tarod had to find her before the Circle did. Only then could he hope to fulfil his self-imposed pledge to confront the gods themselves – for they alone could destroy the stone and the evil that dwelt in it. If touched by the evil in the stone, Tarod would be forced to face the truth of his own heritage, triggering a titanic conflict of occult forces, and setting him on the ultimate quest for vengeance . . .

THE DARWATH TRILOGY
Barbara Hambly

Book 1

The Time of the Dark

For several nights Gil had found herself dreaming of an impossible city where alien horrors swarmed from underground lairs of darkness. She had dreamed also of the wizard Ingold Inglorion. Then the same wizard crossed the Void to seek sanctuary for the last Prince of Dar and revealed himself to a young drifter, Rudy. But one of the monstrous, evil Dark followed in his wake and in attempting to help Ingold, Gil and Rudy were drawn back into the nightmare world of the Dark. There they had to remain – unless they could solve the mystery of the Dark. Then, before they could realise their fate, the Dark struck!

Book 2

The Walls of Air

In the shelter of the great Keep of Renwath eight thousand people shelter from the Dark. The only hope for the besieged is to seek help from the hidden city of Quo. Ingold and Rudy set out to cross two thousand miles of desert. Beyond it they have to penetrate the walls of illusion that separate Quo from the world.

Book 3

The Armies of Daylight

The survivors of the once-great Realm of Darwath shelter, squabble and struggle for power. Meawhile the monstrous Dark threaten their great Keep. Is there a reason for the reawakening of the Dark? The final volume of *The Darwath Trilogy* builds to a shattering and unexpected climax.

DRAGONSBANE
Barbara Hambly

It was said to be impossible to slay a dragon. But Lord John Aversin had earned himself the name of Dragonsbane once in his life and had become the subject of ballad and legend. Fired by the romance of his tale, young Gareth travelled far and wide across the Winterlands from the King's court to persuade the hero to rid the Deep of Ylferdun of the great Black Dragon, Morkeleb, oldest and mightiest of the dragon race. But Morkeleb was not the greatest danger that awaited John Aversin and his witch-woman. Just as Morkeleb posed the hardest test of skill and courage for the Dragonsbane, so Jenny Waynest would find her powers pitted against an adversary as deadly as the Black Dragon, and infinitely more evil.

'This is literary alchemy of a high order, and it confirms Hambly's place as one of the best new fantasists.'

Locus

'. . . a writer of unusual proficiency.'

SF Chronicle

'*Dragonsbane* is an enjoyable fantasy. Barbara Hambly takes a familiar opening, with witches and heroes and dragons, and gives the story unusual twists and vivid, believable characters. A good read.'

Everywoman

'. . . an excellent, beautifully written and thrilling story, and one of the most enjoyable I've read in a long time.'

Johannesburg Star

THE SILENT TOWER
Barbara Hambly

Another thrilling fantasy from best-selling author
Barbara Hambly.

Antryg Windrose, dog wizard student of the Dark
Mage, has been imprisoned in the Silent Tower for
seven long, lonely years.

But have his powers been limited by the spell-bound
tower walls, or is the life-sapping Void and the appearance of appalling abominations throughout the countryside somehow connected to him?

And is he linked to the strange occurrences noticed by
young computer programmer Joanna Sheraton at the
San Serano Aerospace Complex? Joanna has the feeling
that someone is following her, but who, and why? At a
party thrown by her boyfriend Gary, she is soon to find
out: whirled through the Void into an unfamiliar world,
accompanied by a mad wizard and a beautiful sasenna
swordsman, she is about to discover depths within
herself she had never dreamed of, and horrors worse
than any nightmare . . .

THE SILICON MAGE
Barbara Hambly

Concluding the nail-biting story that began with THE SILENT TOWER . . .

The corrupt Archmage Suraklin has taken over the body, brain and computer of Gary, Joanna's ex-boyfriend. Through magic he is already able to leech the life-force out of two worlds to fuel his lust for eternal power and life: now he will harness science as well.

His main adversary, Antryg Windrose, dog-wizard and Joanna's lover, is imprisoned again in the Silent Tower, his mind and body broken. Joanna is on her own. Somewhere, in this strange medieval world full of superstition and corruption, where worship of the Dead God, lord of entropy, has emerged one more, where human sacrifice is practised and abominations abound, Suraklin has hidden his computer. Armed with a back-pack full of software, a worm disc and a .38, Joanna Sheraton is all that stands between the Dark Mage and the death of the universe.

THE LADIES OF MANDRIGYN
Barbara Hambly

Determined to win back their men from the cruel fate assigned to them by the evil Wizard King Altiokis, the Ladies of Mandrigyn set out to hire the services of the mercenary leader Sun Wolf to destroy him. But not even a fortune of gold would tempt Sun Wolf to be fool enough to match his sword against the wizard's sorcery . . .

Sun Wolf awoke, some hours later, on a ship bound for far-flung Mandrigyn, lethal anzid coursing through his veins. The ladies held the only antidode, and Sun Wolf found himself an unwilling participant in a very dangerous game . . .

Following *The Ladies of Mandrigyn*
a new story featuring Sun Wolf and Star Hawk:

THE WITCHES OF WENSHAR
Barbara Hambly

Every female of the ancient house of Wenshar was possessed of a powerful magic: but their line is long dead, their desert city in ruins.

Yet there is still magic in Wenshar: the lady Kaletha has some gift for it and will train her neophytes to free their own talents. After his adventures in Mandrigyn, Sun Wolf, the mercenary, seeks her out to train his own newfound magic.

Shortly after his arrival a series of horrific supernatural killings turns Wenshar into a snakepit of superstitious fear and loathing. Sun Wolf finds himself in deadly danger as vicious tongues begin to wag . . .